Brides for the Greek Tycoons
Marriages maid *in Greece!*

Business is Cristo's and Niko's first—and only—
love. So when marriage becomes necessary to
secure the future of their hotel empire, they vow
to approach it like any other deal.

Chambermaids Kyra and Sofia are stunned
when they receive the biggest tips of their
lives—a diamond ring each! Find out what
happens when the lives of these Cinderellas go
from sweeping the hotel floors to being swept
into the tycoons' wealthy jet-set lives in:

The Greek's Ready-Made Wife
Available March 2016

And discover what shocking surprise
Sofia has in store for Niko in their story...
Coming soon!

THE GREEK'S
READY-MADE WIFE

BY
JENNIFER FAYE

First Published in Great Britain 2016
By Mills & Boon, an imprint of HarperCollins*Publishers*
1 London Bridge Street, London, SE1 9GF

© 2016 Jennifer F. Stroka

ISBN: 978-0-263-91967-7

23-0316

Our policy is to use papers that are natural, renewable and recyclable products and made from wood grown in sustainable forests.The logging and manufacturing processes conform to the legal environmental regulations of the country of origin.

Printed and bound in Spain
by CPI, Barcelona

Award-winning author **Jennifer Faye** pens fun, heart-warming romances. Jennifer has won the RT Reviewers' Choice Best Book Award, is a Top Pick author and has been nominated for numerous awards. Now living her dream, she resides with her patient husband, one amazing daughter (the other remarkable daughter is off chasing her own dreams) and two spoiled cats. She'd love to hear from you via her website, www.jenniferfaye.com.

For Karen.

Thanks for being such a wonderful, supportive friend and big sis. May your future bring you many amazing adventures both near and far. In case your travels don't take you to Greece, here's an armchair vacation for you.

CHAPTER ONE

"MARRY ME."

Kyra Pappas's breath caught in her throat. She hovered in the doorway of the Governor's suite of the Blue Tide Resort, the housekeeping pass card still clutched in one hand and a pink feather duster in the other. Had she heard correctly? Did someone just utter a marriage proposal?

Talk about bad timing on her part. Still, being a romantic at heart, she couldn't resist trying to catch a quick glimpse of the happy couple before making a hasty exit. Her gaze scanned the room until she stumbled across the most gorgeous man wearing a gray tailored suit, sans the tie.

Wait. She recognized him. Yesterday, he'd returned to this suite just as she'd finished freshening everything. They'd chatted briefly about her being American. He'd inquired whether she enjoyed working at the resort. As their conversation had progressed, he'd mentioned some local sites she should visit while in Greece. He'd certainly seemed nice enough.

But right now, he was staring directly at her. Why would he be looking at her when he was in the middle of a marriage proposal? Kyra glanced around. They were alone. And the television was turned off. How could that be?

And then a thought struck her. Surely he wasn't posing the question to her. The breath caught in her throat. No. Impossible.

Her puzzled gaze studied the man with the tanned face. She could stare at him for hours. His dark wavy hair made her long to run her fingers through it, while his startling azure-blue eyes seemed to see all. He kept staring at her as though he expected her to respond. Perhaps she hadn't heard him correctly.

"I'm sorry. What did you say?"

His dark brows drew together as his forehead wrinkled. "I…asked if you'd marry me."

He really had proposed. This stranger wanted to marry her? To say she was caught off guard was akin to saying the Hope diamond was just another trinket.

For just the briefest moment, she imagined what it'd be like if he was serious. Until now, no one had spoken those words to her. On those occasional Saturday nights when she was home alone, she wondered if she'd ever fall in love. But she wasn't desperate enough to fall for the charming words of a stranger—however sexy he may be.

Besides, the last thing she wanted was to be tied down— not now when she'd just embarked on an adventure to find her extended family. She had other priorities and love wasn't one of them. It wasn't even on her lengthy to-do list.

She studied the serious expression on the man's face. He certainly didn't seem to be making light of his proposal. So then why had he proposed marriage to a total stranger? Was he delusional? Or had he made some sort of ridiculous wager with his buddies?

"Are you feeling all right, sir?" Her gaze panned the room again, this time a bit more slowly, looking for an open liquor bottle or a hidden camera. Anything to explain his odd behavior.

"I…I'm not exactly handling this well." He rubbed a hand over his clean-shaven jaw. "I must admit that I've never proposed to anyone before."

"Is this some sort of bet? A joke?"

His face turned gravely serious. "Certainly not. This is a serious business proposition. One that could benefit you handsomely."

Which was it? A marriage proposal? Or a business proposition? Kyra's mouth opened but nothing came out. Perhaps it was for the best. The man must have started drinking early that day even though she couldn't find any signs of it. The best thing she could do was beat a hasty retreat. She took a step back.

"Don't look so scared. I'm really not that bad." He sent her a lazy smile that made her stomach quiver. "I'm usually so much better at these things. Give me a moment to explain."

"I have work to do." She'd heard about rich people having weird tendencies. She kept a firm eye on him as she took another step back. "I...I'll stop back later and...um, freshen up your room."

"Please, don't go." He took a few quick steps toward her.

She held up a hand to stop him. "Don't come any closer or I'll scream."

"Relax. I won't hurt you. I promise." He rubbed the back of his neck. "I'm sorry. I'm really making a mess of things. I guess I should be relieved this isn't a real proposal."

She eyed him up to see if at last he was being on the level. The guilty puppy look on his face was so cute and tugged at her sympathies. He must be in a real bind to suggest something so preposterous. "Apology accepted. Now I really should get back to work."

"Aren't you at least curious about my proposal?"

Of course she was. Who wouldn't be? She studied the man a little more, noticing how the top couple of buttons on his slate blue button-down shirt were undone. It gave her the slightest hint of his muscular chest. She swallowed hard. To keep from staring, she diverted her gaze. On his arm, she spotted a fancy wristwatch. She wouldn't be surprised to find it was a Rolex.

He looked every inch a successful businessman right down to his freshly polished shoes. A man who was used to getting what he wanted. A man who made calculated decisions. And somehow he'd decided she would do for his plan. Interesting.

"Yes, I'm curious." She crossed her arms to keep from fidgeting. What would it hurt to hear him out? "Go ahead. I'm listening."

"Wouldn't you rather come inside and have a seat where you'll be more comfortable?"

"I'm good here." Until she had a clue what was going on, she was staying close to the open door. After all, she grew up in New York City. Her mother taught her at an early age not to trust strangers. Although, she didn't know if her mother would extend that warning to dashing billionaires or not, but Kyra didn't find wealth and class as important as her mother did.

He shifted his weight from one foot to the other. "I realize we don't know each other very well. But I enjoyed our conversation yesterday. You seem like a very interesting young woman, and you have a way of putting people at ease."

She did? She'd never been told that before. "Thank you. But I don't understand why you're, uh, proposing to me."

"I'm trying to secure a very important business deal. The problem is the seller is an older gentleman and a traditionalist. He has certain expectations that I currently fail to meet. Such as being a family man."

He wants to play house with me?

No way. She wasn't doing this. She didn't even know his name. "I'm not the right person."

"You're exactly who I need." His eyes gleamed with excitement.

She made an obvious point of glancing at the time on her phone. "I really need to get going. I have a lot of rooms to clean today."

"You don't have to worry. I'll vouch for you."

What an odd thing to say, but then again, this whole episode could easily be classified as bizarre. Just so she knew who to avoid in the future, she asked, "Who are you?"

His dark brows rose. "You don't know?"

She shook her head. The only thing she knew about him was that no one had a right to look that sexy. "Would I have asked if I knew?"

"True. Allow me to introduce myself. My name is Cristo Kiriakas."

His name did ring a bell—a very loud bell. It took a moment until she was able to place it. Kyra gasped. He was her boss—the owner of the Glamour Hotel and Casino chain that included the newly built Blue Tide Resort. She would have known it was him if only she'd done her homework. This was, after all, the Governor's suite— the best in the resort.

"Nice to meet you, Mr. Kiriakas. I…I'm Kyra Pappas. I didn't recognize you."

"Don't look so worried." He spoke in a calm, soothing tone. "I didn't expect you to recognize me. And please, call me Cristo. My father insists on going by Mr. Kiriakas. So every time you say that name, I'll be looking over my shoulder for my father."

"Sorry, sir. Um. Cristo. You can call me Kyra." At this particularly awkward juncture, she supposed the wisest thing to do regarding her employment while in a foreign country was to reason with the man. "Does my job hinge on me playing along with your wedding plans?"

"No, it doesn't. You don't have to worry. Your job is safe."

She wasn't sure about that. "Surely you have a girl-friend—someone close to you—to marry."

His jaw tensed and a muscle in his cheek twitched. "Yes, I could find someone to marry for real, but the truth is I don't want to be married. Not for keeps."

"Then why jump through all of these hoops? You seem rich enough to do as you please."

"I wish it were as easy as that. But having money doesn't mean things come to you any easier. Some things are still unobtainable without help."

Kyra had lived with money and without money. She found that both lifestyles had their positives and negatives. But she didn't know that other people had similar opinions. Her mother seemed to think that having money was the only important thing in life. And if you no longer had money, like her and her mother, then you pretended as if you did. Kyra didn't subscribe to that way of thinking, but after going round and round with her mother, she knew trying to change her mother's mind was a waste of time.

Kyra eyed up Cristo. "And you want my help to create a paper marriage so you can conclude a business deal?" She struggled to get this all straight in her mind. "And when the deal's complete, we'll go our separate ways?"

"Yes." He smiled as though relieved that she finally grasped what he was saying. "But it's not just any business deal. It'll be the biggest of my career. It'll change everything."

The conviction in his voice surprised her. Even though she didn't quite understand the importance of this deal, she felt bad for him. Why would anyone have to propose to a stranger in order to do business? No one should marry someone they didn't love heart, body and soul. For any reason.

Perhaps he needed a bit of coaxing in order to see things clearly. "There has to be another way."

He shook his head. "If there was, trust me, I would have done it by now."

She paused for a moment and gave his predicament a bit of thought. "Well, if marriage is so important, why can't you just have a fake fiancée? Wouldn't that save you a lot of trouble?"

Not that she was applying for the position—even though his blue eyes were mesmerizing and his mouth looked as though it could do the most delicious things. The fact was she'd come to Greece with her own agenda. And getting caught up in someone else's drama would only delay making life better for her and her mother.

This lady was sharp.

That was a definite bonus.

Cristo smiled. He knew from the moment he'd met Kyra that there was something special about her. And it went much deeper than her silky dark hair with long bangs that framed her big brown eyes. The rest of her hair was pulled back in a ponytail. He imagined how seductive she'd look with her hair loose and flowing over her shoulders.

However, his interest in her went beyond her good looks. From the moment they'd met, he'd noticed the warmth in her smile and the ease in her manner. Who knew she'd end up being the answer to his problems? He hadn't—not until this morning when he submitted his final proposal to the Stravos Trust to purchase its hotel chain. It had been summarily rejected without review.

He knew then and there that he was going to have to play by the off-the-wall rules laid out by the reclusive billionaire Nikolaos Stravos, whether he liked it or not. And he most certainly did not like having his business deals hinge on his personal life.

Although, Kyra's suggestion of an engagement might make the arrangement a bit more tolerable. An engagement wouldn't necessitate the use of attorneys and an ironclad prenuptial agreement. It'd be all very neat and tidy.

His gaze met and held hers. He needed more information in order to make this work. "How long have you been working at the Blue Tide? I don't remember seeing you around here before yesterday."

"That's because yesterday was my first day. I used to work in the New York hotel."

"Did you work there long?"

"A few years."

"And it was in housekeeping?"

She nodded, but the way she worried her bottom lip was a dead giveaway that she was leaving something out. If he was going to trust her with this important deal, he had to know what she was leaving out. "What aren't you saying?"

Her gaze met his as though deciding if she should trust him or not. After a few seconds, she said, "I'm currently taking online courses in international hotel management."

"I don't understand. Why would you be hesitant to tell me that?"

She laced her fingers together. "I didn't want you to think I was ungrateful for my current position."

He smiled at her, hoping to ease her obvious discomfort. "The thought never would have crossed my mind. I encourage all of my employees to further themselves. In fact, we have in-house training sessions periodically."

"I know. I checked into them."

Again, she was leaving something out, but he was pretty sure of what she was hesitant to say. "But we don't offer the classes you are interested in. And if you don't mind me asking, what might that be?"

She straightened her thin shoulders and tilted up her chin. "Property manager."

Of course. He should have known. There was a get-it-done spirit to her. "I have no doubt that you will succeed."

Her lips lifted into a warm smile. "Thank you."

So she had drive. He respected that. But there was still so much that he didn't know about her. The cautious side of him said to pull her personnel file, but there wasn't time. However, his manager made a practice of thoroughly investigating prospective employees. She must have a clean history or she wouldn't be here.

"I enjoyed our conversation yesterday. You're a very insightful young woman. And I would consider it a huge favor if you were to help me out with my business issue."

The panic vacated her eyes as her rigid stance eased. "I

really do like my job with housekeeping. It allows me time to, uh…sightsee and stuff."

"Will you at least consider my proposition?"

"I have. And the answer is no. I'm sorry, but you'll have to find yourself someone else to play the part." She started out the door.

"Please think it over." He threw out an outrageous dollar figure that put a pause in her step. "I really need your assistance."

He was running out of time.

And options.

CHAPTER TWO

THE MOST LOGICAL thing to do right now was to keep walking.

Yet there was that note of desperation in Cristo's voice. Something told her that he didn't say please very often.

Kyra hesitated, her back still to him. Why was this most bizarre plan so important to him? What secrets was he holding back? And why did she care? This wasn't her problem.

"If I didn't really need your help, I wouldn't have proposed this arrangement. I swear." Weariness laced his every syllable. "I will make it worth your while. If that wasn't enough money, name your price."

Why did it always come back to money? "I'm not for sale."

She headed straight for her cart of cleaning supplies. She dropped the feather duster back in its proper spot. Her curiosity got the best of her. She glanced over her shoulder to see if Cristo had followed her into the hallway.

He hadn't. She breathed easier. What in the world did they put in the water around here? Because there was no way that whole scene was normal. After all, they were strangers. No one would ever believe they were a couple.

As she prepared to push her cart to the next suite, she recalled the large dollar figure he'd named and the offer to make it bigger if necessary. Okay, she may not be a gold digger, but that didn't mean she'd turn her nose up at some extra income. But could she really play the part of his fiancée?

Could she pretend to be something she wasn't?

Wouldn't that make her a hypocrite?

Kyra paused in front of the next suite. She recalled how

many times she'd gone round and round with her mother in the past year since her father's death about putting on a show for her mother's country-club friends. When her father had died, so had their silver-spoon lifestyle.

Kyra felt sorry for her mother—first losing the love of her life and then having to go back to work after twenty-plus years as a stay-at-home mom. With her mother buried beneath a mountain of debt, Kyra had moved back in to help meet the mortgage payments. And though this new position in Greece took her away from home, Kyra reconciled it with the fact that it paid more so she could send more money home.

The one other reason Kyra had taken the position was to help her mother—even if her mother swore she didn't need help. With her father gone, her mother was depressed and lonely as her country-club friends had less and less to do with her. With no other family in New York, Kyra had hoped to locate her father's extended family. If she could forge bonds with them, maybe she could make a life for her and her mother here in Greece. By once again being part of a warm, supportive family, perhaps her mother wouldn't feel so alone.

One thought after the next rolled around in Kyra's mind as she cleaned the remaining suites on the floor. All the while, her thoughts moved back and forth between doing what she felt was right and earning enough money to help her mother, who had always been there for her. Did Kyra's principles outweigh her duty to help her mother?

And the fact she was in Greece gave her the freedom to make decisions she wouldn't normally make. Being thousands of miles from New York City meant her chance of running into anyone she knew was slim to none. Well, there was one person at the Blue Tide that knew her, her best friend, Sofia Moore. But Sofia would keep her secret.

Speaking of her best friend, Kyra could really use some advice right now. If anyone could make sense of this very odd opportunity, it would be Sofia. Once the last suite on the floor had been put to rights, Kyra paused next to the large window overlooking the private cove. She pulled out her phone. Her fingers moved rapidly over the screen.

Mop&Glow007 (Kyra): Hey, you're never going to believe this. I met someone.

She just couldn't bring herself to admit that she'd been proposed to by a stranger, only to learn later it was their boss. Somehow, it sounded desperate on his part. And she felt sorry for Cristo.

Seconds turned into a minute, then two, and still no response. Where was Sofia? Probably still cleaning the exclusive bungalows that lined the beach. But Sofia always had her phone close at hand.

MaidintheShade347 (Sofia): As in a guy?

Mop&Glow007 (Kyra): Yes.

MaidintheShade347 (Sofia): What? But how? You swore off guys.

Mop&Glow007 (Kyra): I know. But he found me.

MaidintheShade347 (Sofia): And it was love at first sight?

Mop&Glow007 (Kyra): Not quite. More like a business deal.

MaidintheShade347 (Sofia): He offered to pay you to be his girlfriend?

Mop&Glow007 (Kyra): Yep. A bundle.

MaidintheShade347 (Sofia): You can't be serious. Is this a joke?

Mop&Glow007 (Kyra): No joke.

MaidintheShade347 (Sofia): Is he cute?

Mop&Glow007 (Kyra): Very.

MaidintheShade347 (Sofia): Is he rich?

Mop&Glow007 (Kyra): Very.

MaidintheShade347 (Sofia): And you accepted?

Mop&Glow007 (Kyra): Not yet.

MaidintheShade347 (Sofia): Why not?

Mop&Glow007 (Kyra): You think I should really consider this idea?

MaidintheShade347 (Sofia): Sure. It's not like you have anything better waiting in the wings.

Mop&Glow007 (Kyra): Thx for making me sound so pathetic.

MaidintheShade347 (Sofia): Oops! My bad. Go for it. Gotta run. Talk soon.

Kyra blinked and read Sofia's last message again. *Go for it*. Was she serious? Then again, ever since Sofia had caught her boyfriend in bed with another woman, Sofia's attitude had changed drastically. When it came to men, she didn't trust them and she refused to get serious, but she was open to having a good time. Kyra was happy that Sofia had regained her spirit and was getting out there and trying different things. But should Kyra do the same? Then again, wasn't that part of the reason for this trip to Greece? Trying something different?

Maybe it was time she quit living life so conservatively. Maybe it wouldn't hurt to color outside the lines, just a little. Mr. Kiriakas's tanned, chiseled face formed in her mind. It certainly wouldn't be so bad being his fiancée for a night or two. She had enjoyed talking to him the other day, and when he smiled, it made her stomach quiver. Sofia was right. She had nothing to lose. It might actually be fun.

Before she could chicken out, she turned in her supplies and rushed to the small apartment she shared with Sofia in the employee housing. Once she had showered and changed into yellow capris and a pink cotton top, she rushed to his suite. She didn't have any idea if he'd still be there.

Her knuckles rapped on the door. She hadn't been this nervous since she came home from school with a below average grade on her report card. She didn't know why she was so jittery. Cristo certainly was nice enough. Besides, this whole thing was his idea.

The door swung open and there before her stood her almost-fiancé, all six foot plus of toned muscle. She tilted her chin upward in order to meet his gaze. "I…I thought over what you said earlier, and I have a few questions for you."

He hesitated and then swung the door open. "Come in."

She glanced around, making sure they were alone. As she did so, she took in the difference in decor between this suite and the other units. For one thing, the standard black upholstered furniture was leather in this suite. The art on the walls consisted of prints in the other suites, but in here everything was original, one-of-a-kind paintings. And lastly, the suite definitely had a lived-in feel—a sense of hominess to it.

Behind her, she could hear the door snick shut. It was

just the two of them, alone. Suddenly Kyra didn't feel quite so confident, so ready to strike a business deal. Right now, even the memory of Sofia's encouraging words sounded foolish. After all, she didn't go out on limbs and take big risks. She liked to play it safe.

Cristo cleared his throat. "Should I take your presence to mean you've changed your mind about my offer?"

She forced her gaze to meet his. "It depends on your answers to my questions."

"What would you like to know?"

Comfortable that she'd left herself an out, should she need it, she leveled her shoulders. "The pretense of being your fiancée, it would only be a show for others, right? You don't want me to, um…sleep with you?"

"No. No. Nothing like that."

She breathed a little easier. "And how long would I have to pretend to be your fiancée?"

"I'll be honest with you. I'm not sure."

"So this is going to take longer than a day or two?"

He hesitated. "Yes, it will. But only until my business deal is concluded. It could be a few weeks or as long as a couple of months—"

"Months?" Kyra shook her head. *No way.* He was simply asking too much of her. "That's not possible. I can't pretend to be your fiancée for that long."

"Are you planning to return to the States before then?"

The easiest way out of this mess was to say yes, but in truth she wasn't leaving Greece until she had a chance to track down her father's family. And since she didn't have a starting point, she didn't know how long that would take her. "No. I'm not leaving yet. I…I have things to do here."

"Anything I can help you with?" When she cast him a skeptical look, he rushed to add, "There are no strings attached to that offer. I like you. You make me smile, and it's been a while since anyone did that. Whether you agree to this plan or not, I'd like to help you out, if I can."

Now, why did he have to go and do that? It would have been so much easier to say no to a man who was pushy and arrogant. None of those descriptions quite fit Cristo Kiriakas. He was more like a really hot, Grecian…gentleman.

"Thank you. That's very kind of you. But not necessary."

"It may not be necessary, but I'd like to help. What has you here in Greece?"

His eyes told her that he was serious. He was really interested in her. So what would it hurt to open up and share a little with him?

"I'm here to find my extended family, or what's left of it." Cristo's brows rose with surprise, encouraging her to continue. "My father passed away a little more than a year ago. He'd always wondered about his extended family and had promised one day we'd take a trip here to see what we could learn. Now that he can't finish our research, I'm taking up where he left off."

"It sounds important."

"It is. For me, that is. My mother doesn't understand my need to do this." In fact, her mother had done everything in her power to curtail Kyra's trip, from pleading to offering up excuse after excuse until she finally resorted to a big guilt trip.

"I know some people who go by the name Pappas—"

"You do?" Could it really be this simple? "How do I find them?"

He held up a hand. "Slow down. Pappas isn't exactly a unique name."

"Oh." She'd known that from her research, but after hitting so many dead ends, she just wanted some hope.

"Do you have much family in the States?" Cristo's voice halted her thoughts.

"There's just me and my mother. The rest of my mother's family, small as it was, passed away. I thought my mother would understand my need to find out more about my past, especially after losing my father. But all she did was get angry and resentful any time I brought up a trip to Greece. Finally, I just stopped trying to make her understand."

"So you thought by taking a job here that you would have the perfect excuse to investigate your family's roots?"

She nodded. At the same time, her phone chimed. Expecting it to be Sofia, she grabbed it from her pocket. The caller ID said Mom. Kyra forwarded the call to her voice mail before slipping the phone back in her pocket.

"If you need to answer that, go ahead."

"It's not important. I'll get it later." The last thing Kyra needed right now was to talk to her mother in front of Cristo—a man who had a way of short-circuiting her thoughts with just a look. No man had ever had that kind of power over her. And she wasn't sure she liked it, but another part of her found him exciting—exhilarating—unlike any man she'd ever known.

"Suit yourself." He moved to the fully stocked refrigerator and removed a bottle of water. He glanced over his shoulder at her. "Would you care for one, too?"

What would it hurt? After all, he was being nice enough and she was a bit thirsty. "Yes. Thank you."

Her phone chimed again. It wasn't like her mother to call right back. Kyra did a quick time change in her head and realized that her mother should be at her second part-time job. Perhaps she was just checking in on one of her breaks.

When Cristo handed over the bottle, their fingers brushed. Their gazes met and held. The breath caught in her throat. She'd never gazed into eyes so intense, so full of energy. She'd heard people talk about instant attraction but she hadn't really known what they were talking about until now. Sure, she'd noticed some really good-looking guys, but they'd always been easily forgotten. Something told her that Cristo would not be so easily dismissed.

He stepped back. "If you'd like something to eat, I could order from the restaurant downstairs."

"No, thanks. I'm fine." With the flutter of nerves in her stomach, there was no way she could eat a bite of anything. "About the arrangement. Will we have to be seen in public together?"

"Definitely." His gaze narrowed. "Will that be a problem? Do you have a boyfriend?"

"No. No boyfriend." She glanced down at her casual clothes and then at his designer suit. "But I don't have anything appropriate in my wardrobe."

"No worries. A new wardrobe and accessories will be part of your benefits package."

Just like that he could arrange for a new, designer wardrobe without even a thought. Wow. How much was this man worth?

With a slight tremor in her hand, she pressed the cold bottle to her lips and took a small sip. She tried to recall the other questions she'd wanted to ask, but her mind drew a blank. At least she'd asked the important ones.

He walked over and placed his bottle on the bar. "I know this is rushing things, but I really need to know your answer to my offer."

"You definitely don't give a girl much time to weigh her options."

His voice grew deeper. "Maybe I just don't want to give you time to find an excuse to back out on me. I can already tell you're going to make my life interesting. You, my dear, are quite intriguing. And I find that refreshing."

"Is that all you find attractive?" The flirtatious words slipped over her lips before they registered in her mind.

His eyes lit up as the heat of embarrassment swirled in her chest and rose up her neck. What was she doing? She barely even knew this man. And yet, she was drawn to him like a moth to a flame, but if she wasn't cautious, she'd get burned.

"It's definitely not the only attractive aspect of this arrangement. Not even close—"

"The money you offered, is it still part of the deal?"

He nodded.

"And can you pay me weekly?" She wanted to pay down the mortgage as soon as possible.

His brows rose. "If that's what you'd like."

"It is."

She made the mistake of gazing into his eyes and noting that he looked at her with genuine interest. Did she really intrigue him? Her heart fluttered. Would it be so bad to have a gorgeous fiancé for just a bit? After all, you only live once. What did it hurt to have a little adventure?

And aside from the money, he'd mentioned helping her to search for her family roots. Now she had to make certain it was part of the deal. "And you agree to assist me in the search for my extended family?"

"I do."

She stepped up to him and extended her hand. "You have yourself a fiancée."

Instead of accepting her hand and shaking it, he lifted it to his lips. His feathery light kiss sent waves of delicious sensations coursing through her body. Much too soon he released her.

"When, um…do we start?" She hoped her voice sounded calmer than she felt at the moment.

"Right now. You have a wedding to plan and we need to get to know each other much better if we are going to convince others that we're a genuine couple."

Her phone chimed. It was her mother again. Something was definitely wrong. Kyra couldn't deny it any longer. "Excuse me for a moment while I answer this."

He nodded in understanding.

Kyra moved toward the wall of windows that overlooked the white sandy beach and aquamarine water. She pressed the phone to her ear. Before she could utter a word, she heard her mother's voice.

"Kyra, why didn't you answer your phone? I didn't call

to talk to your voice mail. Do you even listen to your messages? If you had, you'd know this is important—"

"Mom, stop. Take a breath and then tell me what's the matter."

"Everything."

Her mother had a way of blowing things out of proportion. *Please let this be one of those times.* "Mom, are you all right? You aren't in the hospital, are you?"

"The hospital? Why would I be there?"

Kyra exhaled a relieved sigh. "Just tell me what's wrong."

"My life. It's over. You have to come home."

Not melodramatic at all. "I'm sure it's not that bad."

"How would you know? You don't even know what's the matter."

Kyra fully expected this would be another engineered guilt trip. "Mom, just tell me."

"I would if you'd quit interrupting."

Keeping her back to Cristo, Kyra rolled her eyes. Why did talking to her mother always have to be an exercise in patience? Her father must have had more patience than a saint. "I'm listening now."

"They let me go. Can you believe that? After all I did for them. Is there no longer any such thing as loyalty and respect?"

"Who let you go?"

"The cleaning company. They said they lost some contracts and had to downsize. How can they do that? Don't they know I have bills to pay?" Her mother's voice cracked with emotion. "Kyra, you have to come home right away. I need you."

She should have known it'd come round to this. "I can't. I have a job to do."

"But we're going to lose our home." There was an awkward pause. "I don't know what I'm going to do. I'm all alone."

"Don't worry." Kyra may not agree with everything her

mother said and did, but she still loved her. And her mother didn't deserve to lose her home—no one did. "You won't lose your home. I'll help you."

Kyra, realizing that she'd said too much in front of Cristo, wound up the phone conversation. She promised to call her mother back soon.

Not sure how much Cristo had overheard, her body tensed. Her mother always did have the most amazing timing. Still, there was no undoing what had been done.

She turned to him. He was staring at her with questions reflected in his eyes. She couldn't blame him. If the roles had been reversed, she would have been curious, as well. "Sorry. That was my mother."

"I take it there's a problem."

Kyra really didn't want to get into this with him. "There is, but it's nothing I can't deal with."

He arched a dark brow. "Are you sure about that? I mean, if you have to leave Greece, it's best that we end our arrangement now—"

"No. That won't be necessary." And she didn't add that the money he'd been willing to pay her for her time would be a huge help with her mother's plight. Her doubts about whether she really wanted to move forward with this plan had just been overturned. She owed this to her mother. "I'm all yours—so to speak."

CHAPTER THREE

KYRA WAS ALL HIS.

Cristo couldn't deny that he liked the sound of those words. In fact, that wasn't the only thing he could imagine passing by that tempting mouth.

Cristo gave himself a mental shake. What was he doing daydreaming about this woman? He knew better than to think of romance. He'd witnessed firsthand what happened when the romance turned cold. His parents were like the king and queen of Frostville. He got frostbite every time they were in the same room. He refused to end up unhappy like them.

Cristo cleared his throat. "Maybe we should start this relationship over." He held out his hand to her. "Hi. I'm Cristo."

She slipped her slender hand in his. He immediately noticed the coolness of her skin. She was undeniably nervous. That was good because he was, too.

Her fingers tightened around his hand. "Hi. My name's Kyra. I have the feeling this is going to be quite an adventure."

He had the same feeling but for other reasons, none that he wanted to delve into at the moment. "Let me know whatever you'll need to make this arrangement as pleasant as possible."

As she pulled her hand away, surprise reflected in her eyes. "You make it sound like I've just released the genie from the magic lantern."

"Not exactly. But I do want you to be comfortable during our time together." Cristo knew how thorough Stravos was with his background checks of potential business associates. "I need this engagement to be as authentic as possible. Don't spare any detail or expense."

"What expense?"

"For our wedding."

"You're serious? You really want me to plan a wedding that's never going to happen?"

He nodded. "You have no idea what type of man I'm dealing with. Nikolaos Stravos is sharp and thorough."

"But if people know about this engagement, how are you going to explain it when we break up?"

"I thought about it and we'll handle it just like everyone else who calls off their wedding. We'll tell people it's an amicable split and we'd appreciate everyone respecting our privacy during this difficult time."

"That may be fine for the public but not for close friends and relatives."

"I've thought of that, too." He smiled, liking having all of the answers. "We'll tell them we couldn't agree on kids. You want a couple and I want none."

"Are you serious?"

He nodded. "It's a legitimate reason with no associated scandal. We won't be the first couple to break up over the subject."

She paused as though giving the subject serious consideration. "I suppose it'll work."

He cleared his throat. "It's the truth, at least partially. I'm too busy for a family." That wasn't the only reason he'd written off being a father, but it was all he was willing to share at the moment. "If we're going to do this, we have to make the relationship authentic to hold up under scrutiny. Starting with you moving in here."

"But…but I can't. I told you I'm not sleeping with you."

"And I don't expect you to. But if people are supposed to believe we're getting married, then they'll expect us to be intimate." When she opened her mouth to protest, he held up his hand silencing her. "We only have to give people the impression. Nothing more. Is that going to be a problem?"

Her worried gaze met his. He couldn't blame her for hesitating. He knew he was asking a lot of her. But he was stuck between the proverbial rock and a hard place. She'd been a really good sport, until now.

He had to give her an out. He owed her that much. "It's okay if you want to back out. I will totally understand."

For a moment, he thought she had indeed changed her mind—that she was going to head for the door and never look back. His body tensed. He didn't have a plan B. He'd only devised this plan, such as it was, on the spur of the moment.

When she spoke, her voice was surprisingly calm and held a note of certainty. "You're right. People will grow suspicious if we don't act like a normal engaged couple. But won't people talk about me being a maid?"

He shook his head. "You've only been on the job for two days, and I'm guessing you haven't met many guests."

"No. Not really."

"Good. I wouldn't worry." She glanced around the suite as though trying to decide how they would coexist. He could ease her mind. "Don't worry. There's a guest room with a lock on the door. But I'm sure you probably already know that."

She nodded. "When do you want me to move in?"

"Now. I'll send someone to gather your stuff. It'll be less obvious if you aren't lugging around your suitcases. Are you staying in the employee accommodations?"

She gave him the unit number. "But I…I need to tell my friend."

"Remember, this arrangement has to be kept strictly between us. You can't tell anyone about it or it'll never work. Nikolaos Stravos has contacts everywhere."

"Understood."

"Good. You stay here and I'll have your luggage delivered to you." Her mouth opened, then closed. "Is there a problem?"

She shook her head. "I'll have Sofia toss my things together."

"Good. Because we have big plans tonight."

Was this really happening?

Dressed in a maroon designer dress from the overpriced boutique in the lobby, Kyra held on to Cristo's arm. She was glad to have something to steady her as her knees felt like gelatin. Her hair had been professionally styled and her makeup had been applied by a cosmetologist. It was certainly a lot of fuss for a dinner date. What was Cristo up to?

She highly doubted she'd be able to eat a bite. Her stomach was a ball of nerves. They paused at the entrance of the resort's High Tide Restaurant. The place was dimly lit with candles on each table. Gentle, soothing music played in the background, but it wasn't having any effect on Kyra.

Numerous heads turned as the maître d' escorted them to a corner table. Cristo made a point of greeting people. It was like being on the arm of royalty as everyone seemed to know him. At last at their table, Cristo pulled out her chair. Quite the gentleman. She was impressed.

He took the seat across from her. "Relax. You look beautiful."

Heat warmed her cheeks. She knew she shouldn't let his words get to her. Everything he said and did tonight was all an act. "You look quite handsome yourself."

"Thank you." He sat up a little straighter as a smile reflected in his eyes. "Can I order you some wine? Maybe it'll help you relax."

"Is it that obvious?" She worried her bottom lip while fidgeting with the silverware.

He reached out to her. His hand engulfed hers, stilling it. "Just a little."

Her gaze met his before glancing down at their clasped

hands. She attempted to pull away, but he tightened his grip and stroked the back of her hand with his thumb, sending wave after wave of delicious sensations coursing through her body.

She struggled to come up with a coherent thought. "What are you doing?"

"Trying to get my fiancée to relax and enjoy herself. We don't want anyone wondering why you look so unhappy, do we?"

"Oh." She glanced around, making sure they weren't being watched. Thankfully, no one seemed to notice the bumpy start to their evening. Cristo was right, she needed to do better at holding up her end of this deal—no matter how unnerving it was being in this dimly lit restaurant at a candlelit table with the most handsome man in the room while trying to remain detached.

After making sure the server wasn't within earshot, she said softly, "Would you mind releasing my hand?"

Cristo's brows lifted, but he didn't say a word as he pulled away. She immediately noticed the coldness where he'd once been touching her. She shoved the unsettling thought aside as she picked up the menu. *Just act normal.*

"Would you like me to recommend something?"

Her gaze lifted over the edge of the menu, which was written in both Greek and English. "Do you have it memorized?"

"Would it be bad if I said I did?"

"Really?" He nodded and she added, "You take a hands-on boss to a whole new level."

His eyes twinkled as his smile grew broader and she suddenly realized that her words could be taken out of context. It'd been a total slip of the tongue. Hadn't it?

"The chef's specialty is seafood."

She forced her gaze to remain on the menu instead of continuing to stare into Cristo's eyes. Though her gaze focused on the scrolled entrées, none of it registered in her mind. "I'm not really a seafood fan."

"Beef? Salad? Pasta—"

"Pasta sounds good." Especially on a nervous stomach.

Cristo talked her through the menu. His voice was soothing and little by little she began to relax. She decided on chicken Alfredo and Cristo surprised her by ordering the same thing.

"You didn't have to do that."

His brows drew together. "Do what?"

"Order the same thing just to make me feel better."

A smile warmed his face. "Perhaps we just have similar tastes."

Perhaps they did. Now, why did that warm a spot in her chest? It wasn't as if this was a real date. Everything was a case of make-believe. Did that include his words?

He didn't give her time to contemplate the question as he continued the conversation, moving on to subjects such as how the weather compared to New York, and the differences between the Blue Tide Resort and his flagship business, the Glamour Hotel in New York City, where she'd previously worked.

She appreciated that he was trying so hard to put her at ease. It was as though they were on a genuine date. He even flirted with her, making her laugh. Kyra was thoroughly impressed. She didn't think he would be this patient or kind. She had to keep reminding herself that it was all a show. But the more he talked, the harder it was to remember this wasn't a date.

Much later, the meal was over and Cristo stared at her in the wavering candlelight. "How about dessert?"

She shook her head as she pressed a hand to her full stomach. "Not me. I'm going to have to run extra long tomorrow just to wear off a fraction of these calories."

He pressed his elbows to the table and leaned forward.

"You don't have to worry. You look amazing. Enjoy tonight. Consider it a new beginning for both of us."

A new beginning? Why did it seem as though he was trying to seduce her tonight? Maybe because he was. She was going to have to be extra careful around this charmer.

"The dinner was great. Thank you so much. But I honestly can't eat another bite."

A frown pulled at his lips. "I have something special ordered just for you."

"You do?" No one had ever gone to this much trouble for her, pretend or real.

He nodded. "Will you at least sample it? I wouldn't want the chef to be insulted."

"Of course." Then she had an idea. "Why don't you share it with me?"

"You have a deal." He signaled to the waiter that they were ready for the final course. It seemed almost instantaneous when the waiter appeared. He approached with a solitary cupcake.

It wasn't until the waiter had placed the cupcake in front of her that she realized there was a diamond ring sitting atop the large dollop of frosting. The jewel was big. No, it was huge.

Kyra gasped.

The waiter immediately backed away. Cristo moved from his chair and retrieved the ring. What was he up to? Was it a mistake that he was going to correct? Because no one purchased a ring that big for someone who was just their fake fiancée. At least no rational person.

Cristo dropped to his knee next to her chair. Her mouth opened but no words came out. Was he going to propose to her? Right here? In front of everyone?

A noticeable silence fell over the room as one by one people turned and stared at them. The only sound now was the quickening beat of her heart.

Cristo gazed into her eyes. "Kyra, you stumbled into my

life, reminding me of all that I'd been missing. You showed me that there's more to life than business. You make me smile. You make me laugh. I can only hope to make you nearly as happy. Will you make me the happiest man in the world and marry me?"

The words were perfect. The sentiment was everything a woman could hope for. She knew this was where she was supposed to say *yes*, but even though her jaw moved, the words were trapped in her throat. Instead, she nodded and blinked back the involuntary rush of emotions. Someday she hoped the right guy would say those words to her and mean them.

Cristo took her hand in his. She was shaking and there wasn't a darn thing she could do at that moment to stop it. Perhaps she should have realized he had this planned all along, what with her fancy dress and the stylist. If he wanted a surprised reaction, he got it.

Who'd have thought Cristo had a romantic streak? He'd created the most amazing evening. Something told her she would never forget this night. She couldn't wait to tell Sofia. She was going to be so upset that she missed it.

Cristo stood and then helped Kyra to her feet. As though under a spell, she leaned into him. There was an intensity in his gaze that had her staring back, unable to turn away. Her pulse raced and her heart tumbled in her chest.

When his gaze dipped to her mouth, the breath caught in her throat. He was going to kiss her. His hands lifted and cupped her face. Their lips were just inches apart.

She should pull back. Turn away. Instead, she stood there anxiously waiting for his touch. Would it be gentle and teasing? Or would it be swift and demanding?

"You complete me." Those softly spoken words shattered her last bit of reality. She gave in to the fantasy. He was her Prince Charming and for tonight she was his Cinderella.

The pounding in her chest grew stronger. She needed

him to kiss her. She needed to see if his lips felt as good against hers as they'd felt on her hand.

"How did I get so lucky?" His voice crooned. Yet his voice was so soft that it would be impossible for anyone to hear—but her.

If he expected her to speak, he'd be waiting a long time. This whole evening had spiraled beyond anything she ever could have imagined. She was truly speechless, and that didn't happen often.

His head dipped. This was it. He was really going to do it. And she was really going to let him. Her body swayed against his. Her soft curves nestled against his muscular planes.

She lifted on her tiptoes, meeting him halfway. Her eyelids fluttered closed. His smooth lips pressed to hers. At first, neither of them moved. It was as though they were both afraid of where this might lead. But then the chemistry between them swelled, mixed and bubbled up in needy anticipation.

Kyra's arms slid up over his broad shoulders and wrapped around his neck. Her fingers worked their way through the soft, silky strands of his hair. This wasn't so bad. In fact, it was…amazing. Her lips moved of their own accord, opening and welcoming him.

He was delicious, tasting sweet like the bottle of bubbly he'd insisted on ordering. She'd thought it'd just been to celebrate their business arrangement. She had no idea it was part of this seductive proposal. This man was as dangerous to her common sense as he was delicious enough to kiss all night long.

When applause and whistles filled the restaurant, it shattered the illusion. Kyra crashed back to earth and reluctantly pulled back. Her gaze met his passion-filled eyes. He wanted her. That part couldn't be faked. So that kiss had been more than a means to prove to the world that their relationship was real. The kiss had been the heart-pounding, soul-stirring genuine article.

Her shaky fingers moved to her lips. They still tingled. Realizing she was acting like someone who hadn't been kissed before, she moved her hand. Her gaze landed upon her hand and the jaw-dropping rock Cristo had placed there. The large circular diamond had to be at least four, no make that five, carats. It was surrounded by a ring of smaller diamonds. The band was a beautiful rose gold with tiny diamonds adorning the band. She was in love—with the ring, of course.

"Do you like it?" Cristo moved beside her and gazed down at the ring.

"It's simply stunning. But it's far too much."

Cristo leaned over and whispered, "The ring quite suits you even if it can't compare to your beauty. How about we take our cupcake upstairs?"

CHAPTER FOUR

KYRA'S HEART BEAT out a rapid *tap-tap-tap*.

Why was Cristo staring at her as though she was the dessert?

He leaned close and spoke softly. "You're enjoying the evening, aren't you?"

The wispy feel of his hot breath on her neck sent a wave of goose bumps cascading down her arms. "I…I am. It's magical."

"Good. It's not over yet."

This evening had been so romantic that she couldn't help but wonder if he'd almost gotten caught up in the show. Would he kiss her again? Her gaze shifted to his most tempting lips. Did she want him to?

He extended his arm to her and she accepted the gesture. Before they exited the restaurant, she glanced back at the table to make sure she hadn't forgotten anything. "What about the cupcake?"

"It'll be delivered to our suite along with another bottle of champagne." He turned to the waiter to make the arrangements.

Our suite. It sounded so strange. She wasn't sure how she felt about being intimately linked with Cristo—even if it was all a show.

On their way to the elevator, people stopped to congratulate them. Kyra smiled and thanked them, but inside she felt like such a fraud. A liar. Once again her life had become full of lies and innuendos, but this time instead of being a casual observer of her mother's charade, Kyra was the prime star. She didn't like it…but then again, she glanced at Cristo, there were some wonderful benefits. Not that she was confusing fiction with fact, but there was this tiny moment of *what-if* that came over her.

Once inside the elevator, it was just the two of them. He pressed the button for the top floor and swiped his keycard. She knew this was the end of her fairy-tale evening. She needed to get control of her meandering thoughts. It'd help if he wasn't touching her, making her pulse do frantic things. When she tried to withdraw her hand, he placed his other hand over hers.

What in the world?

She turned a questioning glance his way only to find desire reflected in his eyes. Her heart slammed into her chest. Had he forgotten the show was over? They were alone now. But he continued to gaze deep into her eyes, turning her knees to gelatin.

Was it possible he intended to follow up that kiss in the restaurant with another one? Blood pounded in her ears. Was it wrong that she wanted him to do it—to press his mouth to hers? The breath caught in her lungs. She tilted her chin higher. *Do it. I dare you.*

He turned and faced forward. *Wait. What happened?* Had she misread him? She inwardly groaned. This arrangement was going to be so much harder than she ever imagined.

The elevator doors slid open. Another couple waited outside. The young woman was wrapped in her lover's arms. They were kissing and oblivious to everything around them. Caught up in their own world, the elevator doors closed without them noticing. Now, that was love.

It definitely wasn't what had been going on between her and Cristo. That had been—what—lust? Curiosity? Whatever it was, it wasn't real. And now it was over.

Cristo grew increasingly quiet as he escorted her to their suite. He opened the door for her—forever the gentleman. It'd be so much easier to keep her distance from him if he'd just act like one of the self-centered, self-important jerks that her mother insisted on setting her up with because they had a little bit of money and prestige. Her mother never understood those things weren't important to Kyra.

She stopped next to one of the couches and turned back to him. "Thank you for such a wonderful evening." Before she forgot, she slipped the diamond ring from her finger and held it out to him. "Here. You'd better take this. I don't want anything to happen to it."

He shook his head. "No. It's yours."

"But I can't keep it. It's much too valuable." And held far too many innuendos of love and forever. Things that didn't apply to them.

Cristo frowned. "Now, how would it look if my fiancée went around without a ring on her finger?"

"You're serious? You really want me to wear this? What if something happens to it?"

"Yes, I'm serious. And nothing will happen to it. Besides, I like the way it looks on your hand." He slipped his phone from his pocket and started to flip through messages. "Now, if you'll excuse me, I've got some business to attend to."

"Now? But it's getting late."

His forehead wrinkled as though he was already deep in thought. "It's never too late for work."

And just like that, her carriage turned back into a pumpkin—her prince was more interested in his phone than in her. She felt so foolish for getting caught up in the illusion. Why did she think he'd be any different from the other guys in suits that she'd dated?

"No problem. I'll just go to my room."

There was a knock at the door.

Cristo moved to the door and swung it open. "You're just in time. We were getting thirsty." He turned to her with a warm smile. "Darling, dessert is here. Why don't you go get comfortable and I'll bring it in."

A server rolled in a cart with a cupcake tree and a bottle

of bubbly on ice. The man sent her a big smile as though he knew what she would be up to that evening. Wouldn't he be surprised to know that she was going to bed alone?

Kyra was more than happy to head toward the bedroom. Her strides were short but quick. The evening's show had left her emotionally and physically drained. All she wanted to do now was slip into something comfortable and curl up in bed.

"Kyra, you can come back." Cristo turned to her. "Would you like me to open the wine for you?"

She didn't want to return to the living room. And she certainly didn't need any more bubbly. She needed time to sort her thoughts. But on second thought, it was better she went to him rather than having him seek her out.

Reluctantly she strolled back into the living room. "I think I'll turn in early tonight."

"It's probably a good idea. You have a lot to do tomorrow. Good night." He moved to the study just off the living room and pushed the door closed behind him.

How could he turn the charm off and on so casually?

With a sigh, Kyra headed for her bedroom, which was situated across the hall from his. This hotel suite was quite spacious, resembling a penthouse apartment. She should really snap some pictures to show her mother, but Kyra's heart just wasn't in it. Maybe tomorrow.

Her phone chimed with a new message. Still in her fancy dress, she flounced down on the bed with her phone in hand.

MaidintheShade347 (Sofia): Don't keep me hanging. How'd the date go???

Kyra stared at the glowing screen, wondering what in the world to tell her friend. That the night was amazing, magical, romantic…or the truth, it was a mistake. Plain and simple. She shouldn't have agreed to this arrangement. She wasn't an actress. It was just too hard putting on a show. And worst of all, she was getting caught up in her own performance.

Still, she had to respond to Sofia. Her mind raced while her fingers hovered over the screen.

Mop&Glow007 (Kyra): It was nice.

Immediately a message pinged back as though Sofia had been sitting there waiting to hear a detailed report.

MaidintheShade347 (Sofia): Nice? Was it that bad?

Mop&Glow007 (Kyra): It was better than nice.

MaidintheShade347 (Sofia): That's more like. Now spill.

Mop&Glow007 (Kyra): I wore the most amazing dress. We dined downstairs in the High Tide Restaurant.

MaidintheShade347 (Sofia): Good start. So why are you messaging me?

Mop&Glow007 (Kyra): Why not? You messaged me first.

MaidintheShade347 (Sofia): And I'm not with a hot guy.

Mop&Glow007 (Kyra): Neither am I.

MaidintheShade347 (Sofia): You mean the evening is over already?

Mop&Glow007 (Kyra): He's working.

MaidintheShade347 (Sofia): What did you do wrong?

Her? Why did she have to do something wrong? It's not as if they had gone out tonight with romance in mind. The night ended just the way she expected—though she really had thought at some point over dinner that he was truly into her. The man had given an Oscar-winning performance.

Mop&Glow007 (Kyra): I've got a headache. I'm calling it a night. Talk tomorrow.

She kicked off her shoes and stretched her toes. It'd been a long time since she'd spent an evening in heels. She thought she'd left this kind of life back in New York.

Something told her that sleep would be a long way off. She had too much on her mind—a man with unforgettable blue eyes and a laugh that warmed her insides. How in the world was she going to stay focused on finding her family when Cristo was pulling her into his arms and passionately kissing her?

Where was she?

Cristo refilled his coffee mug for the third time that morning and took a long slow sip of the strong brew. He stared across the spacious living room toward the short hallway leading to Kyra's bedroom. Maybe he should go check on her. He started in that direction when her door swung open. He quickly retreated back to the bar, where he made a point of topping off his coffee.

Kyra leisurely strolled into the living room wearing a neon pink, lime green and black tank top. His gaze drifted down to find a pair of black running shorts that showed off her toned legs. Maybe he should have chosen someone who was less distracting to play the part of his fiancée.

When he realized he was staring, he moved his gaze back to her face. "Good morning."

"Morning." She stretched, revealing the flesh of her flat stomach. Cristo swallowed hard. She yawned and then sent him a sheepish look. Her gaze swept over him from head to foot and then back again. "How long have you been awake?"

He glanced at his watch, finding it was a couple of minutes past seven. "A couple of hours."

Her beautiful eyes widened. "You certainly don't believe in sleeping in, do you?"

He shook his head. "Not when there's work to be done. Would you like some coffee?"

"I'd love some."

He grabbed another mug. "Do you take cream and sugar?"

"Just a couple packs of sweetener."

"Which color do you prefer? Pink? Blue? Yellow?"

"Yellow."

He added the sweetener and gave it a swirl. "If you want to make another pot of coffee, you'll find all of the supplies in the cabinet." He gestured below the coffeemaker. "Make yourself at home."

"You won't be here today?"

He handed over the cup. "I have some meetings in the city that I need to attend. Besides, you'll be so busy that you'll never notice my absence."

"Busy? Doing what?"

"You haven't changed your mind about our arrangement, have you?" He noticed how she fidgeted with the ring on her finger. He hadn't been lying last night when he said it looked perfect on her. In fact, if he hadn't made a hasty exit last night, he would have followed up their kiss with so much more than either of them was ready for at this juncture.

"No. I... I haven't changed my mind."

"Good. Because we made the paper." He grabbed the newspaper from the end of the bar and handed it to her.

"We did. But how?" When she turned to the society page, she gasped.

He had to admit that he'd been a bit shocked when he'd

seen the picture of them in a steamy lip-lock. He'd meant for it to look real, but he never imagined it'd be quite so steamy. Had she really melted into his arms so easily—so willingly?

And for a moment, he'd forgotten that it was all pretend. He'd wanted her so much when they'd returned to the suite that it was all he could do to keep his hands to himself. Thank goodness he had the handy excuse of work waiting for him, because a few more minutes around her and his good intentions might have failed him.

"I didn't realize it'd be in the papers." Kyra tossed aside the paper. "This wasn't part of our agreement. This is awful. My mother isn't going to understand. She…she's going to think we're really a couple. That you and I— That we're actually going to get married. This is a mess. What am I going to tell her? How do I explain this?"

"Calm down. You don't have to tell her anything—"

"Of course I do. When she sees that photo, she'll jump to the obvious conclusion. She'll tell all of her friends. It'll be a nightmare to straighten out."

"No, it won't. Trust me." His soft tones eased her rising anxiety.

"Why should I trust you?"

"Because I made sure this photo was just for the papers here in Athens. Nothing will be printed in New York."

Her gaze narrowed in on him. "Are you absolutely certain?"

He nodded. "I am. Trust me. I have this planned out. We may not be on the front page, but we did make a big headline in the society section. Hopefully it'll be enough to garner Stravos's attention."

"Why would you think this man would look at the society section? Isn't that geared more toward women?"

"Trust me. Nothing gets past this man, especially when he's considering doing business with a person. I'm sure he doesn't stay on top of everything himself, but he has plenty of money to pay people to do the research. But since Stravos is a bit of a hermit living here in Greece on an isolated estate, there's no need for our engagement to be announced in the American papers."

"You're sure?"

"I am."

The rigid line of her shoulders eased and she dropped down on the arm of a couch. "The next time, you might want to mention that part first."

"Would it really be so bad if your mother thought you and I were a couple?"

Kyra immediately nodded. "You have no idea how bad it would be. Until recently, my mother had made it her life's mission to marry me off to one of her friends' sons."

"And you're opposed to getting married?"

"No." Her voice took on a resolute tone. "What I'm opposed to is being someone's arm decoration. I don't want to be someone they drag out for appearances and then forget about the rest of the time."

"I can't believe a man could forget about you."

There was a distinct pause. "It's not worth talking about."

She was one of those women Cristo tried to avoid—the ones who didn't understand the importance of business. He didn't want someone dictating to him when he could and couldn't work. His email constantly needed attention. Almost every bit of correspondence was marked urgent. He didn't want to have to choose between his work and a significant other. Because in the end, his work would win. Work was what he could count on—it wouldn't let him down.

And he didn't imagine there was a man alive who could ignore Kyra. Himself included. He didn't think it was humanly possible. Her presence dominated a room with her beauty and elegance. Even he had gotten carried away the prior evening.

If he was honest with himself, the reason he avoided a

serious relationship was because he could never live up to certain expectations. He'd promised himself years ago that he'd never become a father. He'd learned firsthand how precious and fleeting life could be. All it took was one flawed decision, one moment of distraction, and then tragedy strikes.

The dark memories started to crowd in, but Cristo willed them away. He wasn't going to get caught up in the past and the weighty guilt—not now.

Kyra sighed. "My father was a workaholic. He loved us, but I think he loved his work more. My mother would never admit that. For her, he was the love of her life. But I sometimes wonder if she realizes all she missed out on."

"So you want someone who is the exact opposite of your father?" Cristo wasn't quite sure how that would work. What sort of man didn't get caught up in his work?

She shrugged. "Let's just say I'm not interested in getting involved with anyone at this point in my life. But if I were, I'd want to come first. When we're out to dinner, I'd want his attention focused on me and our conversation, not on his phone."

"That sounds fair." He wondered if she was recalling their dinner the prior evening. His full attention had been on her. He wanted to convince himself that it was because he needed to put on a believable show for the public—a besotted lover and all that it entailed. But the truth was the more Kyra had talked, the more captivated he'd become with her. He swallowed hard, stifling his troubling thoughts. "I've left you some information to get you started with the wedding plans. There's every bridal magazine available, the phone numbers of all the local shopkeepers and a credit card to make whatever purchases are necessary."

"You don't mind if I go for a quick run before I start, do you?"

He glanced at her formfitting outfit. It looked good on her. Really good. "Make your own schedule. But just so you know, the wedding is in six weeks. You don't have a lot of time to spare."

"Six weeks?" Her brown eyes opened wide. "You sure don't give a girl much time to plan. It's a good thing this wedding isn't really going to take place. I'm not sure I could work out all of the details in time."

"But you must. There can't be any cutting corners. Nothing that gives the slightest hint this wedding is anything other than genuine."

"I'll try my best." She frowned as she made her way over to the desk to examine the aforementioned items. "How will I know what to spend? Is there a budget?"

"No budget. Use your best judgment. But remember, this wedding is meant to impress important people. Spare no expense in planning our lavish, yet intimate nuptials."

"This is all still pretend, right? You aren't actually planning to go through with the wedding, are you?"

"Of course not."

She sent him a hesitant look as though trying to figure out if he was on the level or not. "I'll do my best. I don't have much experience with wedding planning."

"I'm sure you'll do fine." He grabbed his briefcase and headed for the door, knowing he had lingered longer than was wise. He paused and glanced over his shoulder. "My cell number is on the desk. If you need me, feel free to call. Otherwise, I'll see you for dinner."

"Not so fast. We aren't finished."

CHAPTER FIVE

CRISTO STOPPED IN his tracks.

What could he have forgotten? He thought he'd accounted for everything.

He turned back to Kyra. "Is there something else you need?"

She nodded. "We had an agreement. You said you would help me search for my extended family."

And so he had. But the last thing he had time for at this critical juncture was to go climbing through Kyra's family tree. "Have you tried doing some research online?"

"Yes. But I couldn't figure out how to narrow my search. I thought a trip to a library or somewhere with records of past residents of the area would be helpful."

"Your family, they're from Athens?"

"I'm not sure. I know my grandparents set sail for the States from here."

A frown pulled at his lips. He didn't have time to waste running around on some genealogy project when he had a billion-dollar deal to secure. He'd risked everything on this venture...from his position as CEO of Glamour Hotel and Casino to his tenuous relationship with his father.

Cristo clearly remembered how his father had scoffed at the idea of taking the already successful hotel and casino chain and making it global. Cristo knew if the chain was allowed to become static, that its visitors would find the hotels limited and stale. The Glamour chain would ultimately begin to die off. He refused to let that happen.

Cristo adjusted his grip on his briefcase. "I'll have a car at your disposal. Feel free to visit any of the local villages or the library in Athens."

She pressed her hands to her hips. "I thought you'd be accompanying me. You know, to help search for my family."

He recalled saying something along those lines, but he just didn't have time today. "Sorry. I've got a meeting in the city with a banker."

"And tomorrow?"

Tomorrow he had more meetings planned. He couldn't even get away from the demands on his time in this fake relationship. It just made him all the more determined to retain his independence.

"Cristo?"

"Fine. I'll check my calendar and get back to you after today's meeting."

She nodded.

Before he walked away, he might as well find out what this venture would entail. "What information do you have to go on?" His phone buzzed. "Hold on." He checked the screen. "My car is here. I must go. I'll look at what you have this evening."

As he rushed out the door, his thoughts circled back around to the sight of Kyra in those black shorts that showed off her tanned legs. Even her toenails had been painted a sparkly pink. And then there was that snug tank top that showed off her curves.

His footsteps hesitated. Maybe he should have offered to go running with her. Almost as soon as the thought crossed his mind, he inwardly groaned. He couldn't—he wouldn't—let his beautiful new fiancée distract him from achieving his goal.

He was so close to forging a deal to purchase the Stravos Star Hotels. It was just a matter of time until he heard back from Nikolaos Stravos about that invitation Cristo had extended for a business meeting. That steamy kiss in the newspaper, with the headline of Cristo Kiriakas is Off the Market, should have done the trick.

* * *

Her lungs strained.

Her muscles burned.

At last Kyra stopped running. Each breath came in rapid succession.

She leaned back against the stone wall lining the walkway in front of the resort. She knew she should have run first thing that morning instead of putting it off. But she'd become so engrossed with the wedding magazines that she'd found herself flipping through one glossy page after the next. When she got to the tuxes, she imagined Cristo in each of them. The man was so handsome that he would look good in most anything. She wasn't quite so fortunate with her broad hips and short legs. It took a certain kind of dress to hide her imperfections.

By late that afternoon, she'd felt pent-up and her head ached. She had more questions about the wedding than answers. What she needed was to talk with Cristo. She knew the wedding would never actually take place, but he'd insisted they were going for authenticity and to pull that off she needed some answers.

When she made her way back to the suite, she called out to him, "Cristo? Cristo, are you here?"

There wasn't a sound. *Drat.*

She moved to the bar where he'd left her his cell number. She entered it in her phone in order to send him a text message.

Mop&Glow007 (Kyra): I have some questions about the wedding. Will you be home soon?

She figured it wouldn't be too long before he responded as he seemed to have his phone glued to his palm. She imagined him falling asleep with it in his hands. Then again, she could easily imagine something else in his hands…um, make that someone else in his very capable hands. And this time, they wouldn't be putting on a show.

She jerked her thoughts to a halt. She was already hot and sweaty from her run. No need to further torture herself.

Her phone chimed.

CristoKiriakasCEO: Meeting has turned into dinner. Will be late. Don't wait up.

Just like that she'd been dismissed. Forgotten. Frustration bubbled in her veins. Cristo was just like the other men her mother had paraded through her life.

Mop&Glow007 (Kyra): Don't worry. I won't.

Her finger hovered over the send button. But then she realized she was being childish. It wasn't as if they were a real couple. This was all make-believe, thankfully. Her heart went out to any poor woman who actually fell for Cristo's stunning good looks and charming smile. He would forget her, too.

Kyra deleted her heated comment and instead wrote, Have a good night.

She told herself she should be happy. It'd give her quiet time to study for her hotel management accreditation. She hated to admit it, but she was woefully behind. Getting ready to move across the Atlantic had been her priority and then she'd been focused on learning her new position at the Blue Tide Resort.

After a quick shower, she made herself comfortable on the couch. Her assignment was to read four chapters and then complete the online questions.

Before she had time to do more than read one chapter, her phone chimed. Was it Cristo? Kyra anxiously searched the couch for her misplaced phone. Had he had a change of heart? Was he in fact different than the men she'd known? He certainly kept her guessing.

MaidintheShade347 (Sofia): What are you doing?

A wave of disappointment washed over Kyra. She had to quit thinking Cristo would surprise her by being anything other than a workaholic. Soon their arrangement would be over and she could get on with her own life.

Mop&Glow007 (Kyra): Studying.

MaidintheShade347 (Sofia): What? You land a really hot, really rich guy and you're studying???

Mop&Glow007 (Kyra): Cristo isn't here.

MaidintheShade347 (Sofia): He bailed on you for dinner?

So Kyra wasn't the only one with that thought.

Mop&Glow007 (Kyra): His meeting ran late. He won't be back for hours.

MaidintheShade347 (Sofia): Oh, good. My date bailed on me. I'll be right over.

Kyra glanced at the unread material on her e-reader and then back at her phone. Maybe some company was exactly what she needed. It'd help get her head screwed on straight. She'd study later. Satisfied Sofia would put normalcy back into her life, Kyra smiled.

Mop&Glow007 (Kyra): See you soon.

And Sofia wasn't kidding. Within a few minutes, there was a knock at the door. At last the evening was starting to look up. She rushed to the door.

Sofia was a couple of inches shorter than her and wore her dark hair in a pixie cut, which worked well with her heart-shaped face. She strolled into the living room and gazed all around. "So this is your," she said, using air quotes for the next word, "'boyfriend's' place?"

Kyra nodded. "I told you he's rich."

"You didn't say *how* rich. This place is really decked out. It's fancier than those exclusive bungalows I clean." Sofia stopped next to one of the couches and glanced down. "Hey, what's this?"

Oh, shoot. Kyra had totally forgotten to put the bridal magazines away. Now she had a lot of explaining to do.

"Are these yours?" Sofia's puzzled gaze met hers. When Kyra nodded, Sofia asked, "But I thought you were paid to be his girlfriend? You didn't mention anything about marrying him. I would have remembered that."

"I'm not marrying him."

Sofia glanced at the open magazine on the glass coffee table. "Looks like you are to me."

"Well, I'm not. I...I'm planning a wedding."

"For whom?"

"Um...so what do you want to eat?" Kyra moved to the desk to retrieve the menus from the drawer. She'd found them earlier at lunchtime. "We could get a pizza."

"Don't go changing the subject. Are you really marrying some guy you hardly know?"

Why did this whole arrangement sound so terribly wrong when Sofia said it? "Hey, I thought you said I should go for it and enjoy an adventure."

"But I didn't say to marry the dude."

Kyra knew she'd promised Cristo that she wouldn't tell anyone about their arrangement, but Sofia wasn't just anyone. Sofia was her best friend. She was the sister Kyra never had. And right now, she needed someone to talk some common sense into her.

"Let me order the pizza and then we'll talk."

"You bet we will." Sofia grabbed the magazine and sank down on the couch. "By the way, do you think they have pizza here?"

Kyra shrugged. "Isn't pizza international cuisine?"

"If it isn't, it should be."

In no time, the concierge had them connected with a nearby pizzeria. As the phone rang, Kyra realized it was very likely that the employees only spoke Greek. This would be a problem as Kyra only knew basic Greek at this point. *Gia sou*—hi. *Nai*—yes. *O'hi*—no. *Efcharistó*—thank you. She knew nothing about how to order a large pepperoni pizza in Greek.

Luckily the person on the other end of the phone spoke English although with a heavy Greek accent. And in turn, Kyra learned that when requesting extra pizza sauce they referred to it as gravy. She tucked that bit of trivia away for future use as she loved pizza.

With food on the way, Kyra had some explaining to do. She inhaled a steadying breath. After starting at the beginning of the story, she ended with, "And now I'm planning a lavish wedding."

"To go with that amazing ring. Let me see it again."

Kyra held out her hand. "Do you think I'm making a big mistake?"

After Sofia got done ogling the rock for the third time, she leaned back. "From what you say, he's been the perfect gentleman." When Kyra confirmed that with a nod, Sofia continued, "And you're doing it to help your mother?"

Kyra nodded again. "I've never heard her so worried. She wanted me to drop everything and go home. I tried repeatedly to explain that I could help her better from here, but I don't think it registered."

"Well, since you're doing it for a good cause, I'd say enjoy your no-strings-attached engagement."

"Will you be my fake maid of honor?"

"Hmm…I've never been asked to be a fake before. I don't know whether to be flattered or insulted."

"Be flattered. After all, I'm only a fake bride and this is a fake wedding."

"True." They both laughed.

"But the planning part is going to be all real."

"You mean he's really going to shell out cash for a wedding that's never going to take place?"

Kyra nodded. "He obviously has more money than anyone should be allowed."

"In that case, I'd be more than willing to take some of it off his hands."

Kyra grabbed one of the magazines and leaned back on the couch. "I don't think that'll happen, but you could help me pick out obscenely expensive dresses, flowers and whatever else goes into a society wedding. I asked Cristo to help me, but he bailed on me for some business dinner tonight."

Sofia shook her head. "What is it with guys and work?" And then lines of concern creased her face. "Are you sure he's actually at a business meeting?"

"Yes." Cristo might be a lot of things, but she had no reason to doubt his word. She knew Sofia's trust in men was skewed by the lies her ex had fed her while romancing another woman. "Cristo is a good guy even if his sole focus is his work."

"Too bad. He might have made a great catch."

Just then the pizza arrived. The aroma was divine. They also delivered two espressos and some complimentary limoncello. The wood-fired pizza was fresh and the toppings were plentiful and outrageously good. The evening

was shaping up to be a great one…despite the fact she'd
been stood up by Cristo.

Why exactly was his business so incredibly important
to him?

Did he know what he was missing?

CHAPTER SIX

WHERE HAD THE evening gone?

Cristo loosened his tie and unbuttoned his collar. He stepped into the waiting elevator and pressed the button for the top floor of the Blue Tide Resort. All he wanted to do now was see Kyra's smiling face. He checked his watch. It was almost eleven. Something told him that if she had waited up for him, she wouldn't be smiling.

He'd never meant to be out this late, but after the bank he'd had a meeting with one of the suppliers for the Glamour Hotel chain. Their contract was about to expire and both sides were haggling for better terms. In an effort to soothe rising tensions, one of Cristo's business advisers had suggested they all go out for the evening. It was not what Cristo had in mind, but in the end, an evening away from the boardroom had eased tensions all around. Details were settled in a casual atmosphere to everyone's satisfaction and tomorrow the papers would be signed.

He really hoped Kyra would be waiting up for him. He didn't know why. Perhaps it was just the thought of having someone to unwind with—someone to share the news of his successful evening. Or maybe it was the way Kyra put him at ease as though he could tell her anything.

He slid his keycard through the reader and opened the door. The first thing that greeted him was the peal of female giggles. Giggles? Really?

He stepped into the room and found Kyra sitting on the floor with her back to him. She and another young woman he'd never met were pointing at pictures in a magazine and laughing. Well, it seemed Kyra was quite self-sufficient and capable of making her own entertainment. For a moment, he regretted missing it.

He cleared his throat. "Good evening."

Both women jumped to their feet and turned to him. Their faces still held smiles. The last thing he felt like doing right now was smiling. Yet there was something contagious about the happiness on Kyra's face. It warmed his chest and eased his tired muscles.

"Oops. Is it really that late?" Kyra glanced down at the mess of papers on the floor. "I guess we got caught up with wedding plans."

Cristo's gaze moved to the young woman at her side. "I see you enlisted help."

Kyra smiled and nodded. "I needed someone to help me." The unspoken accusation that he'd bailed on her was quite evident even in his exhausted state. Thankfully, Kyra didn't appear angry. "So I asked my friend to join me. Cristo, this is Sofia. Sofia, this is Cristo."

"It's nice to meet you, Sofia."

"Nice to meet you, too." Sofia leaned toward Kyra. "Wow. You weren't kidding."

What exactly did that mean? He sent Kyra a puzzled look. Then again, he wasn't sure he wanted to know.

"Don't mind her." Kyra waved off her friend, who was trying to smother a laugh and failing miserably.

Obviously they were very good friends. He didn't know why that should surprise him. Kyra was easy to get along with. That was one of the reasons he'd asked her to work with him to secure this deal with Stravos. He hoped she'd be able to charm Stravos. So far, nothing else had worked. But what Cristo hadn't anticipated was that he would be the one charmed.

He cleared his throat. "I'm sorry. I was held up and couldn't get back sooner." It was the truth, though by the look on Kyra's face, she didn't exactly believe him. "It looks like you two had a good evening."

"We did. Sofia has agreed to be my fake maid of honor for our fake wedding—"

"You told her?" His jaw tensed. What part of don't tell anyone about their arrangement hadn't she understood?

"Um...I did—"

"I think I should go." Sofia grabbed her purse from the couch and moved toward the door. When she got near him, she paused. "Don't worry. Your secret is safe with me."

"Thank you. There's a lot riding on it." He glanced at Sofia, who didn't look as though she trusted him alone with her friend.

The smile faded from Sofia's face. "Kyra and I go way back. There's nothing I wouldn't do for her. Perhaps I should stay."

Did Sofia think he was going to retaliate in an ungentlemanly way? That was not his style. Not now. Not ever. "You don't have to worry. Kyra will be perfectly safe here. I promise."

Sofia gave him one last assessing glance. Then she turned back to Kyra. "Call me if you need anything, anything at all."

"I will. Thanks."

Once Sofia was out the door, Cristo turned back to Kyra. "It seems your friend doesn't trust me."

"Should she?"

"I suppose that's up to you to answer." Okay. So maybe he hadn't taken it well that Kyra had broken her word to him about keeping this deal on the down-low, but he really didn't think he'd done or said anything out of line. Maybe it was the stress of having his whole career on the line combined with the lateness of the hour that had him a bit sensitive. "Don't worry. I hope to have this deal with Stravos concluded soon."

"Does this mean Stravos agreed to a meeting?"

Cristo shook his head. "Not yet. But I hope to hear from him in the near future."

"Will our arrangement be over as soon as you have your meeting?"

Was there a hopeful note in her voice? Was she that anxious to get away from him? He hoped not. He kind of liked having her around. She certainly made his life a lot more interesting. "We'll need to keep up the pretense of being a happy couple until I have a signed agreement."

CHAPTER SEVEN

KYRA YAWNED AND stretched the next morning.

The weekend had finally arrived. After all of the changes and upheaval that week, it was good to have a chance to regroup. After a quick run, she planned to sit down with Cristo and find out exactly what he had in mind for this wedding. She had a few of her own ideas now that she'd looked over the magazines, but she didn't know if they were what he wanted.

With her hair pulled back in a ponytail and dressed in her running clothes, she headed for the living room. When she didn't find Cristo drinking his morning coffee or looking over one of the many newspapers he had delivered to the suite daily, she took a glance in his office. It was empty. In fact, there was no sign of him. Was it possible he'd actually slept in? She couldn't fathom it.

She contemplated knocking on his bedroom door just to check on him when he came strolling in the front door. She spun around, surprised to find him wearing a suit and tie. "Don't you ever take a day off?"

"Why would I do that?" He wore a serious expression.

"All work and no play makes Cristo a dull boy."

He arched a brow. "You think I'm dull?"

"I don't know. Perhaps." She sent him a smile that said she was teasing him. But her comment wasn't all in jest. She found it frustrating the way he worked night and day. And from all appearances, every day of the week. "You do know that it's okay to take some downtime once in a while, don't you?"

His dark brows drew together as though what she said did not compute. "The world doesn't stop just because it's

Saturday. You'd be surprised to know of all the business deals that are agreed to on weekends."

She sighed. "Well, what about the work we have to do here?"

His phone buzzed and he held up a finger to indicate he would be with her in a moment. She was seriously tempted to take his phone from him and give him a time-out. She crossed her arms and tapped her foot.

He quickly typed something into his phone before slipping it in his pocket. "Now, what did you need?"

"You."

A broad smile lifted his kissable lips. "Why didn't you say so? If I had known you wanted me, I would have been at your beck and call."

She rolled her eyes. "Does that line really work on the ladies?"

He shrugged. "I don't know. I never tried it."

"Lucky for them. No wonder you were so desperate for a fake bride if that's the best you've got."

"What can I say? I'm not used to picking up women."

She wasn't for a second going to believe he didn't have a social life. No way. Not with his dark, tanned good looks. "So you're saying they pick you up?"

"In a manner of speaking. Would you like to pick me up?"

She shook her head and waved him off. "Not a chance. You've already given me enough headaches with this wedding that you refuse to help me plan."

"I never refused."

"I know. You're just too busy." Her voice grew weary. Cristo needed to realize she wasn't one of his employees to slough tasks off on. They were in this together. Perhaps he just needed to be reminded of what was at stake. "Maybe we should call the whole thing off."

"What? But we can't."

She pressed her hands to her hips. "You're too busy to

help me, and from what I can tell, your plan isn't panning out."

"It's working. Remember, our picture was in the paper?"

"From what you're telling me, this Mr. Stravos is very thorough. You don't think he's going to want to see us together—see if we're really a happy couple?"

Cristo shrugged. "How hard can that be? We fooled everyone in the restaurant."

"That was from a distance. What happens when we have to put on a show for someone—someone who is suspicious of us like Mr. Stravos?"

"So what do you have in mind?"

"Stay here today. We can get to know each other better." When his eyes dipped to her lips, her pulse raced. She swallowed hard. "Not like that. I meant talking. If we're going to portray a happy, loving couple, we should know more about each other."

"But my meeting—"

"Can be rescheduled. This was your idea, not mine. I'm just finding ways to make it work. Unless you just want to forget it all—"

"Okay. I get the point." He sighed. "Let me make a phone call."

"And change into some running clothes." Then, realizing that just because he looked like a Greek god didn't mean he exercised, she added, "You do run, don't you?"

He nodded and moved toward the bedroom. The fresh air and sun would do him good. And if she was lucky, it'd erase the frown from his face.

In no time at all, Cristo had changed into a royal blue tank top that showed off his broad shoulders and muscular biceps. Mmm… This man definitely knew his way around a gym. A pair of navy shorts did nothing to hide his well-defined legs.

Cristo didn't say much on their way to the beach. In fact,

he was so quiet she wondered if he was truly upset with her about ruining his plans for the day.

She came to a stop on the running/walking path and turned to him. "If you don't want to do this, I'll understand."

Cristo started to stretch, lifting both arms over his head. "Are you starting to worry that you can't keep up?"

"Are you serious?"

He didn't say anything, but his stare poked and prodded her.

Her pride refused to let her back down. He might look amazing, but since she'd known him, he hadn't run. She, on the other hand, had been running every morning. "I'm not worried at all. We'll see who keeps up with whom."

He smiled confidently.

Once they warmed up, they took off at a healthy pace. Little by little they kept trying to outdo each other. Kyra was used to running solo, so she'd never been challenged this way.

When she started to get winded, she glanced his way. Cristo hadn't even broken a sweat. What was up with that? Shouldn't a man who spends all of his time going from meeting to meeting be tired by now?

As though he sensed her staring at him, he glanced over at her. "I take it I've surprised you."

What did it hurt to be honest? "Well, kinda. It's just that with you working all of the time, um…"

"You thought I'd be out of shape?"

Her face was already warm from the sun and exertion, so she hoped it'd hide her embarrassment. "I know how busy you are—"

He slowed down to a walk. "Between you and me, I do take time out to exercise."

"But when? You're always going from meeting to meeting."

He sent her a smile. "When something is important enough, you make the time. Sometimes I make it to the gym before heading to the office. Other times I do it at lunch. And on the really stressful days, I go in the evening."

Funny how he found exercise important enough to squeeze in, but he didn't seem to have that same philosophy about his social life. "You must really be health conscious."

"I don't know about that. I still enjoy a nice juicy steak. The exercise is more of a stress reliever for me. I played football all through school and always felt better after a strenuous workout. I guess it stuck."

"Football? Here in Greece?"

"No. I grew up in New York City."

"Small world. So did I." Something told her they may have lived in close proximity but they had led very different lives. "Let me guess. You were the quarterback."

He shook his head. "Sorry to disappoint you. I was a wide receiver, much to my father's disappointment."

"Your father wasn't happy that you played football?"

"He was fine with football, but he thought that a Kiriakas should always be the best. In this case, the quarterback and team captain."

"Surely he was…um, is proud of you."

"We should be getting back. I'll race you." When she didn't respond, he added, "I'll give you a head start."

She wasn't too proud to accept his offer because they both knew with his powerful legs that he could easily beat her. "And winner buys lunch."

She took off, all the while thinking about the relationship between Cristo and his father. Her heart swelled with sympathy for the son who failed to live up to his father's expectations. Was that why Cristo seemed to keep to himself?

Minutes later, Kyra and Cristo relaxed at an umbrella-covered table after their race. She'd ended up winning the race. And though she'd teased him about it, she knew he'd let her win. She hated to admit it, but he could easily out-run her. Maybe there was more to Cristo than profit reports and balance sheets after all.

"Looks like you're buying lunch." Cristo's eyes twinkled with mischief.

"So that's why you let me win?"

"Let you?" He shook his head. "I don't throw races. Are you trying to get out of our little wager?" He sent her a teasing smile.

She wished he wouldn't make her pull everything out of him. It'd be so much nicer if they could chat like friends—like her and Sofia. Open, easy and honest. Kyra squeezed the wedge of lemon over her iced tea. "Do you have siblings?"

He nodded. "Three…erm, two older brothers. And you?"

That was a really strange mistake to make. Who forgot the number of brothers they had? His pointed stare reminded her that she still owed him an answer. "I'm an only child. But Sofia is the sister I always wanted."

"Have you known her long?"

"Since junior high. We've been inseparable ever since. She's the yin to my yang. Although lately she's been a bit more yang." When he sent her a puzzled look, she added, "More sunny rather than shady."

He nodded in understanding. "So does that cover everything?"

She arched a brow. "You're kidding me. This isn't an interview. And we've barely scratched the surface of what I'd want to know about my fiancé, but it's at least a start."

"Honestly, there's not that much to know about me."

She eyed him up, surprised to find he was perfectly serious. Well, the guy may be a workaholic but he certainly couldn't be accused of being conceited.

"There's lots to know about you. Like what's your favorite meal?"

He thought for a moment. "I guess surf and turf."

"Who's your favorite musical group?" She'd bet he was a classical fan.

"U2."

Color her surprised. "Coffee or tea?"

"Coffee."

"Sunrise or sunset?

"Sunrise."

"Left or right?"

His brows drew together. "Left or right what?"

"Oops. Preferred side of the bed."

"Left."

Oh, good. She preferred the right. Not that it mattered, since this relationship was an illusion.

"Now it's my turn." Cristo leaned forward, resting his elbows on the table. He launched into his own rapid-fire questions. She played along, enjoying getting to know him better.

"Top or bottom?" His eyes twinkled with devilment.

Oh, no. She wasn't going there with him. "That's nothing you need to know."

"I disagree." His lips lifted into an ornery grin. "Every fiancé should know these things."

Boy, was it getting warm. Kyra resisted the urge to fan herself. The only thing she could think to do now was change the subject. "So why is this deal with Stravos so important to you?"

Cristo sighed as he leaned back in his chair. He took a sip of his iced coffee. "I plan to expand the Glamour Hotel and Casino chain, which is currently only a North American venture, into a global business. Stravos has an upscale hotel chain that spans the globe. I've heard rumors his grandson is interested in condensing the family's holdings in order to concentrate their funds on expanding their shipping business. This is the prime time to make my interest in the hotel chain known before they publicly announce it's for sale."

He hadn't really answered her question. She still didn't know his driving desire to make his business bigger and better than before. And from what she sensed, it was more than just a strategic business move. But she didn't want to push him too hard now that he was finally opening up to her.

"Now that we've gotten that out of the way, I really should get some work done today." He downed the rest of his drink.

"What about the wedding? Exactly how far do you want me to go with these wedding preparations?"

"The whole way." His chair scraped against the colorful tiles as he prepared to stand.

He wasn't going to get away, not until they got a few things straight. "You know, I didn't sign on to guess my way through this whole wedding. Engaged couples, well, at least the ones I know, make some of the decisions together."

His jaw tensed as a muscle twitched in his cheek. "But I don't know anything about weddings."

"And you think that I do?"

He shrugged. "But you're a woman. Don't all women dream about their weddings?"

"Not this woman. It was never a priority. I figured some-day if I met a guy who could make me his top priority, that we'd settle down together. But I'm not getting married just because it's what my mother expects."

"So what you're saying is you wouldn't marry someone like me—at least not willingly."

She paused, not sure if she should speak the truth or not. But then she figured that a man as rich and power-ful as Cristo Kiriakas probably didn't have many people in his life who spoke openly and honestly with him. After all, what could it hurt?

She took a deep breath. "No. I wouldn't marry you. You're too wrapped up in your own world. You say the right things, but when it comes time to the follow-through, you fail—"

"That's not fair. You're just judging me on this one oc-casion, when I have everything riding on this pivotal deal with Stravos. You have no idea what's at stake here."

"I'm sure I don't. But I'm guessing in your world there's always some huge deal to be made or some catastrophe to resolve. Face it, your business is your mistress. You don't have room in your life for another woman."

His mouth opened, then snapped shut. She had him and he knew it. What could he say to the contrary? Absolutely nothing.

His phone buzzed.

She sighed. "Let me guess. You're going to get that when we're at last having an open and honest conversation?"

He pulled the phone from his pocket. "It could be important."

"Do you ever get a phone call that isn't important?"

He didn't answer her as he took the call and moved toward the rail overlooking the beach, most likely to gain some privacy. And yet again, he'd proven to her why staying single was her best option. She didn't like being shoved aside and forgotten.

The truth of the matter was she wasn't suited for this job. She was getting too emotionally invested in a man and a relationship that would soon disappear from her life. But how did she turn off her emotions?

As Cristo's conversation grew lengthy, her patience shrank. She finished her tea and was about to return to the suite for a shower when she noticed Cristo's voice rising. She glanced around finding that most of the nearby tables were vacant.

"You're just worried, because when this deal goes through—and it will—my hotel chain will rival yours."

Kyra couldn't help but be curious as to what had made Cristo lose his cool. He might be a busy man, but he was very good at the art of deflection. He'd even taken her harsh assessment of him as husband material without raising his voice. Who was on the other end of the phone?

"I'm not disloyal to the family. This is business, pure and simple. Something you taught me as a kid."

She shouldn't be sitting here listening. Yet she couldn't move. She was entranced by this new side of Cristo—this vulnerable aspect.

"I'm sorry you feel that way, Father." His whole body noticeably tensed. "Do what you need to do, and I'll do what I need to do."

Sympathy welled up in Kyra. She knew what it was like to disagree with a parent. She did it more than she liked with her mother.

"You know what? You've always been disappointed in me." Cristo jabbed his fingers through his hair as he started to pace. "Why should this be any different?" And with that, Cristo ended the call.

The breath caught in Kyra's throat. There was a line being drawn in the proverbial sand between the two men. And that wasn't good. Not good at all.

Okay, so maybe she'd had a few heated arguments about her mother's meddling, but it had never gotten that harsh. She knew no matter what she did in life that her mother would love her. She didn't have anything to prove to her mother.

So what in the world had happened between Cristo and his father? Was there always such discord between them? Her heart went out to Cristo as he leaned forward on the rail, keeping his back to her. She could only imagine the turmoil churning inside him.

If she'd had any thoughts about backing out of this arrangement, they were gone now. It was bad enough that his father thought he was going to fail, but for her to pull the rug out from under Cristo when he'd been working night and day to make this deal a success would just be too much.

Suddenly, grabbing a shower didn't seem quite so urgent. "Cristo, I was thinking about ordering brunch. That run really worked up an appetite. Want to join me?"

When he turned to her, his face was pale. Lines by his eyes and mouth were more pronounced. It was as though he'd aged five years during that one phone call. She was tempted to go up to him and wrap her arms around him while murmuring that it would all be better soon. But she knew that his wounded ego would rebuff her sympathies.

Cristo returned to the table and sat down. "That was my father." She'd guessed that much by what she'd overheard, but she didn't say anything as she waited and wondered if Cristo would open up to her. He cleared his throat. "He saw the press release of our engagement."

"But I thought you said it wouldn't be in the New York papers."

"It wasn't. My father has his sources. I just didn't know he had me under such tight scrutiny." Cristo rubbed the back of his neck. "He also found out about my plan to buy the Stravos hotels."

"I take it he's not happy about either of your plans." When Cristo shook his head, she added, "I'm so sorry."

Cristo's dark gaze met hers. "What do you have to be sorry about? You had nothing to do with my father."

"I'm just sorry that you had to argue."

Cristo's brows drew together. "I don't need your pity. My father is a hard, cold man. But once this deal is concluded, I'll have an international hotel chain. It'll even top my two brothers' accomplishments. My father will have no choice but to acknowledge my success. He'll have to admit I'm no longer that irresponsible boy who stood by helplessly while…while, oh, never mind. It doesn't matter now."

On the contrary, it mattered a great deal. But she wouldn't push him. As it was, she understood so much more about him and his driving motivation to make this deal a success. She couldn't even imagine how much it must hurt to need to prove your self-worth to a parent. She would do her utmost to help him.

CHAPTER EIGHT

What did he know about planning a wedding?

Nothing. Nada. Zip. Zero.

Cristo sat on the floor of the suite with his back propped against the couch. His legs were stretched out in front of him with his ankles crossed. He couldn't remember the last time he'd had such a leisurely Sunday.

He frowned as he gazed at the glossy magazine cover that Kyra had just dropped in his lap. His gaze moved over the cover. *Finding the Perfect Dress.* He kept reading. *Wedding Night Confessions.* He groaned.

"Did you say something?" Kyra rushed over to him with an armload of magazines.

"No." He willed his phone to ring with an emergency or anything he could construe as an emergency, but the darn thing for the first time ever remained silent. He was stuck. He stifled another groan.

She settled next to him. "It helps if you open it. I've marked some pages."

He grudgingly started flipping through the pages. What he wouldn't do now for a quarterly profit report to review or the *Wall Street Journal* to peruse. Instead, he was looking at articles on which shade of nail polish go best with your gown. He turned the page to find *Flowers on a Budget*.

"Isn't it amazing all of the subjects they cover?" Kyra sounded impressed. "I've learned quite a bit from reading these magazines."

"I certainly wouldn't have thought of these things." And that was no lie. His gaze paused on the headline *Making Your Wedding Night Unforgettable*. The title evoked all sorts of tempting images of Kyra in skimpy—no, scratch that. She'd be wearing a classy white nightie that tempted and teased. He closed the magazine.

"Are you sure something isn't bothering you?" She sent him a worried look and shifted uncomfortably.

Yes. Lots. He struggled for a different subject to discuss, something that wouldn't have him imagining her on their wedding night. And then it came to him. "Actually, there's something I've been meaning to mention."

She laid her pen down on a pad of paper as though giving him her full attention. "I'm listening."

He set aside the bridal magazine with its taunting headlines and got to his feet. He retrieved his briefcase from next to the bar and removed a manila folder.

"Between meetings, I was able to pull up some preliminary information on your surname." He handed it over to her. Their fingers brushed and a wave of need washed over him. His gaze dipped to her lips. He wondered what she'd do if he were to kiss her again, because that one time just wasn't enough. Not even close.

"You did?" Her face beamed with a hopeful smile.

"Don't go getting too excited. As you probably know, it's a popular name. We're going to need more information to narrow it down. Can you remember any details your father told you? Was he born here?"

"He was born in the States. My grandmother was pregnant with him when they crossed the Atlantic."

"Hmm… That eliminates finding a birth record for your father. Did he ever hear any family names?"

She shook her head. "He said his mother didn't talk much about her family. His father told him it was because she was homesick."

"And your grandfather's family?"

"Died in a flu epidemic. He ended up being raised by friends of the family." Kyra worried her bottom lip. "I do have something that might be helpful in my bedroom."

When she went to stand, he put a hand on her shoulder.

"Let's not get sidetracked from this wedding stuff. We can go over the stuff about your family tomorrow."

"Oh." Disappointment rang out in her voice.

She held out the folder. "Thanks for these names. I know it'll be like finding a needle in a haystack, but it's a start." Her eyes grew shiny. "Who knows, I might be holding the name of a relative in my hand."

In that moment, he realized just how much this search for her family meant to her. With him being so distant from his own, Kyra's need to reconnect with hers intrigued him.

He cleared his throat. "How about we make a trip into Athens?"

"To do what?"

"I thought we'd visit the library. Hopefully they'll have lots of old documents."

She clasped her hands together and smiled. "You'd do that for me?"

He nodded. "I'd like to see you find your family."

"Really?" The smile slipped from her face. "I mean, up until now you haven't seemed very interested in helping."

He raked his fingers through his hair. How did he explain this to her when he hadn't really delved into his motives? Why exactly had this become so important to him?

Cristo cleared his throat. "I guess I know what it's like to feel alone and isolated." Wait. Was that honestly how he felt? He didn't like digging into emotions, but the captivated look on her face urged him on. "And I know that it's different because my family is alive. I chose to walk away. You never got a choice."

"Thank you for understanding." Her eyes filled with warmth. "You know, it's not too late to change your mind about reconciling with your family. In fact, this wedding is the perfect excuse to ask them to visit."

He shook his head. It wasn't going to happen. "Speaking of the wedding, didn't you have more stuff we need to go over?"

* * *

If anyone could help her track down her family, it was Cristo.

The next morning, Kyra awoke before the alarm. As she showered and dressed, thoughts of Cristo circled around in her mind. She had a good feeling about finding her family now that he was on her side. He spoke Greek fluently and could read it. He knew a great many people, including those with the Pappas name. If Cristo could point her in the right direction, she just might meet her distant relatives.

When she rushed into the living room, she found it empty. She made her way to his study. It was empty, too. Was it possible Cristo had slept in? On a Monday—a workday?

Maybe she should check on him. She started toward his room when she noticed a note on the bar. In a very distinctive scrawl with determined strokes, the blocked capital letters were surprisingly legible.

KYRA,
UNEXPECTED PROBLEM AT THE OFFICE NEEDED MY IMMEDIATE ATTENTION. I'LL MAKE IT UP TO YOU. IN THE MEANTIME, BELOW ARE SOME WEBSITES YOU MIGHT WANT TO CHECK. HOPE THEY ARE HELPFUL.
CRISTO

Frustration bubbled in Kyra's veins. Why had she believed him when he said he'd help her this morning? She clenched her hand, crinkling the paper. She should have known he'd be too busy.

She had to get out of the suite. Otherwise, she just might invest in a gallon of ice cream. That would not help slim her hips. Besides, a run in the fresh air and sunshine would hopefully soothe away her disappointment in finding out that Cristo was just like the other men she'd dated. Why in the world did she let herself imagine he would be any different?

She pushed herself long and hard. An hour or so later, she returned to the suite feeling a bit better. She was determined to find her family, with or without Cristo's help. She'd gotten this far on her own. She could make it the rest of the way.

After showering again, Kyra settled on the couch with her laptop. She smoothed out the note Cristo had left her and input the first web address, which took her to a Greek social site. Thank goodness her computer had the option to translate everything to English.

She didn't know how much time had passed when she heard the door open. With effort, she continued to stare at the monitor. Try as she might, she couldn't think about anything but the sexy man now standing behind her.

"Hello, Kyra." His deep voice washed over her.

"Hi." She stubbornly refused to make this easy for him. He was the one who'd broken their date as though she should totally understand that business trumps all else, all of the time.

He moved to stand at the end of the couch. "Aren't you even going to look at me?"

Was that some sort of challenge? She glanced at him and then turned back to her computer, already forgetting the site she wanted to visit next. "Did you need something?"

"So this is how it's going to be?"

She closed her laptop and turned to him. "What is that supposed to mean?"

"That you're mad because I had work to do."

She hated how he made it seem as if her search to find her family was so unimportant. If only he knew how much her mother needed it—how much she needed it. "It doesn't matter. I did fine on my own."

"You did?" There was genuine enthusiasm in Cristo's

voice as he slid off his suit jacket and draped it over the back of a black leather armchair.

She nodded. "I was able to connect with some people online who pointed me toward some helpful information."

"That's great. Were the sites I left you of any help?"

"Yes. Thank you."

Cristo sat down on the couch and rolled up his sleeves. "I know I let you down today, and I'm truly sorry about that." His gaze met hers, making her heart thump. "But I'm here now and I'd like to do what I can to help. And tomorrow we're off to Athens to do research."

She sent him a hesitant look. "You don't have to. I know you have a lot of work to do—"

"And it can wait. I really do want to help. I promise no emergency will hold us up. So is it a plan?"

He'd apologized and it was a soothing balm to her bruised pride. She smiled. "It's a plan."

"Good. Now, why don't I look over what you have so far while you order room service."

That sounded reasonable to her. "I'll be right back." She rushed out of the room, hoping he wouldn't grow frustrated with her lack of documentation. Seconds later, she returned. "Here's everything."

He accepted the black-and-white snapshot of a young couple obviously very much in love. He turned it over to glance at the back before looking at her. His eyes reflected his confusion. "Where are the birth records, marriage certificates or family bible?"

"I…I don't have them. When my mother realized I was going to continue my father's mission, she gave me this photo. Everything else was destroyed in a fire when my father was a kid. That's a picture of my grandparents here in Greece before they moved to the States."

Cristo glanced back at the black-and-white image. "This isn't a lot to go on."

"But it's a start, isn't it?"

He sighed. "I supposed it is. Do you mind if I borrow this?" He hurried to add, "It won't be long. I just want to make a high-quality copy of it."

Her chest tightened. She couldn't stand the thought of losing the only solid link to her past, but as of right now, it was of no help to her. "Go ahead. Do what you need to." Then for her own peace of mind, she asked, "Do you think there are any clues in it?"

He held up the photo. "I'm interested in the background. If we have it enlarged, we might be able to locate where the photo was taken."

"I used a magnifying glass, but I couldn't make out any signs."

"I'm thinking more about the architecture. If it's unique enough, it could point us in the right direction. Now, show me what you came up with online."

Kyra readily opened her laptop, eager to share the tidbits of information. It was a lot like a jigsaw puzzle. She welcomed the help in figuring out how the information fit together and discerning which information didn't belong.

And at last she had Cristo's full attention. Best of all, the more they talked, the more excited he became with the project. He filled her with hope that at last she might find any lingering relatives.

They sat in the living room all evening, scouring the internet and eating room service. Kyra saw a different side of Cristo, a down-to-earth quality. And she liked it. A lot.

Now, how could she get him to let down his guard again? She really enjoyed seeing him smile.

CHAPTER NINE

IT HADN'T WORKED out quite as he'd planned.

Cristo glanced over at Kyra as their limo inched its way through the congested streets of Athens. "I'm sorry our visit to the library wasn't more productive."

"It's not your fault. After all, you helped me search through countless newspapers, journals and books. We may not have uncovered anything, but it wasn't for lack of trying."

He breathed a little easier. "Don't give up. We still have the picture of your grandparents. It's got to have some clues."

She lowered her head and shrugged. "Perhaps."

Even though they weren't able to track down any documents with her grandparents' names, he refused to give up and she couldn't, either. "You know that library is huge. They have thousands of documents. I'm sure we've barely even scratched the surface. We'll just keep at it until we head in the right direction."

"You're right. It's just so frustrating."

"Then think about something else for a while."

"Actually, I do have some questions for you." She withdrew a notebook and pen from her purse. "How many people are you considering inviting to the wedding?"

"You want to do this here? Now?"

"What else do we have to do?"

Some tempting thoughts sprang to mind. "I can think of something a lot more fun."

His gaze moved to the partition that was currently down. If he was to put it up, they'd have all the privacy needed and then he could claim her lips.

A smile tugged at her lips. "That's not what I meant."

"But I promise you'll enjoy it." He playfully reached out for her, but she scooted away. He frowned at her. "Fine. You win. What was it you wanted to know?"

"How big should the wedding be?"

"I'm thinking something small and intimate. Maybe five hundred people."

"Five hundred?" Kyra's mouth gaped. "Are you serious?"

He shrugged. "What were you thinking?"

"Twenty would work for me. But I know you're a very popular person, so how about one hundred people?"

That wasn't many people. There was family, business associates and employees to consider. Still, there was a certain appeal to an intimate gathering. "Considering we'll be having the ceremony here in Athens rather than in New York, I'm guessing you won't be having many guests."

She shook her head.

Surely he could cut back on the invites. He gave it a bit of thought. "I should be able to get out of inviting a number of people because of the location. It'll take some effort, but I think we can make one hundred people work."

She noted something in her day planner. "I've done some online research and there are invitation addressing and mailing services. I think at this late date it'd be our best option. For a fee, I can put a rush on the order."

"Yes. Yes. The price doesn't matter."

She reached in her purse for an electronic tablet. "What's your favorite color?"

"Why?"

"I need it for the invitations." Her fingers moved rapidly over the screen.

"I guess it's blue." He honestly didn't think anyone had ever asked him that question. "And what's yours?"

"My what?" she asked as though she had been lost in thought.

"Your favorite color?"

"It's aqua." She focused on the tablet and then said, "I've got some invitations picked out. It's just a matter of narrowing them down. Ah, here's one that uses both of our colors. How about a beach-theme invitation with the background being the sand and water with a blue sky?" She turned the screen around for him to see a picture of the proposed invitation. "And for a fee they can add a gold ribbon and starfish. They'll be sent in little blue boxes."

If she liked it, that was good enough for him. "Go ahead and place the order. And you're sure it'll get to everyone in time?"

She nodded. "As long as you give me those names and addresses today."

He was afraid she'd say that. "I'll list the names and my assistant can give you the addresses."

"You do know that once we send out the invitations your family and friends will know about this thing between us. How are you going to explain the fact they've never met me or even heard of me?"

He hadn't thought of that. "I'll tell them the truth. That we met here at the resort…and it was love at first sight."

"And you think they'll believe it?"

"Most definitely. You're so gorgeous, how could I not be captivated by you?"

"You're making that up."

"I could never make up something like that. Between your beauty and your warm personality, I'm not sure which won me over first."

He wished he was better with words. If he was, he'd tell her how her big brown eyes glittered with specks of gold. They were utterly mesmerizing. Her cheeks held a rosy hue. And her lips…well, they were so sweet and tempting. He knew that for a fact because the kiss they'd shared was forever imprinted upon his mind.

And when he was alone, it wasn't facts and figures that filled his mind these days, it was figuring out how to steal another kiss. Perhaps he could suggest they practice some more, so that it seemed natural when they had to do it in front of people.

He may not be able to articulate how she made him feel, but he could show her. Going with the moment and refusing to consider the implications, he reached his hand out to her. His thumb traced her jaw. "You're the most amazing woman I've ever known."

She continued to stare into his eyes. His heart pounded against his ribs. Did she have any idea what she could do to him with just a look? He should back away.

But he needed to taste her once more. His gaze dipped to her shimmery lips. Instead of the calm, sophisticated businessman that he liked to portray to the world, right now he felt like a nervous teenage boy.

The tug-of-war between right and wrong raged within him. All the while his fingers continued to stroke her smooth skin. His pulse quickened and the pounding of his heart drowned out the voices.

He leaned forward. His lips claimed hers. Gently and hesitantly. He had no idea if she felt the same way.

But then her hands moved over his shoulders and wrapped around his neck. Her mouth moved beneath his. No kiss had ever rocked his world like hers. He didn't know what was so different about her. He just knew he never seemed to get enough.

His phone buzzed and Kyra pulled away.

Of all the lousy times. Cristo swore under his breath. With the moment ruined, he reached for his phone. "Kiriakas here."

"Mr. Cristo Kiriakas?"

"Speaking." He really should have checked the caller ID, because he didn't recognize the female voice.

"I'm calling on behalf of Nikolaos Stravos. He would like to know if you are available for dinner."

She named a date in the coming week. The acceptance

teetered on the tip of Cristo's tongue, but he held it back for just a moment—just long enough so this employee of Stravos's didn't know just how anxious he was for this meeting. After a slow, deep breath in and out, Cristo said, "As it happens, I could rearrange my calendar."

"He also requested you bring your fiancée. Would that be possible?"

Cristo's gaze moved to Kyra's beautiful face. "Yes, we will both be able to attend."

"Good." The woman filled him in on the details.

When Cristo disconnected the call, he was a bit stunned. His plan was really working. Okay, so he had had a few doubts along the way. And when his father had insisted he was doomed to fail, his confidence had wavered just a bit. But thanks to Kyra sticking by his side, he'd kept moving forward and it had paid off.

Curiosity glittered in Kyra's eyes. "Well?"

"That was one of Stravos's employees. He wants to have dinner."

"Really?" Kyra clapped her hands tightly together. "This is good, isn't it?"

He nodded.

"Yay! Congratulations." A big grin lit up her entire face.

For a moment, he didn't move. He'd been so stunned by her rush of emotions. He wasn't used to people getting outwardly excited. His family and coworkers were quite reserved. But maybe just this once, it wouldn't hurt to follow her lead. He smiled.

"And it's all thanks to you."

"Me?" She pressed a hand to her chest. "I didn't do anything."

He wasn't going to argue with her, but he couldn't have done any of this without her. And it wasn't just the dinner—she'd gotten him to remember that there was more to life than work. And she'd reminded him how good it felt to smile—really smile, the kind that started on the inside and radiated outward.

Cristo cleared his throat. "Dinner is next weekend."

Her smile turned upside down. "But I have absolutely nothing to wear. I'm presuming this will be a formal affair."

"Yes, it will be. Mr. Stravos is very old-fashioned and quite proper."

"What will you be wearing?"

"A black suit." Then witnessing the mounting stress on her face, he added, "You'll want something stunning. Something that will turn heads."

"Really?"

"Most definitely. I want Stravos to see just how amazing you are. Don't worry. When we get back to the resort, I'll ring downstairs and arrange to have the boutique send up their best dresses for you to choose from."

The worry lines faded from her face. "You'd do that for me?"

There was a whole lot he'd do for her, but he kept it to himself. "Of course. After all, you are doing me the favor."

And with that he made a point of answering emails on his phone. He needed some time to straighten out his jumbled thoughts. Kyra had an effect on him unlike any other. And that wasn't good. He needed to be sharp and focused for his meeting with Stravos.

CHAPTER TEN

THE WEEK HAD flown by what with wedding plans and studying.

At last Friday had arrived as well as Kyra's generous paycheck.

She frowned. *That just can't be right.* She disconnected the phone call with a bank in New York after attempting to make a payment on her mother's mortgage. The problem was the bank didn't want to take her money. They said the mortgage had been paid in full. *How could that be?*

She immediately dialed her mother's number. Maybe her mother had moved the mortgage to another bank. That had to be it, because her mother wouldn't have called the other week panicked if the mortgage had been mysteriously paid off.

"Hi, Kyra." Her mother's pleasant voice sounded so clear that it was as if she was next door, not an ocean away. "I can't talk long. I'm at work. At least I still have one job—"

"Mom, we need to talk."

"Okay. About what?"

"The mortgage."

"Have you changed your mind about coming home? I'm sure between the two of us, we can make the payment."

"Where's the mortgage?"

"What do you mean? It's at the bank, of course."

Something wasn't adding up. "The same bank Dad used?"

"Yes. But you don't need to contact them. I'm taking care of everything. I…I explained that the next payment might be late. They were very understanding."

An understanding bank? The words sounded off-key. In fact, her mother wasn't quite acting like herself.

"Kyra, I need to go. We can talk later."

At last Kyra could no longer deny the truth. Her mother was lying to her. The knowledge sliced into her heart. The one person she was supposed to be able to blindly trust was capable of deceit. But why?

"Mom! Stop! I know the truth."

"What truth? I don't know what you're talking about." Her mother's voice was unusually high-pitched.

"I just called the bank. They told me the mortgage has been paid in full for the past year since…since Dad died. How could you do it?" A rush of emotions had Kyra blinking repeatedly. "How could you let me believe Dad had let us down—that he left us in debt?"

"Kyra, you have to understand. I did it all for you—"

"Me? No. You did it for yourself. You lied and connived so you could control me."

"You're wrong! You don't understand. I couldn't lose you, too. We need each other."

"Not anymore." Kyra pressed the end button on her phone.

In a matter of minutes, everything she thought she knew about her life and her family had come undone. She swiped away a tear as it streaked down her face. How could her mother let her think the worst of her father—that he was irresponsible and careless? None of it was true. Her father wasn't perfect, but he had taken care of them.

The walls were closing in.

Kyra paced back and forth in the suite. Her thoughts raced until her head started to pound. What she needed was a distraction—something to calm her down. First she phoned Cristo, then she called Sofia. She struck out twice.

Everyone but her had plans on a Friday night. Cristo was away on business. And even Sofia had plans with some friends from the housekeeping department. That left Kyra on her own. And there was no way she was going to thumb through any more bridal magazines, conduct any further internet searches for a clue to her family or study for her online classes.

She opened the French doors leading out to the private balcony. The moon shone overheard and reflected off the serene cove. She leaned against the rail, enjoying the warmth of the evening air.

How was she ever supposed to trust anyone after this? Her mother had lied to her. And not just a little fib, but an ongoing whopper of a tale. If it hadn't been for her mother, she wouldn't be standing in this extravagant suite pretending to be Cristo's bride. Did her mother have any idea what her lies had done to Kyra's life?

The lapping sound of the cove beckoned to her. It would be just perfect for a nighttime dip. After all, she'd been in Greece for several weeks, and she had yet to stick her toes in the clear, inviting water. Tonight she would remedy that.

Determined to wear off some of her frustration after speaking to her mother, Kyra rushed to her room and slipped on her brand-new turquoise bikini. She scribbled a note for Cristo, just in case he returned sometime that evening and actually noticed her absence. With a white crocheted cover-up and flip-flops, she rushed to the beach.

She discarded her cover-up and towel on the sand. The water was warm and she waded farther in. This would be the perfect way to clear her mind. But even then, thoughts of betrayal ate at her.

Ever since her father died, she had worked so hard to be the perfect daughter, to put her mother's needs first, to play by the rules. But no more. Now she was going to do what she wanted—what made her happy.

Kyra moved farther into the water until it was up to her shoulders. Was it wrong that she sometimes wondered what it would have been like if she and Cristo had met under different circumstances? Would he have asked her out just because he found her attractive or intriguing? She sighed with regret over never knowing the answer.

She fell back in the water and began to float. So far, Cristo had been nothing but a gentleman...when he wasn't working. Which wasn't often. She really wondered if anyone would believe he was madly in love with her. She started to do the backstroke. A few strong strokes and then she coasted.

Thoughts of Cristo crowded her mind. Though he could be sweet and was devastatingly handsome, he didn't have room in his life for a woman because he already had a mistress—his work. And his mistress was demanding—too demanding. Or was he using his work as an excuse to avoid a serious relationship? If so, why?

There was a splash of water behind her. The little hairs on the back of her neck lifted. She wasn't alone. Her gaze sought out the shore. She wasn't far from it, but could she get there before whoever it was caught her?

She started for the shore when a hand reached out and caught her foot. A scream tore from her lungs. She started to struggle, splashing water in her eyes.

"Kyra! It's me. Cristo."

She stopped struggling. "What in the world are you doing? Trying to scare me to death?"

"Sorry. You looked so peaceful floating on the water that I didn't want to ruin the moment."

"Well, you certainly did that. I didn't hear you." And then she caught sight of his muscular chest. Okay, so maybe she wasn't so upset about him joining her. The moon reflected off the droplets of water on his bare flesh, making it quite tempting to reach out and slide her fingertips over his skin. Her fingers tingled at the thought.

"It wasn't my intention to startle you. It's just when I got back to the suite and saw your note, a night swim sounded like a good idea. I thought I'd join you, but if you want me to go, I'll understand."

"No. Stay." She tried to catch a glimpse of what he was wearing, but the water was too dark to make out anything.

So she was left to wonder what sort of swimwear he preferred. Perhaps he was skinny-dipping. Nah, not Cristo. He was too proper. Maybe it was a pair of those itty-bitty bikini bottoms. She immediately rejected the image. Perhaps he wore some shorty-shorts—better yet low-slung board shorts.

Cristo's gaze met hers. "You're sure you want me to stay?"

She nodded, still working up the courage to reach out and run her hands over his chest. "I'm actually happy to see you. I thought you'd be working until late."

"I had something better to do." A mischievous smile lit up his face, making him even more handsome.

Was he flirting with her? It sure sounded like it to her. A smile pulled at her lips. "And what would that be?"

His voice lowered. "Spend time with my fiancée. Didn't you say it was important we learn more about each other?"

"I did. Do you swim much?"

"Wait a sec. This was my idea. I get to ask the first question."

"And what would that be?"

His gaze narrowed. "Have you ever gone skinny-dipping?"

Thankfully the moonlight wasn't that bright, because Kyra was certain her cheeks were bright red. "No."

"Oh, come on," he coaxed. "You can tell me."

"I am. I haven't. But I take it you have."

He nonchalantly shrugged. "I was at boarding school. It was a dare. There was no way I could back out."

She shook her head. "You must have been a handful as a kid."

"And you were a straight-A student and a Goody Two-shoes who did no wrong."

Was she really that predictable? She stuck her tongue

out at him. He let out a deep laugh that made her stomach flip-flop.

Still chuckling, he turned and swam away from the beach. The gentle lap of the water filled the quietness of the evening. No way was he getting away that easily. She followed him.

They paddled around the cove, laughing, playing and enjoying the intimacy of having the water to themselves. Okay, so maybe Cristo wasn't a complete workaholic. Kyra's cheeks began to ache as she continued to smile, but she couldn't help herself. Tonight Cristo was engaging and entertaining. Just what she needed to take her mind off her troubles.

She moved up next to him. "I'm surprised you'd take the evening off to splash around the cove with me."

"What, you thought I'd forgotten how to have a good time?"

She shrugged. "Something like that."

"Well, I'm glad to prove you wrong." He cupped his hands together and sent water splashing in her direction.

She sputtered, caught off guard. She swiped the water from her eyes to find Cristo grinning. No way was she letting him get away with that. She held her arm out at her side and swiped it along the surface of the water, sending a much larger spray in his direction. The next thing she knew they were engaged in a heated water battle until Kyra's arms grew tired and she gave up the victory to him.

"Is my water nymph worn-out?" Cristo moved closer.

"Yes." She leaned her head back, dipping her long hair in the water before smoothing it into place. "Aren't you tired, too?"

"Not too tired to do this." His hands slipped around her waist, pulling her close.

His lips claimed hers. What was up with him? He'd kept his distance from her after the kiss in the limo. Perhaps it had confused him as much as it had her. Whatever it was, she approved.

His mouth moved lightly, tentatively as though testing the waters. Her hands moved to his bare shoulders, enjoying the feel of his muscles beneath her fingertips.

As the kiss deepened, her legs wrapped around his waist. The kiss went on and on. They definitely had this part of their relationship down pat. Then again, maybe a little more practice would be good.

Cristo carried her out of the water. All the while their kiss continued, and Kyra's heart pounded. Could this really be happening? Was she really falling head over heels for this man?

She couldn't think clearly. It was as though the full moon had cast a spell over them—anything seemed possible. And she didn't want this moment to end—not now—not ever.

However, when a breeze rushed over her wet skin, a chill set in. She pulled back. In the moonlight, she stared into Cristo's puzzled gaze.

She attempted to steady her rushed breathing in order to speak. "We can't keep this up. What if someone sees?"

"They'll probably get some ideas of their own." His brows lifted. "You do remember we're supposed to act like we're on a romantic getaway, right? Consider this a dress rehearsal."

His words were like a cold shower. Was that really what he thought they were doing here? Putting on a show? The realization stabbed at her heart. Here she was getting caught up in the moment and he was figuring out how to get the most mileage out of their public display of affection.

She untangled her limbs from him. Goose bumps raced over her flesh, but the heat of her indignation offset the chill of the night air. "It's getting late. We should go inside."

"And continue this?" There was genuine hope in his voice.

"Um…no. I think we have this kissing stuff down pat."

"Are you sure? I'm thinking I might need a little more practice."

"You do remember this is all make-believe, right?" With each passing day, she found it harder and harder to draw the line between their fake engagement and real life. The lines kept blurring and they were starting to fade away.

Cristo sighed. "I remember. And tomorrow night will be our big test. Do you think we can pull it off?"

"I think we have a good chance. But when we're alone, we can't keep forgetting about the boundaries in this pretend relationship."

Cristo stepped back. "Is that what you really want? Because while we were out in the water, I got the distinct impression you wanted more."

For a while there, she thought she could play the part of girl gone wild. The truth was, while her mother's actions had hurt her deeply, she was still the same person inside, just a bit more scarred.

"I...I didn't mean to lead you on." She glanced away.

He placed a finger beneath her chin and lifted until their gazes met. "Talk to me. You're not acting like yourself. What's going on?"

"It's nothing."

"It's definitely something." His voice was low and soothing. "I'm your friend. I'd like to be there for you. If you'd let me."

She moved to where she'd left her towel and cover-up. Maybe it would help to talk about it. Cristo would know that he wasn't alone with his problems coping with his parents.

As she dried off, she chanced a quick glance over her shoulder in order to satisfy her curiosity. He indeed was wearing a pair of dark board shorts with a white stripe around each leg. In the moonlight, his shorts hung low enough to show off his trim abs. His head lifted and their gazes met. He ran a towel over his chest, but he didn't say a word. It was as though he was waiting for her to start the conversation.

She slipped on her crocheted cover-up. She spread out her towel on the sand and sat down. "Join me."

He did. His shoulder brushed against hers. She ignored the nervous quiver his touch set off in her stomach.

"The reason I agreed to play the part of your fiancée was because it allowed me to help my mother. But today, I learned that everything I believed is…is a lie." She went on to reveal her mother's duplicity. The whole sordid story.

When it was all out there, Cristo draped an arm over her shoulders and pulled her close. She let her head rest against his shoulder, taking comfort in his touch. He didn't have to say a word. There was comfort and understanding in his touch.

She didn't know how much time had passed before they started for their suite. This gentle side of Cristo was even harder for her to resist. But she knew that if she let Cristo get too close, he'd wedge his way into her heart. From that point forward, she would forever be comparing every man she met to Cristo. And she already knew they wouldn't live up to Cristo's larger-than-life personality.

She couldn't let that happen. She had to stay strong for a little longer.

CHAPTER ELEVEN

SO THIS IS WHAT it's like to ride in a helicopter.

Kyra gazed out the window as the lights of the Blue Tide faded into the distance. She was never going to forget this experience.

Thankfully she'd had the forethought to document it. She stared down at the new photo on her phone. It was of her and Cristo standing next to the helicopter in their evening clothes. If she didn't know better, they really did look like a genuine couple. Cristo was so sexy in his black suit, black dress shirt and steel-gray tie. Any woman would be out of her mind not to want to be on his arm. She cast Cristo a glance, surprised to see he was staring back at her. Her stomach dipped.

She would have liked to talk to him, but the *whoop-whoop* of the helicopter blades made that difficult. Even the headset Cristo had given her hadn't done much to offset the rumbling sound. She turned to stare out the window. The brilliant rays of pink, orange and purple of the setting sun took her breath away.

She adjusted the beaded, pearl-colored bodice of her strapless dress. Cristo had told her to go with something stunning. She truly hoped this dress was what he'd had in mind. With him being tense over the upcoming dinner, he hadn't seemed to notice her, much less her dress.

Thankfully the saleswoman assured Kyra the dress was made for her. The crystal-beaded bodice led to a beaded waist followed by a hi-low handkerchief skirt of sky blue. She wiggled her freshly pedicured toes in the new silver heels with a rhinestone strap. She couldn't remember the last time she'd been this dolled up.

Kyra glanced over at her dashing escort. She was really hoping he would notice all of her hard work. As though he'd sensed her staring, he glanced her way. Their gazes met. He reached out, taking her hand in his and giving it a reassuring squeeze. His warm touch calmed the fluttering sensation in her stomach. She wanted so desperately to help him today, but she worried whether she'd be able to pull it off.

The helicopter touched down on a fully lit helipad not far from an impressive coastal mansion. The grounds surrounding the white mansion with a red tile roof were illuminated by strategically placed spotlights. Kyra was awed by the enormity of the home.

After Cristo helped her exit the helicopter, she turned to him. "One man lives here? All by himself?"

Cristo's gaze moved to the mansion and then back to her. "His grandson lives with him. And I'm sure there's a household staff."

"I'd get lonely." She turned all around, not finding any signs of neighbors. "This place really is isolated out here on this island."

"Don't worry." Cristo wrapped his arm around her waist and pulled her to his side. He placed a kiss upon the top of her head. His voice lowered. "You're safe with me."

She lifted her chin and gazed into his eyes. She couldn't read his thoughts. But when he ran a finger along her cheek, her heart went *tip-tap-tap* in her chest. Was he being sincere? Or was this just another performance?

"Welcome." A male voice interrupted the moment. "I'm Mr. Stravos's butler."

With great regret, she turned to find an older gentleman standing off to the side of the helipad. Immediately, her heart settled back to its normal pace. So Cristo had seen the man approaching and it had all been a show.

Right now, all she wanted to do was pull away from Cristo. She felt foolish and gullible. But considering their agreement, she was stuck acting as his loving and devoted fiancée. She choked down her disappointment.

Cristo took her hand and placed it in the crook of his arm. They followed the butler to the grand house. The sand and sea were only a few yards away. The lull of the water pounding the rocky cliff filled in the silence. The walkway led them to a portico that stretched the length of the house. Impressive columns were placed every ten feet or so.

At the center of the structure was a courtyard. A wrought-iron gate stood open, welcoming them into the tiled area. A working water fountain stood prominently in the middle highlighted with different colored lights.

Surrounding the fountain sat various groupings of patio furniture, from a wrought-iron picnic table for four to a couple of cushioned loungers. At the far end stood a fireplace. It glowed as a log burned in it. Kyra was awed by the entire courtyard.

A tug on her arm had her realizing they were being led inside. Kyra grudgingly followed along. She had a job to do this evening and she intended to do her best. The sooner Cristo had a signed agreement, the sooner this arrangement between them would end. Cristo would have his precious contract and she'd have her life back.

Though her stomach quivered with nerves, Kyra knew how to do this. At last there was some benefit from the years of witnessing her mother putting on airs for her friends. Kyra knew how to embellish and imply things without outright lying. It was an art of inflection and knowing what to leave out. Her mother was an expert, and it'd only gotten worse since the death of Kyra's father. Kyra shoved the troubling thought to the back of her mind. Right now, she had a job to do.

The living room was quite formal with two full-length white couches facing each other. There were four wingbacked chairs in burgundy upholstery. At the far end of the room was a prominent stone fireplace. On the perimeter were various types of artwork from a bust of some Greek hero to paintings of historical figures and the Greek ruins.

When Kyra went to free her hand from Cristo's in order to further explore her surroundings, he tightened his grip. What in the world? Was he worried that she'd slip away and leave him on his own?

"Welcome." Another man entered the room. He approached them and smiled. But she noticed immediately that his smile didn't quite reach his eyes. "I'm Nikolaos Stravos III, but please call me Niko."

The man was approximately Cristo's age. Niko was handsome in a tall and dark kind of way. But in Kyra's mind, he didn't hold a candle to Cristo. And it was then she realized she was starting to measure other men according to Cristo's yardstick. Not good. Not good at all.

She tried to see Niko clearly without the comparison to the larger-than-life man at her side. Niko had dark wavy hair, which was finger-combed back off his face. It was a very relaxed look for a man whose grandfather seemed so old-fashioned. Or maybe that was why Niko had a casual appearance—it was opposite of what his grandfather would want. The fact he would stand up to the senior Stravos instead of catering to the older man scored him a few points in Kyra's book.

Cristo shook his hand and introduced himself before turning to her. "And this is my fiancée, Kyra Pappas."

She presented what she hoped was a bright and friendly smile. "I'm pleased to meet you."

Cristo cleared his throat. "Will your grandfather be able to join us this evening?"

Niko's face creased with lines. "I hope you won't be too upset to learn that I'm the one who invited you here."

"You? But why?" It wasn't Cristo who spoke those words but rather Kyra. And it wasn't until the words were out there, followed by an awkward silence, that she realized she shouldn't have spoken so freely. The heat of embarrassment rose up her neck as both men cast her raised brows.

Niko lifted his chiseled chin as he faced Cristo again. "As I was saying, my grandfather is quite set in his ways and I've been trying to talk him into making some changes."

Cristo sent her a warning look not to say anything else. He turned back to their host. "And you are the one considering selling off the hotel chain?"

"How about we dine first? Everything is ready now."

"And your grandfather? Will he be joining us later?"

"He has a lot of work to deal with. But I mentioned the dinner to him earlier today." Niko waved the way to the dining room.

At least food would give her something to do, since talking hadn't gone so well for her. Not a great way to start the evening. The problem was her nervousness. Cristo's tension had rubbed off on her and now she had to relax if she wanted to help her fiancé.

Why had Stravos's grandson requested this meeting?

Cristo attempted to keep up the light conversation about football. All the while, he kept wondering if there'd been a shift in power in the Stravos organization. But how would his investigators have missed such huge news? The answer was they wouldn't have.

Though the dinner itself was quite a delicious affair, Cristo had a hard time enjoying it. He hadn't come here for good food and company. He'd wanted to negotiate a deal or, at a bare minimum, find out what it'd take to strike a deal with Stravos. So far, he knew no more than when he'd arrived at the estate.

"Thank you for the delicious dinner." Kyra folded her linen napkin and set it aside.

"It was my pleasure." Niko pushed back his chair. "I thought we would have dessert out in the courtyard."

"That would be wonderful. I just love what you've done

with it." Kyra continued to chatter on about nothing spe-
cific, just making idle conversation to fill in the empty
spots in the conversation—empty spots left by Cristo's prolonged silence.

He knew he should be friendlier. But he also knew the
grandson didn't possess the control needed to make this
venture a reality. Right now, he was left hoping for a mir-
acle.

They made their way to the courtyard. Niko turned back
to him. "Would you care for some more coffee?"

When Cristo declined, Niko moved to the wrought-iron
table with a glass top that held a tray with a coffee carafe as
well as cream and sugar. Once his cup was filled, he took
a seat in the chair opposite Cristo.

Now that dinner was over and they'd made idle chitchat,
it was time to get to the point of this get-together. "I hate
to ruin this lovely evening with talk of business, but I was
wondering what your thoughts are regarding the sale of the
Stravos Star Hotels."

"I've given the subject of selling off the chain considerable thought. My question for you is, why are you so interested in the purchase when you already have a hotel chain
of your own?"

"The Glamour Hotel and Casino chain is a North American venture. What I'd like to see happen is to merge the
two chains and give the discriminating traveler the global
availability of staying with a chain they are comfortable
with—that keeps track of their preferences in our univer-
sal concierge system. That way, no matter which location
they stay in, they'll feel like they're at home."

Niko's eyes lit up. "I take it you have already imple-
mented this feature in your existing hotels?"

"We have, and it has created a large increase in return
clientele. You don't have to worry about the Stravos Star
Hotels. Though the name will change, the quality will remain exemplary."

They continued into a more detailed discussion of what each of them would like to see take place with the sale. For the most part, there was mutual agreement. There were other areas that were a bit sticky, but Cristo didn't see them as insurmountable hurdles. No deal was ever achieved without its share of negotiating.

Niko set aside his now-empty coffee cup. "I know that if the time comes, our assistants and attorneys can hash through all of this, presenting us with long, dry memos, but I suppose I'm more like my grandfather than I care to admit. I like to be personally involved when it comes to the decisions that will change the course of Stravos Holdings."

"I can appreciate the personal touch. My father is the opposite. He would rather sit in his ivory tower and read reports."

"What a shame to spend so much time locked away in an office." Kyra's eyes pleaded with him to follow her conversation. "I'd love to hear what it's like to live out here on this private island."

"It's quiet." Niko smiled as he settled back in his chair.

There was more business he wanted to discuss, but perhaps Kyra was right. And Niko seemed like a decent man. "I bet there's good fishing."

"I must admit that I'm not much of a fisherman." Niko refilled his coffee before turning to Kyra. "I'm sure you'd grow bored out here."

"Unless I found something to amuse me."

Was she flirting with Niko? Cristo sat up a bit straighter. Her gaze immediately swung around to him.

"I could definitely imagine some leisurely mornings." Did she just smile and wink at him?

As the playful conversation continued, Cristo forgot about his business agenda and enjoyed the moment. Kyra was captivating and could take most mundane subjects, turn them on their heads and find an interesting angle he hadn't thought of before.

There was a natural warmth and friendliness about her that he hadn't experienced with the other women he'd dated. He started to wonder if this was what life would be like with an amazing lady by his side, one who supported and loved him. And then realizing the dangerous direction of his thoughts, he drew them up short.

Much too soon the conversation wound down and everyone got to their feet. Cristo didn't want the evening to end. He hadn't been this relaxed and happy in a long time.

"Thank you so much for having us." Kyra smiled at Niko.

Cristo held out his arm to escort her back to the helipad. When her hand looped through the crook of his arm, all felt right again. With her by his side, he didn't have to pretend. It felt as though this was how things were meant to be.

They'd just turned for the gate when there was the sound of footsteps behind them. Assuming it was one of the household staff, Cristo kept moving toward the portico.

"Grandfather, come meet our company."

"Very well." There was a gruff tone to the man's voice.

Cristo turned, having absolutely no idea how this initial meeting would go. The one thing he did know through his abundant research was that the senior Nikolaos Stravos was not a social man. The man preferred his privacy, but he loved his grandson above all else. Hopefully Niko would have some sway with the older man.

Cristo's eyes met a slightly hunched man who in his prime would have towered over Cristo. The man's wavy hair was snow-white and his matching beard and mustache were clipped short. On his nose were perched a pair of black-rimmed reading glasses. It appeared he had been hard at work just as his grandson had claimed.

"Grandfather, please meet Cristo Kiriakas."

Cristo stepped forward and held out his hand. "It's good to meet you, sir. I've heard a lot about you."

The man studied him as though trying to decide if he

wanted to shake it or not. At last the man accepted the gesture. His grip was firm and the handshake was brief.

The senior Stravos pulled back but kept his gaze on Cristo. With his arms crossed, he frowned. Cristo did not have a good feeling about this meeting—not good at all. Was the man always this hostile?

"Grandfather, wouldn't you like to meet Kyra—"

"What I'd like is to know why this man has been digging around in my business and my life." The man's voice was deep and rumbled with anger.

"Excuse me?" Cristo feigned innocence while he figured out how best to handle this situation.

"There is no excuse for the level of digging your men have been doing. Did you really think you'd find whatever you were searching for?"

Perhaps Cristo had been a bit zealous with his quest to make this deal a reality.

Before he could find an appropriate response, Kyra stepped forward. "I'm sure Cristo meant no harm. He's from the States and, well, I think we do things differently from how you do them over here."

Senior Stravos cast her a quick glance. "I should say so. We know when not to cross a line. We have respect—manners."

"Cristo does get excited about business. Sometimes he gets wrapped up in a project to the exclusion of everything and everyone."

Why was she making excuses for him? Didn't she think he could handle this situation on his own? Not that he'd done a good job so far.

"What my fiancée is trying to say is that I like to do my research before I start negotiations. I like to know everything about who I'm about to do business with. I'm sorry if that offended you or if my team overstepped. That was not my intention."

The man's bushy brows drew together. "And what exactly do you think you have to offer me?"

"Money. And lots of it for your hotel chain."

The man's eyes widened. He turned to his grandson. "Did you know about this?"

"I did."

"And I suppose you think it's a good idea."

Niko straightened his shoulders and met the older man's gaze straight on. "You know I do. We've talked about it numerous times."

"But I didn't know you'd gone behind my back to bring in an outsider to try to sway my opinion."

"It's not like that. You knew I was still exploring the idea of selling off the chain and you knew I invited Cristo here for dinner. I asked you repeatedly to join us."

Nikolaos sighed in exasperation. "I told you I was busy. Besides, a dinner won't change my mind about selling."

This was worse than Cristo had been imagining. This man could give his own father lessons in being obstinate. How in the world was Cristo going to sway the older man to reconsider his position?

Obviously money for a billionaire wouldn't be a deciding factor. It had to be something else—something more personal. But what?

CHAPTER TWELVE

KYRA KNEW CRISTO was in trouble.

Everything he'd been working toward was about to go up in flames—if it hadn't already. She wanted to help, but she didn't know how. And she didn't want to make matters worse.

"You have a very beautiful home here." Kyra smiled at the older man, hoping the neutral subject would ease tensions. "Thanks so much for having us. I can't get over how charming your courtyard is. I especially love the flowers."

The man gazed at her for a moment before turning away. But then his gaze came back to her. There was a strange look in his eyes—like one would give to a person they loosely recognized but couldn't quite place. "Are you American?"

"Yes, I am. My family's from New York."

Mr. Stravos moved to stand next to her, blocking Cristo from the conversation. "And you're in Greece on a holiday?"

There was a slight pause as she debated how honest to be with him. When Cristo went to step forward and intervene, Niko shook his head. This was all up to Kyra. She swallowed hard. Honesty was always the best policy. "I actually came to Greece to work."

"Work? You work for Cristo?"

Kyra might not be a high-powered businessman like everyone else in the room, but she wasn't stupid. She knew Mr. Stravos was on a fishing expedition. He wanted to know if she and Cristo were truly an item or if this was just a scam to secure a business deal. "It started that way, but when we met it was love at first sight."

"Hmpf." Mr. Stravos didn't sound impressed. "So you two don't know each other?"

"That's not true." She'd been learning lots about Cristo, but what she didn't know was where things stood between them. Those kisses they'd shared weren't just for show—no matter what Cristo said. There had been red-hot passion in them. And the way Cristo had looked at her the other night beneath the moonlight in the cove had gone beyond putting on a show for others. There had been hunger and need in his eyes. And there was the way he made her heart race, unlike any man she'd ever met. "How much do you have to know about someone to know they are very special?"

The man's bushy brows rose. "I knew my late wife from childhood. It was expected we would marry."

"Ours was a whirlwind courtship. Cristo swept me off my feet. I don't think it matters how long a couple is together. They just know when it's right." None of which was a lie. She truly believed this. She just hadn't met Mr. Right yet. Her gaze moved to Cristo. He certainly made a really good Mr. Right Now.

"Why come to Athens to work? Don't they have work where you come from?"

She decided to turn the question around on him. "Why not come here? Athens is beautiful. It's an adventure."

"And that's it?"

There was one more thing. Why not tell him? It wasn't a secret. And there was the slight chance that Mr. Stravos might know something about her family. "I came here in search of my extended family."

Mr. Stravos's eyes widened. "You have family here?"

"I hope so. My father's side of the family came from Greece."

"What are their names?"

"Pappas. Otis and Althea Pappas. Cristo has been kind enough to offer to help me search for the records."

A frown pulled at the man's face. Without a word, he

turned and headed back into the mansion. Oh, no! What had she done wrong? She cast Cristo a questioning glance, but he was staring at the man's retreating back. This wasn't good. Not good at all.

Kyra turned to Niko. "Was it something I said?"

Niko shook his head. "You were fine."

"Then what just happened?"

"I have no idea." Niko shrugged before turning back to Cristo. "What can I say? My grandfather is always full of surprises. But don't give up. I'll talk to him."

Cristo stuck out his hand. "I'd really appreciate anything you can do."

Kyra cast Cristo a sympathetic look, but he turned away. She understood that he was deeply disappointed, but there had to be another way. Something he hadn't thought of yet.

They started for the gate when Kyra paused. She turned back to catch Niko just before he entered the living room. "Niko, would it be all right if I sent over a wedding invitation for you and your grandfather?"

"That would be quite thoughtful. But I can't promise we'll be able to make it."

"I'll send one anyway," she said and smiled.

She didn't want to push any further. At least it was something. Maybe nothing would come of it. Then again, who knew what the future might hold. She looped her hand through the crook of Cristo's arm, as was becoming natural to her.

So where did they go from here?

She glanced over at Cristo. His handsome face was marred with stress lines. Now wasn't the time to ask him.

Once back at the Blue Tide Resort, they walked along the paved path that led back to the main building. She kept waiting for him to say something—anything so she knew where things stood. Unable to stand the prolonged silence, she asked, "How do you think the meeting went?"

He sent her an I-don't-believe-you-have-to-ask look. "Obviously not well."

Was she just being overly sensitive or was his grouchiness directed toward her? Surely he didn't think she intentionally messed things up, did he? She would never do that to him.

"I'm sorry I didn't do a better job convincing Mr. Stravos that we're a happy couple. Perhaps it would be best if we just ended this whole arrangement right now."

Cristo stopped walking and sent her a hard stare. "You're quitting?"

"Don't you think it would be best? I was absolutely no help to you at dinner. And there's no need for us to be in each other's way."

"No." His voice held strength and finality to it.

No? What did he mean no? "You aren't even going to consider letting me out of this arrangement?"

He shook his head. "When I make a deal with someone, I expect them to keep up their end of the bargain."

"But I don't understand. Mr. Stravos looked at me as though he didn't believe a word I said—it was as though he could see straight through our story. I think this whole engagement is a huge mistake. I'm sorry I failed you."

"It wasn't you." Cristo reached out, took her hand in his and squeezed it. "You have nothing to apologize for. You did everything right, and I appreciate it."

She stared straight into his eyes, trying to determine the depth of his sincerity. "You really mean that? You're not just saying it to make me feel better?"

"Trust me. I mean every word." He shifted his weight from one foot to the other. "If anything, this is all my fault for thinking up such a far-fetched scheme."

"There has to be another way to convince the elder Stravos that the sale is good for everyone. After all, his grandson is all for the deal."

"The problem is I'm running out of ideas." There was a worrisome tone in his voice—one she'd never heard before.

She realized that she'd come to care for Cristo far more than she ever imagined possible, and she just couldn't let him throw in the towel now. If Cristo really thought expanding his business was a way to somehow reconnect with his father, he had to keep trying. Somehow, someway this would all work out. "Promise me you won't give up hope."

He glanced up at her. Skepticism shone in his eyes. "You think it's still possible to strike a deal with Mr. Stravos?"

"I do."

His eyes warmed. "What would I do without you?"

"Lucky for you, you don't have to find out." She squeezed his hand. He squeezed her hand in return. When she went to pull away, he tightened his hold on her. Their fingers intertwined and they started along the beach. "I wonder why Mr. Stravos got quiet when I started talking about my family. Do you think it's possible he might know some of them?"

"I wouldn't get your hopes up. If he had known any of them, I don't see why he wouldn't have mentioned it. I'd just write off his peculiar behavior to a man who is very eccentric."

When Cristo led her straight past the walkway leading back to the lobby of the resort, she got the distinct impression his mind was too preoccupied for sleep. To be honest, she wasn't tired, either. When they reached the sand, they both slipped off their shoes. The evening air was calm and the moon was full. It was as though it had a magical pull over them.

With each step they took, her curiosity mounted about Cristo's motivation to close this deal. Maybe if she understood exactly what was at stake, she'd be better able to help him. "Why is this business deal so important to you?"

"I already explained it to you."

Kyra shook her head, knowing that his passionate need to complete this deal came from a deep personal need. "But there's something more to it. After all, the Stravos chain isn't the only hotel chain in the world. So why does it have to be this one—and why now?"

"It's not worth talking about."

"It is or I wouldn't have asked. Talk to me. I know this has something to do with your father. Do you really think your whole relationship hinges on your success?"

He stopped and turned to her. "Does that always work?"

"Does what work?"

"Wearing a man down with that sultry voice and then asking him to confide his tightly held secrets." He smiled at her letting her know that he was just teasing her.

"I guess that means it's working."

"Perhaps." He leaned forward and pressed a quick kiss to her lips.

And then as though it hadn't happened, he started walking again. Kyra didn't say anything else as she waited to learn more about the man who was holding her hand and making her heart race. She was overcome with the desire to know everything about him—at least everything that he was willing to share with her.

Just when she'd given up on him answering her, he spoke. "I was only fifteen at the time…it was Christmas break from school. We were on holiday at the family cabin in Aspen. My parents, grandparents and my three brothers were there."

So far it sounded like a lovely memory. She tried picturing Cristo as a teenager. Something told her that he'd had a whole host of girls with crushes on him.

Cristo cleared his throat. "I didn't want to sit around the cabin and I didn't want to go into town and see the latest action movie with my older brothers. So I talked my younger brother, Max, into going skiing with me." Cristo's thumb rubbed repeatedly over the back of her hand. "It is one of those moments in life where I really wish I could go back in time and redo it. If only…"

Kyra had a sinking feeling in her stomach. She wanted to tell him to stop the story—as though that would keep the tragedy from happening. But something told her he'd kept this bottled up far too long. If he was strong enough to let out the ghosts of the past, she was strong enough to be there for him.

"Max was a really good kid and, being the youngest, he was usually left out of a lot of things my older brothers liked to do. So when I suggested we go skiing, just the two of us, he was excited. Perhaps too excited." There was a catch in Cristo's voice. He stopped walking and turned to stare out at the water. "I should have kept a better eye on him. Maybe then…"

"You were only a kid yourself. I'm sure you did your best."

"But that's just it. My best wasn't good enough." His body tensed and his grip on her hand tightened to the point of it being uncomfortable. And then, as though realizing he was causing her pain, he loosened his hold, but he didn't let go—they were still connected. "Max was showing off. He always felt a need to prove himself. Our father has always been a tough man to impress. Max must have gotten it into his head that he had to impress me, too. He went zipping by me. I tried to catch up to him but he was too far ahead and…"

Tears stung the backs of Kyra's eyes because she knew what was coming next. It was going to be horrible and unimaginable.

"And the next thing I knew…he hit a tree." Cristo's voice was raw with pain. "I watched helplessly as his body went down into the snow. And he didn't move. I tried to help him. I'd have done anything to save him."

Kyra wrapped her arms around Cristo and held him close as the waves of pain washed over him. She had no idea that his scars ran so deep, not only his brother's death, but also his estrangement from his father.

When Cristo pulled back, he started to walk again. For a few minutes they moved quietly beneath the starry sky. She didn't know what to say—what to do. Was it possible to get past Cristo's guilt?

When Cristo spoke there was a hollow tone to his voice. "After the accident, Max lived for a little bit, but the brain damage was too severe. My...my father blamed me. He said it was my fault—that I should have been looking out for Max because I was older. And he was right. I failed."

She squeezed Cristo's hand, letting him know he wasn't alone.

"My father never forgave me. I've done everything I could to make peace with him. But nothing will ever bring back Max."

"And this deal with Stravos—is this a way to prove yourself to your father?"

"It...it's a sound business decision." His gaze didn't meet hers.

Cristo couldn't admit it, but he wanted his father's approval. Kyra was at last figuring this all out. "You're intent on proving yourself...just like Max was trying to do when he had his accident."

Cristo shrugged. "My two older brothers succeeded at everything they tried. Life always came easy to them. One runs a string of golf courses and the other has a restaurant chain."

And then another thought came to her. "Are you driving yourself this hard to prove something to your father or is it something else that has you up before the sun and working until long after sundown?"

"What are you getting at?" He rubbed the back of his neck.

"That you don't believe you're worthy of happiness—of building a life for yourself—"

"I have a life."

"Going from business meeting to business meeting

isn't a life. It's an existence. But you could have so much more—"

"No!" He shook his head and blinked repeatedly. "Not anymore."

Kyra wrapped her arms around Cristo and hugged him close, hoping to absorb some of his pain. "You deserve love, too."

Kyra's heart ached for the boy who'd lost his brother and the son longing for his father's love and respect. Contrary to her original impression, this deal wasn't about power or money. It was about so much more. It was about family, and she wanted desperately to reunite Cristo with his, even if she never found her own.

After a bit, Cristo pulled away. "Don't pity me. I don't deserve it. I only told you because, after all you've done for me, you deserve to know the truth—the whole truth."

"I understand and I will continue to help you any way I can. We're in this together and that's how we're going to stay."

Then without analyzing her actions, she leaned up on her tiptoes and pressed her lips to his. He didn't move at first, as though she'd caught him totally off guard. Was it really that much of a surprise after the intimate talk they'd just shared?

As her lips moved over his, she felt as though this evening they'd taken a giant leap in their relationship—less fake and more real. She knew there was no turning back now. Cristo had snuck past her neatly laid defenses and made his way into her heart.

Her hips leaned into his. Her chest pressed to his. His hands moved around to her back—to the sensitive spot where her dress dipped low. His fingers stroked her bare skin, sending the most amazing sensations zinging through her now-heated body.

She didn't want this night to end. It just kept getting better and better. If only she could be content with taking second place to his work, maybe they'd have a chance at something lasting instead of something temporary. And just like quicksand, she kept getting in deeper and deeper.

Suddenly Cristo pulled back. His gaze didn't quite meet hers. "We can't do this. It's a mistake."

A mistake?

"I'm sorry." He turned and followed the lit path back up to the lobby of the resort.

What in the world just happened?

Had he rejected her? The thought stung her heart. How could he go from opening himself up to her one minute to pushing her away the next?

The questions plagued her, one after another. And she had no answers for any of them. And the one question that bothered her most was where did they go from here?

CHAPTER THIRTEEN

WHAT IN THE world had gotten into him?

More than a week had passed since Cristo had bared his troubled soul to Kyra. And it hadn't made things better. It'd made them worse. It'd dredged up all of the horrific memories he kept locked away in the back of his mind. And when he faced Kyra, she was quiet and reserved. It wasn't just his father. Now that Kyra knew the truth, she'd withdrawn from him, too. Not that he could blame her.

Cristo moved to the bar in the suite and refilled his mug with freshly brewed coffee. His second pot that morning. And he still didn't feel like himself.

He hadn't slept well in days. He spent his nights tossing and turning. There had been no getting comfortable. All he could think about was Kyra.

They'd gotten so much closer than he'd ever intended. Even to the point where she had him opening up about his past—something he never shared with anyone. And something he would never do again.

In the daylight hours, he continued his search for her family. He was more invested in the quest now than ever before. He needed to know that when this arrangement was over that Kyra would be all right. Because try as he might, he still hadn't convinced her to speak to her mother.

Though it was still early, Cristo had placed a call to the private investigator. He normally received weekly reports on Monday afternoons, but he had no patience to wait until after lunch. This search for Kyra's family had hit too many dead ends. They were due for a bit of good luck—at least Kyra was due it.

The conversation was short but fruitful. Cristo clenched

his hand and pumped his arm as the PI gave him their first valid lead. Cristo assured the man he would personally follow up on the findings.

Determined to see this plan enacted immediately, he grabbed his phone and called his PA. He canceled all of his meetings that day. He had something more important to do. And though his PA sputtered on about the number of important meetings he would be missing, he didn't care. For once, he was putting something—rather someone—else ahead of his own business agenda. Something his father would never do.

Kyra strolled out of her bedroom, yawning as she headed for the coffeepot.

She eyed up his khaki shorts and polo shirt. "Is it casual dress day at the office?"

"No. I'm not working today."

"Really?" Her fine brows rose. "Has there been a global disaster? Is it the end of the world?"

"Kyra, stop." He didn't realize he'd turned out more like his father than he'd ever intended. A frown tugged at his lips. "Why does there have to be something wrong for me to take the day off?"

"It's just that in all the time I've known you, you've never voluntarily taken a day off. So I figure something big must have happened."

Perhaps he'd been a bit too driven where his work was concerned. "It just so happens that I have other plans today."

"Well, I hope you have a good day. I have to study for a test. I've been catching up on my studies. I need to get my certification." She walked over to the coffee table and picked up her laptop. "It's time I really concentrated on my career. After all, our deal will be over soon, and I want a plan in place so that I can move on to the next stage in my life."

"Do you mean move on from me? Or the Blue Tide?"

"Both."

The wedding was in just a few weeks—the time they'd call everything off. This domestic bliss would be over. The thought of her leaving for good, of never seeing her again, was like a forceful blow to his chest. He swallowed hard. "I noticed you've been studying a lot lately. Does it have anything to do with your fight with your mother?"

"No, it doesn't. Is there something wrong with me getting serious about my future?"

"Not at all." Though he still thought she was using it as a distraction from her family problems, today wasn't the time to dwell on such things—not when at last they had a viable lead. "Could you take today off from your studies?"

She shook her head. "I have my finals soon. I almost have my hotel management certification—my ticket to see the world."

"What if I told you I heard from the investigator and he has a lead on your family?"

Her face lit up with excitement. "Really?"

Cristo nodded. "He used the picture you provided and it led him to the small village of Orchidos."

"Orchidos? I've never heard of it. Where is it?"

"You'll see. Come on." Cristo started for the door.

"Wait. Are you serious?"

"Of course I'm serious."

She ran a hand through her hair. "But I'm not ready to go anywhere. I haven't even had my first cup of coffee yet, and I'm not dressed to go out."

"You can have it in the car." He glanced at his watch. "You've got ten minutes and then we're out of here."

Kyra disappeared to her bedroom, leaving him to pace back and forth in the living room. He checked his phone every couple of minutes for texts or voice mails until he remembered that he'd had his phone calls forwarded to his PA. Today was all about Kyra.

When she emerged from her bedroom, she stole his breath away. He smothered an appreciative whistle. He didn't want to scare her off if she knew how attractive he found her. Still, he couldn't take his eyes off her.

Kyra's long hair was piled on her head with a few loose curls softening the look. A dark teal sleeveless dress with a scalloped neckline and tiny maroon flowers made her look as if she was ready for a picnic on the beach. A brown leather belt emphasized her tiny waist. The skirt ended just above her knees, showing off her legs. On her feet were jeweled flip-flops.

"Is something wrong with what I'm wearing?"

He knew he was staring but he couldn't help himself. At last her words registered in his distracted mind. "No. You look great."

"Are you sure?" She smoothed a hand down over the skirt, straightening a nonexistent wrinkle. "I could change into something else."

"No. Don't. You're perfect." In that moment, Cristo realized his words held meaning that went well beyond her clothes. There was a special quality to her—a warmth and genuineness—that appealed to him on a level he'd never felt before.

This recognition left him feeling off-kilter, not quite sure how to act around her. It was as though something significant had changed between them and yet everything was exactly the same. How was that possible?

At long last, she was about to find out a bit of her family's past. And hopefully about the present, too. She crossed her fingers for luck.

Kyra gave Cristo a sideways glance as they walked side by side through the hotel lobby. And it was all thanks to Cristo. The glass doors automatically slid open and there sat a luxury sports car—the kind of car that cost more than most people's houses.

She went to skirt around it when Cristo asked, "Where are you going? This is your ride."

"It is?" Her gaze moved from the electric-blue super car with a gold lightning bolt etched on the back fender to Cristo's smiling face. "This is yours?"

He nodded. "Why does that surprise you?"

She knew he was wealthy enough, but she didn't think he had a fun side. She thought the only entertainment he found was in closing the next big deal. Perhaps there was hope for Cristo after all. "I just didn't imagine you were the type to enjoy a sports car."

"And what type do I seem?"

"Oh, I don't know. The suit-and-tie kind. The type who reads the *Wall Street Journal* in the back of a limo. The on-the-phone-the-whole-trip type."

"Well, I'm glad to know I can surprise you from time to time." He opened the door for her and she climbed inside, enjoying the buttery soft leather upholstery and the new car smell.

Cristo moved to the driver's seat and started the engine, which roared to life. There was no doubt in her mind that this car had power and lots of it—quite like its owner. They set off, and her body tensed as they headed down the long drive. Any minute she expected him to punch the accelerator.

"Relax." Cristo's voice was calm and reassuring. "I promise I know what I'm doing."

"That's what I'm afraid of. That you might go flying down the road like we're on a racetrack."

"You don't have to worry. You'll always be safe with me." He glanced at her briefly before focusing back on the road.

She wanted to believe him, honestly she did, but she had the distinct feeling that just being around him put her heart in jeopardy. There was something about him—something far deeper than the size of his bank account or his impressive toys—that got to her. And she would have to be careful because she wasn't about to end up playing second fiddle to a man's work—not even when the man was Cristo Kiriakas.

When her phone chimed, she retrieved it from her purse. Her mother's name appeared on the caller ID. It wasn't the first time she'd called since Kyra had uncovered her mother's deceit and it wouldn't be the last. Didn't she understand that Kyra needed to process what she'd done?

The one person Kyra thought she could always depend on had betrayed her trust. It wasn't something that could be righted—at least not straightaway.

Cristo turned down the music. "If you need to take that, go ahead. I don't mind."

Kyra sent the call to voice mail. No way was she speaking to her mother with Cristo listening. "It's not important."

"Are you sure?"

"Yes. I'll deal with it later." Much later.

Kyra turned the music back up and amused herself with the passing scenery. It kept her from staring at Cristo. Besides, she'd promised herself when she finally made it to Greece that she'd get out and see the sights, and so far she hadn't had a chance. There was so much of this beautiful country that she wanted to explore.

The car glided over the coastal roadway. The clear blue sky let the sunshine rain down over the greenery dotted with wildflowers from purples and pinks to reds and oranges. On the driver's side was a rocky cliff that led down to the beach.

Almost an hour later, they arrived in the small Greek village of Orchidos. She soon found out that the village was aptly named. Wild orchids were scattered about the perimeter of the village. Huge blooms ranged in color from apricot to maroon with splashes of white upon the delicate petals. It was truly a spectacular sight.

Cristo pulled off to the side of the road. "Are you ready?"

She eagerly nodded. "Do you really think I have any relatives living here?"

He got out and opened her door for her. "I don't know, but we have an appointment later today with the town elder. Maybe he'll have some answers for you. But first, I thought you might want to explore the village."

"I definitely do."

They passed by the modest white houses with red tile roofs. In the center of Orchidos stood a town square with a charming café, Aphrodite's. White columns surrounded the portico. And a stone carving of what she assumed was Aphrodite stood proudly in the center surrounded by little white tables.

They took a seat and were impressed with the delicious menu. When the food was delivered to their table, it did not disappoint. Kyra found herself eating far too much after Cristo ordered almost everything on the menu, from grilled fish to skewers to a salad and a number of delightful treats in between. She was beginning to think she'd never comfortably fit in her clothes again.

Next up on the agenda was walking up and down the roads and steps that connected this almost vertical village. The buildings were all different shapes and sizes. Each was steeped in history. The people of Orchidos were warm and welcoming as they offered smiles and greetings. Kyra felt right at home.

Cristo held her hand the whole time. It was as though the awkwardness they'd experienced had at last slipped away. He told her what he knew of the history of the village. Most of which he confessed to learning on the internet. They climbed wooden steps that wrapped around the hillside. The effort was well worth it as they ended up in the most stunning lookout spot, overlooking a green valley and patches of more orchids. Kyra took a bunch of photos. She thought of sending them to her mother but quickly dismissed the idea. She wasn't ready to deal with her mother. Not yet.

At one point, Cristo checked his cell phone. She waited for him to say that something had come up and he had to cut their outing short. It wouldn't surprise her in the least. Something always came between them when they were having a good time. But this time, Cristo slipped the phone back in his pocket without saying a word. She didn't mention it, either—afraid of ruining the moment.

Minutes turned into hours and before she knew it, Cristo was leading them back to the town square for coffee. It was only then she realized that her cheeks were growing sore from smiling so much. Then again, her feet ached, too. Sandals weren't the best for long walks, but she wouldn't have missed it for the world. To think her ancestors once walked these streets, too, meant a lot to her.

"Thank you for this." She smiled at Cristo. "I've really enjoyed seeing where my grandparents might have once lived. But in all of the excitement, I forgot to ask how you found this place."

"Remember that photo of your grandparents?" When she nodded, he continued. "It was taken in this village. The building in the background once stood in the town square, but a fire destroyed it many years ago. That's why it took the investigator so long to track it down."

"So this is where my family came from?" Kyra glanced around, taking in the village with a whole new perspective.

"We had better get going. We have an appointment that I'm sure you don't want to miss."

Cristo led her a short distance to a nondescript, white stone house with the standard red tile roof, although it had a few tiles missing. He turned to her. "I hope you find your family."

She did, too. Although she already felt as though she'd found something very special with him, she wasn't ready to name those feelings. It was still so new. And she felt so vulnerable.

CHAPTER FOURTEEN

KYRA'S HEART THUMPED with anticipation.

Please let us find the answers to my past.

The red door of the house opened and an older gentleman stepped out. His tanned, wrinkled face lit up with a smile. *"Yasas."*

Kyra turned an inquiring look to Cristo, who greeted the man in fluent Greek. When Cristo turned back to her, he gave her hand a squeeze. "Our host, Tomas Marinos, welcomes you. I'm afraid he only speaks Greek. But I can ask him any questions you might have."

"Can you ask him if he knew Otis or Althea Pappas?"

Cristo translated for her and the man immediately shook his head. Disappointment sliced through her. But she wasn't giving up. They were so close.

When Cristo guided her inside the very plain house, she whispered, "Why are we staying when he doesn't know my grandparents?"

"You asked to research your family and that's what we're doing."

"Here? Shouldn't we go to the local library and search through old birth records and deeds."

He shook his head. "Not in Orchidos. There's no library. Mr. Marinos is the village elder. He has the best records of anyone, such as they are."

"Oh. I didn't know." Heat warmed her cheeks. She hadn't meant to sound unappreciative.

"I warned you in the beginning that tracking down your family based on one old photo wasn't going to be easy." Cristo's steady gaze met hers. "But I know how determined you are to find out about your past, so I used every resource at my disposal to track Mr. Marinos down and make sure he has photos and papers that stretch back to the nineteenth century. If your grandparents ever lived in Orchidos, their names will be in here."

This was it. Her stomach quivered. She was about to find out what happened to her father's family. In her excitement, she whirled around and gave Cristo a hug. "You're amazing."

"You might not say that when you see all of the papers that need sorted. I've been warned there are a lot."

She sent him a worried glance. "I don't know much Greek and—"

"No worries. I'll be right here by your side."

She nodded. In her heart, she believed her father had a hand in guiding her here. *We made it, Dad. At last we'll find out about your family.* She blinked repeatedly, still feeling the loss of her father.

The kitchen table was lined with boxes, as well as the floor. She had no doubt there was a lot of history in those boxes. She moved to the first box and yanked off the dusty lid. Finding the records were in chronological order, they were able to narrow down their search.

Cristo cocked a dark brow at her as she worked at a fervent pace. "You weren't exaggerating when you said you wanted to find your past, were you?"

She shrugged, lifting out a handful of papers. "You probably don't understand what it's like not to know where you came from. My father and I had started tracing the family tree a couple of years before he died. We started with my mother's family. Her side was pretty easy to trace. My father's side was the opposite. We planned to fly here and do research, but he…he didn't live long enough."

"And what if this information isn't what you're expecting? What if it doesn't lead you to the family you've always dreamed of?"

"I guess I'll have to let go of that dream."

"You know that sometimes the best families aren't the ones we're born into, but the ones we make for ourselves."

Kyra paused. She never would have guessed Cristo ever stopped shuffling papers and signing contracts long enough to contemplate something so deep. "Is that what you plan to do? Make a family for yourself?"

"At first, I thought my work would be enough, but lately I've been reconsidering—"

Their gazes met and her heart picked up its pace. The more this day progressed, the harder it was becoming to remember he was her business associate and not just a really sexy guy with an amazing smile. She couldn't resist his charms or ignore how he was letting his guard down around her.

She placed the aged and sun-stained papers on the table. "If you're worried you'll turn out like your father, you don't have to. I could never imagine you being cold and hostile to your child."

Cristo shook his head. "I don't know if I could split my time between my work and my family. As you've seen, I tend to get absorbed in my work. How about you? Will you choose work or family? Or will you try to balance them both?"

"I don't know what my future holds once I get my certification. I'm going to take it one day at a time."

"You know you don't have to leave the Glamour Hotel and Casino. I could find you a position—"

"No. This is something I have to do on my own."

"If you change your mind—"

"I won't."

Heat warmed her cheeks. She couldn't believe he thought that highly of her. "Thank you. But we better get started on these papers before our host kicks us out."

She glanced around, but Mr. Marinos seemed to have disappeared.

"Don't worry. He's out on the porch. But he said he'd be

more than happy to answer any questions." Cristo glanced down at the papers. "Now that we've found the boxes for the right time period, how about you look through the photos and scan the papers for any mention of Pappas. If you find something of interest, you can pass it to me and I can translate it for you."

She glanced down at the papers and realized they were all in Greek. This search was going from hard to downright difficult. But she wouldn't give up. There was a part of her that needed to know where she'd come from and to connect with any relatives that still might be lurking about. And maybe then she wouldn't feel as if there was a gaping hole in her life where her father used to be.

Hours passed as they sifted over paper after paper. Frustration churned in her stomach as a whole section of papers seemed to be missing. But how could that be?

Cristo returned from speaking to Mr. Marinos. "He doesn't know what happened to the papers."

Kyra blinked away tears of frustration as she placed the lid on the box. "So that's it. We've hit a dead end. Whatever there was of my past is gone. It died with my father."

Cristo stepped around the table. He held out his hand to her and helped her to her feet. He gazed deep into her eyes. "This isn't the end. I promise. We will find out about your past. Maybe not today. And maybe not tomorrow. But we will uncover whatever there is to find. Do you trust me?"

She wanted to—she really did. "How am I supposed to trust you when I can't even trust my own mother?"

He reached out, running a finger along her cheek. "I'm sorry she hurt you, but I am not her. I won't let you down."

Standing here so close to him with her heart pounding in her chest, she couldn't imagine him ever hurting her. "I want to trust you."

He smiled. "I'll take that as a positive sign."

All she could think about at the moment was pressing

her lips to his. He really shouldn't stand this close to her. It did the craziest things to her thought processes.

And then as though he could read her thoughts, he dipped his head and placed a kiss upon her lips. He pulled away far too quickly. "Don't give up hope. Sometimes things work out when you least expect them to."

Was he referring to learning about her family?

Or was he talking about this thing that was growing between them?

She hoped it was both.

He'd been so certain this trip would give Kyra the answers she craved.

Cristo felt horrible seeing the disappointment reflected in her eyes. It was his fault. He'd put it there. He should have followed up better before mentioning the lead to her.

The sports car glided smoothly over the motorway on the drive back to the Blue Tide. Usually sitting behind the wheel of a high-performance vehicle relaxed him—gave him a new perspective on things—but not today. The disappointment in the car was palpable even though Kyra tried her best to cover it up.

His investigator had been certain Kyra would find answers in Orchidos. It didn't make sense. Who removed those papers? And why?

It was almost as if any trace of Kyra's family had been purposely removed—erased—as though they never existed. Who would do such a thing? What were they missing?

Cristo rubbed his neck. He was making too much of this. Why would anyone want to hide the history of Kyra's family? It didn't make sense.

He chanced a glance at Kyra. Her head was tilted back against the seat's headrest, and she was staring out the window. She looked as though she was all alone in this world, but that wasn't true. She had her mother and Sofia. People who cared about her, even if it wasn't the way she wanted them to care.

And she had Cristo. He cared. Perhaps he cared more than was good for either one of them. Because he didn't know how to be there for anyone. He'd never learned that as a child.

He'd been a pawn passed between his mother and a string of nannies and then shipped off to a string of boarding schools—when he got in trouble at one, he'd get shuffled off to another. There had been no consistency—or rather he should say that his life had been one long line of inconsistencies. He could never be what Kyra had traveled the globe in search of—family. The thought saddened him. But he wasn't sure whom he was sadder for, her or himself.

Still, he hated seeing Kyra in such turmoil. He couldn't just sit by and let her feel so dejected—so alone.

He moved his hand from the gearshift and reached out to her. But with her arms crossed, he couldn't reach her hand, so he settled for her thigh. Big miscalculation on his part. A sense of awareness took hold of his very eager body. His fingertips tingled where the heat of her body permeated the cottony material of her summer dress.

Kyra's head turned and their gazes met. He glanced back at the road, relieved to have an excuse to keep her from reading the conflicting emotions in his eyes. He knew he should pull his hand away, but he couldn't—not yet. He hadn't made his point yet.

"Kyra, you're not alone." He tightened his hold on her thigh and his pulse quickened. "You've got people who care about you."

"Does that include you?"

The breath caught in his throat. What was she asking him? Did she mean as a friend? Or did she want something more? Right then the urge was overwhelming to pull back—to keep a safe distance. But a glance at the emotional turmoil in her eyes had him keeping their physical link for just a bit longer.

"I'm here as your friend anytime that you need me." *There. That sounded good. Didn't it?*

His cell phone buzzed. He knew he'd promised not to do any work today, but sometimes promises had to be broken. And this was one of those times when he desperately needed a diversion.

He glanced at the phone as it rested in the console. "It's Niko Stravos. I think I should get it, don't you?"

"You're asking me?" The surprise in her voice reflected his own. He'd never asked anyone if he should take a call. When the phone buzzed again, Kyra added, "Answer it. Maybe he has good news. I could use some about now."

Cristo pressed a button on the steering wheel and, utilizing the car's speaker system, said, "Hello."

"Cristo, it's Niko." They continued to make pleasantries and Cristo let him know that he was on the speakerphone and Kyra was with him. "Sounds like I have perfect timing, then. I'd like to invite you both back for dinner later this week."

Cristo, surprised by the invitation, cast Kyra a glance, finding she looked equally shocked. "Thank you. But perhaps we should get together at my resort. Your grandfather wasn't happy about our prior visit—"

"I wouldn't worry about that. My grandfather can be temperamental at times. Don't take it personally." There was a bit of static on the phone line, but soon it quieted and Niko's voice came through clearly. "In fact, this dinner invitation was my grandfather's idea. He sends his apologies for being abrupt the last time you were here and asks that you join us for a more casual dinner Friday night."

Really? What could this possibly mean? Cristo sure wanted to find out. But he knew Kyra had been disappointed by her lack of discovery today, and he didn't know if she'd be up for putting on a happy front for the senior Stravos.

They were almost back at the Blue Tide Resort now. Cristo slowed the car and turned into the long drive. Cristo hated that he might have to back out of this amazing opportunity, but Kyra's needs had to come first. "Can you hold for just a moment?"

"Sure."

"Thanks." Cristo muted the phone in order to speak with Kyra in private. "What do you think?"

She picked at a nonexistent piece of lint on her sundress. "I think it's an amazing opportunity for you. You should go and see what Nikolaos Stravos has to say."

"And what about you? Will you come with me, too?"

CHAPTER FIFTEEN

PLEASE LET HER AGREE.

After all, they were a team.

Cristo prompted her, anxious for an answer. "Kyra?"

She worried her bottom lip. "I don't know. I really wasn't much help to you on the last visit. You might be better off on your own."

He wanted to argue with her and tell her they made a great team, but he held back the words. After she'd just put him on the spot about being in her life, he didn't want to confuse things further. He was already confused enough.

"I understand." He tightened his fingers on the steering wheel. "After today's adventure, you need some time to regroup. I'll let Niko know."

"Thank you for understanding."

Cristo pressed the button for the phone. "Niko?"

"Yes. By the way, I forgot to mention that my grandfather requested Kyra bring any photos she might have of her family. He said he might have some information for her."

Kyra's face lit up with anticipation—it was such a welcome sight. Cristo didn't have to ask if she'd had a change of heart. He just hoped Nikolaos Stravos's information was better than what they'd uncovered today, which was nothing. "We'll be there."

Niko gave them the details, including the request for casual dress. Cristo knew that the Stravoses' version of casual dress was far from jeans and T-shirts. It was more like a suit minus the tie. Which satisfied Cristo just fine. He always felt more in his element when he was dressed up.

He pulled the car into his reserved spot. One of the attendants would clean it before putting it in his private garage. Right now, the care of his prized car slid to the back of his mind. He turned in his seat. "You did it. Thank you."

Her fine brows drew together. "I did what?"

"Got us a second chance to impress Nikolaos Stravos—"

"I just wish it was under different circumstances. I don't like the tales we're fabricating." Anxiety reflected in her eyes. "What if I say the wrong thing? What if he figures out the truth?"

Cristo didn't like this situation any better than her. This wasn't the way he normally did business, but how else were you supposed to negotiate with someone who was so stubborn and set in their ways?

But this relationship wasn't all a lie. No matter how much he fought it, there was definitely something growing between him and Kyra. He couldn't put a name on it. He just knew that she deserved better than him.

"You'll do fine. You'll charm him just like you do everyone." Anxious to erase the worry from her big, beautiful eyes, Cristo leaned over in his seat and pressed his lips to hers.

She didn't move at first. Had he caught her off guard? His muscles tensed, preparing to be rejected.

And then her mouth started to move beneath his. He started to relax—to enjoy the touch. She tasted sweet like vine-ripened grapes. He doubted he'd ever have another sip of wine without thinking of her.

Cristo had only meant to give her a reassuring kiss, but now that his lips were touching hers, he had no interest in pulling away. What he wanted was more of this—more of Kyra. And she didn't seem to be complaining as her fingers lifted to caress his jaw. No other woman could turn him on the way Kyra could. It wasn't even as if she tried. It was just natural—chemistry.

As her fingertips trailed down his neck to the inside of his shirt collar, he knew he had to stop her before things got totally out of hand. This was not the place to take things to the next level. His fingers moved to cover hers, halting their exploration.

With every bit of willpower, he pulled back and stared her in the eyes. "Now, was that a lie?"

She shook her head. "But—"

His lips pressed to hers again, silencing her protest. He didn't want to know what followed her *but*, not at all. They'd tackled enough problems for now.

He rested his forehead against hers. "No buts. There's something between us. Don't ask me to define it because I can't. And don't expect too much from me because I don't want to let you down. The only thing I can offer you is this—right here, right now."

She pulled away from him. "All the more reason for me not to go to this dinner with you."

"And miss out on a chance to find out what Nikolaos might know about your family?" He knew he had her there. Finding out about her past was too important to her to back out now. "Don't worry, I'll be right there next to you the whole time." He'd just reached for the door handle when Kyra spoke up.

"Do you really think keeping up this charade is the right way to go about things with Stravos? Maybe if we explain everything to him, he'll understand the importance of the deal."

There was nothing about Nikolaos Stravos in his past or present that in the slightest way hinted he was an understanding man who could be swayed by sentimentality. He had a cutthroat reputation in the business world—he wasn't used to sitting back and letting people have their way.

But Kyra had a point. Cristo wasn't comfortable with weaving such an elaborate ruse. "Why don't we play it by ear?"

She stared at him for a moment before nodding her head. "If you think it's best."

As they exited the car and headed back to their suite,

Cristo couldn't dismiss her words. He didn't want Kyra thinking less of him. He wasn't conducting this elaborate ruse because it was fun, although it was with Kyra, or because it was his normal business practice, which it certainly wasn't, but rather because it was what this particular situation necessitated.

His father had taught him to do anything necessary to secure an important business deal. After all, business came first, ahead of all else including family. Cristo supposed he'd learned that lesson quite well. Maybe too well. That was why he'd chosen not to have a family. He didn't want to end up like his father.

And in that moment, he recalled something he'd promised himself as a teenager. After observing his father at the office and witnessing the unhappiness he unleashed on a regular basis, Cristo swore he'd do things differently. Less skirting the truth and with more compassion.

So far he was failing.

Perhaps it was time he considered doing things Kyra's way.

Sleep was elusive.

Kyra tiptoed through the darkened suite late Thursday night. Cristo needed his rest. He had a big day tomorrow. And hopefully Nikolaos Stravos had changed his mind and had decided to go ahead with the sale.

But more than that, she wondered what the older man wanted with her. She recalled their prior meeting and the way the man had stared at her before storming off. He didn't like her, so why was he suddenly willing to help her? Something wasn't adding up, but she couldn't put her finger on exactly what it was.

She sighed and leaned against the wall surrounding the balcony that overlooked the private cove. She was letting her imagination get the best of her. It was Cristo's fault. Ever since their outing, she hadn't been able to get him off her mind. She'd finally found out what it was like to have all of his attention and now she craved more.

"Would you mind some company?"

The sound of Cristo's voice caused her to jump. She turned and had to struggle to keep from gaping at his bare chest and the low-slung dark boxers. Had she fallen asleep somewhere along the way and this was a dream—a very vivid, very tempting dream?

She swallowed hard. "Did I wake you?"

He raked his fingers through his already mussed-up hair. "That would imply I was actually sleeping."

"You couldn't sleep, either?"

"No." He moved to stand next to her. "It's a beautiful night. The moon is so full that it's almost like daylight. But I have a feeling that's not why you're out here. What's bothering you?"

She didn't want to get into another conversation about Nikolaos Stravos. Instead, she said, "I couldn't sleep, and I was bored of staring into the dark."

He reached out and put a finger beneath her chin, pulling her around to face him. "Are you still worried about the dinner?"

"It's nothing."

"I don't believe you. Your eyes tell a different story."

"They do?" She glanced away. Did they say how sexy she found him right now? Did he know how hard it was for her to carry on this conversation when he was barely dressed?

"Obviously you have something on your mind, and until you deal with it, you'll be left lurking in the shadows of the night." His voice lowered, making it warm and quite inviting. "Talk to me."

What would he say if she told him what was weighing on her mind at this particular moment? Her gaze once again dipped to his bare chest. His presence was distracting her—teasing her—tempting her.

How did someone look that good? Cristo certainly knew

his way around a weight room. How did a busy man like him have time for exercise? Somehow he fit it in between boardroom meetings and jet-setting around the globe.

"Kyra? What is it?"

She struggled to center her thoughts on something besides how her heart was thump-thumping in her chest. She licked her dry lips. "I… I was just wondering if this is all going to end tomorrow. You know, after the meeting with Stravos. Will you and I go our separate ways?"

"Is that what you want?"

Her gaze met his. She really didn't want this thing between them to end. She was getting totally caught up in this world of make-believe. And what would it hurt for it to go on just a little longer?

Cristo reached out to her, running the back of his fingers down her cheek. "Tell me what you want."

The pounding of her heart echoed in her ears. Her mouth opened but nothing came out. Her mind went blank. Sometimes words just weren't enough. Without giving thought to the consequences, she lifted up on her tiptoes and leaned forward. Her lips pressed to his.

This was most definitely what she wanted.

His hands gripped her hips, pulling her closer. Her breasts pressed against his muscled chest. Her palms landed on the smooth skin of his shoulders. It was as though an electrical pulse zinged through her fingertips and raced through her body. Every part of her body was alert and needy.

Their kiss moved from tentative to heated in less time than it took his fancy sports car to reach cruising speed. And her engine was revved up and ready to go. Tonight she wasn't going to think about the future or the implications of where this most enticing night would leave them. This moment was all about letting down their guards and savoring the time they had together.

Cristo pulled back. His breath was deep and fast. His heated gaze met hers. "Kyra, are you sure about this?"

She nodded. She'd never been so sure about anything in her life. That not-so-long-ago night when he'd proposed to her, he'd utterly charmed her. But today when they'd toured Orchidos, he'd finally cracked the wall around her heart.

If she walked away now, she would regret it for the rest of her life. Her time with Cristo was the stuff that amazing memories were made of. And she wanted a piece of him to take with her—a tender, special moment.

"I'm sure." Her voice came out as a whisper in the breeze. "I've never been more certain."

His lips claimed hers again. His kiss was hungry and rushed, like a drowning man seeking oxygen. Her hands wrapped around his neck. The curves of her body pressed to the solid muscles of his toned body.

In that moment, she could no longer hide from the truth. She loved Cristo. He hadn't snuck around, no, he'd marched right past her defenses and staked a claim to her heart. She'd tried ignoring it and then denying it, but the truth was she loved him.

As though he sensed her surrender, he stopped kissing her long enough to sweep her off her feet. Her pulse raced. If she was dreaming, she never wanted to wake up.

This night would be unforgettable.

CHAPTER SIXTEEN

THE GLARE OF sunshine had a way of making things look different than they had in the shadows of the night.

Kyra had absolutely no idea what to say to Cristo. So she'd avoided him all day, hoping the words would eventually come to her. But by evening, she was even more confused by her emotions.

Where exactly had their night of lovemaking left them? After all, it wouldn't have happened if not for their make-believe relationship. This whole web of role-playing and innuendos was confusing everything. And now they'd just succeeded in compounding matters even further.

As she recalled the magical night of whispered sweet nothings and the flurry of kisses, her heart fluttered. But was this rush of emotions real? Or was it a side effect of their fake romance? How was she to know?

The only abundantly clear fact was that she would have to be extremely careful going forward. Otherwise, her heart would end up smashed to smithereens when this elaborate ruse was over. And she had no doubt this relationship would most definitely end, sooner rather than later. Cristo had made that crystal clear.

Kyra stepped up to the floor-length mirror in her bedroom and examined her little black dress. It certainly wasn't anything fancy by any stretch, but she wasn't sure what casual dress entailed. So in her mind, a little black dress seemed to work for all occasions—she hoped.

There was a tap on her bedroom door followed by Cristo's voice. "Kyra, are you ready?"

"Um, yes. I'll be right there." There was no time for second-guessing or trying on yet another dress. She was going with black. She snatched up a small black purse with delicate beading on the front and headed for the door, hoping this evening would go much better than their first encounter with Mr. Stravos.

On not-so-steady legs, she made her way to the living room, where Cristo was waiting for her. He looked breathtakingly handsome in a stylish navy suit with a light blue shirt. The top buttons were undone and conjured up memories—heated, needy memories. How in the world was she supposed to get through the evening when she was so utterly distracted?

Cristo gave her outfit a quick once-over. "You look beautiful. Are you ready to go?"

She nodded, still uncertain where things stood between them and not sure how to broach the subject. Apparently she wasn't the only one unsure, because she noticed how Cristo was careful to avoid the subject, too. In fact, he was quieter than normal. It only succeeded in increasing her nervousness.

Once again, they were whisked away in the helicopter. This time she welcomed the *whoop-whoop* of the rotary blades. It was a perfectly legitimate excuse to remain quiet. The only problem was the ride was much too short, and before she was ready, they touched down at the Stravos estate.

This time Niko came out to greet them. "I must apologize for my grandfather. He is delayed by an overseas phone call. But have no worries, he will be joining us."

Cristo gave each sleeve of his suit a tug. "Do you know why he wanted to meet with us?"

Kyra translated that to mean *Is he interested in making a deal?* She had to admit she was quite curious, too. Because she had a distinct feeling her future with Cristo hinged on what happened this evening. And she wasn't ready to let him go, not yet. They'd finally turned a corner in their relationship and she was anxious to see if there was anything real—anything lasting.

Tonight, dinner was served outside in the courtyard. Lanterns were lit and strategically placed around the area, providing a cozy ambience.

"Kyra?" It was Cristo's voice and it held a note of concern.

She glanced over to find both men staring at her. "Um, sorry. I was just trying to memorize the layout of this patio area. I'd love to have something similar someday."

Cristo arched a brow, but he didn't ask any questions. "Niko asked if you'd care for something to drink."

"Yes, please. Would you happen to have any iced tea?"

Niko smiled and nodded. "I'll get that for you."

She was surprised to see her host move to the cart of refreshments and pour her a glass of tea. For some reason, she imagined there would be servants tripping over themselves to do Niko's bidding. Apparently this billionaire was quite self-sufficient. Maybe that was why she liked him so much. And she noticed Cristo had warmed up to him, too.

Kyra struck up a conversation about the architecture of Niko's home and its rich history. Cristo surprised her with his knowledge of Greek history. Little by little, she found herself relaxing.

"Excuse me." A voice came from across the courtyard. Conversation immediately ceased as all heads turned to find Mr. Stravos making his way toward them. "Apologies. Work waits for no man."

Cristo got to his feet. Kyra followed his lead, anxious for this visit to go better than the last one. She lifted her lips into what she hoped was a warm smile even though her insides shivered with anxiety. She noticed that Mr. Stravos didn't smile. Was he angry? Or was that his usual demeanor?

After shaking hands with Cristo, the older man turned to her. He took her hand in his, and instead of shaking it, he lifted it to his lips and pressed a feathery kiss to the back of her hand. She continued to hold her smile in place.

Well, he definitely isn't angry. What a relief.

"Thank you for coming back to visit, my dear. I'm sorry our previous time together was so brief."

"Thank you for the invitation. I was just telling Niko how lovely I find your courtyard. Someday I'd love to have a similar one." She struggled to make polite chatter when all she wanted to do was question the man about her family.

Mr. Stravos glanced around as though he'd forgotten what it looked like. "I must admit that I don't spend much time out here these days. Most of my time is spent in my office."

"You must be quite busy. Too bad it takes you away from this gorgeous courtyard and the amazing flower gardens surrounding your home."

As though on cue, dinner was served at the glass table on the other side of the courtyard. The conversation turned to their adventure to Orchidos. Cristo joined in, explaining that it was also his first visit to the village. Everyone took a turn talking about subjects from the wild orchids growing throughout the village to the architecture.

After dinner, everyone moved to the cushioned chairs grouped together. Cristo took her hand and gave it a squeeze. Her gaze moved to meet his. He smiled at her and her heart tumbled in her chest. No man had ever made her feel so special.

"How long are you going to continue with this charade?" Mr. Stravos asked out of the blue.

Kyra's gaze swiftly moved to the older man. His expression was perfectly serious. They'd been busted. And try as she might, she couldn't keep the heat of embarrassment from rushing to her cheeks.

Cristo's neck muscles flexed as he swallowed. "What charade?"

"This." The man waved his hand between him and Kyra. "You think I'm going to sell you my hotels because you put on a show of marrying her. You two hardly know each other. Am I really supposed to believe that you care for her?"

Kyra hoped Cristo knew what to say because her mind was a blank. If she tried to speak now, it'd be nothing more than stuttering and floundering.

"You're right." Cristo released her hand and sat forward. "I knew how important marriage is to you and I wanted you to take my proposal seriously, so I asked Kyra to act as my fiancée." When the older man's gaze moved her way, Cristo added, "Don't be upset with her. She didn't want to do it, but I convinced her. And a lot has changed since then."

Kyra was not about to let Cristo shoulder all of the blame. The more she got to know Cristo, the more she realized how important this deal was to him. "He has been nothing but kind and generous. I couldn't ask for anyone better in my life." Her gaze moved to the man who'd rocked her world the night before. His gaze met hers. In that moment, she had her answer—their lovemaking hadn't been faked. There was something genuine between them.

Mr. Stravos scoffed at her defense of Cristo. "He is only looking out for himself. He wants this deal so much that he will do anything to get it."

"That's not true. He's been helping me track down my family. It's what led us to Orchidos." She sighed, still disappointed they hadn't unearthed any new information. "But we weren't able to come up with any further information. Which is strange because the investigator traced the photo I have back to that village."

The older man's dark eyes narrowed. "Do you have the photo with you?"

At last she'd gained his attention and hopefully his help. "I do." She reached into her purse and withdrew the black-and-white photo. She held it out to the man. "That's my grandmother and grandfather. They both died before I was born."

The man didn't say a word as he retrieved his reading

glasses from his jacket pocket. He moved the photo closer to the lantern to get a better look. Did he recognize someone? The longer he stared at the photo, the more hope swelled in her chest. What did he know about her family? Would he be able to point her in the right direction?

She sat up straight and laced her fingers together to keep from fidgeting. As though sensing her mounting anxiousness, Cristo reached out to her. His fingers wrapped gently around her forearm and gave her a squeeze before sliding down to her hand. She unclenched her fingers in order to hold his hand.

Her gaze met his, where she found comfort and reassurance. It helped calm her racing heart. No matter what Mr. Stravos said, she knew instinctively that Cristo would be there to help her deal with the news.

Mr. Stravos tapped the photo with his finger. "You're sure this is your family?"

Kyra nodded. The breath hitched in her throat. She had the feeling her life was about to take a drastic turn. She just hoped it was for the best.

There was a long pause before Mr. Stravos spoke again. "I... I knew your grandmother."

Really? There was sincerity written all over his aging face. She expelled the pent-up breath, but she was still cautious. "Why didn't you say so when I told you her name?"

"Because I had to be sure it was her. You don't understand."

"You're right. I don't understand at all. Why would you keep it a secret that you knew her?"

"Because she's my sister. And you aren't the first person to come here claiming to be my long-lost relative—"

"I never claimed to be anything of the sort." She could feel Cristo's grip on her tightening just a bit—cautioning her to move carefully.

"I am sorry." The man's voice was barely more than a whisper. "I've grown too cautious over the years."

She had the feeling the apology was rare for him. His words touched her and immediately soothed her lingering ire. "Trust me. I didn't come here expecting or wanting anything from you. We…we should go."

"No. Stay. Please. We have much to talk about."

She cast Cristo a hesitant look. He nodded his consent. She settled back in her seat and coffee was poured. She tried to relax but she was too wound up, waiting and wondering what information Mr. Stravos would have about her grandparents.

"I haven't seen my sister since I was a kid. She was older than me. Many years ago, our family lived in Orchidos."

"I don't understand. Cristo and I just spent a day there, talking with people and searching through old papers. There was no hint of your family or my grandmother."

Her uncle nodded in understanding. "That's because I had some problems in the past with blackmail. I had as much of my family's history that could be located gathered and brought to me. And the people of Orchidos who knew my family promised to keep what they knew to themselves. Having money comes with challenges that some might not expect. Privacy comes at a premium."

"And how do you know I'm not lying to you?" She didn't like being even remotely lumped in with blackmailers and scam artists.

"That's easy, my dear. You look like my sister when she was younger. When I first saw you, I thought I'd seen a ghost."

Which explained why he'd made such a hasty exit after their first meeting. "But I don't understand. Why don't you know what happened to my grandmother? Did you two have a falling-out?"

"No. We didn't. But she had one with our father. She'd fallen in love with a boy my father didn't approve of. My father did everything possible to break them up but nothing worked. When they eloped, my father disowned her and told her she was never welcome in his home again."

A deep sadness came over Kyra. She couldn't imagine what it would be like for her grandmother to have to choose between the man she loved and her family. "That must have been horrible for all of you."

"There was no reasoning with my father. He was a big man who ruled the household with an iron fist. And he never backed down from a decision."

"So my grandmother married my grandfather and moved to the States?"

Her uncle nodded. "That night was the last time I saw her. My mother and I were banned from keeping in contact with her. When I got older, I thought about checking on her, but back in those days there was no such thing as the internet—no easy way to find someone who didn't want to be found."

They continued to talk and fit together the puzzle pieces of her grandmother's life. And then the conversation turned to Kyra and her life. Uncle Nikolaos seemed genuinely interested in her. He at last let down his guarded exterior, showing her a warm and approachable side.

When she glanced around, she found Cristo and Niko deep in conversation. This evening had turned out quite differently than she'd imagined. And it was all thanks to Cristo. If it wasn't for him, she never would have met her uncle and cousin.

As though Cristo could sense she was thinking about him, he glanced over at her and smiled. Just that small gesture sent a warm, fuzzy feeling zinging through her chest. She loved him more than she'd ever loved anyone. And she knew it was dangerous, because in the end, she would get hurt. But for this evening, she was going to bask in the warmth she found being in the company of the man she loved and her newfound family.

* * *

Cristo had a hard time taking his eyes off Kyra.

There was something different about her that night. Was it that dress? Or was she glowing with happiness from finding her long-lost family? Whatever it was, she was even more captivating than before, if that was possible.

"My cousin seems to be charming my grandfather. That's not an easy feat. Trust me. I've tried in the past. That man is quite set in his ways."

"They do seem to be hitting it off." Cristo finished his coffee. He was tired of dancing around the subject. "What do you think my chances are of putting together a deal to buy the hotel chain?"

"Honestly, I've talked with my grandfather at some length and so far he hasn't shown any interest in parting with it. Between you and me, I think it goes far deeper than a business deal. But for the life of me, I can't figure out why he holds so tightly to it, and he won't explain it to me."

Cristo could feel his chance to seal this deal slipping away. And he'd run out of ideas of how to get through to Nikolaos Stravos, who took stubborn to a whole new level.

Niko set his empty coffee cup on a small table before turning back to Cristo. "I think your best hope lies with your fiancée." His brows drew together. "She's still your fiancée, isn't she?"

Without hesitation, Cristo nodded. "She is. If she'll still have me." A thought came to Cristo of a way to make Kyra happy. "Since you're now family, how would you feel about standing up for me at the wedding?"

Niko's eyes opened wide. "I'd be honored."

"Great." The men shook hands. "Kyra will be so happy."

Cristo turned to gaze over at his adorable fiancée. He didn't know how it had happened, but somewhere along the way, he'd begun to picture her in his future. In fact, he couldn't imagine life without her in it. Marriage would undoubtedly change things as he knew them, but he instinctively knew it would be better with her in it.

When it was time to call it a night, hugs were exchanged between Kyra and her newfound family. Cristo couldn't be happier for her and it had nothing to do with his business… or his hopes to iron out a deal with Stravos.

Nikolaos gave him a stern look. "No more charades. Honesty is the only sound basis for a relationship. And my great-niece deserves only the best."

"I'll do my best, sir."

Nikolaos arched a brow. "You should also know that your involvement with my niece will have no bearing on my decision about selling the hotel chain. Do not have her doing your bidding."

Cristo's body stiffened. "The thought never crossed my mind."

The man's cold, hard gaze left no doubt about his sincerity. "Good. Because if you do, mark my words, I will use every resource at my disposal to destroy you."

Cristo bristled at the threat, but he willed himself not to react for Kyra's sake. At long last, she'd found the family she had been longing for—a connection to the father she lost—and Cristo refused to be the reason for discord between them.

Noting the obvious affection in the older man's eyes when they strayed to Kyra, Cristo understood the man's protectiveness. Cristo cleared his throat. "I would expect nothing less of a caring uncle. I am glad you have found each other."

Nikolaos's eyes momentarily widened as though surprised by Cristo's response. "So long as we understand each other."

"We do, sir. We both want Kyra to be happy." And he truly meant it.

Approval reflected in Nikolaos's eyes. "If you two decide to go through with the wedding, I'd very much like to be there."

"You would?" Kyra interjected. A smile lit up her face.

"Most definitely."

Cristo held out his hand to the man. "We'll definitely keep in touch."

Nikolaos cleared his throat. "As for your offer to buy the hotel chain, I will take it under advisement. My grandson seems to think it would be a good idea to divest ourselves of it and focus on our shipping sector, but I like to remain diversified." He glanced down at Cristo's extended hand, then accepted it with a firm grip and solid shake. "I will take your offer to our advisers and see what they have to say."

"Thank you. I appreciate your consideration."

Cristo didn't know what would happen with his business deal, but he was starting to figure out that the most important thing right now was his future with Kyra.

CHAPTER SEVENTEEN

"I CAN'T BELIEVE IT," Kyra spoke into the phone the next morning.

The sound of footsteps on the tiled floor had her glancing over her shoulder. The sight of Cristo made her heart go *tip-tap-tap*. She smiled at him and he returned the gesture. There was just something about his presence that made her stomach quiver with excitement. He headed straight for the coffeemaker.

"Sofia, I've got to go. I'll talk to you later."

Kyra rushed off the phone. She couldn't stop smiling. She told herself it was because she'd connected with her father's family. And though it wasn't exactly the family she'd been expecting, it was a connection to her father nonetheless. That connection was priceless, especially in light of the discord between her and her mother.

"You can't believe what?"

"I'm just so surprised we found my family. Honestly, after we ran into nothing but dead ends in Orchidos, I'd pretty much given up hope of finding anyone or learning anything about my father's family. I can't believe I've found them."

"I'm really happy for you."

Maybe this was the opening she needed to help Cristo find his way back to his family, which was so much more important than the business deal—if only he could see that.

"Do you really mean that?"

"Of course I do. I know how important family is to you."

"It's just as important to you." When he shook his head, she persisted. "It is, or you wouldn't be so tormented by the memory of your brother or doing everything in your power to gain your father's respect."

He continued to shake his head. "You don't know what you're saying."

"This wedding, it could be a bridge back to them." She had no idea if he was listening to anything she was saying, but she couldn't give up. Someone had to make him see reason.

His dark brows drew together as his disbelieving gaze met hers. "And how is that going to work? Invite them here for a doomed wedding? I'm sure that'll really impress them."

"You're missing the point. This isn't about impressing anyone—it's about reconnecting, talking, spending time together. They'll understand when the wedding is canceled for legitimate reasons."

He raked his fingers through his hair. "Why is this so important to you?"

"Because it's important to you. Just promise me that you'll think about it."

He hesitated. "I'll think about it. By the way, you're welcome to visit with your uncle and cousin as much as you want. Just let me know ahead of time and I'll have the helicopter available. I know you're really missing your mother—"

A frown pulled at Kyra's face. "I don't want to talk about her."

"Wait a second. You're allowed to lecture me on making amends with my family and yet you're unwilling to deal with your own mother?"

"It's different."

"Uh-huh." His tone held a distinct note of disbelief. "And how would that be?"

Kyra huffed. "Because she lied and manipulated me."

"One of these days you're going to have to take her call."

"Not today." Kyra glanced at the clock, finding it was already after eight o'clock. She turned back to Cristo. "Speaking of family, I've received RSVPs from your brothers. They send their regrets."

"I told you they'd be too busy to travel halfway around the world for a wedding." His tone was matter-of-fact. "That's why I asked Niko to stand up for me."

"You did?" This was news to her.

Cristo nodded. "And he agreed. So no worries about my absentee brothers."

The fact he hadn't expected more from his brothers was disheartening. She didn't like the distance between Cristo and his family. Maybe it was because the only family she had now was her mother, but Kyra didn't think there was anything more important than staying in contact with those you cared about.

"I just can't believe they'd miss their brother's wedding."

"Believe it. The apple doesn't fall far from the tree."

"What does that mean?"

"It means they are a lot like my father. Business first. Family a distant second."

How sad.

"Were you ever close?"

"My brothers are a lot older than me. Eight and ten years. It wasn't like we had much in common. I was much closer to Max."

And when Max died, Cristo was left alone with his guilt. *How awful.* She wanted to help him find a way back to his family.

"Maybe if you were to call your brothers—maybe if they knew how important this is to you—"

"No." His voice held a note of finality. "I'm fine on my own."

"Are you? Or are you punishing yourself for Max's accident—something that wasn't your fault?"

"You don't know what you're talking about."

"Don't I?"

She wasn't going to back down and let him waste the rest of his life in a mire of guilt for something that wasn't his fault. "You keep thinking that if you'd said something different or done something different that the accident could have been averted, don't you? It's easier to blame yourself than to accept it was totally out of your hands." Her voice wobbled. "Nothing would have changed what happened."

Cristo's brows scrunched together. "You sound like you're talking from experience."

"I am." She'd never told anyone this. "For a long time, I blamed myself for my father's death."

"But why? I thought he died of a heart attack."

"He did. At home. Alone. My mother had driven me to the movies to meet one of my friends. My mother went shopping until it was time to pick me up. There wasn't anyone there to help him. To call 911."

Cristo moved to her side and wrapped an arm around her shoulders, pulling her close. She let her weight lean into him. Together they could prop each other up. "It wasn't your fault."

"Just like it wasn't your fault."

Cristo didn't say anything, which she took as a good sign. Hopefully he'd let go of the guilt that was only succeeding in distancing him from his family.

Kyra blinked repeatedly, trying to stuff her emotions down deep inside. "Shouldn't you be at a meeting or something?"

His brows lifted. "Are you trying to get rid of me?"

"Not at all. It's just that you're always so busy."

He took a sip of coffee before returning the cup to the bar. "You're right. I am a busy man. Maybe too busy."

"Too busy? Where did that come from?"

"I've been thinking about what you said about slowing down."

Really? He'd listened to something she'd said to him. He certainly had her attention now. "And what did you decide?"

"That there's more to life than work."

It was a good thing she had her hip against the couch or she might have fallen over. Since when did this workaholic have time for fun? "What have you done with the real Cristo?"

"I'm serious."

So it appeared. But she did have to wonder how far he was willing to take this makeover. "And what do you have in mind?"

"I saw there's a beach volleyball game this morning. I signed us up."

Her mouth gaped. She had to admit that she never expected those words to come out of his mouth. Not in a million years.

"You do play volleyball, don't you? I thought I overheard you mention it to Sofia."

She nodded. "I played all through high school. It wasn't beach volleyball, but it'll do."

"Good. How soon can you be ready?" There was a knock at the door. "That will be breakfast. I thought you'd want something to eat first."

"Are there any other surprises I should be aware of?"

He sent her a lopsided grin. "I don't know. Would you like some more?"

This playful side of Cristo was new to her, but she fully approved. A smile pulled at her lips as her gaze met his. She wanted the day to slow down so they could enjoy this time together a bit longer. Okay, a lot longer.

He held up a finger for her to wait as he went to answer the door. After the wide array of food had been delivered and arranged on the table, he turned back to her. "Now, what were we discussing? Oh, yes, surprises. Do you want more of them?"

She didn't have to contemplate the answer. "Yes, more surprises as long as they are this good." She lifted one of the silver lids from a plate, finding scrambled eggs, sausage, bacon and orange wedges. She grabbed a slice of orange and savored its citrusy taste. Once she'd finished it and set aside the rind, she turned back to him. "Definitely."

He moved to stand in front of her, and before she knew what he was up to, his head dipped. His lips claimed hers. His mouth moved tentatively over hers. Was he testing the waters? The thought that he wasn't as sure of himself as he liked the world to think turned her on all the more.

She met him kiss for kiss, letting him know that his advance was quite welcome. Her arms wound their way around his neck as his hands spanned her waist, pulling her snug against him. She definitely liked his surprises.

Much too soon, he pulled back. "Don't pout."

It showed? Or was he just getting to know her that well? "But I liked that surprise. A lot."

He smiled broadly. She loved how his eyes twinkled with merriment. It filled her with a happiness she'd never known before. She forced her lips into a playful frown, hoping to get more of his steamy kisses.

He shook his head. "It isn't going to work. You'll have to wait until later."

"You promise?"

"I do. But right now, we have some beach volleyball to get to."

"You're really serious about this, aren't you?" For some reason, she never pictured Cristo as the volleyball type. But then again, with his shirt off and some board shorts hung low on his trim waist…she could envision it clearly now.

"Yes, I'm serious. And if you don't go change quickly, we won't have time to eat."

Kyra groaned as he pushed her in the direction of her bedroom to put on her bikini. This day was definitely going to be interesting. Very interesting indeed.

How could more than two weeks have flown by?

Cristo had never had so much fun.

He'd really enjoyed this time with Kyra. There had been the volleyball tournament followed by leisurely strolls along the beach. There were late mornings wrapped in each other's arms followed by early evenings for more of the same. If only he'd known what he'd been missing all of this time, he might have taken the chance on love sooner.

Somewhere between the moonlit walks on the beach, the stories of her childhood and the stroll through a nearby village, he'd fallen for his own pretend bride. Now he wanted her for his very genuine wife. But how could he prove his honest intentions to her without her thinking he had an ulterior motive?

His feelings for her were not fleeting. This was not a summer romance to reflect upon in his twilight years. No, this was a deep down, can't-live-without-her love. But he knew Kyra was still holding back—clinging to that wall around her heart.

And he knew why—the fake engagement they'd struck at the beginning followed by her mother's betrayal. Combine them both and it was no wonder Kyra was having problems trusting him. But there had to be a way to convince her of his sincerity. But how?

While Kyra was off checking on flowers for the wedding, he found himself pacing back and forth in the suite. She had left him with one task to complete for the wedding—one task that left his gut knotted up. He had to make a phone call to his parents.

He withdrew his phone from his pocket. His finger hovered over the screen. He'd been very selective on which calls to take this week and which to let pass to his voice mail. Did that make him irresponsible? His father would say it did, but Cristo was beginning to see things quite differently. Every person deserved some downtime now and then. Everyone deserved time to find happiness and love.

And he wouldn't have realized any of this if it wasn't for Kyra. He owed her big-time for the happiness that she'd brought to his life. The least he could do was see if either of his parents were coming to the wedding.

With great trepidation, he dialed his mother's number. She immediately answered.

"Hello, Mother."

"Cristo, don't you ever answer your phone these days?"

She'd called him? This was news to him. He was certain there weren't any voice mails from her. He wouldn't forget something like that. "What's the matter? Is it Father?"

"Your father is fine."

"That's good." Why had he gone and jumped to conclusions? Maybe because his mother didn't call often and certainly not repeatedly. "What did you need?"

"It isn't what I need, but rather, what do you need? After all, you're the one getting married."

"I...I don't need anything." Well, that wasn't exactly true. He needed answers, but he wasn't sure his mother was the person to give them to him.

He needed to know if he was putting too much stock into building a lasting relationship with Kyra. When it was all over, would they end up cold and distant like his parents? The thought chilled him to the bone. He didn't think he could bear it if they did. And he certainly wouldn't want his children growing up in such an icy atmosphere.

He tried to think back to a time when his parents had been warm and affectionate with each other. Surely they must have been at one point. For the life of him, he couldn't recall his father sweeping his mother into his arms and planting a kiss on her lips just because he loved her and wanted to show her. How could they coexist all of these years with such distance between them?

"Mother, can I ask you a question?"

"You can ask, but I don't know if I'll have an answer for you."

His mother was a very reserved woman. She didn't sit down with a cup of coffee and spill her guts. Whatever she felt, she held it in. Maybe she was more like his father than Cristo bothered to notice before now.

"When you and Father married, were things different in the beginning?"

"Different? How so?"

"You know, was he always a workaholic?" Cristo just couldn't bring himself to say *icy* and *cold*.

"Your father made it perfectly clear from the start that his work would always come first."

"And you were all right with that?"

There was a slight pause. "I understood how important his work was to him."

"What about Max's accident? Did that change him?" What Cristo really wanted to know was if he was responsible in some way for his father's chilly distance from his own family.

This time there was a distinct pause. "The accident changed everyone. You included. But you can't blame yourself. It was an accident."

"That's not what Father thinks."

There was a poignant pause. "What your father thinks is that the accident was his fault. But he doesn't know what to do with all of that guilt and grief so he projects it on those closest to him. It creates a barrier around him, keeping us all out. He no longer thinks he deserves our love."

"Really?" Cristo had never gotten that impression. Had he been reading his father wrong all of this time?

"I think your father is afraid of losing someone else he loves, including you. I can't promise he'll ever be the father you want—the father you deserve—but sometimes you have to accept people flaws and all. Cristo, I'd love nothing more than our family to heal."

To heal there had to be forgiveness—a letting go of the past. Would his father be able to do that? More important, would Cristo be able to do it? Could he let go of his guilt over Max's death?

Cristo surprised himself when he realized that Kyra had opened his eyes and shown him the importance of family. Kyra had also pointed out a fact that both he and his father had been overlooking—Max wouldn't have wanted this big rift in the family. He was forever the peacemaker.

Maybe the best way to honor Max's memory was to swallow his pride and make peace with his father. But there was something he needed to know first. "Mother, is that what Father wants, too? For the family to be together again?"

There was a poignant pause. "I think he does, even if he can't bring himself to say the words."

His mother was only guessing. Of course his father wouldn't admit that he needed his family. That would make him look weak. "I don't know how you do it."

"Do what?"

"Make excuses for him and give him the benefit of the doubt. Do you really love him that much?"

There was suddenly a distinct chilliness in her voice. "Cristo, what are all of these questions about? Are you having second thoughts about your wedding?"

He was definitely having doubts, but not as she was thinking. He had to make a choice—his work or his bride. He couldn't have them both in equal portions. One had to outweigh the other. But could he let go of his work—his meetings and his endless phone calls—in order to put Kyra first in his life?

"Cristo, you're worrying me. What are you thinking?"

"That I don't want to end up like my father." It wasn't until the words were out of his mouth that he realized he'd voiced his worst fear. And he didn't have any idea how his mother would take such a statement.

"You have a good heart. Follow it. It won't let you down."

His mother rarely handed out advice, so for her to say this, she had to really believe it. His mother thought he had a good heart. A spot in his chest warmed. Maybe what he needed now was to have more faith in his love for Kyra.

"Thank you. This talk helped. I know exactly what to do. I've got to go."

After getting off the phone, he knew the only way to prove his love for Kyra was real would be to turn his back on the deal with Stravos. His heart beat faster. But how could he do that when he had worked so hard to make this deal a reality? He clenched his hands. How could he give up his chance to finally prove himself to his father—to earn his father's respect?

But then Kyra's smile came to mind and his fisted hands relaxed. He remembered the way her eyes lit up when she was happy. He conjured up the memory of her melodious laughter and the way it relaxed him. She knew what was important in life—family and love.

He had to trust in his love for her.

The rest would work itself out.

CHAPTER EIGHTEEN

WASN'T THIS EVERY little girl's dream?

Kyra turned in a circle in front of the large mirrors that had been specially delivered to her suite. The slim-fitting snow-white lace-and-organza bridal gown was divine. This was her final fitting and she didn't think the dress needed another stitch. It was absolutely perfect. The neckline dipped, giving just a hint of her cleavage. The bodice hugged her waist. She smiled at her reflection, imagining what it'd be like to walk down the aisle and have Cristo waiting for her.

She'd tried on countless wedding dresses from frilly ball gowns to hip-hugging mermaid-style dresses. They were either too flouncy, too clingy or too revealing. She had started to think she'd never find the right dress.

It wasn't until her frustration had reached the breaking point that she stopped and wondered why she was working so hard to find the perfect dress for a fake wedding. Why was it so important to her? As of yet, she didn't have an answer—at least none she was willing to accept.

The wedding was only two days away and Cristo had yet to call it off. She didn't understand why, especially now that her uncle had stated their marriage would have no bearing on his decision to sell the hotel chain. Or was Cristo hoping to really go through with the wedding? Did he think by marrying her that her uncle would feel obligated to follow through with the sale?

A frown pulled at her lips. Was she merely a means to an end? The thought made her stomach lurch. Or was she making too much of things—letting her imagination run amok?

She inhaled a deep, calming breath. That must be it, because Cristo had been nothing but charming and thoughtful. He wouldn't hurt her. It was bride's nerves—even if she wasn't truly a bride. And besides, with Cristo holding off on canceling the wedding there was still a chance his parents would make an appearance. Kyra had even sent them a note pleading with them to come for their son's sake. She never heard back.

A knock at the door curtailed her thoughts. The suite had been a hub of activity all morning in preparation for the big day. She'd never had so many people fuss over her. It was a bit intoxicating. If only it was real...

She spun around one more time, enjoying the breezy feel of the luxurious material. She wondered what Cristo would think of it. Would he want something more traditional? Or perhaps he'd rather she wear something more daring—more revealing? Kyra sighed. The truth was she didn't know what he'd think and she never would.

"Hello, Kyra."

Oh, no! It can't be.

Kyra spun around, finding her mother standing in the doorway of the suite. Her arms were crossed. That was never, ever a good sign.

"Mom, what are you doing here? I didn't know you were flying in."

"You would have known if you'd ever check your messages. But I guess we're even now because I didn't know my own daughter was getting married."

Kyra glanced down at her wedding dress. "I can explain."

Her mother's gaze narrowed. "I can't wait to hear this."

Kyra inwardly groaned. Could this day possibly get any worse?

"Explain what?" Cristo came to a stop next to her mother.

This time Kyra groaned aloud. It was her fault. She shouldn't have tempted fate. Now look at what she'd brought upon herself, her mother and her fake groom all in the same room. Wasn't this cozy?

Her mother turned to Cristo. "And you would be?"

"Cristo Kiriakas. The groom. And you would be?"

"The mother of the bride." Her painted red lips pressed together in a firm line of disapproval. Her gaze flickered between Cristo and Kyra. "And now you've ruined everything."

A look of bewilderment filled Cristo's wide eyes. "Excuse me. I don't understand. What did I ruin?"

"Surely someone must have told you the groom can't see the bride in her wedding gown. Now go. Get. You can't be here."

Cristo's brows drew together and his voice deepened. "This is my suite and no one orders me around."

"Must you be so stubborn? Don't you know being here is bad luck? Come back later. My girl and I have some catching up to do."

He sent Kyra a questioning look. She shrugged. Right about now, her face felt as if it was on fire. This just couldn't be happening. This had to be some sort of nightmare and soon she'd wake up.

Cristo sent her a reassuring smile, letting her know he had everything in hand. "I think she looks absolutely beautiful in her gown." He glanced up at the ceiling. "See, no lightning strikes. I think we're safe."

"Really? Are you really going to stand there and mock me?" Her mother sent him an I-dare-you-to-argue-with-me glare.

Kyra inwardly groaned. She knew that look all too well. Cristo would lose and it wouldn't be pretty. Kyra rushed over to the counter and grabbed her phone. Reinforcements were needed and fast.

Mop&Glow007 (Kyra): 911...suite

MaidintheShade347 (Sofia): What's wrong?

Mop&Glow007 (Kyra): Everything. Hurry.

Tension filled the room.

"Mom, what are you doing here?" Kyra tried to redirect the conversation.

For a moment, her mother didn't move. Eventually, she turned to Kyra. "You surely didn't think I was going to let my only child walk down the aisle without me."

"But I'm not—" Cristo sent her an icy stare that froze the words in the back of her mouth.

Her mother's perfectly plucked brows drew together. "You're not what?"

"I'm not," she said as she glanced at Cristo, who shook his head, "getting married right now."

Her mother sighed. "And you expect me to believe that while you're standing here in your wedding dress? I know you're mad at me, but were you really going to get married without telling me?"

Kyra shrugged. She honestly didn't have an answer because she'd never thought about it, since this wedding was never going to take place. But with Cristo signaling for her to keep quiet about the fake engagement, she couldn't tell her mother the truth right now. And if her mother learned the truth, word would spread quickly. The scandal they desperately wanted to avoid would become a reality. So Kyra said nothing. *What a mess.*

"Mom, how did you know about the wedding?"

"I read it in the paper just like everyone else. Honestly, Kyra, do you know how it made me feel to learn about your engagement that way?"

Kyra sent Cristo a puzzled look. He'd promised that news of their engagement wouldn't be in the United States papers. He shrugged innocently.

"Kyra, what's really going on? Are you pregnant?"

"What? No! Mother!" The heat in her face amplified.

Her mother's suspicious stare moved from her to Cristo

and back again. "I'm only saying what others will think with such a rushed wedding."

"That's it. I've heard enough." Cristo stepped up to her mother. "You can't come in here and upset Kyra. I think you've already caused her enough pain."

"Her pain? What about mine? She abandoned me and now she's trying to get married behind my back—"

"That's enough!" Cristo's voice held a steely edge. "Kyra has done nothing but love you and do everything she could to help you. It's you who owes her an apology."

Her mother gaped at him, but no words passed her lips.

"Kyra, I'm here. What's the emergency?" Sofia came to an abrupt halt in the open doorway. Her gaze moved rapidly between Cristo and Kyra's mother. "Oh. Hi, Mrs. Pappas."

For an awkward moment, no one spoke. The tension was thick in the room as Cristo and her mother continued to stare at each other as though in some power struggle.

Sofia sent Kyra a what-do-I-do-now look.

Kyra snapped out of her shocked stupor. "Sofia, why don't you give my mother a tour of the resort while I get out of this dress."

"I don't want a tour," her mother announced emphatically. "I want to know why you're standing there in your wedding gown in front of the groom. There's still time to fix this. We can find another dress—"

"Mom, no. This dress is perfect."

Her mother gave the dress due consideration and then nodded. "It was perfect, but now it's jinxed."

"It is not. I love it. Now, please go with Sofia." Before her mother could argue, Kyra added, "Really, Mom, go ahead. I have a few things to discuss with the seamstress and then I'll be free."

"But what about him?" Her mother nodded toward Cristo.

"He's not superstitious and neither am I. We'll make our own luck."

"Well, I never…" With a loud huff, her mother turned and stormed out of the room.

Sofia sent her one last distressed look.

Kyra mouthed, *Sorry*.

Once they were gone, Cristo shut the door. "Would you mind explaining what just happened here?"

"Tornado Margene blew into town, huffing and puffing." Kyra stepped down from the pedestal, anxious to get out of the dress.

"So I've seen. But what is she doing here?"

"Why are you asking me? You're the one who promised not to put our wedding announcement in the New York papers. If you want someone to blame for this fiasco, look in the mirror."

"I didn't do it." When she continued to look skeptical, he continued. "Why would I? It just complicates things further." He paused as though a thought had just come to him.

"What is it? Don't hold back now." She approached him.

"Considering the timing of your mother's visit, I'm going to guess my mother received her wedding invitation and arranged for the press to be informed. It would be something she'd do. She's always taking care of details like that. She doesn't know we're not—well, um…that the marriage—"

"Isn't real," Kyra whispered, finishing the sentence though it left an uneasy feeling in her stomach.

He raked his fingers through his hair. "This certainly complicates things."

"You think? And I've got my finals tonight." She should be studying this afternoon, not trying to appease her mother.

Cristo's face took on a concerned look. "Can you get an extension?"

She shook her head while catching the anxious look on the seamstress's face. "I've got to change clothes. I'll be back. Don't go anywhere. We aren't done talking."

This arrangement couldn't go on. She shouldn't have

agreed to it in the first place. In the end, it hadn't worked out for Cristo after all. She felt awful for him.

Would Cristo understand when she called everything off? Would they still be on friendly terms? Or would they go their separate ways and never see each other again? The thought of never seeing Cristo again tore at her heart.

But she realized that's the way it needed to be. He had his work. She had her family. That had to be enough.

Kyra wasn't just beautiful.

She was stunning in her wedding dress. Like a princess.

Cristo paced the length of the living room. Over and over. Her mother making a surprise appearance certainly wasn't how he'd planned for their talk to start.

For days now he'd been trying to decide how to propose for real. At last he had everything sorted out. That was until her mother showed up. Why did her mother pick today of all days to fly in?

He stopped and stared down the hallway. There was no sign of Kyra. What was taking her so long? He paced some more.

He envisioned telling Kyra his decision to make this marriage authentic. Her face would light up with joy as she rushed into his arms and kissed him. Excitement swelled in his chest at the mere idea of it. He'd promise her that they could face anything as long as they were together and she'd agree. Life would be perfect. Okay, maybe that was stretching things with her mother being at the resort, but it would all work out. It had to.

At last Kyra emerged from her room in a pair of peach capris with a white lace tank top. Her hair was in a twist and piled atop her head with a clip. She looked absolutely adorable. Thankfully the seamstress had made a hasty departure.

Cristo drew in a deep steadying breath and then slowly blew it out. "Kyra, we need to talk—"

"If this is about my mother, I'm sorry for accusing you of letting the cat out of the bag."

"It's okay—"

"No, it isn't. I jumped to conclusions and I shouldn't have." Her gaze didn't meet his. "There's something I have to tell you. I know we made a deal, but I... I can't go through with this. I have to be honest with my mother—with everyone."

"I understand."

Her head jerked upward and her wide-eyed gaze met his. "You do? You understand?"

His gaze moved to the windows. Suddenly he felt the walls closing in on him. Or maybe it was a case of anxiety. He'd never considered it before now, but what if Kyra turned him down? What would he do then?

"Cristo? Did you hear me?"

"I have an idea. How about some sunshine and fresh air?"

Her brows arched. "What about our talk?"

"We'll talk. I promise." He moved toward the door. "Come on."

"Cristo, I can't. If you hadn't noticed, my mother is here."

"She can wait. This can't."

He led her to the elevator, out the back entrance and down a windy path to the beach area. Maybe he should have rehearsed what he was going to say to her. Where did he even begin? His jaw tensed. What if he made a mess of things?

Kyra touched his arm. "Hey, what's wrong?"

He glanced over at her. Concern reflected in her eyes. The words wouldn't come. They caught in the back of his throat.

"Just relax." She slipped her hand in his. "Whatever it is, we'll deal with it."

His frantic thoughts centered. All he could think about was how her smooth fingertips moved slowly over his palm, sending a heady sensation shooting up to his chest and far-ther. His anxious, rushed thoughts smoothed out. He could do this. Anything was possible with Kyra by his side. They were a team.

Hand in hand they walked along the path away from the crowded beachfront. This time around, he didn't want an audience for what he was about to say. He just needed Kyra.

Alone at last, he turned to her. "I have something I need to tell you."

Worry lines creased her beautiful face. "It's okay. I know what you want to talk about."

"You do?" Was he that obvious? He didn't think so but, then again, Kyra knew him better than anyone. He'd opened up to her far more than he'd ever done with anyone.

"It's my mother. Don't worry. I'll send her packing—"

"No, it's not her. And you don't have to ask her to leave on my account. In fact, it might be better if she stayed—"

"Why? Are your parents coming for the wedding, too?"

He shook his head. "My mother called. Neither she nor my father will be attending. She blamed it on my father's hectic work schedule."

"I take it you don't believe her?"

He shrugged. "It doesn't matter. I don't need them here. But it might be nice if your mother stayed—"

"Stayed? Why do you keep saying that?"

He took both of Kyra's hands in his. "It's okay. You don't have to worry. I have a plan."

"A plan? Isn't that what just blew up in our faces? First with my uncle and now with my mother—"

"I guess you wouldn't exactly call it a plan."

Frustration reflected in Kyra's eyes. "Would you please explain what you're talking about?"

He was beating around the subject and making this con-versation far more complicated than it needed to be. "The truth is, I called Nikolaos today. And I withdrew my offer to buy the hotels."

"What? But why? That deal means everything to you."

"Because somewhere along the way, you taught me there are other things more important than business and beating my father at his own game."

"I did that?"

Cristo nodded. "You taught me that and a lot more."

He dropped down on one knee. "I know I am supposed to have a ring when I do this, but seeing as you're already wearing it—"

"Cristo, get up!" Her eyes widened with surprise. "What are you doing?"

"You know what I'm doing. I'm proposing, if you'll let me get the words out."

"You can't. This isn't right." She pulled her hands from his.

Wait. What? She was supposed to be jumping into his arms. Lathering his face with kisses. Not standing there looking as though she was about to burst into tears at any second.

He was so confused. He thought at last he'd gotten things right—choosing love over business. But it still wasn't working out with a happily-ever-after.

Where had he gone wrong?

CHAPTER NINETEEN

THIS COULDN'T BE HAPPENING.

Cristo was saying all of the right things at exactly the wrong time.

Kyra took a step back. She couldn't—she wouldn't—be the woman he sacrificed everything for. The fact he'd withdrawn his offer for the Stravos hotels was too much. Though she loved him dearly, she couldn't let him turn his life upside down to be with her. She wouldn't be able to bear it when later he ended up resenting her.

"I can't do this." Her hands trembled as she slipped the diamond ring from her finger and pressed it into his palm.

"Kyra—"

"I'm so sorry." She turned on shaky legs, hoping they'd carry her back to the hotel.

"Don't walk away. Kyra, I know you care. Why are you doing this to us?"

She paused. If she was honest with him, he would just explain away her worries. He'd be more concerned about the here and now. He wouldn't give the future due consideration. But she could. She had to be the strong one—for his sake.

With every bit of willpower, she turned back and met the pained look on his face. "You have to understand that we've let ourselves get caught up in this fairy tale. Neither of us has been thinking straight."

"That's not true." His eyes pleaded with her.

"Everyone can see we don't belong together. Your parents can't even be bothered to meet me. Why can't you see that this is a mistake?"

"My parents know nothing of love. If they ever loved

each other, it was over years ago. But I do love you. I guess the real question is, do you love me?"

Kyra's gaze lowered to the ground. "You need and deserve more than I can give you. You're an amazing guy. Someday you'll find the right lady and she'll make you happy. You'll see—"

"What I see is you refusing to admit that you love me, too." He reached out to her.

Kyra sidestepped his touch. She knew that if he touched her—held her close—she'd lose her strength. She'd never be able to let him go—to let him find happiness. "I don't want to hurt you. I never wanted to do that. But you have to realize that this dream world we created isn't real. You and I as a couple, it isn't real."

His eyes grew dark and a wall came down in them, blocking her out. Even though they were standing beneath the warm Greek sun, a shiver ran across her skin.

"And that's it? You're done with us?" His voice vibrated with frustration.

"I think it's best we call the wedding off immediately and go our separate ways before we hurt each other any more."

He stared at her long and hard, but she couldn't tell what he was thinking. And then he cursed under his breath and started back toward the hotel—alone.

Kyra pressed a hand to her mouth, stifling a sob. She couldn't let her emotions bubble over now. She had to keep it together a little longer—until Cristo was out of sight.

He would never know how hard it was to turn him away. But she couldn't make the divide between him and his parents even wider—because they'd made it clear with their silence that they didn't approve of her. She was a nobody by their social standards. Her chest ached at the thought they wouldn't even give her a chance.

And now Cristo had sacrificed his chance to merge the Glamour Hotel chain and the Stravos Star Hotels. The enormity of the gesture finally struck her and a tear dropped onto her cheek. No one had ever sacrificed something so important for her. How was she ever going to move on without him?

Kyra dashed away the tears. Somehow she had to make things right once again for Cristo.

But how?

Her phone chimed. She pulled it from her pocket.

MaidintheShade347 (Sofia): Do you want to hang out?

Mop&Glow007 (Kyra): Can't.

MaidintheShade347 (Sofia): Busy with Cristo?

Mop&Glow007 (Kyra): No.

MaidintheShade347 (Sofia): No? What's up?

Mop&Glow007 (Kyra): It's over.

MaidintheShade347 (Sofia): What's over?

Mop&Glow007 (Kyra): Everything.

MaidintheShade347 (Sofia): Where are you?

Mop&Glow007 (Kyra): The beach.

MaidintheShade347 (Sofia): I'll be right there.

Kyra moved to the sand and sank down on it. It didn't matter if Sofia showed up or not. No one could fix this. No one at all. She'd done what was needed. Somehow she had to learn to live with the consequences, as painful as they were.

CHAPTER TWENTY

THE WEDDING WAS TOMORROW.

Correction. The wedding was supposed to be tomorrow.

Still in yesterday's clothes, Cristo paced back and forth in the empty suite. Kyra hadn't returned to their suite since they'd spoken yesterday—when he'd made a complete and utter fool of himself. He'd never begged a woman not to leave him. And yet, baring his soul to her hadn't seemed to faze her. He didn't understand her. He didn't understand any of this.

Kyra was different from any other woman he'd ever known. And he was different when he was with her. She brought out the best in him. And now that she was gone, he had all of the time in the world to catch up with business, but he didn't have the heart to do it. For the first time ever, he'd lost his zealousness for making boardroom deals.

What was wrong with him?

So what if a woman had dumped him? He knew better than to invest too heavily in a relationship. He knew they were likely to turn sour at a moment's notice just like his parents' unhappy union.

He should be happy he'd gotten out of the engagement unscathed. He could have ended up married to a woman who didn't love him. That would definitely be a road map to unhappiness.

How could he have let himself think any of it was real?

They'd been having fun. They'd been laughing and talking. That was all. He'd let himself get caught in those smiles of hers that lit up her whole face. He'd fooled not only those around them, but himself. He'd let himself believe in a fantasy of them creating a lasting relationship. And absolutely none of it had been real.

No matter how hard he tried, he couldn't make himself believe that last part. It had been real, at least for him. And that was what made this so difficult.

Thank goodness his father didn't know what a mess he'd made of things. It would have just reinforced his father's opinion that he was incapable of making important decisions—decisions for a multimillion-dollar business.

Cristo's hands balled as every muscle in his body stiffened. He was losing his edge. And that couldn't happen. He had to get a grip on his life and get it back on track. But how? It was as if by losing Kyra, he'd lost his rudder.

A knock at the door jarred him from his thoughts.

Kyra!

His heart raced. His palms grew clammy. He had to handle this the right way. He would be calm, cool and collected. He inhaled a deep breath and then blew it out.

His footsteps were swift and direct. He yanked the door open. "You came back."

Niko's brow knit together. "I wasn't here before."

"Oh. Never mind. I thought you were someone else." Cristo inwardly groaned as he turned and walked farther into the room.

Niko closed the door behind him. "So, are you ready for tonight?"

"Ready for what?"

"How could you forget? Tonight's your bachelor party. Your last night of freedom."

In truth, Cristo had forgotten, but he wasn't about to admit it. He wasn't about to let Niko read too much into his forgetfulness. "Sorry. I've been busy."

Niko glanced around the suite. "You don't look busy now. Want to grab some dinner before the party?"

Cristo rubbed his stiff neck. "I'm not hungry."

Niko sat down. "So tell me what's wrong."

"Why do you think something's wrong?"

"I didn't want to say anything, but you look like hell. So do you want to tell me what is going on?"

Cristo spun around and faced his friend, who had agreed to be his best man. Cristo hadn't asked him to fulfill the role because of the potential business deal, but rather because they'd struck up an easy friendship. Plus, Niko was going to be family and what better way to draw Kyra into her newfound family than to invite her cousin to be part of the wedding?

But so much had changed since that decision had been made. Cristo might as well let Niko know it was over. What was the point in holding back? Soon everyone would know the truth.

Cristo balled up his hands. "The…the wedding…it's off."

"What? But why? You and Kyra looked so happy together at dinner the other week."

Cristo choked down his bruised ego and pushed past his scarred heart to tell Niko the whole horrible story. He started with Kyra's mother making a surprise appearance and how her mother had lied to her. Then he mentioned the disastrous proposal. Cristo had hoped that by getting it off his chest he'd start to feel better about everything. But in the end, he didn't feel any better. In fact, he felt worse—much worse.

Niko looked him directly in the eyes. "Do you love her?"

Cristo sank down on the couch. "I thought I did but… but I was wrong."

"You don't believe that any more than I do. I know your ego is wounded. Any man's would be. But is it worth walking away from the love of your life?"

"You're just saying that because she's your cousin."

"No, I'm not. I'm saying this because I've never seen

a man look so miserable. Look at you. You're an absolute mess."

Cristo glanced down at his wrinkled clothes. He ran a hand over his hair, finding it scattered. And he didn't even have to check his jaw to know he had heavy stubble. His face was already getting itchy.

"Have you eaten anything recently?"

"I'm not hungry." Though his empty stomach growled its disagreement, he just didn't have any interest in food.

"There has to be a way to fix this." Niko sighed as he leaned back. "Did you ever consider she might have had a case of bridal nerves?"

Cristo shook his head. "It's not that."

"What do you think went wrong?"

"I don't know. That's what I spent all night and today trying to figure out. In the beginning, I never intended to care about her, but somewhere along the way this pretend relationship became the genuine thing."

"Did you tell Kyra this?"

"I started to, but she cut me off and told me I was making a mistake. She thinks everything I'm feeling is just an illusion."

"And is it?"

He shook his head. "It's real. I even called your grand-father and withdrew my offer to buy the hotel chain, hoping to prove my sincerity to her. But it didn't seem to faze her. In fact, it had the opposite effect."

"Trust me. I'm no expert on women and love, but if she means that much to you, you should go after her. Make her understand this isn't some illusion—that your feelings for her are real."

Cristo rubbed his neck again. "I don't know. Why would she believe me this time?"

"Maybe because this time you aren't going to blindside her with a proposal right after an emotional run-in with her mother. Maybe by now she realizes she made a monumental mistake, but she's too embarrassed to come back and face you."

Niko's words struck a chord in him, but Cristo's ego still stood in the way. One rejection was bad enough. Being rejected twice was just too much. "Why should I go after her when she was the one to back out of the wedding in the first place?"

Niko arched a brow. "Would you give up this easily on a business deal?"

Cristo inwardly groaned. His friend knew how driven he was, but that was business and this was...was different.

When Cristo didn't answer, Niko continued. "Wouldn't you try to do everything in your power to secure the deal—even if it meant risking a second rejection?"

Cristo knew all along that Niko was right. At this point, he didn't have anything more to lose. But he did have a chance to gain everything that was truly important. It was a chance to hold Kyra in his arms once more. A chance to gaze into her eyes and tell her how much he loved her. His love for her trumped his wounded pride.

Cristo jumped to his feet. "Don't call off the bachelor party." He started for the door. "I'll catch up with you later."

"Cristo, wait." When he turned around, Niko added, "Don't you think you should shower first?"

"I don't have time for that now. I have something far more important to do."

Now that he had a plan, he couldn't wait around. He had to go to Kyra. He had to apologize for throwing everything at her at once.

At last he realized he'd been so caught up in his own feelings and plans that Kyra's feelings hadn't registered. It hadn't struck him until now how her mother's appearance would make Kyra feel vulnerable. Instead of being there for her, he'd been pushing his own agenda as if their marriage was some sort of business deal.

Now he needed to apologize and be there to support Kyra as she dealt with her mother.

Whatever she needed, he'd do it.

He loved her.

He would wait for her…as long as she needed.

CHAPTER TWENTY-ONE

"STOP! I DON'T need to hear this. It's over. Done."

Kyra glared at Sofia, willing her to drop the subject of her now-defunct wedding. She couldn't take any more of being badgered by her best friend and her mother. They were getting on her case for calling off the wedding. They just didn't understand. She'd lost the only man she'd ever loved and to compound matters she'd just completed her finals even though she'd hardly been able to concentrate on them. Thankfully her test results wouldn't be in for another week.

She sat on Sofia's couch and stabbed a spoon in the now-soft ice cream. She could only deal with one tragedy at a time. And missing Cristo was as much as she could take at the moment.

"Obviously you need to listen to somebody as you're not making any sense." Her mother crossed her arms and frowned at her.

"And you're lucky I'm even speaking to you after the way you lied and manipulated me. How could you do it?"

The color drained from her mother's face. "I told you I'm sorry."

Kyra swirled the spoon in the ice cream. "And that's supposed to fix everything?"

"No." Her mother sounded defeated. "I was wrong. After your father died, I wasn't thinking clearly. I couldn't bear to be alone."

"Why couldn't you have just said that instead of creating elaborate lies and scheming to get me to move back in with you?"

Her mother lowered her arms and then laced her fingers

together. When she spoke, her voice was soft. "You had your own life. Your own friends. I thought you'd say no. And I would be all alone for the first time in my life." Tears splashed onto her mother's cheeks. "I was so lost without your father. He was my best friend."

The anger Kyra had been nursing the past few weeks melted away. As her mother softly cried, Kyra set aside her ice cream in order to put her arms around her. No matter what, she still loved her. "It's okay, Mom. You aren't going to lose me. Ever."

Her mother straightened and Sofia, looking a bit awkward, handed her some tissues. Her mother's watery gaze moved from Sofia back to Kyra. "Really? You forgive me?"

"I'm working on it." It was the best she could offer for now. Her mother's lies had cut deeply. It would take time for the wounds to completely heal. "But you have to promise to always be honest with me…even if you're scared."

Her mother nodded as the tears welled up again. "I promise." She dabbed the tissues to her damp cheeks and then turned her bloodshot eyes to Kyra. "But you can't let what I've done ruin your future with Cristo. I've seen the way he looks at you. He loves you—"

"Mom, don't! That isn't going to help. What's done is done. I don't want to talk about it."

Her mother got to her feet. "You're making a mistake."

Once her mother retreated to the tiny balcony of Sofia's efficiency apartment, Kyra flounced back against the couch. No one understood she'd done what was necessary. Cristo was better off without her.

Sofia moved to stand in front of her. She planted her hands on her hips. "You aren't going to scare me off. So don't try."

Kyra retrieved the carton of rocky road from the end table and took another bite. "Why doesn't anyone believe this is for the best?"

"Because you don't believe it yourself or you wouldn't

be shoveling that ice cream in your mouth with a serving spoon."

"That's not true. It's a soup spoon." She glanced down, realizing she'd single-handedly wiped out half of the large container. This wasn't good. She set aside the melting ice cream and stood. "I need some air."

"Want some company?"

She shook her head. "I have some thinking to do."

"Think about the fact you might have been wrong about Cristo. He really loves you."

"You're just saying that because you want to believe in happily-ever-after." Kyra headed for the door.

"I never stopped believing in them. It's just that they are for other people, like you, not me. I have a habit of picking out the wrong guys."

Kyra opened the door and stepped into the quiet hallway before turning back. "You'll surprise yourself one of these days and find yourself a keeper."

"Oh, yeah, listen to who's talking. You've got yourself a keeper and you're tossing him back."

As Kyra walked away, she realized Sofia was right. Cristo was a keeper for someone—just not her.

The sun was setting as she walked along the path that snaked its way along the beach. The lingering golden rays bounced off the water, making it sparkle like an array of glittering diamonds—like the one that used to be on her finger. She glanced down at her bare hand. Tears stung the backs of her eyes. She blinked them away. Her emotions felt as though they'd been shoved through a cheese grater. Why did doing the right thing have to be so difficult?

As she walked, she kept replaying snippets of her time with Cristo. She loved how he'd started to let down his guard with her—how he'd started to enjoy life instead of going from one meeting to the next. She hoped now he wouldn't revert to his old ways. There was so much more to life than business—even if his future wasn't with her.

"Kyra."

She knew the sound of his voice as well as she knew her own. It was Cristo. How had he found her? Silly question. Sofia and her mother would have tripped over themselves to tell him where to find her.

She turned to him, too exhausted and miserable to put on a smile. But when her gaze landed on him, she found she wasn't the only one who wasn't doing well. Cristo's hair was a mess. His suit looked as though it had been in a hamper for a week. Wait. Weren't those the same clothes from yesterday? And then there were the dark shadows beneath his bloodshot eyes.

She stepped up to him. "Cristo, what's the matter?"

He didn't say anything. He just stared at her. All the while, her concern mounted. Maybe he was ill. Maybe something had happened to his family.

"Cristo, please say something. You're scaring me. Is everything all right?"

"No. Everything is not all right."

"Tell me what it is. I'll do what I can to help."

"Do you truly mean that?"

"Of course." She had already sacrificed her heart and her happiness for him, what was a little more?

CHAPTER TWENTY-TWO

CRISTO WANTED TO believe her.

He wanted to believe Kyra had at last come to her senses.

He wanted to believe she'd been caught off guard yesterday when he'd proposed. But the only way to find out was to put his scarred heart back on the line. His pulse raced and his palms grew moist.

With the lingering rays of the setting sun highlighting her beautiful face, he also noticed the sadness reflected in her eyes. Maybe Niko was right. Maybe too many surprises had been thrown at her yesterday. Maybe it had been bridal nerves. He sure hoped that's all it was.

Cristo stared deep into her eyes, knowing this would be the most important pitch of his life. "Kyra, I'm sorry about yesterday. I shouldn't have sprung that proposal on you after you had the shock of seeing your mother again. I was anxious." His head lowered. "I wasn't thinking clearly."

"It's okay. I'm not mad at you."

He lifted his head to see if she was telling him the truth. In her eyes, he found utter sincerity. "So if you aren't upset, why did you push me away?"

"We don't belong together. These past weeks have been an amazing fantasy and you've been wonderful, but it can't last forever. Things end."

"Are you thinking about your mother and father?"

She shrugged but her gaze didn't quite meet his.

"Well, I'm not your father. And no, I can't promise you that we'll have fifty years together. But you can't predict we won't. The future is a big question mark. But there is one thing that I do know."

"What?"

"That I love you." When she went to protest, he pressed a finger to her lips. "And it isn't part of my imagination. It's a fact. I love the way you laugh. I love the way you can see the important things in life. And I love that you are forever putting other people's happiness ahead of your own."

She removed his finger from her mouth but not before pressing a kiss to it. "It's more than that. I know how much you want your father's approval. They will never approve of a nobody like me."

"First of all, you're not a nobody."

"You mean because I'm Nikolaos Stravos's long-lost great-niece?"

"No. Because you're a ray of sunshine who makes this world a better place just by being in it."

"But your parents—"

"Will come around."

"Really? They won't even come to our wedding. I… I wrote them a note pleading with them to come to the wedding for you. And still they say nothing. I really thought I could get through to them."

His hands cupped her face. "See, there's another thing you've taught me—to quit working so hard to gain other people's approval. Fulfillment has to come from within— knowing that whatever I choose to do in life, I do it to the best of my ability."

"But they're your family."

"No. You're my family. I love you, Kyra. And I will be here to love you and support you."

There was a moment of silence. Oh, no. He prayed he'd gotten through to her.

"I do. I love you." Her eyes filled with unshed tears.

"I love you, too. And when you're ready, I have a question for you. But I won't pressure you. I'll wait. I'll wait for as long as it takes."

She sniffled and smiled up at him through her happy tears. "I'm ready now."

"You're sure?"

She nodded.

He slipped the ring from his pocket and held it out to her. "Kyra, will you marry me?"

She nodded as a tear splashed onto her cheek. "Yes. Yes, I will."

He'd never been so happy in his life. For so long, he thought seeking out bigger and better business deals would bring him the peace and happiness that he'd desired. How had he been so wrong?

"From this point forward, you and I are family." He leaned forward and pressed his lips to hers.

EPILOGUE

Next day...

"Talk about a perfect day."

"Do you really mean it?" Kyra looked up into her husband's handsome face as they swayed to a romantic ballad. All around them were wedding guests, smiling and talking.

"Of course I mean it. How could you doubt it?"

"It's just that I know this isn't how you'd been hoping things would turn out—"

He placed a finger to her lips, silencing her words. "We agreed we weren't going to discuss business today."

"I know. I just feel really bad you weren't able to work out the deal for the hotel chain. I think me turning out to be Nikolaos's great-niece hurt you instead of helped you."

Cristo arched a brow at her. "I've learned there are more important things in life than a successful business deal... such as an amazing wife and a monthlong honeymoon to look forward to."

Her heart swelled with love as she gazed into Cristo's mesmerizing eyes, and it was there she saw her future. "Do you know how much I love you?"

"Not as much as I love you." He leaned forward and pressed his lips to hers.

Being held in his strong arms and feeling his lips move over hers was something she'd never tire of. It was like coming home. Because no matter where they were, Cristo was her home, now and forever.

He led her from the dance floor and was about to get her a refreshment when Uncle Nikolaos approached them. She immediately noticed his face was markedly pale. "Uncle, are you feeling all right?"

He waved off her concern. "I'm fine. Just a little tired. I guess I'm not used to getting out and about. But enough about me. I wanted to congratulate you again. Your grandmother would have been so proud of you. You're such a beautiful bride."

"Thank you." Kyra leaned forward and pressed a kiss to his weathered cheek.

Uncle Nikolaos turned to Cristo and stuck out his hand. "Welcome to the family."

"Thank you, sir. Don't worry. I plan to make your niece very happy."

"I'm going to hold you to that promise. And I hope what I have to say won't distract you from the happiness you've found with Kyra, because nothing is more important than family."

Cristo wrapped his arm around her and pulled her close. "Trust me, sir. I've learned that lesson."

"Good. Then if you are still interested, expect a call soon to make the arrangements to have the Stravos Star Hotels sold to you. Consider it a wedding present."

For a moment no one spoke. At last Cristo found his voice. "Thank you. I am quite honored you trust me with the chain. I won't let you down."

"Thank your wife and Niko. They're both quite persuasive. An old man can only hold out so long."

All eyes turned to Niko, who had quietly stepped up and kissed Kyra's cheek. "Congratulations, cousin. You didn't do so bad in your choice of a groom."

"Thanks. I'm kind of fond of him." She flashed a big smile at Cristo.

Niko shook Cristo's hand. "Looks like we'll have a lot of details to sort through when you get back from your honeymoon."

"I'm hoping we won't have to wait that long—"

"Cristo, you promised." Kyra wasn't about to let him off the hook. This month away was supposed to be all about them, not his work.

He sent her a sheepish look. "I haven't forgotten. You won't even know that I'm working."

She really wanted to put her foot down, but she knew better than most how important this sale was to Cristo—it was his chance to step out from his father's shadow. She couldn't deny him this opportunity. "As long as you keep it to an hour in the morning while I'm enjoying my first cup of coffee and getting ready to tackle the day."

He held out his hand to her and they shook on it. "It's a deal."

She pulled on his hand until his face drew near hers and then she pressed her lips to his for a quick kiss. "Now it's a deal."

Everyone laughed.

"It was a beautiful ceremony," said a female voice.

Heads turned to find the new addition to their gathering.

He'd know that aristocratic voice anywhere.

"Mother." Cristo's voice rose with surprise mingled with happiness. "When did you get here?"

"We arrived a little bit ago."

We? Cristo glanced around. His gaze came to rest on his father. Was it his imagination or had his father aged considerably? There was considerable graying at the temples and the lines on the man's face were deeply etched.

When their gazes connected, Cristo detected the weariness reflected in his father's eyes. Cristo was so stunned by his father's appearance that he was at a loss for words. What did this all mean?

"Congratulations, son." His father held out his hand to him.

His father had taken time out of his busy schedule to be here. He wouldn't have done that voluntarily. Cristo suspected his mother had a lot to do with clearing his calendar. Cristo's gaze swung over to his mother, who had a hopeful gleam in her eyes. And then he noticed Kyra prodding him with her eyes to accept his father's gesture of goodwill.

He slipped his hand in his father's warm, firm grip. A smile eased the lines in his father's face. His father pulled him close and hugged him, clapping him on the back.

The hug didn't last long. Cristo quickly extracted himself from the awkward position. He hadn't been hugged by his father since he was a kid. He glanced at the ground unsure of what to do next.

"Thank you both for coming." Kyra stepped forward and held her hand out to his father, who in turn surprised everyone when he hugged her, too.

Cristo's mother stepped up next and gave Kyra a brief hug. "Welcome to the family."

Kyra stepped back to Cristo's side and took his hand in hers. "Thank you. I'm looking forward to getting to know you both."

"I was hoping you'd say that." His mother beamed. "When you return to the States, you're both invited to stay with us. You and I can house-hunt while the men are off tending to business."

Kyra smiled. "You have a date."

This was a surreal moment. Cristo tried to make sense of what had taken place just now. Sure, he was all hyped up by the rush of emotions from the wedding, but deep down, he had the feeling it was a new beginning for all of them.

His mother bestowed a warm smile on them. "May you both have a lifetime of happiness."

Cristo hoped the same thing. He wanted nothing more than to be able to make Kyra smile every day for the rest of their lives.

Kyra turned to her husband. Her husband. She loved the sound of those words. And she loved Cristo even more.

Tiny crystal bells placed at each table setting started to chime in unison, signaling it was time for the bride and groom to kiss. Kyra smiled as she turned to Cristo. He didn't waste any time sweeping her into his arms and planting a loving kiss upon her obliging lips. Her heart fluttered in her chest as if it was their first kiss.

Far too soon, he pulled away. Just then a romantic ballad started to play. Cristo held his arm out to her. "May I have this dance?"

As they moved around the dance floor, Kyra spotted Sofia at the bridal party table alone. Kyra frowned. She'd told her to bring a date, but Sofia had insisted there was no one she was interested in enough to ask to the wedding.

"What's the matter?" Cristo's voice drew Kyra out of her thoughts.

"Nothing."

"Come on now, I know you well enough to recognize the signs of you worrying about something or someone."

He was quite astute. "It's Sofia. She's all alone tonight and I feel bad. Perhaps I should have had you set her up with one of your friends."

"I'm glad you didn't ask."

Kyra stopped dancing and pulled back just far enough to look into her husband's eyes. "What's that supposed to mean? You don't think Sofia is good enough for your friends—"

"Slow down. That isn't what I meant at all."

"Then what did you mean?"

"That I'm not comfortable playing matchmaker. I think it's better when people find each other on their own. Like we did."

She hated to admit it, but he did have a good point. She moved back into his arms and started swaying to the music. "I suppose you're right."

"What did you say? I didn't quite hear you."

"I said you're right." And then she caught his sly smile. "Oh, you. You just wanted me to say you're right again."

"Hey, look." Cristo gazed off into the distance.

"Don't try to change the subject. You're just trying to get out of trouble."

"Is it working?"

"No." She sent him a teasing smile.

"But I'm serious. You should check out the bridal table again. I don't think you have to worry about Sofia having a boring time. Your cousin seems to have taken an interest in her."

"Really?" Kyra spun around to check it out. Sofia was smiling. And so was Niko. "Do you really think anything will come of it?"

Cristo shrugged. "Hard to tell. Niko seems quite wary of relationships. But aren't you rushing things? They just met."

"True." She sighed. "I guess I just have romance on my mind."

"And so you should, Mrs. Kiriakas. This is just the beginning of our story."

"I can't wait to see what's next."

"Neither can I. I love you."

"I love you, too."

* * * * *

MEET THE FORTUNES

Fortune of the Month: Lucie Fortune Chesterfield

Age: 27

Vital statistics: Pretty as a princess, Lucie is tall, graceful and hopelessly single—or so she thinks.

Claim to fame: The accomplished daughter of Lady Josephine Fortune Chesterfield, Lucie is known for her charity work and her consistently calm demeanor.

Romantic prospects: While many men have attempted to woo her, Lucie has never lost her heart… at least not since high school, when she fell for a brash American cowboy at summer camp. Readers, she married him. *But no one ever knew.*

"They say you never forget your first love, but I've tried. Hard. And until a few days ago, I would have assured you that Chase Parker was firmly in my past. But that was before he showed up at my apartment in Austin.

"I can't believe our teenage marriage was never annulled! I can't believe Chase is here after so many years. And most of all, I can't believe, after all this time, I dissolve at the mere sight of him. He's only here to get our annulment taken care of—we both agree it's for the best. And yet, I can't help but imagine what could have been…"

The Fortunes Of Texas:
All Fortune's Children—Money. Family.
Cowboys. Meet the Austin Fortunes!

FORTUNE'S SECRET HUSBAND

BY
KAREN ROSE SMITH

First Published in Great Britain 2016
By Mills & Boon, an imprint of HarperCollins*Publishers*
1 London Bridge Street, London, SE1 9GF

© 2016 Harlequin Books S.A.

Special thanks and acknowledgement to Karen Rose Smith for her contribution to the Fortunes of Texas: All Fortune's Children continuity.

ISBN: 978-0-263-91967-7

23-0316

USA TODAY bestselling author **Karen Rose Smith**'s eighty-seventh novel was released in 2015. Her passion is caring for her four rescued cats, and her hobbies—gardening, cooking and photography. An only child, Karen delved into books at an early age. Even though she escaped into story worlds, she had many cousins around her on weekends. Families are a strong theme in her novels. Find out more about Karen at www.karenrosesmith.com.

To my grade school friend Liz,
who married young, too. We made it!
Thanks for being my friend.

Chapter One

Lucie Fortune Chesterfield was late!

It was her own fault. She'd forgotten her phone and had to run back to the Austin, Texas, apartment she was subletting to retrieve it. In a rush now on her way out again, after disembarking from the elevator in the lobby, she stopped cold.

Was she seeing things? Was that Chase Parker leaving the building? Not possible. Just because he still invaded her dreams—

The doorman stood at his counter and she ran to him and pointed to the departing tall, broad-shouldered man whose Stetson was tilted at an angle she thought she recognized.

The doorman did a double take. "Lady Lucie, I thought you'd left."

Irving hadn't been at his station when she'd rushed

back in for her phone. "I forgot something and had to return to my apartment. Do you know who that man is?"

Lucie was very used to doormen and chauffeurs and pomp and circumstance. Born in England and living on the Chesterfield Estate, she was considered "almost" royalty. Her mother's adopted father had been an earl. Her own father had been knighted. In England and the United States, her family was sometimes hounded and followed by paparazzi searching for that money shot. After the scandal her sister had become involved in, Lucie was more than aware of her actions and couldn't just run into the street chasing a tall Texan who resembled a ghost from her foolish past, a ghost so secret not even her family had known all the details about her association with him.

Irving, in his fifties and balding, turned red to his scalp as he reached out to the shelf under the counter and retrieved a business card.

"I'm so sorry, Lady Lucie. I saw you the first time and assumed you'd left for the morning."

She'd been following a routine. Each morning after breakfast, she'd been scouting out properties for an office for the Fortune Foundation, which was planning to open a branch in Austin.

Irv, as he preferred to be called, went on to explain further as he handed her the business card. "The gentleman gave me this and said he'd be back later."

Lucie read the card aloud in a low tone. "Chase Parker—" There were two numbers listed.

At the idea of Chase being in close proximity, she felt a tremble race through her. At seventeen, she'd been on a youth trip to Scotland. And then…

She had to forget about Chase Parker, ghost or not,

and concentrate on this trip to visit her relatives in Texas. She had agreed to help the Fortune Foundation set up a branch in Austin for the benefit of children there.

"What do you want me to do if he comes back again?" Irv asked.

She fingered the card in her hand. What did Chase want with her now? He obviously knew she was here. Why hadn't he called first? Should *she* phone *him*?

No. He'd forgotten about her easily. The past was in the past. If he had a reason to see her, she'd find out soon enough what that was.

Answering Irv's question, she said, "If I'm in, buzz me just as you do with everyone else."

"As you say, Lady Lucie. There is one other thing—"

She really had to be going, but Irv looked worried about something, so she waited.

"That reporter's been out there again from the news station. I saw him yesterday afternoon, but he was gone until you got back."

"As long as he stays outside, there's really nothing we can do about him."

"I don't want him accosting you as you leave," Irv maintained, "or as you return. You know, we can always arrange for your driver to pick you up in the garage instead of at the front entrance."

"He'd soon catch on to that because he knows I'm usually out and about. I'll deal with him if I have to, Irv. Please, don't worry about me."

"But I do," Irv said with a boyish smile. "Somebody has to. With your relatives living in Horseback Hollow, you need somebody to worry about you here."

Everyone thought they knew her family's history— from the articles in the tabloids and in the more respectable media. Irv was right, though. Her relatives were in Horseback Hollow about five hours away.

"I have friends here, too. In fact, I'm supposed to be meeting them for brunch. So I really need to be going. Barry is waiting to drive me. You have a good day."

"You, too, m'lady."

The temperature in Austin, Texas, in March was around sixty during the day and went to a low of forty at night. Lucie had chosen a grass-green suit for this brunch, a professional look, since she would be visiting office spaces with a real estate agent afterward. The three-quarter-length sleeves of her jacket were perfect for the weather.

As she pushed her straight brown hair over her shoulder and stepped from the car, she checked the sky. All blue, not a cloud in sight.

Thanking Barry, telling him she'd text him when she finished brunch, she headed for the restaurant that her friends had chosen for this get-together. It was a bit of an elite location. Cavette's catered to a crowd that didn't have to worry what they spent on brunch, lunch or a late dinner. No paparazzi were allowed inside, and there was a security guard stationed in the restaurant who would react quickly if he had to. Celebrities in the area who often stopped in at Cavette's were assured of their privacy and a backdoor exit should they need it.

The restaurant was tastefully decorated with lots of real greenery. Lucie stopped briefly at the hostess's desk but spotted her friends at a table against the wall. Ella Thomas had recently returned from her honeymoon with Ben Fortune Robinson. Vivian Blair was engaged to Ben's twin brother, Wes. Ella spotted Lucie first.

Ella was a beauty with thick, long, wavy auburn hair

and blue-blue eyes. Lucie respected her. She wore minimal makeup and preferred to be admired for her brains rather than her body. She'd dressed today as she usually did, in dress jeans, a Western-cut blouse and expensive boots. In contrast, Vivian was taller than Ella with hazel eyes and honey-streaked brown hair that she wore pulled back today. She also wore glasses—very stylish ones. A computer programmer, she'd dressed in a navy pantsuit with a red blouse. She was shyer than Ella but smart and fun. Lucie liked both of these women immensely and was glad to call them friends. As she took a seat with them, she noticed they'd already ordered her a mimosa.

"You don't have to drive this morning," Ella counseled her. "Let loose. Champagne and orange juice are a good way to start your day."

Lucie laughed. "I can't let too loose. I want to choose the right office space for the Fortune Foundation. It has to be utilitarian, but classy, too, with just the right square footage to fit what they want to do."

"And what is that?" Vivian asked after a quick hug.

"What I'm looking for would mostly be a functional space. If we have programs for kids, they would probably be at other sites."

"Or maybe at a community center?" Ella offered. "I can see the Fortunes building one of those."

"Just how long are you going to be in Austin?" Vivian asked.

"I'm free until April, when I fly to Guatemala with my mother to start a project there."

"How do you like living in Austin? I know your sister likes living in Horseback Hollow."

Lucie took the napkin from her plate and spread it onto her lap. "Amelia loves Horseback Hollow. But truth be told, I prefer Austin. It's more metropolitan than Horse-back Hollow."

Vivian and Ella both exchanged a look. "You won't get any arguments there," Vivian said. "In Horseback Hollow, everybody knows everybody's business."

"And in Austin," Vivian supplied, "they just know Lady Lucie Fortune Chesterfield's business. Any reporters lately?"

"Irv says one's been hanging around, but I haven't run into him face-to-face yet." She took a sip of her mimosa. "You both look good," Lucie said to them, narrowing her eyes. "Are you happy?"

Ella sighed. "I couldn't be happier."

"Me either," Viv agreed. "And not only with Wes. We think the app I developed, My Perfect Match, is going to continue to be a huge hit. I mean, after all, it brought me and Wes together, though not exactly in the way I intended."

Although she was listening to Viv, Lucie couldn't help letting her mind wander again to Chase leaving his card with Irv. "Just when you think you have life planned out, fate shoves it in another direction."

"Exactly," Viv responded. "And I'm trying to think of a way to balance My Perfect Match. Tell me something, Lucie. Do you think it's better to hook up with someone you know you're compatible with, or should you hook up with someone who sets your heart on fire?"

Wasn't that a question for the test of time? Because of her own experience, Lucie responded sadly, "Flames die down. Compatibility might be better long-term."

"That sounds like experience to me." Ella motioned to Lucie's mimosa. "Come on and drink that, and tell us who taught you about flames."

Lucie had slipped Chase's card into her jacket pocket. Now she touched it, and when she did, she remembered all too vividly the touch of his hands. Her cheeks grew warm, and she blamed that on the mimosa. What could it hurt to talk about it a little? "Come on," Viv coaxed. "You know all about *our* love affairs."

"What was his name?" Ella prompted.

"His name was Chase."

"Now, that's a good Texas name if I ever heard one," Viv noted. "But he couldn't have been a Texan if you were living in England."

"Oh, but he *was* a Texan. His father owned an oil company and they were wealthy. I was seventeen when we met in England at the start of the trip to Scotland. Chase was a group leader. I thought it was love at first sight, but I guess it was just lust at first sight. We got caught together in the hostel room. So much about it was against the rules. A leader consorting with one of the tourists, being in his room alone together, both of us undressed…" She trailed off. "Chase got fired, and I was sent home." At least that was the gist of the story.

Contrite, feeling disgraced in the eyes of her parents, Lucie had vowed to herself to never do anything so reckless again. She'd maintained that vow by pouring all of her energy into setting up orphanages with her mother in developing countries. Their lives were about helping needy children.

"You never saw or heard from him again?"

"I received a letter. I wrote him many, but I never heard from him after that first one."

"You didn't call him?"

"Not what a proper lady would do," Lucie answered

almost teasingly, though there had been other reasons not to call, too.

Should she tell them about Chase dropping off his card at her apartment? No. He might not even come back. She was sure nothing would come of it.

Lucie had learned early on the best way to turn attention away from herself was to listen to another's story, and she knew these women had stories to tell. Ella's husband, Ben, had recently found out he was a Fortune and that his father, whom he'd always known as Gerald Robinson, was really Jerome Fortune, who had disappeared years ago. Ben was now on a quest to locate other relatives. The Robinsons might be Fortune cousins.

"Has Ben gotten any further in proving that his father is really Jerome Fortune?"

"His father is thwarting him at every turn," Ella said with a frown. "His sister, Rachel, who uncovered the connection and confronted their dad, is sure their father is hiding something. Ben wants the truth. He has seven siblings who want to know about their roots, whether his father wants to deny the past or not. Thanks to you, he located Keaton Whitfield, who's his half sibling."

In one of those quirks of fate, Lucie had already known Keaton, an architect in London. He'd designed a house for one of her mother's friends, and he and Lucie had run into each other at a few parties. He was what the Americans would call a stand-up guy. When Ben had asked for an introduction to him, she'd readily complied.

"Hasn't he located anyone else who might be related?" Lucie asked. Apparently Ben's father had had several affairs.

"Right now he's on the trail of Jacqueline Fortune,

who may or may not be his paternal grandmother," Ella revealed.

"This is a mystery unraveling before our eyes," Viv said with enthusiasm. "I can't wait for the next install-ment."

Brunch was full of more Fortune stories, including the party Kate Fortune had planned for her ninetieth birth-day. Lucie, Viv and Ella kept their voices low because Kate Fortune's residence at the Silver Spur Ranch near Austin was still a secret, except to the Fortune family. In the past, Kate had been the target of blackmail and kidnapping attempts. Now, looking for an heir for her company and not wanting media attention about it, she intended to keep her presence in Austin quiet.

When Lucie checked her watch, she saw the day was moving ahead without her, and she really had to get on with looking at properties. After goodbyes to Viv and Ella, she called the real estate agent who was advising her. They agreed to meet at the first location on Lucie's list and then tour the others together afterward.

By late afternoon, while Lucie sat in the car on her way back to her apartment, she was quite discouraged. None of the spaces had seemed quite right. She was be-coming more and more sure that she might also have to help find satellite locations for the actual kids' programs themselves—summer lunches, music, art, sports. Build-ing a community center might be a possibility, unless the foundation could find already established and deserving programs to fund.

Barry pulled up in front of her apartment building. She was tired and all she wanted to do was soak in her tub. After she climbed from the car, Irv came to meet her at the curb. That was unusual, since the doors had an electric sensor.

He said quickly, "Just in case you wanted to get back in your car and go in the other direction, I wanted to warn you, the man who was here this morning is waiting at my desk."

Lucie stood at the curb and peered through the glass doors into the lobby. Her heart began to beat in triple time. The man at Irv's desk *was* Chase Parker. She couldn't tell exactly how much he'd changed from when he was twenty-one. After all, he'd be thirty-one now. But she could tell he was still as tall and straight-shouldered. The Western-cut jacket he wore fit him impeccably, his black jeans and boots just as much so.

He turned toward her now, and that tilt of his Stetson told her some of the young man still remained.

"It's fine, Irv. Apparently he has some business with me, and I have to see what that is."

She squared her shoulders, forgot her fatigue and started forward to meet her past head-on.

Lucie walked through the glass doors and approached Chase, thinking his dark hair was still the color of the finest imported chocolate. His dark brown eyes seemed to take in everything about her all at once. Even in that wonderfully cut jacket, she could tell he was more muscular than he'd been at twenty-one but not too bulked up. He was long and lean and still looked like everything good about Texas.

Before Lucie took another step toward the unknown, she turned to Irv who'd come in behind her. "Not a word of this meeting to anyone, not anyone." After all, Irv knew Chase's name from the business card. If the press associated their names, if reporters started digging, a new scandal could erupt.

"Not a word, Lady Lucie. You know you can count on me."

"Thank you, Irv. You don't know how much I appreciate that. Was that reporter around here at all today?"

"I didn't see him…or the news van."

She nodded and stepped up to Chase. She felt as if all her composure had slipped away, though she knew that was crazy. After all, she'd practiced that her entire life.

With that stiff upper lip Brits were accused of having, she said simply, "Chase?"

"You've grown up." His gaze traveled over her suit, seemed to linger on her tiny waist, then idled on her long, straight brown hair. She wondered if he could see all the questions in her hazel eyes. She wondered if he had any idea of what seeing him again did to her—increased her heart rate and brought back vivid pictures of the two of them together, but, most of all, squeezed her heart until it hurt.

He nodded to the corner beside the elevators that was away from the doors, Irv's counter and everyone else for the time being. She walked with him and stood beside a potted palm.

Before she could ask a question, he inquired, "Do you know how hard it is to track you down, even though you and your family and your stories are spread across the tabloids?"

Lucie was flummoxed. So he'd kept up with articles in the tabloids as if they were true.

He went on. "I thought you were in London. Then I found out you were in Horseback Hollow. After consulting a PI, I learned you were here in Austin, where my father's company is located. If you only knew how much time I wasted—"

After all these years, he was acting as if seeing her was an emergency. "My life is full of people and activities, as I imagine yours is."

"I don't globe-trot. I was beginning to have visions of my traveling to some developing country to see you."

"Would that have been so bad?" she asked, sensing his agitation but still not understanding any of it.

He took off his Stetson, ran his hand through his thick hair and shook his head. "None of that came out right. I read the stories about your work with orphans and refugees. I know you and your mother are selfless in your cause. But I had to find you."

"Why such urgency?"

"Because…" he started. He leaned close and lowered his voice to a whisper. "We're still married."

Chapter Two

Chase felt as if he'd been kicked in the gut. Lucie Fortune Chesterfield was even more beautiful now than she'd been at seventeen. That glossy, dark-brown hair and those expressive hazel eyes… He remembered the dimple that only appeared when she smiled, but she wasn't smiling now. She looked worried and upset and very pale.

She confirmed some of his conclusion when she warned him, "Come up to my apartment so no one overhears us or sees us."

She was obviously worried about information getting into the wrong hands. He knew the paparazzi hounded her family. Put an earl in your background, or a sir, as in Sir Simon Chesterfield, her father, and the press thought the whole world wanted to read about you. Maybe they did.

Lucie pressed the elevator button with an impatient finger as she snuck a glance at him. He wanted to smile at her, but he had a feeling this was no smiling matter.

"We'll get it worked out," he said in a low voice.

Chase had been twenty-one and a group leader when he and Lucie had secretly married in Scotland. There, at seventeen, Lucie hadn't needed permission. However, another member of her tour group had caught them disrobed in Chase's hostel room and reported them. Chase's father had swooped in with a lawyer and confidentiality agreements with promises of an annulment. Everyone had been sworn to secrecy.

When the elevator doors swished open, Lucie didn't respond. Maybe she was so upset because of her sister's recent scandal. He'd read the tabloids about Amelia's status as a run-away fiancée and that she'd become pregnant from a cowboy lover. That had probably made Lucie even more skittish of public opinion. The tabloids ran with stories that weren't even true. He knew that. Though he *had* followed Lucie's engagement a few years ago with interest, and couldn't help being irrationally relieved when it had come to naught.

When Chase's elbow brushed hers, Lucie stepped away. He found himself taking a step closer. He was stabbed by the same desire for her now that he'd felt at twenty-one. Yet he was sure she must hate or resent him because of the way they'd been broken up…because of the way his father had handled it. After all, she'd never answered his letters.

When they stepped off the elevator, Lucie motioned to the left. Chase noted there were two apartments on the floor. "I'm surprised you don't have a penthouse. Then you wouldn't have to worry about nosy neighbors."

"I don't have to worry about nosy neighbors." She took her keys from her purse and unlocked her apartment door. "The other apartment is rented by a businessman who travels a lot. He's in Hong Kong right now for the month while I'm here. So I basically have the floor alone. Win-win all around."

She'd made her voice light and airy, but he had a feeling nothing was light and airy. There was a note of anxiety beneath her words.

After she unlocked the door and he stepped inside the apartment's foyer, he gave a quick glance around. "This doesn't look like you," he said automatically.

She gave him an odd look. "How do you know? You've had nothing to do with me for ten years."

That sounded like an accusation, but he didn't stop to wonder about it. The apartment was decorated in chrome and glass, black and white. There was a row of flowered throw pillows on the sofa and he wondered if Lucie had added those.

"You weren't chrome and glass at seventeen, and I doubt very much if you are now."

"I'm only going to be here a month, Chase. The sublet was furnished. Now tell me, why are we still married?" She went over to the sofa and sank down on it, motioning for him to do the same.

He rounded the long, glass-topped coffee table and lowered himself beside her, careful not to let any parts of their bodies touch. He didn't know why, but it just seemed to be the wise thing. Discarding that sentimental thought, he gazed into her eyes and wisdom seemed to fly out the window. This was Lucie, the girl who had stolen his heart. But then he snapped his thinking back to what it should be. She was a public figure now and here only for a month.

He explained quickly, "I applied for a business loan

separate from my father's company. It has nothing to do
with him."

He saw the remembrance pass through her eyes that
he'd once told her he'd never work for his father and never
be anything like him. Circumstances had changed that,
but now they were going to change again.

"After I filled out all the paperwork at the bank," he
went on, "the loan officer called me to tell me I needed
my wife's signature before they could put the payment
through. I couldn't believe what I was hearing. My parents said our marriage was annulled. But then I did research of my own and discovered it is still on the books.
I wanted to tell you in person in case the information
leaked out and somehow made the tabloids. I know how
much your family has been hounded by the media."

Lucie looked even paler. In fact, she looked ill, as if
she might faint.

"Are you all right? Can I get you something? I don't
want you to pass out."

She straightened her shoulders and tossed her hair
back. "I've never passed out in my life, though this might
be a good time."

Apparently she still had a sense of humor. Right now,
though, he didn't think it made either of them feel better.

"Did you see the media storm my sister went through?"
she asked.

Chase nodded. "I did. And I don't want us to experience anything like it. That's why I'm here. To tell the
truth, I'd never be caught dead shirtless outside my house
with a shotgun aimed at reporters like Quinn Drummond."

Quinn was Amelia's husband, a cowboy commoner
in the eyes of everyone but Amelia and now her family.

"He was driven to it," Lucie protested. "You can't imagine what it's like living in a fishbowl with every decision or faux pas analyzed to death by the media."

Chase felt disgruntled at her assessment. Maybe he really didn't know what it was like. "I understand your concerns. My parents and I can't understand what happened with the annulment. My father maintains that he had the marriage dissolved. It must have been a snafu in the paperwork. He and I have spoken with our family's lawyer, as well as an international attorney. We're going to settle this as soon as possible. If I have to, I'll get a whole law firm on it."

Lucie wasn't looking at him but rather at the wall. She seemed to be in a daze. Maybe he should stay a little while. On the other hand, maybe he should go quickly. He handed her another business card.

She started. "I have your card."

But he shook his head. "You have my personal one. This is the ranch card. Note the address for the Bar P. It's about a half hour from here."

"You live on your parents' ranch?"

"I live in the guesthouse. That's going to change soon."

"And you work for your father?" There was surprise in her voice. He'd been right. She did remember.

"For now, but that too will be changing. It's a long story. You have all my numbers. If you want to talk anytime, just call me."

She studied the card and kept studying it as if she was thinking about him working at Parker Oil, as if she might be thinking about all the things that might have been.

He stood, believing she needed time to absorb the news. He had started to cross for the door when Lucie

suddenly popped up from the sofa and rushed to him.
She took his arm. The feel of those fingers of hers, even
through his suit jacket, made his body respond.

He could tell she was a proper lady now when she
said, "I'm sorry for my reaction. The shock of the news
of being married to you really upset me. You must be
just as upset."

"I'm not upset. I'm just concerned about what it means
for you, too. When I couldn't find you, I panicked a bit.
I didn't want this to come out without us talking first."

Talking. Not only talking but falling right back into
memories. As he had in the elevator, he caught the scent
of her perfume, light and airy. It teased him, even though
she always tried to be so proper. She hadn't been proper
in bed. That was something he'd never forget—their wedding night.

"Maybe after this sinks in and we absorb it, we can
have lunch or something."

She was gazing up at him in that way she'd always
had, and he thought he could tell she still felt drawn to
him, just as he felt attracted to her. But it didn't mean
anything. It couldn't. A wife was the last thing he wanted
right now. He intended to buy property that was all his
own and move the horse rescue operation he'd started on
his family's huge spread to his own place. This project
would be all his and have nothing to do with the Parker
family name. He'd owe his dad nothing but a good day's
work when he consulted with Parker Oil.

Chase stepped away from Lucie and toward the door.
She didn't follow him. Maybe she'd decided a husband
was the last thing she needed, too.

He opened the door, but he couldn't help saying, "Remember, if you want to talk, call me." He didn't wait for her response. He left before he stayed.

Once outside the apartment complex, he headed down the street. Unfamiliar with the building and its parking restrictions, he'd left his pickup in a public lot down the block. He headed for it now and made a decision. Instead of going to his family's ranch, which was about a half hour away, he was going to book a hotel room near Lucie. He'd give a call to his mother later and let her know he wasn't going to be back tonight.

His mother had persuaded him to live on the Bar P. She'd asked him to stay there after his dad's stroke several years ago. His dad had recovered, but she lived in constant fear he'd have another stroke. She wanted Chase to keep him from overdoing it, and that was what Chase had done on all levels for the past five years. But recently, when a college friend was killed, he'd realized he had to live his own life, not the life his parents wanted him to live. The horse rescue ranch would be a first step in that direction.

Thinking again about a hotel room, he felt he needed to stay close by Lucie so she didn't disappear again or fly off somewhere. The reason? He couldn't get his life restarted until their situation was cleared up.

What other reason could there be?

When Lucie's alarm woke her, she wasn't only startled by the sound; she was startled by the dream she'd been having. It starred Chase and was anything but tame. She was still married to the man! Her subconscious had apparently been trying to process that and had inserted him naked into her dream.

She remembered his body all too well. She recalled

every detail of the way he'd touched her—not simply in the dream, but on their wedding night.

"I'm still married to the man," she repeated aloud, remembering all too well everything about it, including being sent home in shame.

Her parents had known about her reckless affair with Chase, but not the marriage. Why hurt them with an impulsive escapade that had been erased from the books? Lucie had promised Chase's father she'd never breathe a word about any of it to anyone. After all, her family would have been embarrassed and humiliated even more if the word of her marriage ever got out. They were constantly in the public eye.

She had to talk to someone about it, and she had to talk now.

If she called her mother… First of all, she couldn't. Her mum was in a remote village without cell phone towers for miles. Second of all, she'd tell her mother in good time. After all these years, her mum might be hurt that Lucie hadn't told her in the first place.

Lucie sighed. The questionable decisions of youth. She'd thought the passage of time had healed all this, but she'd been wrong. Because the annulment had never gone through?

Yes, that was certainly the reason.

She'd call Amelia.

She didn't even bother to brush her teeth first. Amelia lived on a ranch with Quinn and she'd be up early. She had a baby, so *certainly* she'd awake. Thinking about her niece, Clementine Rose, made Lucie miss her. She picked up her cell phone and dialed her sister.

"You're up early," Amelia said without preamble. "Going to look at more office spaces?"

"I wish I was. I mean, I will be. I mean—"

Lucie heard a shout…a deep male voice.

Amelia called, "I'll be right there, Quinn. I'm on the phone."

He must have shouted something back.

"It's Lucie," Amelia called back. "Can't you get Clementine her breakfast?" A pause. Then Amelia asked Quinn, "She tossed all the cereal on the floor?"

Obviously this wasn't a good time for Lucie to have a talk with her sister, not about something as serious as a marriage Amelia knew nothing about.

She said, "Amelia, I'll talk to you later when you're not so tied up."

"Lucie, really, if you want to talk, I'm sure Quinn can handle this."

"No, it's okay. You two give my niece a big kiss from me. I promise I'll hug her soon. Have a good day."

"I'm coming," Amelia called to Quinn. "You, too," she said to Lucie, meaning it.

Lucie stared at the phone after she ended the call. Maybe her brother Brodie could help, in more than one way. He might be able to give her some professional advice. He was a publicist who would know how to handle this news, especially if it got out.

But when her call went through to Brodie, all she got was a voice mail message. Next, she tried her brother Jensen. He didn't have voice mail and he didn't pick up.

That left one person she could call. Her brother Charles, who was still in London. She found his number in her contact list and pressed Send.

"Hello, Lucie," he said cheerily. "You're up early."

It was around noon in London. "I have reason to be. Do you have time for a chat?"

"With you? Sure. What's wrong?"

"Why do you think something's wrong?"

"You're my sister. I know the tone of your voice. Spill it."

Charles was the youngest son, a bit of a playboy and charming. He sometimes had trouble being serious, but he was now as he waited for her to talk about whatever it was she needed to discuss.

"Do you remember when I went to Scotland when I was seventeen?"

"Of course I do. There was a ruckus when you were sent home. My sister, who was usually an angel, the perfect sibling, had gotten herself into a mess. Mom and Dad did some fast pedaling with the press, if I remember correctly."

"You mean, they managed to squelch the story that I was sent home from a trip because of a boy."

"That about covers it."

"Actually, no, that didn't cover it. Now don't say a word until I finish telling you everything."

"My lips are zipped."

Was she making a mistake telling Charles? She hoped not. "Promise me you will tell no one else until I say you can."

"Lucie, you're starting to scare me."

She plunged in. "I didn't just have an affair with Chase Parker in Scotland, I married him," she blurted out. "But when we were caught, his father flew in, didn't give either of us a chance to breathe and started paperwork for an annulment."

Charles whistled.

"I'm not done," she protested.

"Still zipped," he assured her.

She rolled her eyes. "Chase found me and came to

see me yesterday. The annulment never went through. We're still married."

She wasn't exactly sure what she expected from Charles, but she definitely didn't expect his burst of laughter.

"Oh, my gosh! Miss Goody Two-Shoes got herself into a mess. I didn't know you had it in you."

"Stop it," she warned him, "or I'll hang up right now."

His laughter simmered down to a smile in his voice as he coaxed, "Ah, you wouldn't hang up on me, not your favorite brother."

"Charles—"

"Oh, Lucie. So you made a mistake and it was never rectified. That doesn't mean it can't be now. A good lawyer will straighten it out. What does Parker say?"

"He says he has lawyers on it, that I should call him if I need to talk, that we'll figure this out. Charles, if this gets out to the press, Mum will be mortified. Think of the scandal. I was engaged while I was still married. All my work at the orphanages will be looked at as some hypocritical jaunt. I can't stand the idea of it."

"The paparazzi are one matter," Charles agreed. "But Chase Parker is another. Are you going to call him to talk about it?"

She remembered her dream. She remembered all the feelings that went with it.

"I don't know," she said in a low voice.

"Lucie, are you telling me everything?"

"What do you mean?"

"What did you feel when you saw him again?"

She went back to that moment yesterday, and she didn't want to admit what she'd felt.

"Aha!" Charles said.

"What do you mean, 'aha'? I didn't say anything."

"Exactly. It was never over with this man, was it?"

"Of course it's over. It's been ten years."

"Sometimes our hearts don't count time. More than anything else, Lucie, you'd better figure out what you want. You can't face the world with news like this with any uncertainty if it does get out."

"I have to think. I need some time."

Suddenly Lucie's bedside phone rang. From caller ID, she could see that it was Irv downstairs.

"Is that your phone?" Charles asked.

"Yes, I have to get this. It's the doorman. Someone must be downstairs. I have to go. Promise me, Charles, you won't breathe a word of this."

"I promise."

She ended the call with her brother and picked up the phone. "Yes, Irv?"

"Mr. Parker is here to see you. Shall I send him up?"

"Tell him to give me five minutes," she said, suddenly out of breath.

"Yes, Lady Lucie. I'll make sure he gives you five minutes."

She didn't have time to do much, but she did have time to brush her teeth. She was wearing pink-and-white-flowered sleep pants and a pink tank. No time to think about clothes. She ran a brush through her hair and grabbed a long pink satin robe, belting it tightly.

There was a knock at her door.

She ran to it and looked through the peephole. It was Chase. Today he was dressed more casually. His chambray shirtsleeves were rolled up, and he'd left his suit jacket somewhere. She undid the chain lock and then the dead bolt. When she opened the door, she just stared at him.

Breaking out of whatever spell that came over her

when she looked at him, her senses returned. "Did any-one see you down there?"

"No one was around but your doorman."

"We have to be careful, Chase. If we're seen together, there will be questions and gossip. If anybody finds out Irv is buzzing me to let you up, someone will investigate."

"I get it. We'll have to work something out," he said, as if seeing each other might become a common occur-rence. Because of paperwork? Because of resolving their situation, of course.

"We can't be seen together here," he reiterated. "I un-derstand that. But certainly there are ways you go out when you don't want to be recognized, right?"

"I have a wig."

He nodded. "Come to breakfast with me. I know a hole in the wall, otherwise known as a truck stop, where you won't be recognized and neither will I. There's won-derful food there. We can talk about all this and what we're going to do."

She thought about it. Sometimes she did feel as if she were a captive in her apartment. Having a normal life was tough in her position. In her family, it had always been that way. Maybe that was why she'd been so reck-less in Scotland when she met Chase. She just wanted to be normal. Since then, she'd accepted the fact that her life would never be that.

However, today—

"We can't just walk out of here together," she warned him.

He took his phone from his belt, tapped on his picture gallery and handed her the phone. "That's a photo of my truck. It's a blue pickup. I'll drive into the parking ga-rage and meet you up on the third level. Will that work?"

"That works, but I need at least ten minutes to get dressed."

He looked her up and down. "I don't know. What you're wearing works for me."

She blushed, and his grin and the sparkle in his eyes told her he was remembering when her being dressed in her robe or *without* her robe would have been just fine.

But that had been another time and place.

"I'll meet you up on the third level, parking row C," she confirmed.

"Got it," he agreed, then went to her door and opened it. As he left, however, he threw another look to her that told her that, dressed or undressed, he still found her attractive. Just what was she going to do about that?

Fifteen minutes later, Lucie had her wig firmly in place, her sunglasses on her nose and all her wits about her. She would not let Chase rattle her. She couldn't. There were too many consequences if she didn't control this situation.

Finding Chase's truck easily, she opened the passenger door and climbed inside.

Chase gave her a smile, nodded and started the engine. As he exited the parking garage, turned and drove down the street, he cut her a sideways glance. "You look hot as a redhead."

So much for not being rattled by him. She didn't respond.

She didn't recognize the route he took, but then she didn't know the city all that well yet. Ten minutes after they'd left the parking garage, he pulled up next to a gas station where several semis were fueling up. There was a restaurant attached—the Lone Star Diner.

Lucie had dressed in a more casual way than she usually did. After all, she didn't want to be recognized. She'd worn jeans and a T-shirt and a blouse on top of that. Her auburn wig was curlier and fuller than her own hair and the chin-length strands brushed her cheeks. She had to hurry to keep up with Chase's long strides as he led her into the diner.

"It's totally impersonal," he told her. "The waitresses rotate shifts, so the same ones are never on at the same time."

"Do you come here often?"

"There are times when I like to be nameless, too. When I agreed to stay at the ranch, I told my mom I wouldn't be there for regular meals. I didn't want anybody keeping tabs on my comings or goings. So I drop in here now and then. The waitresses seem to have a high turnover. I haven't run into the same one twice."

All of that was good to know, not that she'd be coming back here again.

"The thing is," he said in an aside to her, "this isn't a royal kind of place."

"I'm not a snob, Chase."

He sobered. "That wasn't an insult. I was just teasing."

Yes, her sister and brothers teased her, but no one else did. She wasn't used to it.

There were a few stools open at the counter, but Chase led her to a booth in the back, and she was glad of that. He was definitely aware of her need for anonymity.

The waitress arrived immediately and Chase said, "Two coffees and lots of cream for her."

When the waitress moved away, he asked, "You still take it that way?"

"I do. But, you know, Chase, I'm not used to a sterling carafe to pour it from. When I go to developing countries to help with orphanages, sometimes I physically help to build them. My life isn't all silver spoons and Big Ben."

After a long, studying look, he nodded. "Noted. I won't take the tabloid stories about you seriously anymore."

"I'm surprised you read them."

"Only when you're on the cover."

So he'd been curious about her and what was going on in her life? She was curious about him. "So, tell me what you've been doing for the past ten years. In Scotland, you explained you'd never work for your dad because he was manipulative and hard, and he had to control everything."

"Yes, I told you that. After Scotland, I joined a construction crew, but I found I missed the horses on the ranch. So I signed on as a trainer at a quarter horse spread. I liked the work, and I liked being separate from my family."

"But then?" she prompted.

"But then Dad had a stroke. At first we thought his one side would be completely paralyzed. But it's amazing what rehabilitation can do now. I helped him with it. He's so stubborn and independent that we set up a home gym. My mom asked me to live there and watch over him. When he went back to work, she asked me to be his right-hand man there again."

"*He* didn't ask you?"

"Are you kidding? He always expected me to work there, so that's where I've been the past five years. But it's time for a change. It's time for me to leave. My plans are in the works. That's where the loan and me finding out about our marriage have come into play."

Because Lucie had known Chase before, she felt she could read into his expression and his words. He'd felt trapped for five years, and he couldn't wait to break free. Now, however, he was trapped in a marriage he'd assumed had been dissolved.

"You want out. You want to be free."

His gaze locked to hers. "Don't you?"

She did, didn't she? In a month, she'd be in Guatemala working on a new orphanage. In a month, Chase would be putting his plans into action. At that time, they'd be going their separate ways. That was the plan, wasn't it?

Gazing into his eyes, she wasn't so sure.

Chapter Three

Lucie sat beside Chase in his truck as they drove back to her apartment. She folded her hands in her lap, and she could swear they were trembling a little. Why was that?

After their initial dip into what she was doing and what he was doing, they'd talked about mundane things. Maybe because both were afraid to go too deep into anything…maybe because the tension between them was evident to them both. There was tension for lots of reasons—regrets, resentment, something unfinished. Most of all, sexual tension remained. When his knee had brushed hers…when her fingers had tangled with his, reaching for a creamer…

Touch was taboo.

Suddenly Chase said, "You said you'll be in Austin for a month. Is that a solid deadline?"

"Yes, it is," she answered. "I'm meeting my mother

in Guatemala on the first of April. She has set up introductions to officials who can get the ball rolling as far as construction goes."

"You have a site picked out?"

"We do."

He changed the subject a bit. "So you're officially a Fortune?"

"Yes, I am. When my mother found out about her heritage, that she had a long-lost sister and brother, she changed her name to Josephine Fortune Chesterfield, and I changed mine. It seemed right. Her sister and her family have come to mean everything to Mum. Now that Jensen and Brodie and Amelia all live in Horseback Hollow, our visits can become more raucous than royal."

Chase chuckled. "Would you say your family's become closer?"

"Amelia and I have definitely become closer. I know that seems odd, with her living in the United States and me living primarily in England. But when we were growing up, there always seemed to be a wall between us. I'm not sure exactly why. Maybe because we had nannies and were at boarding school. Maybe because our lives were very formal."

"With her married to a cowboy, is her life as formal now?" Chase asked.

"Quinn is down-to-earth. With their baby, Amelia's just like any new mom. Maybe we all just seem more human in Texas. I don't know."

When Chase drove into the parking garage, Lucie was almost sorry. In spite of the tension, she'd enjoyed breakfast and all of their conversations. He was more mature now, with a broader view of life than he'd had at twenty-one. She could tell he wasn't as impulsive and he thought things through. He wasn't so wild, though she could still see deep passion in his eyes. His father's stroke had apparently changed his focus on life. Now he seemed to know what he wanted for his future.

Chase said, "I'll park and walk you back to your apartment."

"It will be safer if you don't do that," Lucie informed him. "You can watch me until I'm in the elevator if you'd like, but then I'll be safe from prying eyes or from a stray reporter. The wig and the clothes help, but anyone who spies on me regularly could probably identify me. We don't want anyone to identify *you* with me."

Chase was silent as he drove up to the second level, through the garage and around the bend and then followed the exit sign to another ramp. No cars trailed them. No one with a camera was evident. Chase should probably change the level he parked on if they ever did this again.

There was no reason to do this again. Legal documents could be sent back and forth by courier.

Instead of just pulling up outside the glass doors that led into the elevator bank, Chase slowed, braked and then backed into a parking place.

"What are you doing?"

"If I'm going to stay until you get on the elevator, I don't want to block traffic."

That made sense. She fingered her purse, a simple, natural leather bag that didn't snag anyone's attention. She knew she had to look at him. That was only proper. But she also knew that when she did, she'd get caught by the dark, knowing expression in his eyes.

Stalling, she unfastened her seat belt, but then she

angled toward him and realized he was already gazing at her. "I enjoyed breakfast."

"The chocolate chip pancakes there are the best."

"It wasn't just the pancakes," she admitted. "It was good catching up with you."

He unfastened his seat belt and turned toward her. She wasn't really so very far away from him. She caught a whiff of either soap or aftershave. Like lime, and manly. She fell under the spell of his dark eyes and the way his hair dipped over his brow. He'd tossed his Stetson into the back, and she could remember the feel of the thickness of his hair sliding through her fingers.

The tremble was back in her hands, and she felt she had to make conversation to hide her nervousness. "I like to do things that make me feel like a real person. This breakfast did that."

He moved only slightly, but he was big and the cab of the truck seemed small. He was closer to her now as he reached out a hand and smoothed strands of hair from her wig away from her face. "You are a very real person, Lucie Fortune Chesterfield. I've always known that."

"Even when the tabloids make me look like a cartoon?"

He smiled but didn't move his hand from her cheek. She was both hot and cold and afraid to move.

"You could never look like a cartoon. You're much too beautiful for that."

Her father had called her beautiful, and her mother told her she was. But they were her parents. She accepted compliments as the polite conversation they were, but this was different. This one came from a man she'd once loved and was still sorely attracted to. She didn't know what to say. Maybe it was better she said nothing, because they were both leaning toward each other.

Chase's thumb swept across her cheek. "Ten years have given you refinement, polish and a generous spirit."

He was going to make her cry. No, he wasn't. She wouldn't let him. When she found her voice, she whispered, "Ten years have made you wiser, stronger, motivated."

"So this really was a get-to-know-you breakfast."

"Maybe so."

But then she asked herself the important question: Why were they getting to know each other when they were going to end something between them?

As if he sensed that question flitting through her mind, he said, "We may be clarifying that there was no marriage between us, but that doesn't mean we can't have a friendship."

Clarifying that there hadn't been a marriage? But they had been married, and they'd done what married people do. How did you just wipe that away forever?

Now he reached out his hand to the other side of her cheek and held her face between his palms. "Are you happy?"

"We all define happiness differently. But yes, I am. I have every earthly need met. I'm helping children, so they can have their own needs met. My family and I are closer than we've ever been. Amelia's baby daughter is such a blessing, and I love her deeply. My only regret is that Dad isn't here to see it all. Sometimes I wake up and my heart hurts because I want him to be involved in all this, too. The Fortune Chesterfields are changing, and I want him to see that change and be as excited about it as I am."

"I can believe he's with you, Lucie. I can believe he nudges you in the right direction when you might go in the wrong one. Energy is energy and it doesn't disappear. Your father could be your personal guardian angel whispering in your ear."

"And who's *your* guardian angel?"

"My guardian angel is a college friend I lost. He died way too young, without accomplishing a quarter of what he wanted to. I feel him sometimes pushing me. Really, I do. And not in the direction my father wants me to go, but one that will give me the most fulfillment in life. Not money, but value. Value that can help horses and people, too."

"As I said, you've matured."

"And you have grown into a woman many men would be proud to be married to."

His face was before hers, and hers was before his. Neither of them were blinking. Neither of them were breathing. If she didn't breathe soon…

He brought his lips very close to hers. "Do you want to kiss?"

"If we kiss, we could be starting something instead of ending it. Is that what you want?"

"I want to know what's beneath the Lady Fortune Chesterfield facade."

Lucie thought about her task here for the Fortunes. She considered her upcoming mission in Guatemala and her responsibilities as a Chesterfield. She considered the way her mother had depended on her since her dad died. She didn't have time for a dalliance.

Chase ran his hands down over her arms and held her hands. "Do you want an annulment?" he asked.

There was only one answer. "Yes. I'm committed to

my life. I don't see it changing. What about you? Do you want it?"

"Oh, yes, I want it. Starting over at my own place, with no one telling me what to do but me, taking responsibility for it all, the horses, the finances and management, the vet bills. I've been counting the years until I could do this."

When he talked about the work, she could see it made him happy. "So one day you're going to leave your dad's and not go back again?"

"No, it won't be like that. I'm grooming someone in my office to take over my position. Jeff has been apprenticing with me, and he can do it. He just needs to have the confidence that he can. I'll stay part-time for a while until everybody gets used to the idea. Then I can slip away and just be used for consulting services."

"We're on the verge," she said softly.

With his gaze unwavering, he agreed, "We are. I enjoyed breakfast, too. Maybe we can do this again."

When he tilted his head, she thought he was going to kiss her. It wasn't full-blown. He kissed her on the cheek. She still felt it all the way down to the toes of her boots. She almost grabbed him and laid one on his lips, but she'd been taught better. Decorum could be everything. She'd never been forward and she wouldn't be now.

She hurriedly opened her door, slid over to it and dropped her legs around to take the giant step down from the running board.

When it seemed as if he was going to come around the truck, she shook her head vigorously. "No, you stay. I'm fine." Shaky, but fine.

She could feel his eyes on her as she walked through the glass door into the bank of elevators and greeted the security guard. She pressed the button and the doors swished open immediately. She stepped inside. Fortunately there was only time for a small wave before they closed in front of her.

She breathed a sigh of disappointment, regret, but also joy. She'd enjoyed being with him. She'd enjoyed feeling alive with him. She'd enjoyed the fact that Chase Parker still turned her on.

At his desk later that afternoon, Chase tried to concentrate on examining the work records, evaluations, and overall résumé of Jeff Ortiz. Jeff was now Parker Oil's CFO, and had done a bang-up job ever since Chase hired him three years ago. He was a good manager with great public relations skills. Not only that, he was intelligent, informed about the industry and would go far either at Parker Oil or for some other company who might try to steal him. He was Chase's pick to replace him when he left. The feat would be getting his father on board with the idea.

Turning away from his computer, Chase thought about breakfast as he had on and off all day. He couldn't shove Lucie out of his mind. Had it been easier ten years ago? He'd had no choice then. If she hadn't been so young, maybe things would have been different. If *he* hadn't been so young, maybe he would have known better what he wanted.

He took his cell phone from his belt, pulled up his contacts and studied her number. She'd given it to him in case he had to reach her about the paperwork...about the annulment...about ending something that had hardly started.

He jabbed the green phone icon.

He half expected her voice mail. After all, she'd said she was going to look at more properties this afternoon with a real estate agent. But he didn't get voice mail. She answered.

"Hi, Chase."

Her tone was cautious, but at least she hadn't avoided his call. Without preamble, he asked, "Are you finished with business for the day?"

"I just got home."

He hesitated only a moment. "We have about an hour of daylight left. How would you like to see the ranch I plan to buy?"

Her silence lasted a few moments and he realized he was holding his breath. But then she answered, "I can be ready as soon as you get here. But you'd better pick me up on a different level this time. Let's try level two."

"I'll be there in ten minutes," he assured her.

When he ended the connection, he wondered how she lived her life like this. She had to think about every twist and turn in the road, and how the public would view it. When did she ever get to do what *she* wanted to do? Would she be wearing her wig again?

Standing, he pushed in his desk chair and realized he couldn't wait to find out.

Ten minutes later, when she ran to his truck and hopped inside, he saw instead of a wig she was wearing a baseball cap with a large bill that practically hid her face. Jeans, a plaid shirt and boots rounded out her outfit. She didn't look royal, and he supposed that was the idea. She used a persona for her public appearances.

Who was the real Lucie?

They didn't speak until they were well out of Austin. He noticed her checking the rearview mirror a few times. He had checked it, too. From what he could tell, no one had followed them. She seemed to relax the farther from Austin they drove.

Finally she said honestly, "I was surprised you called… about your ranch."

She was obviously wondering why he'd asked her to come along. He wasn't entirely sure. "Maybe I just want a second opinion on the place."

"No one else has seen it?"

"No one else."

"How many horses do you plan to run on this property?"

"I'm bringing five over from the Bar P. I adopted two out last month, but I'd like to triple or quadruple that. A lot has to happen first, though. Some horses have to be quarantined. Others need their own pastures. There are no wild mustangs, per se, in Texas. That's the way most people think about horse rescue. But in stiff economic times, people are abandoning horses on private and public lands. As far as the wild mustangs go, the Bureau of Land Management has adoption events in Texas. I purchased a few, gentled them, and then sold them."

"It's a wonderful idea. What made you start doing it?"

"Dad added property to the Bar P when I was a teenager. It was a rundown ranch. The owner was selling. Two of his horses were malnourished and hadn't been cared for. I convinced Dad to let me take them on that summer. I turned them around. One of them became Mom's favorite to ride. After Dad's stroke, I guess I needed an outlet for living there again, something else to keep me occupied while I was there. So I began rescuing horses."

"I looked you up online yesterday."

He cut her a glance. "Oh, you did."

"There's an article about you in one of the Texas magazines about being the most eligible bachelor in Austin."

He kept silent to see where she was going with this.

"It's just—with your money, looks and reputation, you could be leading the good life."

"Fast cars, bars, clubbing every night?"

"Something like that."

"That might have been me in my teens and early twenties, but it isn't now. Scotland changed me, Lucie. Didn't it change you?"

"Before Scotland, I was never impulsive or reckless the way you were. I think maybe I let you sweep me away to prove that I could be. The thing was, after the humiliation the whole episode caused my parents, being sent home from the trip in disgrace, I was never that way again."

Had she reverted to type, or had she just curbed her passionate tendencies? Maybe that was something he wanted to explore.

Lucie's face wore an interested expression as he veered onto the gravel lane to the ranch. Suddenly the thought that this was a bad idea assaulted him. The ranch was run-down. The main barn needed to be refurbished. The second barn with its apartment on the second floor needed a makeover, too. This property was certainly nothing like the Bar P or the Chesterfield Estate in England. He'd seen video clips of her home. What was she going to think?

"I have to repair the fence, of course." He nodded to the worn stakes and supports along the road.

"Lots of caretaking involved," Lucie commented as if she knew.

"It will be a lot of work at the outlay, but then upkeep won't be so bad. The land alone is worth the price. With the rest, I'll add to its value."

As the truck bumped along, the barns and then the house came into view. They could see the forest beyond now and Lucie was looking in that direction.

As they parked at the house, they both climbed out.

"I'm going to have the house sided, of course," Chase said. "I'm thinking tan with brown shutters."

She wrinkled her nose. "Pale yellow siding with black shutters would be more inviting."

He grinned. "I knew there was a reason I brought you along."

They went up the three porch steps to the house. The porch was a large one, rounding three sides.

"It's locked, of course," Chase explained. "But you can peek inside. It's empty, so you won't see much. The plank flooring is good, if a little worn. In time, I'll redo the kitchen."

Lucie peered in the window, devoid of shades or curtains. "The living room looks nice-sized," she noticed.

"There are four bedrooms upstairs. One's a little small. The whole place has that original ranch house feel."

She stepped back from the door and glanced toward the barn.

"Do you want to explore a little? The barns aren't locked."

"Sure. Old barns can be like treasure chests. They take you back into another era."

"Exactly."

They were on the same page with that. The early 1900s feel of the barns and the house was the reason he liked them so much. If he had his way, he'd restore all of them as much as he could and keep the original wood and architecture.

He went ahead of her and opened the heavy, creaking barn door. She came up beside him and when she passed him, the light perfume she wore teased him. Once inside, however, the smell of hay, old wood and rusting tools was evident. There was a loft with an old, rickety ladder propped against it.

"I wouldn't use that ladder to look around up there," she warned with a smile.

"I brought my own in to have a look around. But when I own the place, I'd like to replicate the original."

Basically the barn was one open space.

"You'll need stalls, right?" she asked.

"Oh, yes. Lean-tos and a fenced corral. I'm looking into enlarging the second barn."

"Wow. You have your work cut out for you."

"I do and I can't wait to start. I want to do some of the work myself, especially in the house."

They were standing close to each other near a support beam. He had one hand on the support and his other he dropped by his side. She was standing right in front of him, close enough to touch. Dim light shone in the foggy windows. Last light from a long day shadowed the barn. The hushed atmosphere inside made him aware of his breath as well as hers.

He tipped up the bill of her cap. "This really doesn't disguise you very much. The wig does a better job."

"It hides my hair, though, and part of my face. It works, Chase."

Her life seemed to be all about what worked, what fit in, what didn't stir the pot. What if he stirred the pot?

As he swept the hat from her head, her hair fell down around her shoulders. He couldn't help touching it. He couldn't help sliding his hand under her hair, along her neck. He couldn't help bending his head.

A beep made them both start. It was as if someone had walked into the barn and caught them there.

Lucie stepped away from him and said, "My phone. I'd better check to see who it is."

Slipping it from her pocket, she said, "It's Amelia. I have to take this. She and I never ignore each other's calls."

Chase didn't have a brother or sister, but he understood that if he did, he wouldn't ignore their calls either. He turned away and walked to the other side of the barn to give Lucie some privacy. The idea of kissing her had revved him up. Better if she didn't understand just how much.

Chapter Four

Lucie was abominably rattled. She knew Chase had been about to kiss her and she'd wanted him to do it. Good sense hadn't stepped in. Recklessness had almost taken over. Thank goodness Amelia had called.

She was breathless when she glanced at Chase, who'd turned away and walked across the barn. She answered her phone. "Hi, Amelia."

"I'm sorry I was so distracted yesterday morning. It was late last night until I realized I hadn't called you back. So I made time right now. The baby's sleeping and Quinn's out in the barn. Are you at your place?"

Her place. Only it really wasn't hers, because she'd be flying away again soon.

"No, I'm not at the apartment. I'm exploring a ranch."

Amelia sounded puzzled. "For the Fortune Foundation?"

"No, not for them. I'm with…" She couldn't go into a long explanation with Chase in the same room, so to speak. "I'm with a friend."

"I'm so glad you're making friends in Austin. Are you with Ella or Viv?"

"No, not them. Amelia, I really do want to chat. We have a lot to talk about. But now isn't a good time."

"I entirely understand. Maybe midnight would be better, when the day is calmed down. The problem is, then Quinn wants all my hours—"

She stopped as if she'd said too much.

"Of course he does. You're still newlyweds."

"It feels as if we are," Amelia admitted happily. "And truthfully I don't want it ever to end. You should try it."

Wasn't that a touchy subject? She couldn't talk about finding Prince Charming with Chase in the barn with her.

As if Amelia understood something was going on, she asked, "So you can't talk freely?"

"Not now."

"Okay, so you don't have any privacy, and I know you probably have a bunch of international calls coming in later with regards to your trip."

Lucie had almost forgotten about those. She checked her watch. She had told contacts who were donating supplies to call her after eight tonight. Or was it nine? Chase had her so rattled. The whole situation had her rattled. This wasn't like her at all.

"Have you heard from Mum?" Amelia asked.

"Not since last week. And now she's traveling in an area with no cell phone connection. Did she tell you about that?"

"Yes, she did. When I spoke with her last, she seemed

to be in her element again. She loves the work…just as you do."

Lucie's life had been about helping orphaned children. But had she chosen the work for the right reasons? Or because her mother had needed her to be just as involved as she herself was? The orphanages had become a passion project after her husband died.

Now she wanted to tell her mother about her marriage to Chase. She wanted to prepare her in case news of it got out.

"Text me when you're free," Amelia went on. We'll have that talk. We can video-chat."

"I'll text soon. Give Clementine a kiss for me."

"Will do."

After Lucie ended the call, her gaze found Chase. He was over at the loft looking up, maybe deciding what he wanted to do with it. He was acting all casual, as if he hadn't been listening.

But as he turned to Lucie, he asked, "So I'm a friend now?"

He'd obviously heard her conversation with Amelia. Suddenly frustrated with the whole situation, Lucie blew out a breath. In a fit of unusual pique, she said, "I don't know what you are. We're in a kind of limbo. We want to live in the now, but the past is interfering. Yet we can't resurrect the past—"

Apparently Chase believed the simplest thing to do to get her to stop thinking was to encourage her to stop talking. She noticed a moment of doubt in his eyes. Then suddenly his arm was around her, his hand on the small of her back, urging her closer. His gaze never left hers.

First she felt surprise, swiftly followed by anticipation. Would a kiss be as explosive as it had been ten years ago?

There was only one way to find out. She let it happen.

Chase's lips covered hers before she could second-guess her decision.

In his adult years, Chase had prided himself on his self-control. But kissing Lucie almost destroyed it. It was the scent of her, the softness of her, the feel of her in his arms again. He wasn't thinking about the past or the future as his tongue breached her lips, and he took the kiss deeper, wetter, more intense. The fire was still there—fire that burned away any reservations, fire that had urged him to propose to her. The main reason…she'd been a virgin. Now, when she gripped his shoulders and he felt the sweet clutch of her fingers, his desire ramped up until it was almost dizzying.

Nevertheless, as quickly as it had started, it ended. Lucie broke away, brought her hands to his chest and put a foot between them. When he gazed into her eyes, he saw she was reeling from the kiss, too. Past dreams had been resurrected just for an instant. However, reality had rushed in, and he could see her good sense was telling her to run. That was exactly what she did, if not literally, figuratively.

He heard her swallow hard. He heard her deep intake of breath. He needed a swig of air himself. He needed to calm sensations that he'd forgotten.

She said, "I have to go. Can you take me back to my apartment? I have incoming international calls that I'm expecting tonight, and I can't be late."

He couldn't help asking wryly, "Isn't that what cell phones are for?"

"They'll be coming in on the landline," she informed

him. "I want to make sure my conversations aren't cut off."

Sure she did. She was doing important work. She'd be leaving in a month to build another orphanage. She probably had suppliers to talk to, directors to engage, donors and sponsors to extract money from. And she was telling him in a not-so-subtle way that that kiss had changed nothing, that the past was in the past, that their lives were very different and separate now.

"Let's go," he said, motioning to the barn door. "I'll have you back in no time at all."

And he did. They drove in silence, and when she climbed out in the parking garage, she said, "Goodbye, Chase."

He watched her walk to the elevator bank. He watched her nod to the security guard, then disappear inside, regretting every word they hadn't spoken, regretting the fact that Lucie's life was headed in one direction and his was headed in another.

The walnut-paneled study at the Silver Spur Ranch was the perfect place for Lucie's meeting with Kate Fortune the following day. Lucie studied this icon, who had recently turned ninety, as she sat in a huge leather chair that seemed to swallow her up. Kate had ended up in the hospital recently and was still recovering, but she looked at least ten years younger than her age, maybe more. She had more wealth than anybody could make use of, thanks to the success of the Fortune Youth Serum, which she'd discovered and perfected in the '90s. She was a walking advertisement for the efficacy of the product. But the future of her company was on her mind and she was looking for the right person to run it. For some reason, the two of them had seemed to connect at Kate's birthday party and Lucie had accepted this invitation to coffee, glad to see this remarkable woman again.

"How are you feeling?" Lucie asked.

Kate waved her hand. "Better each day. As you know, I'm still looking for the right Fortune to work at my company. I can't seem to find someone with all the attributes that are necessary, though the family tree does seem to be growing."

Kate motioned to the coffee and pastries that a butler had set up on a tray near them both. "Eat, my dear. You're much too thin."

Lucie did eat, and she was fortunate that she didn't seem to put on pounds because of it. She picked up a petite cherry Danish and took a bite. "What about you? Are you going to have some?"

"I have to watch everything these days—sugar, cholesterol, caffeine. I suppose it all matters. This morning I'm just going to enjoy your indulgence in the pastries. Tell me what you think about Ben Robinson's claim that his father is a Fortune."

"Could it be true?" Lucie asked, unsure how to answer.

"Anything can be true, I suppose," Kate mused.

"I had brunch with Ella and Viv," Lucie said. "They both seem very happy. Ben and Wes both are their Prince Charmings."

"Prince Charming is one thing, a Fortune is another," Kate proclaimed. "Ben can be very bold, as he proved at my party, but I believe he's sincere. I've tried to contact his father since I've been out of the hospital to verify Ben's claim that his father *is* Jerome Fortune. But Gerald Robinson hasn't returned any of my calls or my emails. Ben might claim his father is Jerome Fortune, but the man doesn't seem eager to prove it. His children deserve to know the truth, and so do I."

"They also want to find any half siblings they might have," Lucie explained.

"You're the one who connected Ben with Keaton Whitfield, correct?"

"Yes. I happened to know Keaton. It was amazing, really, that Keaton confirmed to Ben that Gerald Robinson is his father, too." Keaton and Ben were now working together to uncover other possible blood relatives that Gerald might have sired. The Fortune family was complicated and messy, and if Gerald Robinson was truly Jerome Fortune, Kate would have a lot to sort out.

"I know what you're thinking, my dear—that maybe finding family and trying to control my legacy might just be too complicated for someone my age."

"I'm not thinking that at all," Lucie protested. "Maybe I would be thinking that if you were the type of woman who sat in a parlor with an afghan covering your lap, knitting all day." She waved to the study with the computer, the printer, and the state-of-the-art smart TV for video-conferencing. "But you're not that type of woman. You like to be in charge. You like to know what's happening. You want to have a finger on what happens after you leave. I think you're up to the task."

Kate laughed. "I'm glad to see someone's on my side."

"I'm sure lots of people are."

"I've been reading more about how you and your mother work together to build orphanages and provide schooling for children who don't even have the necessities. Emmett Jamison, the head of the Fortune Foundation, told me you're hunting for office space to open a branch of the foundation in Austin. How is the hunt for space progressing?"

"I've seen a few possibilities. Probably the best strategy is to tap into programs that are already running. If we set up the office, then on-site events for kids can be anywhere. For instance, if there's a sports program that needs funding, we can do that. If there is a music therapist involved in community action, we can help her find space and a place to teach. We could also help provide college scholarships for girls interested in science."

"Emmett told me you'd put a lot of thought into this. It will be a remarkable undertaking."

"We would have an Austin Fortune Foundation Central, so to speak," Lucie concluded. "Then all the outreach programs would be like satellites."

"That sounds practical," Kate agreed. "Any program that is worthwhile can apply."

Kate gave Lucie a sly smile. "I have no doubt you're capable of getting this ball rolling. But I have been wondering something."

"What's that?"

"You travel the world with your mother helping others, but that doesn't leave much time for a personal life, does it?"

"No, it doesn't."

"Do you ever intend to marry?"

Lucie didn't know how to answer that honestly, because the truth was, she was already married!

When Lucie seemed stumped for an answer, Kate went on. "It's none of my business, of course. Charitable work is wonderful. But you know, don't you, it can't replace the love of a husband and family."

Lucie wondered if Kate was right. On the other hand,

though, her mother had had both during her second marriage, as well as now, though now she spent more time and intensity doing her charity work. Lucie realized she would never want to give up helping children, even if she had a husband and her own family.

If she had her own.

Just what kind of father might Chase Parker be?

She pushed that thought out of her head.

"Would you like to go for a walk?" she asked Kate. "It's a beautiful day outside."

"A change of subject is in order, huh?" Kate smiled. "Sure. Let's go for that walk. You can tell me about your sister Amelia and all about Horseback Hollow. You can also regale me with stories about how your royal life is different from mine."

Lucie laughed. "You *are* a royal, Kate Fortune, and you know it."

Kate gave a slight nod, agreeing.

Chase's workday had seemed long and tedious for several reasons. Soon he had to tell his father his plans and was trying to figure out how to do that. His dad was away in Galveston meeting with cronies, checking on a branch of their office there. But when he got back, Chase would have to be honest with him. And speaking of being honest, his last encounter with Lucie was heavy on his mind, not to mention that kiss.

So when he got home from Parker Oil, he headed toward the barn. That was his place where he could work off stress, communicate with the horses and chill. At least that was what he hoped. After a quick change into jeans and a T-shirt at the guesthouse, he checked on one of the last horses he'd rescued. The owners had left the property and abandoned him in the pasture. Chase didn't know how people could be so cruel.

Now he went to the fence and clicked his tongue against the roof of his mouth. Dusty, a chestnut, loped toward the fence and eyed Chase.

"Well, at least you come when I call now," Chase said conversationally.

The horse snorted, pawed at the ground, then turned tail and headed in the other direction.

"Making progress?" a female voice asked from outside the barn door.

Chase turned and saw his mother. She rarely ventured out here. She went on rides now and then, but those were few and far between since his dad had had his stroke. Was she afraid to be away from the ranch house in case he was taken to the hospital again? When he was in the house, did she feel she had to be with him?

"You should ride more often," Chase said now.

"Do you think I need the exercise?"

"I think you need the escape."

There were so many subjects they didn't talk about. There were so many feelings they'd never expressed. That was just the way it had been between him and his parents. Somehow he'd gotten the idea that boys should turn into men like his father—buttoned up, stoic, inflexible. After the Scotland fiasco, he'd rebelled against everything he'd learned as a child. He'd found his own way with work and horses, if not with women. He'd learned what was important to him and how he should feel when he treated others rightly or wrongly. He'd learned there were many shades of gray, and black and white were just illusions that his father and mother lived under. Since his dad's stroke, all of it had become even clearer to him. All of it had led up to this point.

"You didn't stop in at the house or text me to let me know you were here."

"Were you worried?" he asked, really wanting to know.

"No, I suppose not. But you didn't come over to the house last night either. Is something wrong?"

Whether he liked it or not, his mother could read him. Maybe all mothers were like that. Still, he felt he had to deny it.

"Nothing's wrong."

"We haven't heard from Mr. Sylvan yet. There's so much red tape."

Mr. Sylvan had been his family's lawyer for years. He was the one uncoiling the complications with the international law firm.

"You told me that when you met with Lady Fortune Chesterfield, she said she wants this dissolution as much as you do."

He thought about breakfast with Lucie, as well as kissing her. He'd seen the resolution and commitment in her eyes when she asked him to take her back to her apartment. "Yes, she wants the annulment. She wants to get on with her life, too, a very public life. She was even engaged under the glare of the media. Imagine how it will look if the news of our marriage gets out."

"You've had your picture taken at society events with beautiful women on your arm. The same would be true for you."

Chase was already shaking his head. "It wouldn't be the same at all. We mere mortals don't know what the royals go through."

"The Chesterfields aren't exactly royals," his mother maintained.

"That all depends on the way you look at it. The way Lucie tells it, her mother was first married to a man who was an earl. Lucie's father, Simon Chesterfield, was knighted for his service in the RAF and gained the title of "sir." He was also as wealthy as Dad is. So her family is in the royal public eye. We don't have paparazzi on our property every other day or even once a week. Once in a while someone wants to do a story on us, like Norton Wilcox, who set up the interview with me about horse rescue. But if I had said no, he would have accepted that for now. It's not that way for Lucie. The press actually hounds her family. They even follow her. And if they're on public property, there's nothing she can do about it."

"So you've talked about this?" his mother asked.

"Not just talked about it, lived it, in a small way. I took her for breakfast. We went in my truck and she wore a wig and jeans so nobody would recognize her or connect her with me. Right now that's our big problem—not being able to be associated together. We have to meet up in secret."

"Why do you have to meet up at all?"

Chase sighed. Why indeed? Ignoring that question, he said, "Mom, there's something we have to talk about other than Lucie. I was going to tell you and Dad together, but maybe it's better if I talk to you first."

His mother's face looked drawn, the lines around her mouth and eyes cutting deep. She looked almost scared.

"I've given the last five years to Dad and I don't regret any one of them. I don't regret living here for a while to help take care of him, and I don't regret being on the property these past few years. I don't know how much closer it's brought us, but at least we have the illusion of being together."

"It isn't an illusion," his mother protested heavily. "We *are* together."

"Together, Mom, means talking. Together means understanding. Together means compromising to find the best way for everybody."

"And in your not-so-subtle way, you're trying to tell me you want to compromise."

"What I'm telling you is that I'm going to make changes. I'm going to leave the company in the CFO's capable hands. Jeff is trustworthy, intelligent and knows every aspect of what we do. Dad's never going to retire, and if he does, he can sell Parker Oil for a hefty profit. He won't need me to be there."

"And just what would *you* be doing? Riding around the great state of Texas, collecting horses that are left on private land?"

"Maybe. Maybe those horses can find homes with loving families. Maybe they can find the lives they were made for."

His mother gave a resigned sigh, as if she didn't approve, but also as if none of this was a great surprise. "I understand that you're determined to see a horse rescue ranch come to fruition, and now you're determined to leave Parker Oil. When are you going to tell your father?"

"When he returns from Galveston. I won't jump on him. I assure you, I'll wait until the time is right, once I'm a free man and can obtain my loan."

"Have you discussed your plans with Lady Fortune Chesterfield?"

"I've mentioned my plans, and she's told me hers. A

month from now, she'll be in Guatemala, helping her mother build another orphanage."

Again, all he thought about was the last time he'd seen Lucie. All he could think about was that kiss.

His mother watched his expression carefully, watched him poke his hands into his pockets, watched him walk over to the fence and stare at Dusty.

"I know you don't often go along with my ideas, but maybe you should listen to this one," she suggested. "How about if you ask Lady Fortune Chesterfield to come to Sunday brunch? We can all handle this whole dilemma with civility."

Chase wasn't sure what to think about that. But it would give him the opportunity to talk to Lucie again. After all, she wouldn't be staying in Austin that long.

Lucie had had her driver stop at the market on her way back to her apartment. She'd picked up everything she'd need for a chicken and vegetable stir-fry. Swishing it around in the pan on the stove, she added soy sauce and breathed in the aroma as it cooked. When her cell phone beeped, she thought about letting it go to voice mail. But she didn't.

Turning the burner down to low, she picked up her phone on the counter, spotting the name and number there. Her heart beat crazily. She willed it to slow down, to not act so foolish. She hadn't liked the way she and Chase had parted. Maybe he hadn't liked it either.

The only way she'd know was to answer the phone. "Hello," she said cheerily.

"Lucie, it's Chase. Did I catch you at a bad time?"

She stared at her simmering dinner on the stove. "Not at all."

Neither of them spoke for a moment; then Chase stepped into the void. "How would you like to come to brunch on Sunday at the Bar P?"

Brunch? That didn't sound like an invitation Chase had issued himself. A moment later, she found out she was right.

"My mother suggested I invite you."

"Your mother did," she repeated. "Can I ask the reason why?"

"She just thought it would be a good idea. She'd like to keep this dissolution friendly—"

Lucie cut in, "Friendly? It's not as if I've been friends with your parents, Chase."

She heard him blow out a breath.

"Heck, Lucie, I don't know what she's thinking. Dad's away and maybe she's just lonely, or maybe it's her way of getting me to brunch. But she suggested it, so I am offering the invitation."

"Do you want me to come to brunch? Do you care if I do?" She wasn't sure why she was pushing. She just wanted to know where everybody stood. That would make going forward easier.

"We didn't part last night on the best of terms, and I'm not even sure why. That kiss—"

In the minute that followed, Lucie imagined they were both remembering exactly what had happened when Chase had kissed her. She imagined she could still taste him. She imagined his arms around her. She imagined…way too much. Maybe she shouldn't go. Maybe she should just break off this relationship right now.

What relationship?

Trying to weigh the pros and cons in less than a second, she finally answered, "All right, I'll come."

"Do you want me to pick you up?"

"No. And I won't have my driver bring me. I'll rent a car myself. I've done that before."

"Can you drive in the US?"

"I have an international license and can usually manage to stay on the right side of the road." *With concentration,* she added to herself.

"Are you sure you don't want me to pick you up?"

Chase had always had protective instincts. She'd felt them ten years ago, and she felt them now. But she couldn't let him protect her or do anything for her. After all, he'd cut off their relationship by not answering her letters. That had hurt more than she'd ever admitted.

"I'm positive. What time would you like me to be there?"

"How's ten a.m.?"

"That sounds fine. Give me the address."

"Text me your email address and I'll send you directions."

"Chase, I'm sure the car I rent will have a GPS."

"I'm sure it will, but I want to make certain you don't get lost."

By the time she ended the call with Chase, she already felt lost—lost in the past, lost in a feeling she couldn't decipher, lost in the knowledge that Chase Parker was going to disrupt her life.

Chapter Five

"This is the smaller dining room," Florence Parker explained to Lucie on Sunday morning. "We have our more intimate meals here."

Lucie, Chase and his mother had passed the large dining room with its ten-foot table and twelve hand-carved oak chairs. This place could rival any British estate! The smaller dining room Florence spoke of hosted a table for six in deep walnut. White lacy place mats sat beneath the Spode china. Crystal juice glasses sparkled from the sun shining in the bank of windows.

Chase pulled out Lucie's chair and she sat. She resisted the urge to glance over her shoulder at him. If she did, this breakfast would indeed be more intimate. She was sure that wasn't what his mother had in mind.

Chase went around to his mother's side of the table and helped her with her chair. When she smiled at him, she looked about ten years younger. Florence Parker possessed classic beauty with her high cheekbones, patrician nose, blond-gray hair that curved just under her chin and wide blue eyes. Lucie imagined she'd had china-doll beauty as a young woman. For brunch Florence had chosen pale lilac slacks and a matching sweater.

Lucie hadn't known how to dress. She'd worn a flowered blouse and navy slacks. As an extra touch, the pearls her mother had given her on her sixteenth birthday lay around her neck, visible in her open collar.

A maid in a black dress with a white collar brought in a tray that was loaded with breakfast entrées—waffles, pancakes, bacon and scrambled eggs. She set the dishes on the table and Lucie could see they were going to be served family-style. That was nice. It made the room feel less like a restaurant and more like a home. As they'd passed through the grand foyer and entrance hall, wound around the curved staircase, passed the high-ceilinged living room, Lucie noticed the Western décor, lots of leather, cowhide and suede. But what she hadn't noticed were any homey touches. Was this house really lived in?

Since she didn't know where to begin a conversation with Chase's mother, she began with something easy. "Your estate is beautiful."

"It's a ranch, dear. You might have estates in England, but we have ranches in Texas."

"Mother," Chase scolded with a warning look.

Lucie, trying not to connect with Chase, even with her eyes, said, "Your mother's right to correct me. I'm still learning about idioms and Texas idiosyncrasies."

Florence Parker laughed. "Idiosyncrasies like wanting our steak rare?"

Lucie smiled. "I prefer mine medium-well."

"You don't have a heavy British accent," Florence noted.

"My mother tells me I once did, but we traveled so much I seemed to pick up intonations from every dialect."

"At seventeen, you were British all the way," Chase said in an undertone.

This time Lucie couldn't help looking at him, and when she did, their eyes locked, and a little tremble went through her. That had to stop.

"I should have traveled to Scotland with Chase's father all those years ago," Florence concluded. "Maybe then the two of you wouldn't be in the fix you're in. But he said he'd handle it, and back then, I guess I listened to him more than I do now."

Chase laughed at that. "What Mom's saying," he explained to Lucie, "is that she's grown independent over the years."

Florence smiled fondly at her son. "When I was first married, I hung on my husband's every word. I took it as law. I wanted to please him. It's not true, you know, that you don't find yourself in marriage. I certainly did, and I think Chase's father respects me more for it."

In a way, Florence reminded Lucie of her own mother. She had a bit more of an edge, but Lucie liked the woman's frankness. Maybe this brunch wasn't a trap after all, though she wasn't sure why Florence wanted to get to know her when she'd be leaving Chase's life.

"Tell me about your work with orphanages," Florence suggested.

For most of the brunch, that was exactly what Lucie did. Florence asked leading questions and Lucie didn't hesitate to answer them. Finally, when the maid poured cups of coffee all around again, Florence revealed, "I work with many charities, too."

That didn't surprise Lucie. Florence Parker probably had a high standing in the community and led fund-raising attempts.

"Word is going around that the Fortune Foundation will be opening a branch in Austin. Is that true?" she inquired.

"Yes, it is. I've been spending much of my time looking for office space."

"Not space to run programs?" Florence prodded.

"No. The programs will be satellite connections to the main office. We'd like to work within the framework of already established ones. That would stream funds to children quicker."

"I see," Florence said, looking thoughtful. "I like that idea. At present I'm trying to find funding for my church's after-school program. Money will soon run out and the minister might have to close it down. Would the Fortune Foundation be interested in something like that?"

Was this why Chase's mother had asked her to brunch? "I can ask Emmett Jamison, who runs the foundation."

"I didn't know if the Fortune Foundation's expansion to Austin was truth or gossip."

"I guess every town has its chatting chain."

"Chatting chain?" Florence asked.

"Grapevine," Chase interpreted with a smile for Lucie. When he smiled at her, her toes curled.

"Yes, this chatting chain you speak of is one of the reasons you and Chase want to get this annulment quickly, correct?" Florence determined.

Neither of them spoke.

Finally Lucie said, "It's in both of our best interests."

"I see," Florence murmured. "You of course mean because of the media attention?"

"Yes. I took a circuitous route to drive here today to make sure I wasn't followed. Usually I have a driver who does that, but neither Chase nor I want to bring embarrassment to our families if the word of our marriage seeps out."

"There's no embarrassment in getting married," Florence said with a sly look at her son.

"Don't start, Mom. You know I have too much on my plate to even consider getting married and having kids, though I know that's what you want me to do."

"I would like grandchildren before I'm too old to enjoy them." She studied Lucie. "Do you have someone special in your life?"

"I'm not dating anyone now," Lucie admitted.

"There was talk of an engagement a while back."

"That didn't work out."

"Can I ask why?"

"Mom," Chase said with exasperation.

Lucie laid her hand on his arm to stop his protest and then was sorry she did. Her fingers burned against his skin, and she quickly withdrew her hand. However, she said, "It's okay, Chase." She was practiced at this. A little bit of truth went a long way. She didn't need to reveal that Terry's dishonesty had left her doubting most men. As much as that, she didn't need to reveal that his critical attitude toward her at the end of their engagement had left her with insecurities that weren't easy to shake off.

"I thought about my broken engagement a lot. I was involved with orphanage work with my mother. Much of my relationship with Terrence was long-distance. Nevertheless, I don't think that was the problem. His family knew mine. We had common interests. But I finally realized I didn't love him the way I wanted to love a man who was going to be my husband and he didn't love me the way a man should love a wife. There was no big clash or conflict or anything like that, even though the tabloids hinted that there was. We just weren't right for each other."

Florence looked from Lucie to Chase. "Yes, I guess one comes to realize who the right person might be as one grows older, doesn't one?"

Lucie suddenly felt uncomfortable and wasn't even sure why.

But then Florence changed the subject and addressed her son. "You *are* going to show Lucie around the place, aren't you? Do you have time?" she asked Lucie.

"I have time," Lucie assured her. "I'd love a tour."

"So it's settled," Florence said.

But Lucie wasn't sure anything was settled.

A half hour later, Lucie and Chase walked in silence through gardens and finally along a path that wound around the barns. He said, "Maybe we should have taken my truck. There are roads through the ranch that lead to the different pastures."

"You have three barns."

"Yes, we do. One leads to the pastures where we keep the horses that have always been on the Bar P and any new ones Dad might find that he'd like to ride. The second barn is for horses who might come in and out, and we want to keep them separate from the others."

"And the third barn?"

"The third barn used to be for storage. But I cleaned it out and now it's for my rescue horses. The stalls each lead to fenced-in areas, in case they don't get along well with others or are afraid of them. It takes a while to gentle them sometimes. That's true of the wild mustangs, too. They can take weeks or months, depending on the temperament of the horse."

"Let's look at the third barn," she decided.

When she cut a glance at Chase, she could see the smile that slipped across his lips. Every time she looked at him, she remembered their kiss. Every time she looked at him, she remembered more than that.

His T-shirt accentuated his muscled arms. His broad shoulders never slouched. That told her he was confident in his stature as a tall man and as a person.

She was glad she'd worn slacks as they walked over packed ground and gravel and through some grass. Now and then, she had to hurry a little to keep up with Chase's stride. He was giving her a tour as his mother had suggested, not stopping to talk or touch. That was what she wanted, wasn't it?

The barn was only about twenty feet away when Chase increased his pace a little more, probably so he could open the door for her. She was looking at him, not watching where she was going. The stones were larger here and one turned under her foot. She gave a little yelp as she felt herself starting to fall, but she never hit the ground. Chase was there, his arms around her, helping her right herself on her feet. She just wished she could right herself in her heart and her head, because when she was standing in the circle of his arms, looking up at him, she felt as if her world would never go back to spinning normally again.

"Are you okay?" he asked, his eyes concerned.

"I'm fine. I should have worn sneakers."

"Did you turn your ankle?"

"No, I just basically slipped. Thanks for saving me."

They stared at each other for a long time, but then Chase blew out a breath. "Come on, let's see the horses. You can only get close to one of them—Gypsy. She's going to be a great riding horse for someone. I hope I can find a family who wants her."

Now Chase took Lucie's arm as they walked. She almost pulled away but decided what could it hurt? She liked the feel of his fingers on her skin. She liked having Chase that close.

"You don't keep any of them?" she asked.

"I'd like to keep them all. When you put time and care and gentling into an animal, you create a bond that really can't be broken. But practically speaking, I can't keep them all. I have to transfer that bond to someone else who will love and appreciate them."

"But if you find a special one—"

"You mean like Gypsy? Yeah, if this deal goes through for my own place, I might just have to keep her."

They stepped over the threshold to the barn. This structure had eight stalls, four on each side. No horses were housed there at the moment. They were enjoying the March day.

Chase opened one of the stall doors and beckoned for Lucie to come in. Walking through, Lucie could see the mare in her own little pasture. She was a gray with a silver mane.

Chase clicked his tongue and the horse came running to him.

He put his arm around her neck and rubbed her. "Hey, girl, how are you today?"

She nudged the back pocket of his jeans.

He laughed. "She knows I keep snacks in there." He took out what looked like a cookie.

"All natural," he said. "She's getting back the shine on her coat and the sparkle in her eyes."

"Can I touch her?" Lucie asked.

"She hasn't seen many people. Mostly me. Just approach her slowly and we'll see what she does."

Lucie did just that.

Chase handed her another piece of cookie. "Give her that. Just hold it in your palm. She doesn't bite."

Lucie's father had taught her to ride. She'd been around horses who were biters, horses that were gentle, and horses who would obey every command. In the Chesterfield stables, Lucie had a special horse, and she understood all about communication between mount and rider and bonds that had formed since childhood. Her horse, Mayfield, took her on trail rides and listened to all her woes and joys.

Holding her hand still with the cookie treat on her palm, she waited. Gypsy snorted and seemed to look Lucie over. Then she took a step forward, snuffled Lucie's fingers and licked up the treat. As she chewed, she stared at Lucie, and Lucie took another step forward. Gypsy didn't retreat and Lucie saw that as a good sign.

"Can I pet you?" she asked the horse.

Gypsy stood by Chase's side, not moving, so Lucie ruffled her fingers under the mane, slid them along the smooth neck and petted Gypsy's flank. "You're a beauty."

"Yes, she is," Chase said, but he wasn't looking at Gypsy. He was gazing at *her*. He gave Gypsy another treat and said, "I'll take you for a run later."

As they walked back into the barn, the magnetic pull

toward Chase was getting stronger and stronger, and Lucie knew there was only one way to break it.

"I really should get going," she said.

Chase didn't argue with her. "I'll walk you to your car."

Silence again stretched between them as they returned the way they had come. Once they arrived at Lucie's car door, she opened it. When she looked up at Chase, she wasn't sure how to say goodbye. Maybe he wasn't sure either, because he reached out and ran his thumb over her cheek. He brushed her hair behind her ear and looked down at her with longing that she so wanted to appease.

Suddenly he said, "We're in this mess because I convinced you to marry me ten years ago."

"You didn't need to work hard to convince me. It was as much my decision as yours. You didn't coerce me, Chase. I married you freely. We were reckless and impulsive, and now we just have to be mature about what we do next."

"Mature. Grown-up. Doing the right thing. Sometimes it's hard to know the right thing, isn't it? I thought I was doing the right thing by staying here after my dad's stroke. But now it's going to be that much harder to tear myself away. For them, not me. I don't want to hurt them, but I need my own life."

"You don't want to feel trapped," she empathized.

"And neither do you. You're trapped by the paparazzi, by the life you've led up till now, by a marriage that wasn't really a marriage."

"My life isn't going to change that much, one way or the other," she assured him. "I've accepted my role."

"Life should be more than a role," he advised her.

Perhaps he was right. She hated the fact that she didn't

know when she would see him again. But she shouldn't be looking forward to it. There were so many shouldn'ts in her life and maybe too many shoulds.

When she climbed into her car, Chase still didn't close the door. Lucie gazed up at the house and thought she saw a curtain move in a second-story window. Was Chase's mother watching them?

Chase leaned down and rested his hand on Lucie's shoulder. "You will look into whether the Fortune Foundation wants to fund the program my mother suggested?"

"I will look into it, then I'll give her a call." She wouldn't have to talk to Chase again, not really.

Maybe he saw the determination in her eyes, or maybe he just heard it in her voice. He leaned away and straightened. Then he backed up and shut the door for her.

That closure sounded like an end rather than a beginning.

That was the way it had to be.

The following morning, after Lucie spoke with Emmett, she called Florence Parker. She wasn't nervous about the call. After all, she didn't have to worry about Chase picking up. He was in the guesthouse. He would most likely not answer the phone at his mom and dad's residence.

She was right, because the maid answered. Lucie recognized her voice from the brunch the previous day.

"I'll fetch Mrs. Parker right away. Hold on please."

In no more than a minute, Florence Parker herself was on the line. "I'm so glad to hear from you. That was quick."

"Emmett answered my question immediately. He assured me the Fortune Foundation could fund the program you mentioned. But I need to take a look at it and make notes about the program itself. Would your minister be okay with me dropping in?"

"I'm sure he would if he has a little notice. When are you thinking about?"

"How about tomorrow after school? I just want to observe and make some notes about the age groups and their needs."

"What time were you thinking?" Florence asked.

"Around three?"

"I'm sure Reverend Stanhope will be fine with the idea once he knows he can get funding to keep the after-school program open. I'll call him, then call you back. Would that be all right?"

"That would be fine."

"I'll try to be there myself," Florence said. "I often volunteer and can show you around if the reverend is busy. Sometimes he's shorthanded, and that's one of the problems I'd like to cure. Volunteers are wonderful, but sometimes a paid position is necessary to keep it all running smoothly. Let me give you the address of the church."

"Is the program right on the premises?"

"It is, in the church's social hall. Do you have a pen and paper?"

"I do."

Florence rattled off the name of the church and the address. "Thank you so much again for taking this to the Fortune Foundation."

"I was glad to be able to help."

After Lucie ended the call, she felt as if she'd done something worthwhile. She would give the after-school program a thorough evaluation and then present her findings to Emmett.

* * *

Lucie arrived at the interdenominational church the following afternoon with a smile and her electronic tablet in her purse. She already had evaluation forms set up on there, and she could just type in her observations. She was excited about this first Fortune-funded project in Austin and ready to speak with the reverend and Florence Parker.

However, when she opened the door to the social hall and stepped inside, she didn't find Florence. She found Chase!

She stopped in her tracks, her mint-colored A-line dress swishing around her knees. She didn't think twice about asking, "What are you doing here?"

The first words out of his mouth surprised her even more than she expected. "Pretend you don't know me," he said in a low voice.

"What?"

Glancing over his shoulder to the room inside, where there was noise and commotion, he repeated, "Pretend you don't know me. My mother was supposed to be here to meet you, but she wasn't feeling well and she asked me to come in her stead."

Lucie had never known Chase to be anything but honest. As far as she could tell, he was being sincere now. But what about Florence? Did she really not feel well? She couldn't be trying to push them together, could she?

Knowing Chase was right and that no one could know their connection, Lucie forced herself to smile and extend her hand.

Chase took it and shook it, but he held on a few moments too long, and she felt the ripple of sexual awareness travel through her whole body. Pretend they didn't know each other? These would have to be Oscar-winning performances.

As if they had just met, Chase motioned her into the larger room and led her to the minister. After introductions, Reverend Stanhope, a tall, thin man with wire-rimmed glasses that fell down his nose, nodded to the children, who didn't seem to be organized well.

He pushed his glasses to the bridge of his nose. "I know you're here to evaluate our program. Please ask any questions you'd like. We're open to suggestions to make it better, even if you don't take us on as a project."

She was used to working with children at the orphanages. All ages. Here, she could see exactly what needed to be done first. There was one motherly looking woman at a table participating in an activity with the smaller children, encouraging them to color and draw pictures. But the rest of the kids were pretty much on their own and not doing a good job of keeping themselves busy. There was squabbling in one corner and raucous roughhousing in another.

"You just have one helper today?" Lucie asked.

"I do. I'm down two volunteers to the flu."

"The first thing we need to do is divide the children who are ages five to seven in one group and eight to twelve in the other. Do you mind if we do that?"

The minister looked relieved that someone had a suggestion he could incorporate. "I don't mind at all."

"I can take the older kids outside," Chase offered. "Do you have a ball?"

She admired Chase's desire to help and wondered if he'd be good with the kids. "That would be a great idea."

She clapped her hands to gain the children's attention, introduced herself and Chase to them and began to organize.

* * *

After an hour of dodgeball, Chase felt he'd had a workout. He rounded up the children and took them back inside. Once they'd chosen books from a shelf and settled in a reading corner, he directed them to choose a partner. They could read to each other.

Suddenly, he heard a little boy crying, and he looked over to see Lucie crouched down with one of the five-year-olds.

"But I can't find it," the little boy wailed.

"What color is it?" Lucie asked gently.

"Red with white letters. It says my name—Dave."

"Okay, Dave. Let's think about where you had it last. When was the last time you wore your cap?"

"I had it on before we were dancing. I had it on before we were singing."

Dancing and singing. Lucie was probably good at both. He could imagine her leading the kids.

"How about before that?" she asked the child.

Dave poked two fingers into his mouth. "I had it on before I played hopscotch." He suddenly grinned. "It's on the bench outside. It fell off and I left it."

"Come on," Lucie said with excitement. "Let's go see if it's still there."

Sure enough, two minutes later, when they both came back inside, Dave was wearing his cap. He wrapped his arm around Lucie and gave her a huge hug. "Thank you. My mom would be mad if I lost it. She bought it for me when we went to San Antonio."

"I'm sure she'd be more concerned that you were upset. But now you have it. How about drawing a special picture of that cap?"

Chase was aware of every word Lucie spoke to the

little boy, but he wasn't only aware of that. He was aware of her arm around the child's shoulders, the tone of her voice that was compassionate and ready to help any way she could. Sure, she'd had practice. She'd helped children around the world. Would she ever think about a life of her own and children of her own?

Parents began arriving to pick up their kids. Lucie saw the reverend say goodbye to his last volunteer, who was looking kind of pale.

The minister came over to Lucie and Chase, shaking his head.

"I think I'm going to have to close down the program for the next few days. I certainly can't handle this crowd on my own. My last volunteer thinks she's coming down with whatever is going around."

"Let me talk to Mr. Parker a few minutes before you make a decision," Lucie suggested to the reverend.

She and Chase went to a quiet corner.

"What do you have in mind?" he asked.

"I know this is awkward, and I know we have to pretend we didn't meet each other before, but do you think we can help the next few days? I hate to see Reverend Stanhope close down the program in the midst of deciding whether we're going to fund it or not. I've had background checks done for the work I do. I don't know if we can get you cleared or not."

"I know the police chief," Chase informed her. "Maybe he can get a background check through quickly for me. It only takes about twenty-four hours. I want to help you with this. And as far as pretending we don't know each other goes, we can pull it off."

They'd done a good job this afternoon, but she'd been inside and he'd been outside.

"Can you spare a couple of hours away from Parker Oil tomorrow?"

"It will be a good test for my CFO. I want to see if he can handle whatever comes up on his own. If he can do that, I'll know I'm leaving the company in good hands when I leave."

"And if he can't?"

"Then I'll find someone else. I trust Jeff, though. I don't think he'll let me down."

"So we're going to offer to help?"

"It's a done deal," he said, holding out his hand again so they could shake on it. This time she slipped hers into his and then quickly pulled it back again.

Chase's knowing smile said he knew what she was doing. She didn't fool him one little bit.

"Since you have your own car and I have my own car, why don't you follow me again to the truck stop? They have great breakfast-for-dinner specials."

Lucie knew she shouldn't. Chase Parker was a temptation that could land her in all kinds of trouble—with her family, with the press, with her life. On the other hand, chocolate chip pancakes and Chase were very hard to resist.

At the truck stop, Lucie didn't see Chase's car. He apparently hadn't arrived yet. She was overtaken with the knowledge that she shouldn't have come. She was sending Chase the wrong message that she wanted to spend time with him. Time with him was not going to help their situation. Time with him was only putting her in a tailspin. Time with him was reminding her of time in the past, when they'd held each other and kissed and made love.

She had stowed her wig in the car for emergencies and she put it on now, combing it into place. Exiting her car, she glanced around and then entered the diner, passed down the row of booths, finally taking a different one than where they'd sat in the last time...just because. Never do the same thing twice. Always do the unexpected. Don't give the media a pattern to follow.

Finally Chase came into the diner and slid into the bench seat across from her, wearing his sunglasses.

She had to smile. "I can recognize you even with the sunglasses," she said.

"And I can recognize you even with the wig."

Was it true that they still knew each other so well after ten years? Maybe so.

Lucie was grateful when a different waitress waited on them this time and took their order. A different shift. That was good.

When she said as much to Chase, he reached across the table and took her hand. "For ten minutes, Lucie, just ten minutes, forget who you are and what you have to do. Just enjoy your chocolate chip pancakes with the whipped cream and talk to me about whatever matters to you."

She wished she could just let go of everything that easily, but for ten minutes—"I'll try."

He nodded and squeezed her hand. She felt that squeeze deep inside, but then he let go and sat back. Taking off his sunglasses, he pocketed them.

She unwrapped her silverware, took the napkin and spread it on her lap. Silence hovered between them.

Lucie asked, "Do you really want me to talk about what's important to me?"

"I do."

"Those kids back there are important to me. I feel like I'm doing something worthwhile when I'm singing a song with them or teaching them a dance. You can see knowledge exploding in their eyes when you show them something new. There is so much innocence there and precociousness and curiosity. Don't you wish we could all keep some of that as we grow older?"

"I wish we could. But that seems to be impossible. Problems and stress weigh us down."

"But they have stress, too. They see their parents argue. They don't get along with a brother or sister. They're scared to come to school. They don't know how to play a game and they're afraid the kids will laugh at them. They don't seem like big stresses to us, but they are to them."

"You really know a lot about kids, don't you?"

"I've probably been with them more than adults over the past eight years, anyway."

The waitress brought them mugs of coffee. After she disappeared again, Chase put his elbows on the table and leaned in. "So, tell me about your life and your dreams. You obviously love children. How many do you want someday?"

To her amazement, she admitted the truth. "I haven't given it much thought."

"And if you did?" he prompted.

If she did… Her mouth suddenly went dry. If she had children, she imagined having them with him! Impossible.

She had to answer his question because he was sitting there, studying her, waiting for her response. "Thinking about it, I think I'd like three."

"Or four?" he countered with a teasing glint in his

eye. "Two girls and two boys, so none of them feel out of place or outnumbered. Of course, we'd have to throw in some horses, and maybe a dog or two."

She laughed, a genuine laugh that had nothing to do with the past or the future and everything to do with now.

As they discussed the kids in the after-school program and what activities they'd devise for the next day, their pancakes arrived.

They both dug in with gusto.

Chase downed his faster than Lucie did. He was finishing up when he reached across the table again. This time, not to hold her hand but to swipe a bit of whipped cream from the corner of her lip. His finger, his touch, was gentle but sensual. She wished she could touch him in the same way. She wished she was kissing him.

They couldn't seem to stop looking at each other.

They both started when Chase's cell phone buzzed. He took it from his belt and studied the screen. "Work," he grumbled.

"It's after hours," she said.

"There are no after hours in this business. I have to take this."

She nodded and didn't even try to keep from listening.

"I understand, Jeff," he said after about a minute of complete attention to his employee on the other end of the line. "He doesn't want to meet with you, he wants to meet with me. Do you want me to give him a call? Fine, you call him."

Chase checked his watch. "I can be there in a half hour."

There was a pause, and then Chase said, "There's no need to apologize. You can't dictate what someone else does or wants or demands. But I want you to sit in on

the meeting, too. Channing is going to have to realize
he has to trust you as much as he trusts me."

After Chase ended the call, he brought his gaze back
to Lucie's. "I have to go."

"A crisis at work?"

"Something like that."

"Do you really think you can ever leave the company?"

Chase pulled his wallet from his pocket and took out
a few bills. He laid them on the table with the check and
then pulled out a tip, too.

"I can leave the tip," she protested.

"My treat," he insisted. Then he stood, loomed over
her and answered her question. "I don't know if I can
ever leave the company, but I'm going to try to make it
happen. Maybe I'm deluding myself that I can change
the course of my life, but I'm certainly going to give it a
good try. I'll see you tomorrow at the church."

Lucie watched Chase leave the restaurant, her heart
feeling heavy. She doubted if Chase would show up at
the after-school program the next day. After all, an oil
magnate had better things to do.

And if he did show up?

She'd have to pretend she didn't feel closer to him
again. She'd have to pretend she wasn't attracted to him.
She'd have to pretend that she didn't wish things were
different.

Chapter Six

It was almost midnight as Lucie sat on her bed, her laptop adjusted so that Amelia could see her face through her webcam. They often video-chatted since she'd been living in Austin. It was one way of seeing each other face-to-face.

"Do you really have time to talk?" Lucie asked her sister.

"I do. Quinn helped me put Clementine to bed and then he crashed. He also said if I'm up late talking to you, he'll get Clementine up in the morning. Isn't he wonderful?"

Lucie couldn't help smiling. It was so good to see her sister happy. "Spoken like a woman in love."

"I am and always will be. So, what do you need to talk about?"

Now that the time had come to say it out loud, she didn't know if she could. She'd kept the secret for so long that she hesitated to share it. But that was silly. This was Amelia, her sister. She deserved to know. Just as her mother deserved to know, especially with Chase back in her life. Well, not really back in her life. Just sort of.

"I've been keeping a secret."

"Really? You don't keep secrets. You're an open book."

"Maybe not as open as you think."

Yes, she was the one who usually followed all the orders. She was the one who followed the rules. She was the one who was proper. Maybe not anymore.

"Do you remember that trip I took to Scotland when I was seventeen?"

"Barely," Amelia admitted. "I was involved with riding competitions that summer. I do remember you were sent home early and there was all kinds of hush-hush about it. Mum and Dad wouldn't talk about it. They just said you'd broken a rule."

"They didn't find out this secret. They only knew part of what happened."

"What happened?" Amelia asked, her eyes widening.

"I got caught with a boy in his room. Not a boy, but a man. Chase was twenty-one."

"And that's why you were sent home?"

"It was, and he was fired. He was from the US. Texas."

"Uh-oh. Do I know what's coming? Are you having a reunion?"

"Not exactly."

When she couldn't seem to find the words, Amelia jumped in. "So, what was the secret?"

"Before I was found in his room, Chase and I got married."

Amelia's mouth dropped open. Her eyes grew even

bigger and wider. She stared through the computer screen at Lucie as if she had two noses. "You got what?"

Amelia's voice had grown louder and Lucie said, "Shhh, you'll wake Quinn."

Amelia brushed that thought aside with her hand. "I might wake him on purpose after *this* conversation. So, what else happened? You got married and just came home?"

Lucie told Amelia about Chase's father and his oil company and his plans for his son that didn't include an English girl.

"So Chase's dad sent you home with a threat that he'd cause a scandal if you didn't keep quiet."

"That's pretty much it."

"And you gave in to that?"

"I had broken rules. I wasn't going to break any more. My time with Chase was an experiment that didn't work. I didn't want to cause more embarrassment to Mum and Dad."

"Would that ever have been a scandal across the tabloids! It would have involved two countries."

Leave it up to Amelia to look at it that way, but it was true.

"So, what brought all this to the surface now?" her sister asked.

"Chase tracked me down and found me here. It turns out, the annulment never went through. He and I are still married."

A frown immediately adorned Amelia's face. "Uh-oh. You were engaged to Terrence."

"Yes. This is another scandal in the making."

Amelia was looking down at her hands, so Lucie couldn't see exactly what she was doing. But she must have been looking Chase up online on her phone because she let out a little squeal. "Chase Parker. You sure know how to pick 'em, don't you? What a hunk. Almost as hunky as Quinn."

"Amelia—"

"So, what have you been doing with him? Is he the friend you were with the other night when I called?"

"Yes, he was. He's buying a ranch. That's how all this came up. In the paperwork. He took me there to show it to me. He wants to rescue horses."

"And you have a keen love of horses."

"I do."

"And?" Amelia prompted.

Should she reveal it all? Should she confide everything to Amelia in a way she hadn't before?

Her sister was perceptive, because she asked, "Are you telling me Chase found you, and the marriage isn't over?"

"It's not over legally."

"I'm talking about emotionally. Do you still have feelings for him? Have you thought about him all these years?"

"I have thought about him," Lucie returned quietly. "But they were merely dreams that came and went. I never expected them to materialize."

"But now they can?"

"Oh, it's not like that. We've had a couple of breakfasts together at a diner. I even wore my wig. If anybody connects us, we're in big trouble for his business dealings and my reputation. We're being very careful, but now things have gotten complicated again. His mother asked if the Fortune Foundation could fund a program at their church. I looked into it and they're going to. The volunteers there have gotten sick. Somehow Chase and I ended up volunteering today and played with the kids. We're helping there again tomorrow and maybe the next day."

"Is he good with kids?"

"He seems to be."

"That's good, because you're a natural. You need a bunch of your own."

Lucie went silent.

"What would be so bad about hooking up with him again? You need some fun in your life, if not someone you can dream about."

"We're intense when we're together. There's tons of chemistry. We're asking for nothing but trouble if we become involved again."

"You kissed him, didn't you?"

Lucie felt herself blushing. "*He* kissed *me*."

Amelia rolled her eyes. "Same difference in this situation. Tell me again why it wouldn't work."

"Because he's changing his life. He's separating from his parents and going out on his own with this new business venture. He's found his vocation just as I have. But mine takes me around the world. I don't want to give up what I do. It's important work. And our mother depends on me."

"Did you ever consider that she depends on you too much?"

"Is that possible? I work with her. She has to depend on me."

"It's more than that and you know it. Ever since Daddy died, she looks to you for emotional support. She's closest to you," Amelia said matter-of-factly without any jealousy.

"I'm beginning to wonder if it's good for her or me."

"I believe you have a lot to think about, my lady,"

Amelia decided. "None of this sounds like you. You really do have to tell Mum as soon as you can."

"Do you have any advice about Chase?"

"Not advice, exactly. I can tell you I tried to deny my attraction to Quinn and that didn't work. If you care about Chase, you shouldn't put the brakes on. You should see where it goes."

"And if it goes nowhere? Or if it takes a wrong turn and goes wrong?"

"Then you'll know. After what I've been through with Quinn, I know I can get through anything. You can, too."

"I'll think about everything you said. I promise. In the meantime, why don't you and Quinn come up here and go on a night on the town? I'll babysit. I'd love to spend some time with Clementine Rose."

"She goes through fussy spells for no reason sometimes."

"That doesn't matter. I'll be here for her and with her. You do trust her with me, don't you?"

"You know I do. You're so good with her." Amelia was silent for a moment—she appeared to be thinking about Lucie's suggestion. "Let me talk to Quinn. Maybe we can get away for at least a night. That would be nice. So, tell me when you're seeing Chase again."

"Tomorrow afternoon at the after-school program, but as I said, we have to pretend we don't know each other. This is going to take a bit of acting."

"You can do it. And after you're done acting?"

"I'll come back here and he'll go back to the Bar P. That's the way it has to be, Amelia, at least for now."

"Don't live in fear of what might happen. Live for what *is* happening. Got that?"

"I got it."

"I'll get back to you about an overnight, and you can tell me what happened. And I want full disclosure."

Lucie laughed. "Full disclosure. And, Amelia, please don't say anything to anyone else about this...except Quinn."

"I won't. I promise."

Lucie knew Amelia kept her promises. "I'll talk to you soon."

When Lucie closed her laptop, she thought about Chase and tomorrow afternoon. A thrill of anticipation bubbled in her stomach. She just couldn't help wanting to see him.

The following afternoon, Lucie knew she had to put on the brakes. She just had to. She felt as if her heart were careening down a highway going the wrong way.

A ten-year-old named Jasper quickly kicked the ball her way and she stepped sideways so she wouldn't be out of the dodgeball game.

Today the minister had taken the smaller kids inside, so unfortunately she was outside with Chase and the older children. They weren't anywhere near each other. He was across the circle. However, when their eyes met...

She expected lightning to strike—either from the chemistry between her and Chase...or the storm that was brewing in those gray clouds up above.

When parents began arriving to pick up their children, Lucie ducked inside the social hall. The kids didn't recognize her, but it was possible one of their parents might. She didn't want a three-ring circus to ensue. She busied herself straightening up the activity room until all the children were gone. At least she thought they were all gone. One little blond girl remained.

Reverend Stanhope checked his watch. "I have a meeting and Michelle Tillot, Chrissy's mother, isn't answering the phone number she gave me. I don't think she has a cell. She can't afford it."

"I can stay until her mother picks her up," Lucie offered. The little girl looked tired and maybe a little scared.

She looked up at Lucie and said, "Mommy always comes."

"She'll come, honey. I'll stay with you until she gets here."

"I'm not going to leave you here alone," Chase said. "I'll stay, too."

"There's no need…"

The reverend looked from one of them to the other, and Lucie knew she shouldn't protest too much. That would just raise a red flag.

Chase asked the minister, "Do you want the folding chairs taken down and stacked against the wall?"

Reverend Stanhope nodded. "That would be terrific. It's good that the two of you work well together. Chase, you tell your mother I hope she's feeling better soon."

"I'll do that."

"I'll check back here after my meeting to make sure Chrissy got picked up and then I'll lock up."

After the minister left, Lucie attempted to ignore Chase's presence as he began collapsing chairs.

She asked Chrissy, "Would you like me to read you a story? There are plenty of books over there. We can do that until your mom comes."

Chrissy poked a finger in her mouth and asked around it, "Can I sit in your lap?"

"Sure you can. Let's use that bigger chair over there."

It was the one the volunteer used for story corner that could easily hold her and Chrissy.

It wasn't long after Lucie began reading *Where the Wild Things Are* that Chrissy fell asleep. Lucie just held her securely, her chin resting on the little girl's head. When she looked across the room, Chase was watching her.

"You and children seem to go together," he said quietly.

She didn't comment because she didn't know what to say. Was he thinking of her with children of her own, and possibly imagining what they'd look like? She could imagine a boy with his dark hair and eyes.

Nope, she wasn't going there.

Fortunately she heard a car pulling into the lot outside. Chrissy's mom, she hoped.

Apparently Chase had heard it too and he went to look. A petite woman with light brown hair and dark brown eyes came rushing in. Spotting Chrissy in Lucie's arms, she looked relieved.

She introduced herself and began apologizing at once. "I'm so sorry I'm late. My car battery went dead and it took a while to find a Good Samaritan to help me jump-start the car. I'm afraid the same thing's going to happen when I start it up again. Is the reverend around? I was going to ask him if I could borrow some money from the emergency fund." Michelle looked embarrassed to have to say it.

"He had a meeting," Lucie said kindly.

Before she could say more, Chase took a card from his pocket, quickly went to a table where pencils were still strewn and jotted something on the card.

Then he held it out to the woman. "If you go to this

garage, a new car battery will be waiting. I'll make sure it is."

Chrissy's mom took the card, surprise in her eyes. "Are you sure about this? I'll repay you, I promise. I'm just short this month."

Chase was already shaking his head. "That's not necessary."

"I don't know how to thank you."

"No thanks necessary. When you have the opportunity, help out somebody who needs it."

Chrissy awakened, fluttered her eyes and saw her mom. Scrambling from Lucie's lap, she ran to her and hugged her around the knees. "Mommy, Mommy, you came."

"It's time to go home, sweetheart. How about macaroni and cheese for supper?"

Chrissy bobbed her head. Michelle mouthed another thank-you to Chase and Lucie and then left, holding her daughter's hand.

Chase stood at the door and watched them climb into the car that was still running. Apparently Michelle had been afraid to turn it off.

"I hope she can get to a garage in the morning," he said.

"Maybe she'll have a neighbor who can help her jump-start it if it doesn't work. That was a nice thing you did." Lucie studied him.

He shrugged. "I couldn't see depleting the church's emergency fund."

"Do you do that kind of thing often?" She was so curious about him and his life and didn't want to be. She was still trying to figure out who he was now compared to who he had been.

"Probably not as often as I should. Giving to an impersonal charity foundation is one thing. Giving help to someone who really needs it, who was right in front of me, is another."

"I see."

"What do you see? Why did you ask?"

"I'm still trying to figure you out. I wondered if maybe you did that to impress her."

"Impressing anyone isn't high on my to-do list," he returned, almost angrily. "Do you do what you do to impress people?"

"Of course not."

"All right, then why suspect that of me?"

"Because I don't know what to believe where you're concerned. I mean, ten years ago, you asked me to marry you. I did. Then your father swooped in and I basically never heard from you again."

She could see the anger disappear from his face and he looked perplexed. "You're the one who didn't write back because your royal life got in the way."

"That's not true. I received one letter from you, and then nothing else."

They stared at each other, not knowing what to believe.

Why did Chase look confused? He'd written one letter and that was it. And why did he insist her royal life had gotten in the way, when she'd written time and time again? Apparently neither of them trusted the other. That was because ten years and a whole lot of history had passed between them. Maybe they hadn't known each other back then any more than they knew each other now.

"It doesn't matter." Lucie gathered up her purse.

Chase's pride seemed to kick in and he crossed his

arms over his chest in a defensive stance. "No, I guess it doesn't. After our marriage is annulled, we won't see each other again."

After their marriage was annulled… She might be flying off before that even happened. There was no point to this conversation. No point to what had happened and what hadn't happened. No point in standing in the same room with Chase and feeling a longing she didn't want to feel.

The gray sky had turned even darker and the wind had picked up. The last thing she needed was to get caught in a storm. "I want to beat the rain getting back to my apartment. Take care, Chase."

She'd call the minister later and see if any of the volunteers were coming back tomorrow. Although she thought she and Chase worked well together, she couldn't be in his presence again tomorrow. She just couldn't.

Chase let her leave without a word. What was there to say? Don't go? It was silly of her to even think he *could* say it.

To her dismay, Lucie didn't beat the rain. As soon as she pulled out of the church's parking lot, sheets of it beat down, heavy and thick. She really *wasn't* used to driving on the right side of the road, especially not with the weather front moving in.

Her conversation with Chase played in her head. Why had she said what she'd said to him? Maybe she just didn't trust men, and that was why she hadn't dated since her broken engagement. After all, hadn't Terrence lied to her on more than one occasion? Hadn't he told her he was having business meetings when he'd gone to his club? Hadn't she seen a text from more than one woman on his phone? Hadn't he admitted not enough sparks were there between the two of them, and he'd seemed to blame her because she wouldn't show cleavage, because her skirts weren't short enough, because she didn't wear enough makeup?

He'd implied all that, and part of her had believed him. Look at the way the tabloids characterized her sometimes. She meant it when she'd said to Chase that they made her into a cartoon. They constantly held up a distorted mirror. Chase had read those tabloids. That was what he'd known about her in the past ten years. He was far ahead of *her* because she'd known nothing about him, certainly not enough to trust his intentions and his motives.

Tears welled up in her eyes and she wasn't even sure why. Because she hadn't believed Chase seemed to be the man that he portrayed himself to be?

The rain was almost blinding now. She tried to take her time to remember where she was and how to drive in this mess. Suddenly, with another cloudburst, she simply couldn't see. The windshield wipers weren't fast enough. Her tires dipped into an immense pothole puddle. The car slid. She wasn't even sure which way.

All she knew was that she came to a banging halt with her shoulder slamming into the door frame. All she knew was that the car tilted sideways. All she knew was that she was in trouble, with no help in sight.

Chase was driving away from Austin toward his family's ranch when he decided to turn around. The weather was miserable and so was he. His pride had gotten the best of him, and he'd become too defensive with Lucie. He shouldn't have let her drive off into the storm like that.

Instead of having more regrets, there was something he was going to do about it. He was going to go after her.

Taking the first side road, he made a quick turn and headed back the way he'd come. The rain was pouring down with no regard for anything in its wake. That was nature. As he drove past the church, he saw that the lot was empty. No surprise there. Continuing toward Austin, he tried not to think. He was on a mission. He didn't know what the result would be, but it had to be better than what he was feeling now. Was Lucie in the same state of tumult?

His windshield wipers swiped as fast as they could, but had trouble keeping up with the downpour. He almost missed the car along the side of the road. Almost.

Thank the Lord, he didn't.

He recognized the shape and color of the vehicle that was barely visible through the rain. But a sixth sense had made him notice, and his gut clenched because he didn't know what he'd find when he pulled off the road.

It wasn't hard to tell that the car was firmly entrenched in a muddy ditch. He climbed out of his truck, ran up to Lucie's car and banged on the window.

When she opened the door, she looked scared and pale. "Oh, my gosh, Chase, you gave me a fright. I didn't know who you were at first."

"Are you all right?"

"I'm fine, but the car won't start and I can't get it out of here."

He was getting soaking wet, and she would be, too, until they got out of this. But there was no help for it.

"Come on," he said.

But when she tried to get out of the car, she winced and grabbed her shoulder.

"You're not fine. I'm taking you to the ER."

"No. The media will be down on this if you do that. Really, I'm just bumped up and bruised a bit. I need a hot cup of tea and my car rescued."

His arm around her now, he hustled her into his truck and helped her into the passenger seat. Then he ran around to his side and climbed in. "I'll get the foreman at the ranch to pull your car from the ditch. Tomás knows how to keep his mouth shut. I'm going to take you back there."

She bit her lower lip. "I can go back to my apartment." There wasn't a whole lot of force behind her voice.

"If you won't go to the ER, I need a second opinion, and Mom will give it. It's the Bar P or the emergency room. Your choice."

"The Bar P," she said with a sigh, giving him a look that told him she didn't like any of this.

They drove to the ranch with only the sound of the rain rat-a-tatting on the truck roof. Using his hands-free device, Chase pressed the button on his mirror and called Tomás. After giving instructions, he ended the call.

"Aren't you going to call your mom and warn her that I'm coming?" Lucie asked.

"I don't want her to worry before she has to."

"Spoken like a man," Lucie murmured.

Chase cut her a glance but didn't argue with her. He knew his mom. She was great in a crisis. But she worried up, down and sideways beforehand. They'd be there in five minutes.

"Is she still ill?" Lucie asked.

"She's feeling better." Though he suspected his mother hadn't told him the truth about the matter. He wasn't sure anything had been wrong with her. He didn't know why she'd wanted him to be at the church instead of her-self. Certainly she wouldn't be trying to push him and Lucie together when she'd supported his father as he'd pulled them apart. Sometimes he didn't understand his parents at all.

By the time they reached the house, the two of them were soaked to the skin. Chase didn't ring the bell but walked right in.

"I could take you to my guesthouse, but I didn't think that would be proper...just in case anybody does find out about this. We want to go through the right channels so there's no reason for gossip."

"Gossip? We're married, Chase. There'd be gossip for the next three months about that."

"All right, so we're going to keep it from happening. Mom, you here?"

His mother came strolling through the dining room. "Of course I'm here. Where else would I be? Oh, my goodness! You've got Lucie, and look at the two of you. What happened?"

Chase wrapped his arm around Lucie's shoulders and took her over to the sofa. "Mom, can you get some tow-els, maybe a blanket? Her car hit a pothole filled with water, hydroplaned and went off the road. She's a little bumped up."

Lucie looked up at Chase's mom. "I hit my shoulder on the door. It's a little sore. With an ice pack, I'm sure I'll be fine."

Florence plopped her hands on her hips and studied Lucie carefully. "You, my girl, need some tender, lov-ing care. Ice on that shoulder is going to make you cold. Coffee or tea?"

"Tea, please." Now Lucie sounded like a small child. That was the effect his mother had on people.

"And the seat belt probably cut you across the ribs. Are you having trouble breathing?"

"It hurts a little when I breathe."

"I wanted to take her to the ER, but she wouldn't have it," Chase explained.

"I can understand that. Come on, Lucie, why don't you come with me? Instead of making the sofa all soppy, I'll put you in the guest bedroom. You can get a warm shower, and I'll give you some spare clothes I have up there. I'll make tea and then we'll see about that ice pack."

"I don't want to put you to any trouble."

Florence waved her hand in front of Lucie's nose. "Nonsense. It isn't trouble. After all, you are still one of the family."

At that, Chase could see Lucie felt totally out of her depth.

"Go with Mom," he said. "I know how to put the tea-kettle on. You should probably eat something, too, something with salt. You're much too pale."

"I'm rattled," she responded vehemently. Yes, she was. First from their argument, and then from that slide off the road.

The two of them had forgotten for a moment that Mrs. Parker was listening.

"There will be time to fix whatever's wrong," Florence deduced wisely. "Come on, Lucie."

Lucie slipped off her shoes. "I don't want to leave marks on this beautiful floor."

"Juanita takes care of that," Florence said. "No need to worry. Chase, did you see to Lucie's car?"

"I did. Tomás will bring it back here and we'll see if there's any damage. He'll clean it up, too."

As Lucie and his mother walked out of the room, Chase headed for the kitchen. He had to keep his hands busy. He'd wanted to put them all over Lucie to figure out if she was okay, of course, but for more reasons, too. Her pale skin with the slightest amount of freckles on her cheeks, that dimple at one corner of her lip begged to be touched. Her hair, even though wet, was silky and sexy. He'd wanted to sling her over his shoulder, toss her into the back of his truck and make love to her right there. How stupid was that? It wasn't as if she was the type of woman who would do anything like that. It wasn't as if he had any right. It wasn't as if they had any reason other than lust for coming together.

No, he had to bury those caveman tendencies. They'd gotten him into trouble with her ten years ago, and he wouldn't let it happen again. He was also grateful his father wasn't home. Then he might have had to take her to the guesthouse and hide her!

A half hour later, his mother had brought Lucie back to the kitchen. They were almost the same size, except Lucie was taller. So the slacks she wore were a little short. But the peach-colored silky blouse hung on her just right. She didn't have a blanket around her, but his mother had apparently offered her one of her cashmere sweaters. It matched the blouse.

"Herbal tea or regular?" Florence asked her.

"Herbal would be nice. Something with cinnamon?"

"Orange spice."

Chase picked up a carafe that sat on an electric warmer. "Just the right temperature."

"You know about that?" Lucie asked, surprised.

"I've been taught by a master. Mom's an expert on tea making, brewing and choosing."

He found an ice pack in the refrigerator and wrapped it with a kitchen towel. Then he gently placed it on Lucie's shoulder while his mother poured tea.

"Just a bit of sugar," Lucie said.

Florence wrinkled her nose. "I like it straight."

Chase had made himself a pot of coffee. "And I like it black." He cast his mother a glance before he broached the next subject.

She seemed to read his mind, because she looked over at Lucie and nodded.

"I think you should stay here tonight," he said. "If those muscles around the ribs swell and you have trouble breathing, someone needs to be with you."

Chase could see the warm tea was calming Lucie down, and fatigue was setting in. Instead of protesting, she asked again, "Are you sure it's no trouble?"

"No trouble," Florence said. "I'll feel better knowing you're safe. Wouldn't you rather have us come to your aid if you need it than a doorman?"

Lucie targeted her glance at Chase. "You told your mother about Irv?"

"I told her he was protective, and that's a good thing."

Lucie had left her purse on the coffee table and now her phone rang inside it. She said, "I'd better check it."

When she did, she said, "It's my mother. She must have reached an area with cell phone towers."

"Do you need privacy?" Florence asked.

Lucie hesitated a moment. "No, I'm fine." She said it as if this were going to be a short call.

Chase guessed Lucie wouldn't be having a heart-to-heart about her marriage to him.

Florence walked away to give Lucie privacy. "I'll see what we have in the refrigerator that we can have for supper."

Chase, however, stayed right there in the living room with Lucie. He wanted to overhear this conversation.

Lucie answered the call. When she did, she pretended everything tonight hadn't happened. "Hi, Mum. How are you?"

Chase couldn't hear what her mother told her, but whatever she said made Lucie happy. At least until her mother added something that drained the color from her face again.

"Yes, I suppose I can do that," she answered. "I'll see where I am with the Fortune offices in two weeks and then I'll let you know. Arriving a week early shouldn't be a problem. No, nothing's wrong."

Uh-oh. Lucie's mother must have good intuition, too, if she'd asked what was wrong. Obviously she could sense something was up, but Lucie was giving nothing away. However, by the time she ended the call, Chase could see she was in turmoil.

"I thought you were going to tell your mother about our marriage the next time you spoke with her," he said.

"I just couldn't do it now."

"Why? You're here. I'm here. The accident happened. You didn't even tell her about that."

"I don't want her to worry."

"Famous last words," he muttered.

He crossed to the sofa and sank down beside Lucie, taking her hand. "Why didn't you tell her? Because I was here and you didn't have privacy?"

Lucie lowered her voice. "I didn't tell her for the same

reason you haven't told your father you'll be moving out and quitting Parker Oil. It's not an easy thing to do."

She was right. Soon they'd both have to deal with those harder aspects of their life. Soon they'd be signing papers dissolving a union that shouldn't have happened to begin with.

Florence called from the kitchen, "I found leftover roast beef and mashed potatoes that we can warm up to have with it. I can rustle up some fresh broccoli. What do you think?"

Chase thought food was the least of their problems. He had no appetite, at least not for what his mother would be cooking up in the kitchen. He had an appetite for Lucie, and he was going to have to deal with that soon.

Chapter Seven

Sun poured in the window of the guest room at the Bar P as Lucie awakened slowly, stretching to try to figure out what hurt. Her shoulder was a bit sore. Her ribs felt better.

Last night had been mostly a blur after the phone call from her mother. Maybe it was stress from the accident or stress from being with Chase. She wasn't sure which. He'd shown her to a pink and lilac room decorated with a luxury comforter and satiny cream-colored sheets. His mother had brought her an ice pack and a heating pad, too. Chase might have stayed, but Florence had insisted Lucie rest and get a good night's sleep. After some hesitation, he'd left. And she'd fallen asleep.

Until a few minutes ago.

There was a slight tapping on her door. She realized someone didn't want to wake her if she was still asleep. But she had to start her day and return to her apartment.

"Come in," she called, tensing a bit because she thought her visitor might be Chase.

However, it wasn't. It was Florence. Chase's mother wheeled in a tea cart that smelled wonderful. There was a large plate with a stainless steel cover, a teapot, a teacup and a plate of pastries.

"Are you hungry?" Florence asked.

"Now that I smell food, I am," Lucie said with a smile. "But you didn't have to do this."

"You didn't have much supper." She took the lid from the large plate that held scrambled eggs, bacon and a stack of silver dollar pancakes. "Warm syrup is in that little pitcher, and butter's in the cup."

"This is wonderful."

"How's your shoulder?"

"Not bad," Lucie said.

Florence reached to the shelf under the top of the tray. "I brought you another ice pack. I thought you might want to put it on before you get dressed."

"You've thought of everything."

Florence frowned. "Not quite. I'm sorry this happened to you. I never imagined you'd be hurt helping me with the church program. You don't have to worry about today," she added. "I called the minister, and he has volunteers again."

"Do you know if my car is ready?"

"You'll have to ask Chase about that."

"He didn't leave for work?"

"No. He always spends some time with the horses in the morning, especially when he's trying to figure things out."

"Figure things out?"

"He's making changes, and I'm not sure he's used to

the idea of them yet. I know *I'm* certainly not. I'm going to miss not having him in the guesthouse, and I know his father will, too. I just hope Warren doesn't explode when Chase tells him what he's going to do."

"I hope he doesn't either. That won't be good for either of them." She did not have fond memories of Warren Parker, and Florence seemed to sense that.

"Chase's dad isn't the ogre Chase makes him out to be sometimes. He's just very old-school and set in his ways. But he has a good heart, and he wants the best for Chase."

"He always wanted that," Lucie agreed, thinking about the plans he'd had for his son when Chase was twenty-one.

"Hmmm," Florence said to that, and that was all. "I'll leave you to your breakfast. Do you remember your way to the barn?"

"I do."

"Well, good. I'll be in my study if you want to say goodbye before you leave."

And with that, Florence left the room.

The food called to Lucie and she ate with a hunger she hadn't had in a while. Afterward she dressed, wishing she had fresh clothes. But she'd be back at her place soon.

A half hour later, she was finding her way to the barn, hoping Chase was still there. When Lucie found him, he was...mucking out stalls! She grinned as she approached him.

Seeing her expression, he laid the pitchfork aside and put his hands on his hips. "What?"

"This isn't quite what I expected you to be doing."

"Horses have needs, too, and clean stalls are one of them. At my own place, I'll probably be doing this even more than I do it here. How are you feeling?"

"Like someone put me in a milk shake mixer."

He chuckled. "Vanilla, strawberry, or chocolate?"

"Chocolate all the way."

He sobered and came toward her. When he reached her, he asked, "Are you sure you're all right? I can take you to my mother's private physician. He'd keep the visit quiet."

"There's no need. Really, Chase. I'll keep icing my shoulder and I'll be fine. Is my car ready?"

"Tomás has to wash it down yet. The truth is, I'm not sure you should be driving. Why don't you let me take you back to your apartment, and he can bring your car in and park it later?"

She was about to protest when he shook his head. "Don't tell me it's too much trouble. Those are words you use too often."

When he was standing this close, she couldn't think straight. "Maybe part of the problem is I don't want to owe you anything."

Really close now, he let his hand drift to her shoulder, then up her neck into her hair. "I don't think of *owe* or *not owe* when it comes to you."

She could hardly push the words out, but she wanted to know. "What do you think of when it comes to me?"

He nudged her closer, and she didn't pull back. "The same thing I was thinking of last night while I lay in the guesthouse and you were at my mom's. Which was probably a good thing because when I'm with you, Lucie, I want to take you to bed again. That's the long and short of it. Our fire didn't burn out ten years ago."

No, it hadn't, but how long could it sustain glowing embers? She and Chase were being pulled in different directions. How could any fire last that way?

"I thought about coming to your room last night," he said honestly. "Even if it was just to hold you through the night."

"My guess is, we wouldn't have just held each other."

His eyes blazed with that fire they were just talking about. "You're right. That's why I didn't come. I didn't want to take advantage of you being vulnerable."

She felt all too vulnerable around him. But when he laced his hand through her hair and came in for a kiss, she didn't protest. Chase's kisses had always been filled with excitement and fervor, and demanded an answering response from her.

When his tongue swept her mouth, she held on to his shoulders as if her life depended on it. As his thumb caressed her cheek, his tenderness swept over her with repercussions she didn't even have the sense to consider. She remembered his kiss all those years ago—the very first one. She recalled how she'd trembled as soon as his lips touched hers, how his coaxing ardor had led her to press against him, the way she was pressing against him now. His jeans weren't that much of a barrier against his passion. Feeling it, she knew she'd welcome satisfaction as much as he would. Chase's arms were as possessive as his tongue was seductive.

He'd just laid fresh hay in the stall next to this one. She'd seen it.

What was she thinking?

A truck door slammed outside, and with that noise, the web of passion around them was torn asunder.

Chase released her, then shook his head and muttered, "Whew. We keep that up, we'll light the barn on fire."

"If we keep that up, we're both going to get hurt."

Chase's gaze raked over her face. "Why didn't your engagement work out?"

She blinked because the change of subject was so abrupt. But the truth was, she didn't really want to talk to Chase about it.

"It just didn't. I'm sure you've dated women and then decided they weren't right for you."

"I've never gotten as far as an engagement. That's serious. What made you decide he wasn't right for you?"

"For one thing, I was traveling and we had distance between us."

"That's not insurmountable if two people care."

He was going to probe and probe until she gave him something, she just knew it. "He lied to me. He went clubbing and wasn't alone when he did."

"Honesty is everything," Chase agreed. "But there was something else, wasn't there?"

"Chase, I don't see why we need to talk about this."

"Tell me the reason you broke up with him wasn't because of the fire we'd experienced. Maybe you just couldn't match that and you didn't want to accept less."

Was that the true reason her relationship with Terry hadn't worked? Maybe with Chase she would have felt sexy, coy and flirtatious. Maybe with Chase—

Flustered now from him delving too deep, she shot back quickly, "You don't have much ego, do you?"

"This isn't about ego, Lucie. I know I've been looking for that same kind of passion ever since."

"We were young...with raging hormones."

"And what's our excuse now?" he asked wryly.

"Maybe when we know we can't have something, we want it even more. Isn't that human nature?"

Chase glanced around the barn, and then he looked

back at her. "Maybe it is. I'd better get you back to your apartment and I'd better get to work. Dad will return within the next few days, and I want to make sure everything at Parker Oil is ready for my departure."

"You've decided on your replacement?"

"I have. Jeff will be perfect. I just have to organize the paperwork with all his accomplishments, so Dad can see my point. Do you need to go back to the house before we leave?"

"I really should say goodbye to your mother. She was so kind."

"All right, then. I'll finish this last stall and meet you in front of the house."

As Lucie left the barn, she felt as if she'd been dismissed. She didn't like that at all, but she knew what Chase was thinking. He had a lot of hard work ahead of him. He would be trying to juggle a new venture while still keeping his foot in at Parker Oil. She'd be building an orphanage in Guatemala. A night in bed, or a tumble in a stall, wouldn't make divergent life paths suddenly coincide.

Lucie couldn't help feeling defensive on the ride back to her apartment. She and Chase could always find things to talk about, but the sexual tension between them was difficult to deal with. This day, conversation didn't come easily. She was aware of his solicitous glances every once in a while, and in a way she resented them. She'd been taking care of herself just fine for the past ten years. If she had a sore shoulder, she'd take care of it. He didn't have to worry.

But he didn't seem to believe that.

By the time they neared her apartment building, she couldn't wait to hop out of his truck. However, about a half block from the building, Lucie noticed a red car with a news station logo on the window. She murmured, "TXLB. I wonder if he's in the lobby."

"TXLB?" Chase asked. "The TV station?"

"Yes. The reporter's car is parked right back there."

"I'll be doing an interview with Norton Wilcox at TXLB for his talk show *About Austin* in about ten days. The station's highlighting the horse rescue. I'm going to reveal all my plans and hopefully encourage public support."

"Wilcox is the reporter who phoned me for an interview. But then he began hanging around. He doesn't want to take no for an answer. He keeps showing up, hoping I'll change my mind."

"He didn't give *me* a hassle. But then, I said yes to the interview because it will help my cause. Maybe I could act as a buffer for you."

She shook her head. "I don't need a buffer. I'll handle him."

As they neared the entrance to the garage, Lucie said quickly, "Keep on going."

As Chase passed the garage entrance, he asked, "Why?"

"Just go around and let me out a good block away. I'll double back."

"Okay, so you don't want a buffer. But if you need me to act as your bodyguard to lead you to your place, I will."

"I don't need a bodyguard. And unless you want your life turned as topsy-turvy as mine is, we need to do this my way. Just think about Amelia and all those tabloid photos. Do you want your face plastered on the front of

one of those? Do you want this reporter associating you
with me and digging up our marriage?"

"I don't like this, Lucie. I don't like letting you off a
block away. You were hurt yesterday, whether you want
to admit it or not."

She sighed. "I'm a little sore, that's all. Please, Chase,
just do this for me."

As he rounded a corner to take the detour around the
block, his jaw drew tense and his lips tightened into a
straight line. Finally he agreed. "All right. I'll do as you
ask under one condition."

"What?" she asked warily.

"Call me as soon as you're inside your apartment. Not
five minutes later, but as soon as you're inside."

"That doesn't sound like a condition. It sounds like
an order."

"You are a very frustrating and stubborn woman."

"And you're reaching into territory you shouldn't be."

"Maybe so," he agreed without apology.

She could see he wasn't going to back down. He might
not let her out of his truck if she didn't agree.

"I'll call you as soon as I'm inside, I promise. I'm
going to walk straight into the lobby and deal with whatever I have to deal with. You can expect my call in about
five minutes. This is a good spot. Just let me out here."

Chase pulled over to the curb a block down from her
apartment complex. Neither of them said a word as she
climbed out. She did so quickly so no one would notice, and soon she was incognito in a line of pedestrians
going their separate ways. She didn't glance back over
her shoulder. She didn't see if Chase pulled away. She
guessed he would, though. That was the smarter thing

to do. But he might just drive around the block again until she called him.

Picking up the pace, she neared her apartment building and took a long, deep breath. Irv was standing at his counter and she immediately recognized the other man standing there with him—Norton Wilcox.

After he'd called for an interview, she watched his spot on the evening news. That hadn't changed her mind about sitting down with him. Irv was frowning, but Wilcox was smiling. It was one very fake smile, but it was an attempt. Wilcox had on-air anchorman good looks, or at least he thought he did. His hair was brushed to the side and gelled. He was wearing a suit with an open-neck shirt and no tie. The casual professional look. She wished her clothes hadn't seen her through an accident, but she squared her shoulders and stood as tall as she could.

Wilcox's blue eyes were alert as Lucie walked toward him. He studied her down to the purse in her hands.

"Hello, Lady Fortune Chesterfield," he said in an ingratiating way. He extended his hand. "It's good to meet you in person. I'm Norton Wilcox from TXLB. I called you a week ago to ask you for an interview, but you declined. I've been trying to connect with you since then, but I keep missing you."

Being as civil as she was able, she said, "Yes, I declined because, as I told you then, I'm not looking for publicity."

"Your charity could use it."

"That's possibly true," she agreed, awarding him the point. "But I'm not on a fundraising mission."

"What mission are you on? Rumor has it you're looking for office space for the Fortune Foundation. Why don't you tell me all about it?"

"No interview, Mr. Wilcox." She didn't know if the foundation was ready to go public until the programs were up and running.

His smile slipped from his lips. "Where were you already this morning? Looking for office space? I ran down a lead that you'd contacted a real estate agent. Or maybe something personal came up?"

The worst thing she could do was become defensive. In her sweetest voice, she answered, "I had an early errand."

His face took on a look that said he was determined to search out the truth. "You weren't here last night either when I asked your doorman to buzz you."

Keeping her composure, she stated blandly, "I must have been in the shower. Have a good day, Mr. Wilcox."

Then she walked quickly to the elevator, punched the button and was grateful when the door swished open. The doors closed and she sagged against the back wall. She'd dodged that bullet. So far so good as far as Chase was concerned, she hoped.

Once inside her apartment, she took her cell phone from her pocket, found Chase in her contact list and pressed the number for his cell phone. When she did, she remembered his expression as she'd left his truck. She remembered their conversation in the barn. She remembered their kiss.

He answered immediately. "Are you in your apartment?"

"I am and all is well." Though she knew it really wasn't for one very important reason. She was falling in love with Chase Parker all over again.

There was momentary hesitation on his end. "Hold

on a minute. I'm going to pull over and park. I like to concentrate on my conversations."

Just what did he have to concentrate on? This conversation was over, wasn't it?

"I'm parked," he said. "So the reporter left?"

"I hope so. I made it into the elevator and I imagine Irv got rid of him."

"He'll be back if he's good."

"Maybe." She sighed. "I can always pull some strings and quiet him, but I don't want to have to do that, at least not yet."

Suddenly Chase asked, "How would you like to run around with your wig on again tomorrow?"

"We'd be tempting fate."

"No, not with what I have planned."

"And what would that be?" In spite of herself, she was interested. In spite of her better judgment, she liked being with him.

"The South by Southwest Conference is in full swing. No one will recognize us in a crowd at the music venues, especially if we wear disguises. If you wear a wig or a baseball cap, you'll be good."

The thought of being free enough to enjoy a music festival intrigued her. "And what disguise will you wear?"

After a moment, he answered, "I'll find a fake mustache and wear cheap boots."

She couldn't help laughing. "I know I shouldn't do this."

"But you want to."

Yes, she wanted to. She thought about the reporter, about having her every move scrutinized. What if she could escape that for a day? "All right," she agreed. "But this time *I* have a condition."

"Uh-oh."

She could tell he wasn't happy about that. "If your foreman brings my rental car back later today, I'll drive myself tomorrow, and I'll meet you on a back street. I really don't think you should be seen anywhere near here."

"You have a sore shoulder."

"By tomorrow, it'll be even better than it is today."

"I don't like meeting you on a back street," he protested.

"We have to meet somewhere where there aren't any security cameras. Convenience stores have them, grocery stores have them, big box stores have them."

"Your knowledge base is a little different than most people's," he grumbled.

"I'll tell you what. I'll let you pick the location, since you're familiar with Austin. Just pick a street where we can both park. I don't care how far we have to walk. I just don't want to be noticed."

"As soon as I'm at my office, I'll check a map and I'll email you."

"That sounds good. And wish me luck today. I'm hoping to find the right space so I can start the paperwork and get the Fortune Foundation office set up." She'd made another list and was determined to find the right space.

"I wish you luck."

She smiled at the sincerity in his voice. "Email me the location and time you want to meet and I'll be there."

"That's a promise?" he asked.

"It's a promise," she vowed.

"I'll see you tomorrow." There was a sexy huskiness to his words that made her anticipate the time with him as much as she anticipated a short time of freedom.

Their conversation stayed with her as she ended the

call. It stayed with her as she searched her contacts for the real estate agent's number. She wouldn't be able to forget about Chase easily today…or their plans for tomorrow.

South by Southwest, a music and media conference in Austin, was a huge event. Lucie had read up on it last night and she understood it was full of aspiring songwriters, from almost-making-it stars who sang their hearts out to musicians who just wanted to play music. A singer might play four live sets in twenty-four hours to get noticed, to engage an audience, to elicit applause. Refreshments were plentiful, from jalapeño margaritas to the best barbecue sandwiches. There were indoor and outside stages, private parties and plenty of public brouhaha. It was one big party, and Lucie found herself grinning from ear to ear as she met Chase.

He seemed to know all the ins and outs and exactly where he wanted to go. He had a printout and a backpack, water bottles and hats emblazoned with a South X Southwest emblem for both of them.

"It seems like I'm going to be taking a trek into the wild," she joked, feeling at home in her wig and her gauzy blouse and skirt…at home with him.

"It can get pretty wild."

"Do you come every year?"

"I try to."

Lucie found herself letting go of anxiety and worry they'd be discovered when Chase hooked his arm into hers. They stood at showcases, listening to everything from indie rock to hip-hop. Most of the time they couldn't talk because the music was loud and the crowds were thick. They walked around Sixth Street and hopped in and out of restaurants as well as a few bars to hear alternative and traditional music.

"I'm glad you took my advice and wore flat shoes," he said, studying her espadrilles.

"I always take good advice."

Chase laughed.

After having to use earplugs at one venue—Chase had thought of those, too—they stopped at a shop for iced coffee and then walked some more.

Music, food, people of all shapes and sizes in all types of attire abounded.

Country music poured from a restaurant they passed and Chase snagged Lucie's arm and pulled her inside. There, they found a high table for two.

After they ordered ribs and cheese fries, Chase said, "We could go somewhere with more refined fare, but I thought you'd want to stay in the center of the action."

There was a small dance floor filled with people. Chase nodded to them. "Have you ever danced the two-step?"

"I've never learned that one," Lucie admitted, eyeing the couples warily.

"It'll be a while before our food gets here. Come on." He stood and grabbed her hand.

"Chase, I don't know. I don't want to make a fool of myself. I know how to waltz and fox-trot, but—"

He eyed her and interrupted her protest. "Don't you ever try anything you're not sure you're good at?"

"Not usually," she confessed.

He laughed out loud. "Well, today's a first. Come on."

Standing, he held his hand out to her. Finally after a few seconds, she took it and let him lead her to the dance floor. When Chase's arm went around Lucie, she felt electrified. They weren't even that close. He took her right hand in his; his right arm came about her, his hand resting on her shoulder blade.

"I'll lead. You follow," he said with a smile.

He kept a few inches between them, and that seemed to be even more enticing than being smack against each other. His hold was light but firm, and she didn't think she'd ever enjoyed a day as much as today. She caught on quickly to the four steps—two quick, and then two slow. It was easy to follow Chase, just as it had been ten years ago.

She found they were in line with the other couples moving around the perimeter of the dance floor. The whole thing felt so natural she couldn't believe it. She jumped into the spirit of it, truly enjoying herself. They were dancing so fast at one point that when Chase executed a spin with her, her wig slipped. Chase righted it for her and they both laughed as they gazed into each other's eyes as she felt stirrings she'd never felt with another man.

When the number ended, Chase directed her back to their table. They sat around the corner from each other and Chase reached out, straightening a few wayward strands of her wig. Now they were close as his hand lingered on the side of her face. Everything they'd done together from the past until today seemed to surround them.

Chase leaned forward and she moved toward him. His kiss was soft, sweet, with a touch of his tongue. Then he backed away.

Just in time, too, because their waitress brought their meals. She winked at them. "You're a cute couple. Enjoying your time here in Austin?"

So, many of the festival-goers weren't local. Lucie answered, "Very much."

But when she and Chase locked eyes again, the realization hit that they weren't a couple.

Picking up one of her cheese fries, Lucie looked away from Chase and outside the plate glass window. But the person she saw out there made her cringe. She grabbed Chase's arm.

"Chase, I think that's Wilcox out there. Do you think he could have followed us?"

"I don't see how that would be possible."

The window was the type that seemed to be darkened glass. The patrons inside could see out, but anyone standing outside couldn't see in.

"If he comes in here, I'm going to have to hide in the ladies' room."

"Hold on," Chase said, keeping his hand on her forearm, keeping her in her seat. "We're not going to let him spoil dinner if we don't have to."

"But Chase, if he sees us together—"

"I don't see how he could recognize us," Chase twirled the end of his mustache and slipped his sunglasses back on.

As they waited, Lucie held her breath. Wilcox pulled open the door and Lucie was all set to run. But Chase kept her still. There were so many people, so much noise, such loud music. After a glance around, Wilcox stepped back outside and headed away from the restaurant.

Lucie breathed a sigh of relief, yet she knew it was possible they were still in jeopardy.

Chase gestured to her ribs. "I know you're worrying that he's lying in wait. Let's eat our dinner, and then I'll find a back way out. He can't be two places at once."

"I don't like this, Chase. Do you think it was a coincidence?"

"I don't know, but we'll evade him. You should come back to the ranch with me. If he *is* trying to follow you, he'll end up at your apartment again. Besides, I'm not ready for this day to end, are you?"

No, she wasn't.

If she went with Chase to the ranch, she'd be digging herself deeper into love. But she didn't know how to stop. She hadn't experienced a day quite like today since… Scotland. She liked…no, *loved* being with Chase. What could it hurt to indulge herself for a few more hours?

Chapter Eight

Chase and Lucie stood by the paddock fence, watching Gypsy. Dusk was starting to fall as the shadows in the pasture began melting together. The sun was tipping over the horizon.

"You don't think Wilcox saw us run out the back door, do you?" She must have asked Chase that about ten times, but she needed reassurance. She'd left her wig and baseball cap in the car after they arrived at the Bar P, but she almost felt as if she should be wearing her disguise even here.

"I'm sure he didn't. There's no way he could have recognized you in that crowded bar, let alone suspected we'd run out the back. There were so many people everywhere, Lucie. There was no way he could have seen you or kept track of you."

"It couldn't have been sheer coincidence he was there, and you know it."

"Maybe, maybe not. It could have been bad luck we ended up in the same place as he was. He was probably all over Austin looking for stories at the festivals."

She sighed. "I hope you're right. I'd hate to think he was tracking me."

He rested his hand on her shoulder. "You're safe here. We both took such a circuitous route, I'm sure no one followed us."

She could feel the heat of his hand through the fabric of her blouse. She looked up at him, feeling that thrill she always felt when she was with him. "Your mom seemed interested in the festivals. Doesn't she go?"

"Too much walking, too many people. At least that's what she tells me. But I don't think she wants to go alone."

"She doesn't have friends she could go with?"

"She did before my dad's stroke. But since then, she's devoted herself to him, all her time and all her energy. When she did that, friends dropped away. She still has contacts on charity boards and at church, but those aren't the kinds of friends you want to run around South by Southwest with."

"No, I imagine you want a close friend for that, one who appreciates all of it as much as you do."

Today she'd felt close to Chase. She'd felt as if they were on an adventure again together as they had been in Scotland. They'd communicated, bonded and laughed together.

He must have been thinking about that, too. "You're even more beautiful now than you were ten years ago," he murmured.

"And you're…" she started. "You're as sexy and as

hard to resist now as you were back then. Even without your fake mustache."

His lips twitched up in a smile, right before he bent his head and wrapped his arms around her. She was surrounded by sensations that almost made her tipsy. There was the scent of Chase, the evening muskiness of damp earth and pine. A light breeze stirred her hair as Chase laced one hand in it. She savored the idea of his kiss as much as she wanted it. The anticipation was a heady aphrodisiac.

He must have thought so, too, because he wasn't rushing anything. He rubbed his cheek against hers and she could feel his evening beard stubble. She breathed him in again, waiting for the inevitable. He began with a nibble at the corner of her lip that left her hungry for him. When his lips finally took hers, she'd ringed her arms around his neck and held on tight.

Chase's tongue dashed against hers, then returned for a lighter stroke.

She responded, giving the same as he had given her. She curved her fingers into his taut shoulder muscles and remembered how he'd looked shirtless. Everything about Chase turned her on.

Their kiss became their world.

Lucie was so involved in a passion she'd almost forgotten that she barely heard the rustle of grass, the crunch of boot heel on stone, Gypsy's quiet neigh.

"What in the blazes, Chase, do you think you're doing?" Warren Parker suddenly yelled. "Your mother told me you were out here with…her. We could have handled this without you getting in touch with her. There was no need for you to see her, and now to find you like this—"

They'd broken apart at the first sound of his father's voice. However, they stood shoulder to shoulder now, facing him as Warren sputtered and fumed.

Lucie was all but fuming herself. The man had been rude ten years ago, and apparently his temper hadn't improved.

"Hello, Mr. Parker," she said evenly, hoping in the dimming light he couldn't see she looked well and thoroughly kissed.

"I hear you're a Fortune now," he said, but not as if he respected the idea. "I read about your mother being united with her long-lost sister—Jeanne Marie Fortune Jones—but I didn't know if it was true. Florence tells me that it is. Apparently you have family on top of family in Horseback Hollow now. Such a quaint two-horse town."

"Yes, it is true my mother and her sister, as well as their brother, were reunited," Lucie responded quietly. "And I have family in Horseback Hollow now."

"Well, bully for you. None of that means anything to us."

"Dad," Chase said sharply.

"Well, it doesn't, Chase. Your marriage is going to be dissolved. Why would you want to consort with an airhead royal who cares about pomp and ceremony and getting her photo all over the news?"

Her temper well past the boiling point, Lucie didn't know which misconception to address first.

But she didn't have to address any of it because Chase stepped in. "You're wrong about everything," he insisted before she could. "First of all, Lucie's anything but an airhead. She's highly intelligent, and she's finding office space for the Fortune Foundation in Austin so they can expand their programs here. Point two—when she's building orphanages in developing countries, the last thing she cares about is pomp and ceremony. She cares about the children she's helping. Point three—as far as getting her photo in the news goes, do you think she wants her life laid out like that?"

But Mr. Parker didn't seem to have heard anything his son had said. He was jabbing his finger at Chase. "You need to be single-minded about your career at Parker Oil as I have been all these years. An up-and-coming CEO needs to have a woman by his side who's an asset, not a disadvantage because of scandal and innuendo being printed about her at every turn of the tabloid page."

Apparently Chase had had enough. He stepped forward, boot to boot with his father. "I didn't want to do it this way, but you're leaving me no choice. I told Mom, and I was waiting until the time was right to tell you."

"Tell me what?" his father snapped.

"I'm leaving Parker Oil to establish a nonprofit horse rescue ranch. I didn't want to merely buy property with my loan for some distant future. I intend to do something worthwhile with it right now. I put down earnest money on the old Schultz land."

"You did *what*? That place is falling down!"

"Not entirely. It needs work, but it'll be worth it, and I'm going to do it."

Warren Parker had been a burly man who'd lost weight since Lucie saw him last. He wasn't so burly now. He looked older, much older. His Western-cut suit was of superb quality, but the jacket was wrinkled, and so was his shirt. That didn't stop him puffing out his chest and blustering.

"I didn't put an end to this romance before to have it rise from the ashes again."

"You didn't put an end to the romance. The annulment did that," Chase concluded. Yet something in his father's expression must have alerted Chase that Warren might have schemed further. "That is what you mean, isn't it?" Chase asked.

"You mean the annulment that didn't happen? Sending *her* back to where she belonged?" Warren scoffed. "That wouldn't have been enough. I saw the way you two looked at each other. I intercepted your letters, and they never went out to her. I got hold of her incoming ones, so you never saw them. That was putting an end to a dalliance that never should have happened."

Lucie saw Chase's jaw stiffen, his mouth press into a straight line. But more than that, she saw his eyes widen, and the look in them hurt her, too. He was stunned by what his father had done, and she imagined he was feeling totally betrayed.

Her suspicion was confirmed when he took her hand and pulled her toward the barn. "Let's go," he said.

His father called, "Chase, you come back here. We're not done."

Chase threw over his shoulder, "We're more than done. I was going to stay on part-time and then consult at Parker Oil. You can forget about that."

And then he was almost running with her. Outside the barn, he took keys from his pocket and headed to a red pickup truck that was close by. There was a ferocious look on his face and she realized he was just as angry as he was betrayed.

"Where are we going?" she asked.

"For a drive. Get in."

"But this isn't your truck…"

"It's a ranch truck Tomás usually uses. He won't care."

She didn't argue. She'd never seen Chase look like this before, and it scared her a little. Yet she wasn't going to let him drive off alone. They were in this together.

As soon as she slid onto the bench seat inside the older truck, she fastened her seat belt. Chase took off. She didn't ask again where they were going, because she suspected he didn't know. He just wanted to drive out of frustration and hurt. He was a controlled man in many ways, or at least he'd learned to be. That control was worn thin tonight, and she suspected he wanted to yell a few things, too, but wasn't doing it because she was with him.

"Say whatever you need to say, Chase."

"Your ears couldn't handle it."

"My ears have handled a whole lot more than you think they have."

He cut her a quick glance, put on his high beams and roared down the back road of the ranch, straight into the forest.

"I guess you know where this leads." No matter where or how fast he drove, she oddly trusted him.

"It leads into another back road and then another one after that. This property is large enough to need its own map."

"Is this helping?" she asked as he zoomed down the road and bumped over a pothole.

"Not much."

They had to be at least a mile from the house now, maybe two. She could feel the vibrations still pulsing around Chase like a ferocious aura that couldn't be quieted. His hands had a death grip on the steering wheel.

Finally she said, "Chase, we can't fully blame your father for what happened."

At that pronouncement from her, he slowed the truck, pulled over to the side of the road and braked. "What do you mean we can't blame *him*? He intercepted our letters."

She needed to be closer to him and she couldn't do that with the seat belt on. She unfastened it and angled toward him on the bench seat.

"If I had had less pride, fewer insecurities and more common sense, I would have contacted you somehow. The same goes for you. Why did you give up without a fight? Why did I? There could only be one reason. We weren't ready for a relationship, let alone a marriage. Not if we could let go that easily."

Chase switched off the ignition, unfastened his seat belt and moved closer to her. "Easily?"

When she gazed into his eyes, she saw so many things. He was devastated by what his father had done. The loyalty Chase had given to him, the years of his life—he might now feel they were wasted.

He reached out and caressed her arm. That was the tenderness she liked so much in Chase.

"I'm sorry for what my father did," he said huskily. "I'm sorry you got caught up in his need for control."

Then without warning, Chase was kissing her. It was wild and took her back ten years. It was so like their first kiss, unbridled. It was so like the first time they'd made love.

Darkness was falling with a vengeance now. The forest surrounded them. His hands touched her as if he wanted more than a kiss as he leaned her back against the door. She found herself pulling his shirt from his waistband. She wanted to feel his skin. She needed to. Their day together reminded her how much she loved being with him, how infatuated she'd been, how hard she was falling again.

He broke away only long enough to murmur, "I have a condom in my pocket."

She didn't stop to think about that. Had he known this was going to happen? Had she, deep down, known, too, because of desires she'd kept secret all these years?

"Are you sure?" she asked him. "Are you sure you're just not angry and frustrated at your father and you want to get back at him?"

"Lucie, this has nothing to do with getting back at my father. Believe me. Do you know how many nights I've dreamed of doing this again?"

Yes, she did. Because if she was honest with herself, she had dreamed about it, too.

In no time at all, he unzipped his jeans. Somehow she divested herself of her panties while he tore open the condom packet. Then he was pulling her onto his lap. He was holding her as she faced him. This wasn't roses and champagne. It wasn't a hostel in Scotland. It was a pickup truck on the Bar P and she knew it. She also didn't care. This was a side of her Chase brought out. This was a side of her she wanted to be free.

She maneuvered herself up until he slid inside her; then she lowered herself onto him. With his groan, she knew she felt the same satisfaction he did. With her moan, he was sure he was pleasing her. He had a condom, and even though they were using it, if he hadn't had one, she'd still be making love with him like this.

He found his release as she reached for the stars and grabbed them. Delicious prickles ran through her whole body and after they ebbed away, she felt boneless. Chase was embracing her, and she was so glad he was. Still, as the night breeze blew through the windows, both of them were silent.

The colder night air made her shiver, and Chase said, "I'll give you a little room to get…straightened up. I'll be right back." He helped her onto the seat and then he stepped out of the pickup.

She wondered what was going through his head. She hadn't known for ten years, and she didn't know now.

He gave her a good five minutes. Her cheeks had cooled down, and so had the rest of her body by the time he climbed back into the truck.

Staring out the windshield, he said, "Maybe that will give us closure."

"Is that what we needed?" She had a feeling what they'd just experienced would never bring closure.

Since Chase's silence told her he obviously wasn't ready to express his thoughts or his feelings, she sighed. "I'd better get back, not only to my car but to my apartment. I don't want rumors floating around that I'd been out all night. And you—you need to make sure your father's okay."

Instead of looking out the front window now, Chase faced her. "How can you even think about my dad?"

"I can think about *your* dad because I lost mine." Not a day went by that she didn't miss him.

"I never want to go back to our ranch."

Softly she offered, "But you will. You're that kind of son." It was one of the reasons she admired him so.

They didn't speak on their return drive. Lucie could see some of Chase's excess energy had subsided. He was definitely calmer and not in as much of a hurry. Eventually they pulled up at the barn at the Bar P.

Lucie said, "I'll come inside with you, just to make sure everything's okay."

Chase wrapped his arm around her, pulled her in for a tight hug and then let go.

They climbed out of the truck and met at the back. They didn't hold hands as they walked up to the house. In fact, in some ways, she felt more separated from him— maybe because they were both confused, maybe because too much was happening at once.

Chase's mom met them in the living room. It was obvious to see she'd been crying. Lucie saw the guilty look on Chase's face and then he masked it.

Florence wasn't accusatory when she said, "Warren told me what happened, and he's in his den. Chase, I did *not* know about the letters. Please believe me."

Lucie could see that Florence was afraid Chase would pull away from her, too. He would associate his dad with his mom and think of them as a unit that had tried to destroy his happiness.

But apparently Chase could easily see that she was telling the truth. "I believe you, Mom."

"Please don't let this put a permanent wedge between you and your dad."

"I don't know how it won't."

Lucie lightly touched Florence's arm. "I think the two of you should talk this out. I need to get back."

"I'll walk you out and make sure you get on your way safely," Chase said firmly.

He did that without reaching for her, without touching her, without kissing her.

At her car, he suggested, "You call me once you're back inside your apartment. I want to know you're safe."

"I'll call," she agreed without protest, not only to ease

his mind, but to ease hers, too. Maybe by the time she called, he'd know how to proceed with his parents. She meant what she'd said to him about making things right with his father. You never knew how long you had someone you loved. Chase would deeply regret that he didn't fix this if something happened to his father. The time was now.

On the way back to Austin, Lucie was determined not to let happen what had happened the other night—getting distracted while driving. She kept her concentration on the road, not on Chase. The traffic wasn't light, but it also wasn't so heavy that she'd feel insecure driving. She was exhausted, though. The day of sun and music and walking, the night of emotion that had blown up in their faces, had worn her out. She was sure Chase was tired, too.

She traveled up the ramp into the parking garage and around the first level into the second, then pulled into her assigned space. It was about twenty car slots down from the elevator. She'd walked it many times and wasn't the least bit nervous about it. Tonight, though, she suddenly stopped walking.

Had she heard footsteps behind her?

She listened. She heard nothing. She was becoming paranoid.

She hurried to the bank of elevators, nodded to the security guard, entered the car, then took the elevator to her floor. Once inside her apartment, she went to her sofa and sank down on it. She pulled her phone from her pocket and dialed Chase. He answered immediately.

"How are you?" she asked.

"Shell-shocked," he answered succinctly.

Just how much had their lovemaking contributed to that?

"How's your dad?"

"I haven't talked to him, but Mom checked on him. She even took his blood pressure. He seems okay. I don't know when we'll hash things out."

"Chase, do it soon, for your sake, as well as his. Don't let this fester. It will only make the situation worse."

"I don't see how it can be much worse. He wants to control my life, and I'm not going to let him. One of us has to win."

"Instead of winning, instead of trying to be right, can't each of you find what will make you happy?"

"Not if we don't agree on what happiness is. Lucie, this isn't your battle. I'm sorry you got mixed up in it."

Was that a dismissal? Was that an I-don't-want-to-think-about-this-anymore end to the conversation?

They were both exhausted, and that had to factor in.

"Chase, try to get a good night's sleep. That will help. Things have to look better in the morning."

"No, they don't have to. But someone like you always thinks they will. It's just another reason I like you, Lucie. I had a great time today, and it's not something I'll soon forget. I hope you enjoyed the day, too."

"I did."

They could talk about the day, but not about what had happened in the pickup truck. Their silence became the end of their conversation. Chase said, "Good night. Take care of yourself."

"You, too."

He ended the call.

There was no talk about seeing each other again, no talk about further conversation. She'd have to see him to sign the annulment papers, wouldn't she?

Time would tell.

She made herself get up from the sofa, take a shower and go to bed.

Everything would look better in the morning; she was sure of it.

Wasn't she?

Chapter Nine

Lucie had finally found the perfect office space Saturday morning, filled in all the details and had all the paperwork sent to Emmett Jamison at the Fortune Foundation headquarters. She would help him set up the office quickly so that the funding could flow. To celebrate, she'd called Ella and was meeting her at an out-of-the-way but excellent deli for lunch. Ella arrived first, and happily waved when Lucie walked in. Her friend had chosen a back-corner table where they'd be pretty much out of sight. It was early for the lunch crowd, so the deli was quiet enough for them to have a decent conversation.

Lucie plopped her purse on the table and said, "I want the works today. Barbecued pork club, cheese fries and sweet peach tea. I'm forgetting the salad in celebration."

Ella laughed. "A job well done. From what you described, this space sounds perfect."

"Two main closed-door offices and plenty of room for cubicles," Lucie added. "Now all they need are more programs to funnel the funds to. I'll be on the lookout for those while I'm still here."

"Now that that task is off your shoulders, tell me what's been filling your time. You said you wanted to talk to me about it. I get the feeling it's a *who*, not a *what*."

"How could you know that?"

"I know women, and I'm getting to know you. It's the sound of your voice. I'm right, aren't I?"

Lucie had told Ella she wanted to discuss something personal with her. She could talk to Amelia, but their snatches of time were so limited that she'd decided to confide in Ella.

"There's a man from my past who's been a secret for ten years."

Ella's eyes widened. "Give me the details."

So Lucie did.

Ella listened intently, not interrupting even once. By the time Lucie was finished, she was surprised she almost felt like crying. Because she didn't know what to do next?

"So your pickup-truck interlude yesterday—was that serious for him, too?"

"I don't know. He was in such turmoil about what his dad did."

"Don't you feel betrayed, too?"

"I feel manipulated, but his father did that from the beginning, so intercepting the letters doesn't come as a huge surprise. If I'd been sure of my relationship with Chase, if I'd been older, I might have flown back here to Texas to see him. But I didn't and he didn't. Neither of us acted."

"And you take that as a sign you weren't meant to be together?"

"Not then," Lucie admitted.

"But you two are headed in different directions now." Ella could see the obvious problems.

"We are, but maybe I shouldn't keep thinking about what my mother expects from me and my responsibilities. Maybe I should think about how I feel."

"Seeing what I've just been through, I think you should take any risk for love. Would you consider settling in Austin permanently, stopping your work, maybe finding something as important to do here?"

"It's a lot to think about," Lucie said, confused by it all. "I suppose I'll figure it out eventually." She sighed. "There's no solution now, so let's talk about something else. Is Ben still on his hunt for other Fortune relatives?"

"Actually something sort of monumental happened."

"Tell me," Lucie coaxed.

"Ben went to meet with Jacqueline Fortune, Gerald Robinson's mother."

"What did he discover?"

Ella shook her head and frowned. "Unfortunately the woman is in a nursing home and suffers from dementia. When she heard the name Jerome Fortune, she started yelling, 'There is no Jerome Fortune. Jerome Fortune is dead.'"

"Oh, my goodness. Ben must have been so disappointed," Lucie sympathized.

"He's not stopping there. He believes there's more to the story. He's working with Keaton to get more information."

"So Keaton's in the area?"

"Actually he's in Austin. Why?"

"I have a charity event to attend and I need an escort. Of course, I wish Chase could take me, but that's not possible, not without everything splattering all over the tabloids and newspapers and cable channels. But since Keaton's here, maybe he'll escort me."

"Go ahead and give him a call now. I'll go place our orders. It's not like I can forget what you want for lunch."

Lucie laughed and pulled out her phone. Checking her contacts, she found Keaton's number, not expecting him to answer. But he did.

"Keaton, this is Lucie Fortune Chesterfield."

"I heard you're in Austin finding space for the Fortune Foundation's new office."

"I've accomplished that. How are *you* doing? I heard that you just started a job at a brand-new firm that only handles the most prestigious projects. Is that fact or fiction?"

"It's fact," he responded. "I'm just taking a break before I start."

"I'm glad you're in Austin. I have a favor. Can you take me to the Museum of Plein Air Artists' fundraising gala tomorrow night? Are you possibly free?"

"Of course I'm free for you. I don't have an active social calendar right now."

"Do you want me to text you the details?" Lucie asked.

"That sounds good. Do you want to meet there or do you want me to pick you up?"

"Do you mind the publicity if you pick me up?"

"Not at all. We'll be seen together at the gala, and I'm sure there will be photos, maybe TV coverage. We might as well go all out."

"Thank you, Keaton."

"Anytime. I usually have my phone on, so text me whenever you want."

When Lucie ended the call, she felt…odd. Her date—if you could call it that—with Keaton would help cover up what was going on with her and Chase. She was debating with herself about how she should tell her mother the whole story. But her mum was out of cell phone contact again and she'd said she'd call when she was back in civilization.

Lucie was beginning to hope that would be sooner rather than later.

Back at the apartment, Lucie was worried about Chase and his dad, about the annulment, about everything. She only knew one way to appease some of her worry. Picking up her cell phone, she went to her contact list and pressed Call for Chase's cell phone number. He answered on the first ring.

"How are you?" he asked, forgetting about small talk.

"I'm good. How are *you*?"

Evading her question, he responded, "I'm getting ready to leave for Masey's Horse Auction Center. Would you like to come along?"

"Where is it?"

"About a half hour from here. I can pick you up, you can come to the ranch, or I can meet you there."

She thought about the implications of all three choices. "Will you be there long?"

"Probably a few hours."

She considered being followed and what she could do to prevent that. If she used her driver, that car was a definite target. She might be better off in the rental again.

"I'll meet you at the auction house. Does that work for you?"

He gave her the address. "That works just fine. Are you thinking you can make sure you're not followed?"

"Exactly."

"And you feel comfortable driving there?"

"Chase, stop being protective. I'm fine. I only got into trouble the other day because of the rain and the potholes and…our argument. I'm not distracted now and today's a sunny day. I'll text you when I arrive at the auction house and you can text back where to meet me."

"Sounds good."

An hour and a half later, her wig in place, her jeans hugging her hips and legs and an oversize green T-shirt completing the ensemble, Lucie parked on the gravel parking lot of the auction house. She texted Chase and he wrote back that she should meet him at the snack cart right outside the main entrance.

I'm wearing my wig, she told him in a return message. He sent her back the thumbs-up sign, and she smiled.

She doubted he'd be wearing his mustache and sunglasses. If they ran into somebody he knew, he could introduce her as his new girlfriend or as a long-lost relative. She'd worn a lot more makeup than she usually did, outlined her lips a little more. Her wig and her clothes should throw anybody off her trail. She'd made sure she wasn't followed to the auction house by taking a winding route.

Lucie couldn't believe how happy she was to see Chase when she spotted him. She found herself wanting to run to him, to be held in his arms. But she couldn't do that. She considered what she *could* do. *Could* she have an affair with him during the time she had left in Texas?

As he gazed down at her with one of those Chase

smiles, she thought it was a definite possibility. Her head was telling her one thing—*No, no, no*—but her heart was telling her another—*Yes, yes, yes.*

"Come on," he said. "I really shouldn't buy any horses today with everything in flux, but there's one I'm going to bid on. She's pregnant."

He looked absolutely excited by the idea. This really was his passion.

He went right up to the barricade and gestured to a beautiful bay with an almost black mane. She was dusty and looked as if she needed more than one good meal.

Chase obviously understood that, because he assured Lucie, "She'll be a beauty when she's taken care of."

Looking over the horses, Lucie wished she could bid on one or two herself. They all needed care and gentle hands and love.

She touched Chase's arm. "I could sign on the dotted line for you right now. You could get the loan and buy the ranch."

He shook his head. "Word would get out, you know it would. Our marriage would be public. We'd have to explain not only that, but the annulment, too. It would be a nightmare. But thank you for the thought."

He wasn't even questioning that they were getting an annulment. She shouldn't be either. Didn't they both want to start over with a blank slate?

But at some point in her life, she wished she could just throw up her hands and not care what anyone said or thought, not care about what was printed or recorded, not care about rumors and innuendos and the public peeking in behind closed blinds. Would that happen when she was fifty, sixty or seventy…eighty or ninety? Could it ever happen?

She hadn't been raised not to care, and that was the problem. She always thought about her family and how what she did would reflect on them. Obviously Chase cared about his family, too. He wouldn't have stayed at the ranch after his dad's stroke if he didn't. He wouldn't listen to his mother's worries if he didn't. That was why she wondered what would happen now that his father knew he wanted to leave not only the ranch, but Parker Oil.

As they walked over to the bleachers to take a seat for the auction, they settled next to each other on the hard bench. Her leg fell beside his and she didn't move away. Neither did he. Pictures played in her head—legs against legs, his chest against her breasts, his mouth on hers. When she cut him a glance, he was looking at her, and she knew he was remembering, too. So she talked about what had led to what happened between them.

She'd leaned in close to him, and almost spoke into his ear. "Have you ironed out everything with your dad?"

When Chase shook his head, she wanted to run her hand over the strong line of his jaw and ease the creases from around his eyes. But they were in public, and even though she wore a disguise, it would be a foolish thing to do.

"I can't talk to him, Lucie. I'm still so angry about what he did. And he's made no move to talk to me. There's a silent wall between us now. He went into work today and I didn't. I gave Jeff instructions about everything that had to be done. He's going to deal with Dad today, whether Dad likes it or not."

"But you could act as a buffer. You could ease the way for their relationship."

"That's what I intended, and yes, I could. But do you think Dad's going to let me? He's going to bluster and yell until he has everyone in a tizzy. On Monday, I'll go in and talk to Jeff and see what can be done about the whole situation. But I'm beginning to think that the sooner I leave, the better. The sooner I move out, the better."

And that meant, the faster the annulment happened, the faster Chase could get his life back on track.

"Since you found an office for the Fortunes, what else are you going to be doing?" he asked her.

"I'm supervising the setup. I've chosen the computers and they're going to be delivered next week. Painters are coming in, too. Everything's going to be a light robin's-egg blue and yellow, both soothing and enlivening, don't you think?"

"So now you're a decorator?" he asked with a grin.

"I wear many hats," she assured him. "I'm wearing my fundraiser hat this week. There's a charity gala I'm going to tomorrow evening. The Museum of Plein Air Artists wants to fund a children's wing. Art programs are being cut in schools and this could be a benefit for children's education."

"Art and music aren't just extra subjects that can be tossed by the wayside," Chase agreed.

"No, they can't."

They were quiet for a few minutes as they watched all the activity, the bidders filing in and out of the bleachers, the horses milling about the pens, the desk where the winners of the auction could pay up.

"Is this gala a black-tie-and-ball-gown type of occasion?" Chase asked, looking straight ahead as if he weren't really interested in the conversation.

"It is," she said simply.

"Are you going alone?"

Was that the basis of his question in the first place?

She hesitated a moment but then told him the truth. "No, I'm not going alone. Keaton Whitfield is taking me. He's an architect I know from London. He's in Austin now on family business. I needed an escort and he agreed to be it."

"How old is he?"

"He's in his thirties. Why?"

"No reason."

But Lucie knew there was. She nudged his elbow. "Why are you asking?"

"Maybe I'd hoped he was sixty and bald."

He hadn't looked at her when he said it, and maybe she was supposed to take it as a joke. But she could take it another way, too. Maybe Chase was jealous.

He said, "After the auction, I'll be taking the horse home with me in the trailer. Do you want to come back to the ranch?"

Could she have an affair with Chase? she asked herself again. Could she throw caution to the wind? The more they were together, the more likely it was someone would let something slip or someone would find out.

"I don't think that's a good idea, on several levels. I don't want to make things worse between you and your dad. My presence on his ranch would do that. You know it would."

"My mother would welcome you."

"She wants what's best for your father, too. And, Chase, seeing each other again… It's not a good idea, is it? I mean, even today is a risk. Yes, I'm disguised. But if someone looked really hard at me and then at you, they'd learn our secret."

The secret that she was falling in love with him again?

Her secret that maybe she didn't think an annulment was the best way to go?

Possibly all of the above.

"You're right," Chase said. "Maybe we are being foolish."

The bidding was about to start, and Lucie was glad of that. They couldn't talk their way out of this situation. Discussing it every which way wasn't going to help.

She didn't know what would. Because going their separate ways just seemed like a mistake.

Chase glanced at the news clip on the big-screen TV for the second time that evening. It had run fifteen minutes earlier at the top of the program. The charity fundraiser at the museum with its glitz and glamour had been a good way to capture the interest of the audience. It had sure captured his, especially when he'd seen someone push a microphone in front of Lucie's face. The thing was, it wasn't only Lucie who had caught his attention. It was the man beside her, his arm linked in hers. This Keaton Whitfield she'd spoken of was tall with dark brown hair. He was a good-looking guy. When the camera zoomed in, Chase could see he had blue eyes any woman might go for.

Lucie had looked beautiful in a black sequined gown, her hair shiny and sleek. She was *so* beautiful. She hadn't seemed at all awkward with Whitfield, and they'd looked like a couple.

Chase had been pacing for the past fifteen minutes with an idea bouncing around in his head. Probably not the best-framed idea he'd ever had, but one he was going to act on. Lucie wanted to be wise about seeing him. He could be wise about seeing her.

Had Lucie gone home with Keaton Whitfield? Had the night been more than a convenient date?

He dialed her cell.

"Chase! Hi. I just got in."

"Is Mr. Whitfield there with you?"

Maybe taken aback by the blunt question, she didn't answer for a moment. But then she responded, "No. He walked me to my door and then he left. Why?"

He wasn't going to explain the thumping jealousy he'd felt. He wasn't going to make excuses either.

"I want to see you, and we don't have to be foolish about it. It just takes a little planning. How about if I come over for a nightcap? I'll use the parking garage and the service elevator. No one will notice me."

After a few seconds' hesitation, she said, "I can make sure the security guard sends you right up. Are you hungry? I didn't have much for supper and I'm ravenous. I was going to make an omelet."

"I never turn down food," he said with a smile in his voice. "I'll be there in a half hour."

"That'll give me time to change into something more comfortable." As if she realized what she'd said, she went on. "I mean, I don't want to sit around in this sequined gown while we have omelets."

"I'll keep that in mind," he responded ambiguously, thinking about himself unzipping her gown, thinking about the garments she might be wearing underneath, thinking about Lucie naked.

Chase nodded to the guard at the elevator after he'd arrived at Lucie's apartment and parked. Lucie must have given the guard his description, because he nodded, yet still asked for ID. After Chase flashed his driver's license, the guard tipped the bill of his cap and said, "Have a good night, sir."

Chase didn't know what this night was going to bring. He just knew he wanted to spend time with Lucie.

He rang her doorbell and when she answered, she was dressed in a swirling multicolored garment with a scooped neck, winglike sleeves and a length that went to her ankles. It had all the colors of the rainbow. Her lipstick still looked fresh, her eyelashes long with mascara, her brown hair as silky as it had looked on TV. But she wasn't on TV. She was right in front of him.

He reached out and tapped the sparkling, dangling earring at her ear. "I saw you on TV. You looked beautiful tonight."

She put her hand to the earring. "Oops, I forgot to take these off. It's fun to get all dressed up and act like a princess once in a while."

He followed her inside the apartment as she removed the earrings. "Go into the kitchen. I'll be right in."

When she came back, he asked, "Those were diamonds?"

"Yes, a gift from my father. I wear them whenever I can."

So she didn't just like wearing jewels. She liked wearing jewels with memories, or maybe anything with memories. He was still learning facets of her personality.

In a glance, he'd taken in the frying pan on the stove, the bowl with what looked like whipped eggs, the chopped pepper and tomatoes and onion.

"How about ham pieces in with all the rest?" she asked, motioning toward the ingredients.

"Are you telling me you know how to cook?"

"Of course I do."

"Haven't you always had servants?"

"We have, but they didn't keep me out of the kitchen. After all, don't you know I'm well-rounded?"

As soon as she said the words, she blushed, and Chase couldn't help taking advantage of the moment. He took off his Stetson and tossed it to the table. Then he closed in on her, his hands teasingly sweeping down her shoulders, down her arms to her waist and then over her hips. At her hips, he stopped, his hands moving the silky material of the caftan and slipping around the back.

"Well-rounded, huh? Everything happened so fast the other night, I couldn't even tell."

She stood perfectly still, and he wasn't sure what she was going to do. Pull away? Push him away? Run? But maybe accepting the inevitability of what they had between them, she didn't do any of those.

All she said was "Chase" in a way that made his blood run hot and his sexual hunger for her increase. The sparkle in her eyes said she was ready for his kiss and whatever came after. After all, she wouldn't have invited him to come over if she didn't have the same thing in mind that he did.

Still, he wanted to make sure. When he kissed her, he caressed her back and rocked her hips into his. It was obvious what he wanted. Did she want it, too?

She pressed against him, chased his tongue into his mouth, and moaned deep in her throat.

He wanted to yank her silky garment off her, but he wouldn't resort to caveman tactics. No, he was a civilized man, right?

His hand went to the zipper at her neckline. He slowly pulled it down, metal on metal, making a sound that was obvious in its purpose. When he reached her waist, she did push against him then, and he thought maybe the night was over.

Smiling, she wiggled her arms and the fabric fell, leaving nothing to his imagination. She'd been naked under the gown and she wanted him to know it. He hadn't been alone in what he wanted for tonight. Apparently she was with him all the way. He cupped her breasts and bent his head to one of them. She cried out when his tongue circled her nipple…when he teased it and then seriously kissed it. She hung on to him as if he was everything she'd ever desired.

Scooping her up into his arms, he carried her through the living room into her bedroom.

After he gently laid her on the bed, she looked at him and teased, "You're overdressed."

While he shucked off his clothes, she pulled back the covers. Soon they were entwined on the high-thread-count sheets, kissing and touching, remembering and making new memories. Chase took it slower than he had done in the pickup truck. He wanted to give her as much plea-sure as he could. From her sounds and her smiles and her kisses, he knew he did.

He left her for only a few moments to reach into his pants pocket for the condom. She helped him roll it on, and he felt as if his whole universe was in her eyes. As he entered her, he was electrified, excited, consumed by passion. With Lucie he felt ten feet tall, strong, a master of the universe. She clung to him and he held on to her, never wanting the moment to end.

Chapter Ten

The sound of her doorbell woke Lucie and she had trouble orienting herself. She was wrapped in Chase's arms! But she was in her bed.

Why was the doorbell ringing without Irv buzzing her first? Or had he done so and she hadn't heard?

No, he wouldn't have just sent someone up.

Last night with Chase had been…exquisite. She couldn't think about the repercussions from it now, not with someone at her door, and not with Chase still in her bed.

"What do you want me to do?" Chase asked, his deep baritone in her ear. He was already alert and thinking about their compromising situation.

"Just stay here. Leave the door open a crack so you can hear who it is. I can't imagine Irv wouldn't have buzzed me first."

The doorbell rang again.

She quickly extricated herself from Chase's arms, grabbed her robe, slipped it on and belted it and then remembered she was wearing nothing underneath. That wouldn't do.

She quickly shucked it off, pulled on a nightgown from her closet, slipped her robe on top of that and belted it. So much for fashion. Nothing matched.

When she went to the door and peered through the peephole, she gasped. It was her *mother*.

She tossed a glance over her shoulder and called to Chase, "It's my mum. There won't be any hiding you, so you might as well get dressed and come out. I have to explain all this sometime anyway."

Then she threw open the door, happy to see her mother no matter what the circumstances.

Josephine Fortune Chesterfield took one look at Lucie and her eyebrows arched. "Give me a hug before you explain to me what's going on."

"How do you know something's going on?" She hugged her mother and then pulled away, trying to fortify herself for this explanation.

"Because you never come to the door looking like this!"

Lucie sighed. No, she didn't. She always made sure she looked properly royal first!

Just then, Chase emerged from the bedroom. He didn't hesitate to come forward and extend his hand. "Lady Fortune Chesterfield, I'm Chase Parker."

It only took a few seconds for Lucie's mother, who had a memory that could rival any genius's, to make a connection. "You couldn't be *the* Chase Parker from ten years ago, the one who sullied my daughter's reputation?"

Again Chase didn't hesitate. "Yes, I'm that one."

Josephine looked from her daughter to Chase and then back to Lucie again. "I think you'd better get dressed and make a pot of tea."

Chase laid a hand on Lucie's shoulder, and she remembered everything they'd done last night. He asked, "Do you want me to stay or go?"

Lucie studied her mother's expression, which was cautiously patient. All the feelings Lucie had experienced last night when she and Chase made love, slept and then made love again were careening around inside her. It was really hard to think straight. Having Chase here while she was trying to explain would cause even more turmoil and be even more confusing.

She dredged up a smile for him and suggested, "Why don't you go? I know you have to get to work."

He looked as if he wanted to take her in his arms again. He looked as if he wanted to kiss her. Yes, she wanted to kiss him, but certainly not now in front of her mother. Certainly not now, when everything was so mixed up.

Were they having an affair? Where was that going to go?

Chase went to the kitchen for his hat, which was still on the table there. Returning to the living room, he said, "It was good to meet you, Lady Fortune Chesterfield."

"Good to meet you, too, I think," Lucie's mother said politely, without a hint of a smile.

Then Chase was leaving. But Lucie wanted to pull him back inside.

However, after he closed the door, she faced her mother. "I have so much to tell you."

Her mother stared into the kitchen where all the dishes

and vegetables were still splayed across the counter from last night. She waved at it. "Your dinner was interrupted last night?"

"It wasn't dinner. It was a late-night snack. Keaton took me to a charity function and brought me home, and then Chase came over and we were both hungry—"

She was rambling and getting all tangled up in events.

Although her mother was wearing a casual, pale blue pantsuit, she said to Lucie, "Go get dressed. I'll start cleaning this up."

"You don't have to do that."

Josephine waved her away.

Lucie blew out a breath and headed for her bedroom.

Ten minutes later, she was back in the kitchen with her mother. Her mum had started the teapot on the burner.

"You didn't have to straighten up," she said, noticing even the counters were empty and cleaned off.

"No problem. I like to be useful. You know that."

Lucie pulled two cups and saucers from the cupboard and set them on the table. "Are you hungry? I can whip up something."

"I take it you didn't have your breakfast?" her mother asked with a wise look.

"No, not yet."

"Then by all means, you have something."

"Why didn't you tell me you were flying in?"

"Because I wasn't sure when or where I'd be in. I did send you a text when I landed late last night."

Lucie's phone was somewhere around here, but she didn't know where, and she certainly hadn't heard it. "Mum, I'm sorry. You probably wondered what was wrong when I didn't text back."

"Yes, I was a bit concerned, and that's what I told your

doorman, Irv. Apparently he knew who I was from the tabloids, and when I showed him ID, he was definitely certain of that. He didn't even hesitate to let me come up. Was I wrong to do that, Lucie?"

Her mother was giving her a probing look, and Lucie felt like a teenager again. "No, you weren't wrong. Chase and I... That was the first night he stayed."

The teapot whistled and Josephine crossed to the stove and took it from the burner.

"I only have teabags," Lucie told her mother, "but they're herbal."

Again Josephine just gave her an arched eyebrow. "You really haven't moved in, have you?"

"I knew I'd only be here temporarily."

Her mother nodded. "Yes, that is the plan. Now, why don't you start at the beginning?"

Lucie closed her eyes for a moment, her throat tightening with emotion. The beginning seemed like yesterday, yet so far away, too. She began with falling in love with Chase in Scotland, their days of touring and talking... their attraction. Finally with difficulty, she described marrying him and what had happened afterward.

She'd never seen such surprise on her mother's face as Josephine asked, "Why didn't you tell me? All these years and you've kept it to yourself? Didn't anyone else know? Does Amelia know?"

"No, no one knew. That was the agreement I had with Chase's father. He would dissolve the marriage and we'd act as if it never happened. He would get his son back on the track he'd planned for him, and I wouldn't have a scandal. You wouldn't have a scandal. He hushed up everything at the school about what happened and you hushed it up at home. You told the press I had the flu and cut the trip short. Just imagine the splash if they'd known I'd married. So I kept to the agreement with Mr. Parker and all went as smoothly as it could."

"You were the one who always played by the rules," her mother said, studying her. "Your father and I were shocked when you were sent home in disgrace. I thought the travel program somehow managed to keep it all quiet. I see now Chase's father had a hand in that."

"I'm so sorry I didn't tell you. I thought keeping the secret was for the best. I had been so foolish. I loved Chase, at least I thought I did, but I was too young to know what love and commitment were. That episode, my confrontation with his father, all of it taught me to always control my emotions, never act impulsively. It brought home the truth that I should think about the big picture, not just my part in it. I thought I was doing what was best for everyone." Her voice caught because she realized how much her mother might be hurt by being left out of the loop.

After a deep breath, she went on to explain to her mother how Chase's father had intercepted her letters to Chase and his to her.

Her mother shook her head and frowned as Lucie ended. "Mr. Parker probably thought he was doing the best thing for everyone, too. *He* was looking at the big picture," Lucie said as she finished.

"That's all well and good, Lucie, but sometimes truth is better than a good public relations spin. Sometimes truth can be liberating. If Chase Parker was here all night, it sounds as if old feelings are all stirred up. What are you going to do about that? You have responsibilities. You have a life of traveling to help the greater world. Certainly you're not thinking of giving that up."

Was she? Without knowing exactly how Chase felt? She did have responsibilities that couldn't easily be delegated. After all, she was Sir Simon Chesterfield's daughter. However, she responded honestly, "I don't know. The lawyers are going through with the annulment."

Her mother reached across and took her hand. "Lawyers, annulment, a marriage that was too early to take hold. The feeling in our hearts can't be dictated by lawyers or due process. You made a foolish decision ten years ago, but you have to be careful you don't make another one now. You have a lot to think about because you have a lot of responsibilities. I depend on you, Lucie. You know that."

Yes, she was the dependable one. She was her mother's confidante, sidekick, helper. Chase was starting a new life. That ranch would take his attention night and day.

Trying to shake off last night's hold on her heart, as well as the vivid, sensual memories from it, she remembered who she was and what her life and her mother's was all about. Just what part did the feelings in her heart play in this?

She couldn't let her mother down, not for a romance that might not have any place to go. "I'll be flying off to Guatemala in less than two weeks. The annulment is going to go through any day. I'll be keeping my commitments, Mum."

Yet Lucie's heart felt as if it was breaking. Leave Chase? It was the wisest path to take. Yet it didn't feel wise at all.

After spending the day with Lucie, her mother had left for Horseback Hollow and her condo there. Lucie felt drained. They had spent a good portion of their time together going over plans for their Guatemala trip and the to-do list once they were there.

Lucie had cooked them dinner and then her mother had left, her driver picking her up out front. Lucie had accompanied her downstairs to say goodbye and had no sooner returned to her apartment than her cell phone beeped.

She saw the caller was Florence Parker.

"Hi, Florence. How are you?" Lucie asked conversationally, but not feeling like engaging at all.

"I'm fine. I have a favor to ask."

Lucie braced herself for whatever was coming. She hoped it had nothing to do with Chase, or her resolve to resume her regular life would weaken.

"Reverend Stanhope didn't want to impose on you himself, but I told him I'd call you. He'd like you to attend Family Day at the church on Saturday. You can meet the parents of the children you're helping with the after-school program."

There was no reason she couldn't do this for the church, and for the Fortune Foundation, as well. Except…"

"Will Chase be there?"

"Probably."

"If he attends, we'll have to pretend we don't know each other."

"I'm sure he understands that," Florence said.

"I'd call him," Lucie responded, "but I'm not even sure our cell phones are secure." Her mother had brought up that point, and she was right.

"I understand, Lucie. Really, I do. And I'm sure Chase does, too. Don't worry. I'll make your wishes clear to him."

Lucie just wished her wishes were clear to herself.

* * *

Had a reporter like Norton Wilcox followed Lucie to Family Day at the church, all he would see would be her enjoying the day with children and their parents. He might be able to dig up the fact that the Fortune Foundation would be funding the church's after-school program, but that was it.

When Chase's mom had called her, asking her to come to this event today, Florence understood full well that Lucie couldn't be associated with her or Chase in the public's eye. Lucie was the Fortune Foundation's representative, and she'd be attending on those grounds. She'd stay only a short time and if anyone recognized her, she'd simply wear her busy public persona.

Simple. Besides, if anyone did do a story about this, more programs that needed help would come forward and the foundation could select where the money would be best spent.

Win-win all around.

At least that was what she thought until she spotted Chase in jeans and a T-shirt, his Stetson tilted at that just-right angle, hauling hay bales onto a wagon. She imagined the minister needed help with all sorts of things, and Chase could provide strong manpower.

She attempted to keep her distance from him at every turn. She avoided eye contact with him. There were a few awkward moments when she ran into Chase's mother and father and she made polite small talk. "Isn't this a wonderful event? It's a beautiful day. Have a great time." Then she moved on.

No one seemed to recognize her, because she was out of her element. She was wearing jeans and an oversize blouse. She wasn't on the Chesterfield Estate. She wasn't in a foreign country building an orphanage. She wasn't dressed in a gown as she had been for the gala. She was trying to be just Lucie for a short while and get away with it. She was fine, really, she was, until one of the mothers recognized her.

With a wide smile, the woman rushed over to her and said, "You're Lucie Fortune Chesterfield, aren't you?"

Lucie put her finger to her lips. "I've tried to keep that under wraps, but yes, I am."

"I heard the Fortune Foundation was investing in our after-school program and I put two and two together. I knew you looked familiar."

Lucie gave her a conspiratorial smile. "I'd like to keep everyone else from doing that. The attention today is on parents and their children, and I'd like to keep it that way."

"Oh, I understand completely, except…could I bribe you to sit next to me on the hay ride? I promise I won't tell a soul, but at least I can say I sat next to Lady Fortune Chesterfield."

Lucie didn't want to make a scene. She didn't want to prolong the conversation. On a hay ride, children would be scurrying about and their parents would be focused on having them behave. No one would be looking at her.

"It's about to take off again." The woman motioned to the hay wagon. "Come on, please?"

Lucie couldn't say no. She followed the mom over to the hay wagon, but then stopped cold. Chase was climbing in. He sat on a hay bale with a small child beside him. The boy must have been about four. When their gazes met, he gave her a shrug and a *what can I do?* look. Maybe Chase was watching the little boy for his parents.

What could *she* do?

The woman hopped into the wagon in front of her and motioned to one of the large bales, where the two of them could sit side by side. The problem was, it was right next to Chase. She was getting a headache...or maybe a heartache.

The hay wagon soon filled up with kids as well as adults. As Lucie had predicted, the adults were busy keeping the children in line. No one paid any attention to her, except the woman on the bale next to her. She chatted, "I've seen your estate on TV." In a lower voice, she said, "Does it really have stables and everything?"

"It does," Lucie assured her. "I learned to ride when I was small."

Her gaze met Chase's again, and just that contact rocked her. Anybody watching them could feel the electricity between them. She quickly directed her attention to the small child across from her who was trying to scramble into his mom's lap.

When her phone buzzed, she wasn't going to answer it. But she decided any distraction would help. As the wagon bumped along, it jostled her and the woman beside her, making the kids giggle, making her even more aware of Chase.

She slipped out her phone. The text was from Chase. This is ridiculous!

She quickly texted back, This is the way it has to be.

She didn't look at him. She didn't dare. She just hoped this was going to be one short hay ride.

Florence Parker had convinced her husband to attend the church's Family Day. Since his argument with Chase, he'd been sullen and in a bear of a mood. But she was hoping today would change that.

They'd each picked up slices of homemade apple pie and carried them to a picnic table set in the shade. The hay wagon was just returning from another run. She'd been so glad to see Lucie climbing on when Chase was already on it. Serendipity?

She hoped so.

"They're pretending not to know each other, and that's fine as long as they don't look at each other," she said as she cut off a bite of pie with her fork.

"It's the stupidest thing I've ever heard of," Warren said. "But what else can they do?" he muttered. "I don't think Chase would care about a scandal anymore, but *she* certainly would. Her family's hoity-toity with their fox-hunts, royalty for guests and highfalutin parties."

"You don't know Lucie, Warren, you really don't. I've had a chance to spend a little time with her, and she's nothing like you suspect. I don't know why you had your mind set against her from the beginning, when you knew how Chase felt about her."

"How he felt about her," her husband scoffed. "He was too young to ruin his life with the wrong woman. They were an ocean apart. You know that never would have worked."

"He would have gone over there to live. You know he would have."

"And that's why I had to squelch it. Besides, she was too young to know her own mind."

"When she looks at him now, do you think she's too young to know her own mind?"

"She's not looking at him," Warren noted, as if he'd been watching their every move this afternoon, too.

"Every once in a while, they can't help glancing at

each other. Don't you remember when we looked at each other like that?"

Warren pushed his pie away as if he'd suddenly lost his appetite. Then he looked at her, really looked at Florence, as he hadn't in many weeks, maybe even months. "I'm not the man I once was. That's why we don't look at each other that way."

Was this what her husband had been thinking since his stroke? Was this the reason he didn't come close to her at night? Florence reached out and touched his hand with hers. "I still see you as the young man I married. I still look at you that way because I love you. You're the one who sees yourself differently. Is that why you can't let go of Chase, because you're afraid you'll need him again?"

Warren pulled his arm back, and she was afraid she'd erected a new barrier between them. But then he directed his focus toward the hay wagon. He watched Lucie jump off; then he saw Chase lifting a little boy onto the ground. When their son straightened, his gaze seemed to meet Lucie's. They were frozen, only for a moment. But as Chase's father, Warren seemed to recognize what that moment meant.

"Maybe I *am* afraid to let go of him," he murmured. "What if something happens to me and the company can't survive without him? What if I have another stroke and he's not here for you or here for me?" he murmured.

"We raised our son to be a caring man with a good heart. He wouldn't want to start the horse rescue ranch if he didn't have a good heart, if he didn't care. The fact that he still cares for Lucie after all these years tells you something about him, too. Just because he leaves the company, just because he tries to find his own life, doesn't mean he'll forget about us."

"What if he flies off to England to be with her?"

"If he's chosen the right woman, they'll figure it out, don't you think?"

"I planned his life. I separated them so he would find his full potential."

"He *is* finding his full potential, but in his way, not yours. If you don't let him go, Warren, he won't come back to us. I've come to realize that, and you have to, too."

She took his hand again and squeezed it. "We do love each other. And we've been happy, haven't we?"

"Those first years were rough, when the company wasn't doing well and we didn't have much. But yes, we've been happy."

"How can you deny Chase that?"

"You know I don't want to deny him anything. That's the whole problem. How can he find happiness with her when she's not even in the same country?"

"Her sister lives in Horseback Hollow with her rancher husband. Don't you think Lucie is made of the same kind of stuff?"

"They're pretending they don't know each other. Chase hasn't stopped the lawyer from proceeding with the annulment."

"Maybe that's because they're not listening to their hearts yet. Maybe the time's not right. But that's not for us to decide. Think about giving your son your blessing, would you?"

Warren sighed and pulled his pie back in front of him. "I'm sure you won't let me forget thinking about it."

Her husband's voice was resigned, but his mood seemed lighter.

Watching a child find his happiness could do that.

* * *

It was noon on Sunday when Chase tried to coax one of his rescue horses to eat from his hand. He wasn't having much luck. The horse could feel the tension oozing all around him, or the frustration. The situation with Lucie had him tied up in knots. Pretending not to know her yesterday had seemed like sheer stupidity.

When you gentle a horse, you have to be calm, he reminded himself. He wasn't calm. He'd wanted not only to talk to her yesterday, but to kiss her silly. Especially after they'd finished the ride on the hay wagon. But she'd disappeared, practically vanished into thin air. He'd texted her, but she hadn't texted back. That was her way of dealing with their situation. He had to be levelheaded about it and respect her wishes, but he didn't like being levelheaded, not after the night they'd spent together. He wanted a repeat. Didn't she?

His mother had reminded him conversations could be overheard on all phones for someone like Lucie. Who knew what devices were out there that a tech-smart press spy could use? With Lucie's mother in the country probably reminding her of her Chesterfield duty, her sister's fiasco not all that far behind her, Lucie was trying to be supercautious.

Chase heard the sound of tires on gravel and figured it was Tomás's truck. But after another attempt to feed the chestnut mare and getting nowhere, he heard a male voice determine, "She's not ready for that yet."

Chase spun around, and when he saw he had a visitor, he smiled, immediately left the fence and approached Graham Robinson, Ben's brother.

"I came to see how your plans are coming along," Graham explained.

Chase nodded to the doorway leading into the barn. "Let's go into my office in there, and we can talk about *your* plans, too."

Graham was six feet tall and every inch a cowboy. He wore his light brown hair short under his Stetson. Even though he was only thirty-two, the lines around his blue eyes told a story that had sobered the man because of an unfortunate teenage escapade. Graham's best friend had died in his arms when they were only teenagers. Graham's father, Gerald Robinson, hadn't been the best father, so Graham had sought out another role model, his best friend's dad. They'd helped each other through the grief, and now Graham was working with Roger Gibault on the Galloping G Ranch. The two men had developed the same dream and wanted to help troubled teenagers find their place in the world.

Once in the office, Chase sat behind the battered desk in an old-time wooden chair that creaked as he adjusted his weight in it.

Graham took a seat on the other side of the desk.

"It's been a while," Chase said. "Would you like a beer?"

"Sure," Graham agreed, and Chase pulled two from the small refrigerator back in the corner. He handed the long-necked bottle to Graham.

"I've been busy," Graham said. "Roger and I are trying to get the place in shape. We're remodeling a bunkhouse and thinking about adding a cabin or two. We're going to have kids coming in around June first and we want to be ready."

"Do you feel ready to handle troubled kids?"

"I once was one."

Chase nodded sagely, not pushing. He knew Graham would say what he wanted to say in his own time.

Graham removed his Stetson, ran his hand through his hair and plopped the hat back on his head. "Roger and I are consulting with a professional, too. We're smart enough to know there are a lot of things we don't know."

"Good idea," Chase agreed.

"How about you?" Graham asked. "I heard you're buying the old Schultz place. I thought maybe we could help you out, take a horse or two off your hands once they're ready to go to a good home. If kids have something to care about and care for, it helps. Gentling a horse could teach them a lot of life lessons."

"I have one or two now that you might be interested in. Maybe by June I'll have my ranch up and running, and we'll have more to choose from. I hit a roadblock that's stalled me."

"Something serious?"

The Galloping G wasn't that far from the Bar P. He and Graham had known each other for a long while. In fact, Graham was one of the few men he'd consider a friend, a friend he could trust. Maybe he could cope with the whole situation a lot easier if he could talk to someone about it.

"Can I trust you to keep what I tell you confidential?"

"You know you can," Graham assured him.

"I'm married. I have been for ten years and didn't know it. We both thought the marriage had been annulled, but it wasn't. When I tried to get a loan approved, I found out."

Graham gave a low whistle. "So this isn't just a business mess."

"No, it isn't. And to make matters worse, this woman

is in the public eye. If our marriage leaked out, it could cause a major scandal for us both."

"You've got to be kidding."

"Nope." Chase blew out a breath. "The marriage happened in Scotland. A lawyer's trying to get it resolved, but we have to keep everything quiet or there will be a scandal to end all scandals. I haven't been celibate and she was engaged."

Graham's gaze suddenly fell on the printout that lay on the corner of the desk. "Why are you printing out ads for engagement rings if you're seeking dissolution of your marriage?"

"It's complicated."

"Believe me, I understand complications."

There was a look in Graham's eyes that told Chase much was going on beneath the surface. But Graham would tell him what that was when he was ready.

Obviously not wanting to talk about himself, Graham asked perceptively, "Are you thinking about staying married?"

Chase shook his head. "It's an impossible situation. She's leaving Texas in a week. She has commitments. I can't ask her to stay to see what develops because her work's her life. Even if we could somehow compromise on that, if she gives up her present job, wouldn't she resent me for it?"

Graham took a long swig of his beer, then shook his head. "I never thought about getting married myself, and I can't see that ever happening. But I sure wish you luck whichever way it goes."

Chase suspected he needed a lot more than luck.

Chapter Eleven

Amelia's long dark hair swayed across her back as she cooed and rocked Clementine on Sunday evening. "Who's the cutest little girl in the whole wide world?"

Quinn Drummond, who claimed he was a small-town rancher who merely wanted a simple life, responded for his child. "*You* are, Clementine Rose Drummond, and no one else." His thick dark brown hair fell over his sun-tanned forehead as he said it, and his hazel eyes twinkled.

Clementine Rose wiggled and wiggled until her mama put her down. She toddled over to Lucie and held up her arms.

Lucie, of course, obliged, sweeping her off the floor. "So, what hotel are you staying at?"

Quinn answered, looking smug, "We're staying at the Dominion."

The Dominion was an old Austin hotel with lots of

history and a presidential suite and bridal suites that could rival any posh resort.

"I reserved the bridal suite for a mini second honeymoon," Quinn said, looking proud of himself. "I got a fine deal on it, too. An old friend from high school is in a management position now. This was last minute because they had a vacancy and a cancellation, and he wanted to fill it."

"Your bargain is my good luck," Lucie said, nuzzling Clementine. "We'll have a grand time here and you'll have a grand time there," she teased.

A look passed between Amelia and Quinn that said it all. They were still deliriously happy.

"Since Mum is back in Horseback Hollow, she offered to babysit." Amelia rooted in her purse. "But I told her you wanted to spend time with the baby, and we'd be back tomorrow night and she could see Clementine Rose all she wants then. She's catching up with Jeanne Marie and everybody else while we're out of town. She likes her place at the Cowboy Condos to have people in for an intimate conversation or to have a group party. She's much less stuffy than she used to be, don't you think?" Amelia asked Lucie.

Quinn came up behind Amelia and wrapped his arm around her shoulders. "You're much less stuffy than you used to be, don't you think, princess?"

She wrinkled her nose at him. How many times had her sister told Quinn she wasn't a princess? But he still treated her like one anyway.

He said now, "Amelia is a wonderful mother and doesn't take a break from Clementine, except to do chores. So now and then, I like to indulge us both."

"Taking care of Clementine and helping you make the

ranch succeed is what I intend to do with the rest of my life," Amelia assured him.

Clementine pulled on Lucie's hair and babbled. They all laughed.

"Are you ready to go?" Quinn asked Amelia.

"We have such little time to visit," she said to Lucie, handing her a sheet of paper. "This has all the emergency numbers. You have my cell and Quinn's, but this is the hotel number, too. And a pediatrician in Austin who I spoke with, just in case Clementine would need a doctor."

"Look at her," Lucie advised. "She's perfectly healthy. It's just going to be overnight. We'll be fine. I have all the food you brought for her in the refrigerator and on the counter. Quinn set up the crib in my bedroom and I have this cute little collapsible play set in here that she can nap in, too. I have the monitor set up in the bedroom so I can hear her if I'm in here and she's asleep. Her toys practically filled up her crib. She has enough clothes for the next three weeks."

Amelia brushed Lucie's conclusion away. "Don't exaggerate. Babies can go through three or four outfits a day. Just wait until you feed her. You might not only have to change her outfit. You'll have to change *yours*, too."

"You didn't put red beets in as part of her diet, did you?"

"They're an essential part. I gave you a variety of foods to use. I marked them breakfast, lunch and supper, and you can vary them."

Lucie checked with Quinn, "Does she plan this much with you, too?"

"She tries to, but most of the time, I get her to roll with the punches. Just go with the flow, Lucie, and you'll be fine. Clementine does have a fussy time, though. When she's like that, we just carry her around and try to entertain her, no matter when it is."

"I'll remember that. I have a couple of lullabies up my sleeve."

Quinn said to Amelia, "Time's a-wastin'."

Amelia gazed over at her baby daughter. "I want to be with you, but I hate leaving her."

"Call me whenever you'd like," Lucie said. "Or text me."

After waves all around and blown kisses, Amelia and Quinn left.

Lucie half expected them to pop back in, but they didn't.

Clementine toddled over to a stuffed toy Amelia had left for her on the sofa. She picked up the pink dog and gurgled at it. Just as Lucie was about to pick her up again—she loved holding her niece—her cell phone beeped. When she glanced at the screen she saw an unfamiliar number. She could let it go, but the call might have to do with her trip.

She answered. "Hello."

She was surprised to hear Chase's voice when he said, "I bought a burner phone that can't be traced. You should, too. I want to see you."

She thrilled at the words. But she was hesitant to repeat them back. If she and Chase kept up an affair, they were going to get hurt.

"I'm babysitting Clementine," she told Chase, regretful yet also, in some ways, appreciative for the excuse.

After a few moments of silence, he asked, "Does that mean you're tied up, or would you like a visitor?"

"You can visit if you're ready to babysit. Clementine

Rose needs all my attention." That type of dedication usually warded off men's attention.

"I've never been around babies," he admitted in a low voice.

She expected him to back off. Some men were downright afraid of babies because they considered them to be little alien creatures. You never knew what they were going to do next. Chase had been good with older children, but this was different.

However, this was Chase Parker, who didn't seem to know what backing off meant. "I'll borrow Tomás's truck so no one recognizes mine, and I'll sneak in the back way."

Lucie's heart sang a little that he was willing to join in her babysitting efforts. Or was he?

"Chase, I really meant it when I said Clementine needs all my focus. We can't—" She stopped, unable to put their passion into words. She had no doubts that if they were here alone, they'd be in each other's arms in her bed.

"I understand, Lucie, I do. And it's all right. I'll be there in a half hour."

Keeping to his word, Chase arrived precisely at her door a half hour later. She laughed when she opened the door to him. He was wearing a baseball cap instead of his Stetson, and he had that fake mustache pasted on above his lip again.

"You went all out," she joked.

"I did."

Once inside, he captured her shoulders and gave her a kiss on the forehead, his mustache tickling her skin. Then he leaned away and said, "Introduce me to Clementine."

Amelia and Quinn's little girl didn't seem to mind strangers, maybe because of the big family in Horseback

Hollow. She was used to many people fussing over her as if she were a little princess. She was too young to be really spoiled yet; Amelia and Quinn thought that was okay and so did Lucie. Children needed to know they were loved, and Clementine Rose did.

Chase took off the ball cap and tossed it to a nearby table. Then he peeled off the mustache and stuffed it in his pocket. "I'll let you see the real me," he teased as he approached Clementine.

"Have I seen the real you?" Lucie asked as Chase smiled and held out his hands to the little girl.

"You saw the real me on that country road after I learned about my dad's betrayal."

Yes, she did. She'd seen the Chase who really cared and was passionate about family and loyalty and maybe everything else.

He picked up a green elephant that rattled and wiggled it in front of Clementine. "What do you think of this, honey?"

Clementine grabbed at it and he laughed. Then he picked her up at the waist and held her high in the air. "Do you like it up there?"

Clementine giggled.

Maybe he'd never been around babies, but he sure had a way with them. Lucie suddenly felt…odd.

Almost to herself, she said, "The tabloids have called me conservative and stiff, or maybe even a little frozen. Sometimes I feel that way when I'm around you."

He cast her a quick glance over his shoulder and plopped Clementine into the crook of his arm. Instead of saying, *Oh, no, the tabloids don't see you that way*, he asked, "Do you see yourself as conservative and stiff?"

She considered his question. "I see myself as unusually cautious, and I try to stay calm, no matter what the circumstances. I never know when my photo's going to be shot, even from a long-lens camera. So almost every moment I'm outside and with people, I have that in the back of my mind. Hence, the pasted-on smile that might look frozen."

"Your smile is anything but frozen," Chase said vehemently, "and as for seeing the real you, that night on the country road, you were pretty free yourself. Don't beat yourself up over the *public* you and the *personal* you. As long as you're genuine with the people who love you, that's what matters."

She'd always thought that, but she wasn't so sure sometimes. "I try to be genuine when I do an interview, but almost every word is turned upside down and sideways, so it's hard."

"I saw the one you did after your father died. You were quite genuine, and the reporter thought so, too. She even had a tear in her eye. Don't you see your public life as a job?"

"Do you show one personality at work and another at home?" she inquired, really wanting to know.

He thought about it and sat with Clementine on the sofa. The baby was suddenly fascinated by the buttons on his shirt.

"I try to be professional at work and watch my words. So yes, I guess I'm different there than I am at home. Maybe that's another reason I want to run the horse rescue ranch. I can just be who I am."

She liked who Chase was and who he'd become.

"Speaking of the press," he said, "I'm doing that interview tomorrow with Norton Wilcox."

"I forgot all about that. Is there anything you have to prepare for?"

"No. It's going to be all about the horse rescue, so there shouldn't be any curveballs. I was talking to a friend yesterday about the ranch. He's the manager of the Galloping G, and they're going to be taking in troubled youth starting in June. We might coordinate some of our efforts. Giving kids a horse to gentle could solve some of their problems, too."

"That sounds like a plan. It also sounds like something the Fortune Foundation might want to help fund."

"I don't know. You're talking about proud men here, who want to run a program their own way. If you accept money from a foundation, there are usually strings attached."

She didn't think these funds were going to work that way, but what did she really know? All she was doing was setting up the office and suggesting programs to aid.

"I think it's time we started supper," she suggested. "Amelia provided baby food, but she also said Clementine liked mac and cheese, so I thought we'd have that, burgers and green beans. With you here, it'll be that much easier to put it all together. I wasn't sure if Clementine would sit in her high chair while I did it."

"I'll keep her occupied. That sounds like a great dinner."

"You're looking at me again as if you're surprised. I am a normal person, Chase. I really do cook. I even knit."

He blinked. "You knit?"

She just rolled her eyes. "I knitted Clementine a baby blanket. What do you think I do on long plane rides?"

"Read," he said with a straight face.

"Come on," she said, motioning him to the kitchen.

"Clementine likes to play with the pots and pans. You can help her clang lids together."

In the kitchen, Lucie made sure she kept at least three feet between her and Chase. That wasn't hard as he raced after Clementine, made sure she was occupied and Lucie started dinner. She also made sure she didn't look at Chase too often, because if she did, she'd want to kiss him. No, Clementine couldn't carry tales yet, but Lucie was very aware she was Clementine's aunt and didn't want to do anything untoward when she was in her company. Chase seemed to realize that and respected it. Except...

There were times they couldn't avoid touching. Lucie dropped an onion. He scooped it up. When he handed it to her, their fingers almost entwined. A muscle memory, that was all it was.

Lucie's version of macaroni and cheese involved a white sauce, melting the cheese in it, then pouring it over the macaroni to bake. After that was in the oven, she patted the burgers and inserted them under the broiler.

"Are steamed carrots okay for you?" Lucie asked. "Clementine loves them."

"Carrots are fine with me."

"And for dessert, we have cookies Amelia baked, something with oatmeal that's supposed to be good for Clementine."

"Do they taste like dog biscuits?" Chase asked.

Lucie cast him a look that was in the least scolding, at the most maybe a little coy. "No, they don't taste like dog biscuits or horse biscuits. They have cinnamon and raisins. If Amelia says they're good, I'm sure they are."

"Do you believe everything she tells you?"

"Mostly. Why?"

"I just wondered how that was between sisters."

"We bonded together against the boys."

"Your brother Charles isn't married either, is he?"

"No, the tabloids have gotten that right. He's been engaged twice."

"The reason for the breakups?"

"He's not ready. Charles is a go-with-the-flow kind of guy, and I'm not sure he wants to seriously be tied down."

"Maybe nobody does," Chase said. "Maybe everybody wants what they want when they want it. Do you actually know many men or women who could compromise? Just in my work alone, we sometimes have to navigate decisions as if we were in peace negotiations."

"I know what you mean, but a marriage shouldn't be about negotiation. It should be about giving on both sides."

They stared at each other while Clementine clinked lids together, like cymbals, cymbals that were going off in Lucie's head. How did they get into this discussion?

"Can you watch the burgers for a while?" she asked, changing the subject. "I'll take Clementine to the bedroom and change her. After that, dinner should be ready."

"You know, I can cook, too."

"Main dishes?" Lucie asked.

"Burgers and tuna fish sandwiches."

They both laughed.

"We could probably put a weekly menu together," she teased and headed for the bedroom.

Chase had never had more fun, had never enjoyed conversation more, had never realized a child was a constant energy suck. But an adorable one. He and Lucie had spoken hypothetically about having kids, but tonight, acting like a couple with a child, he could actually see himself in the role. What would it be like to come home to Lucie and a little girl, or a little boy? To fit everything else around their children because they would be the most important beings in their world?

The whole concept was foreign. If this deal went through on the Schultz property, he'd have mega-renovations to do, and that was going to take time. What woman would put up with having her place torn apart, piece by piece, room by room, floor by floor, appliance by appliance? Lucie was used to the best of everything. Oh, she might go on trips to foreign places and make do while she was there, but when she came home, she came home to conveniences and things she might never even ask for, like walk-in refrigerators, the highest-quality ranges.

He wasn't sure she knew what she had. She just expected it to be there. He wanted to renovate the ranch house nicely, but not at the highest cost he could find. He wanted to be economical and practical about every renovation he made. And if Lucie chose to live there—

He blanked that thought away. She wouldn't. That was the end of it.

By the time Lucie brought Clementine back to the kitchen, the little girl was fussing.

"I think she's just hungry. Let's get it on the table and see if she'll eat."

Lucie and Chase tried to please Clementine. They really did. But the little girl had missed her nap, and Amelia had warned Lucie that might mean she would be cranky. But Lucie hadn't wanted to believe it. So she tempted Clementine with bites of burger, spoonfuls of macaroni and cheese, steamed carrots soft enough for her to chew. Their meal was constantly interrupted by a spilled dish, an overturned spoon, macaroni in Clementine's hair.

Clementine was squawking now as Chase tried to wipe cheese from her hair.

"She's going to need a bath, isn't she?" he asked.

"Probably so. I don't know how much fun that's going to be. But Amelia included her little bathtub and her toys, so it might calm her down a bit. Do you want to postpone coffee and dessert until I try it?"

"That sounds like a good idea. I can get the bathtub set up."

"Okay, but not too hot."

"I'll check it with my elbow."

"Where did you learn that trick?"

"Some program I was watching one day. I'll test the water on my wrist, too, and make sure it's just right. Don't worry, Lucie, I've got this. While you're giving her a bath, I'll clean up."

They were negotiating, sort of…or were they just compromising? Whatever the case, if Chase kept it up, he'd be a darn good husband. Could he keep a compromising attitude?

Clementine was not warm and snuggling after her bath, and not even one of the oatmeal cookies could quiet her. Her voice started in a low cry and then built until she was practically screaming.

Lucie walked her back and forth in the living room. "Amelia told me she sometimes gets like this. She's overtired. She's in a strange place with strange people."

"She's going to make herself sick," Chase muttered, taking her from Lucie's arms. "We can't let her keep this up."

"I hate to do it, but I'm going to call Amelia."

Amelia answered her cell, sounding breathless. "Is something wrong?"

"I'm sorry to interrupt, but I don't know what to do with Clementine. She's crying and won't stop."

"She has a fussy spell sometimes after supper. Did she eat?"

"Yes, she did. Some."

"Well, good. That's important," Amelia explained. "Now all you have to do is get her to sleep. Put her on the phone."

"What do you mean, *Put her on the phone*?"

"Just bring her to the phone. Quinn will sing her a lullaby and she'll fall asleep."

"Just like that?" Lucie asked.

"Just like that."

Lucie told Chase what her sister had said. He shrugged and carried Clementine to Lucie, who put the cell phone to her ear. She was still wailing at that point, but after about a minute, the sound began to diminish. Lucie could just hear Quinn's baritone over the speaker phone as he sang to his daughter. Finally the cries vanished into little hiccups. Her eyes started to shut, and Lucie cradled her in her arms.

When the baby was quiet, Lucie said to Quinn, "You're a magician."

"No, I'm just a dad who knows what to do to make his daughter fall asleep. Now, if that happens again, and sometimes it does, call your friend Chase and have him sing to her."

Lucie looked up at Chase, and she couldn't lie to her sister and brother-in-law. "He's here."

"Well, good," Quinn said. "Then you definitely don't need us. We'll see you tomorrow, Lucie." And he hung up.

Lucie stared at her phone. "I think I feel like a baby-sitting failure."

Chase shook his head. "You're not a failure unless you have to call them again. That is the last thing you want to do."

"Hopefully I won't have to. Let's put her down for the night."

Putting Clementine down for the night lasted for about fifteen minutes. Lucie and Chase had tiptoed out of the bedroom and gone into the kitchen to have a cup of coffee. Lucie was pulling cookies from a container on the cupboard when Clementine began crying again. She and Chase exchanged a look.

Then she said, "I'll see if I can quiet her."

But there was no quieting Clementine Rose when she didn't want to go to bed, when she didn't like sleeping in a strange room, when she wanted her mum and dad.

Soon Chase peeked into the room. "Bring her out here again. If we play with her for a little while longer, maybe she'll fall asleep on her own."

"Wishful thinking," Lucie murmured, standing with the crying baby and rocking her back and forth. "Come on, little one. Let's go see what other toys your mum picked out to send with you."

On the sofa, Clementine stuck her thumb in her mouth and held her stuffed elephant, her cheeks still wet from tears. She smiled, however, when Chase took out a hand puppet and danced the dog across her knees. She pulled her thumb from her mouth to yank on the dog's ears.

Lucie said, "I'll get us both some coffee. I think we're going to need it."

And they did, because Clementine just wasn't going to

sleep. Every time they tried to put her down, she began crying.

Finally Chase decided, "She's manipulating us, and if she doesn't sleep tonight, I have a feeling she'll be a holy terror in the morning."

"You know what we haven't tried yet," Lucie suggested.

He sighed. "Me singing her a lullaby. All right. Why don't we both cuddle on the bed with her and we'll try it?"

Lucie gave him a long look.

"Seriously. We'll all be comfortable and if she falls asleep, we'll just let her sleep."

It was almost 2:00 a.m. "You don't mind staying the night?" she asked him.

"I don't mind." His voice was low and sexy, and she couldn't help wishing he was staying for another reason other than singing a lullaby.

Bringing a few of Clementine's toys with her, Lucie sat on the king-size bed—Clementine in the middle. Chase crawled onto the other side, propped up on two pillows. It should seem odd, having him in her bed. In some ways it did. But in other ways, it felt very natural. That scared her. Everything about her situation with Chase scared her. She might as well admit it.

Clementine picked up rattles, one in each hand, and began shaking them.

"What lullabies do you know?" Lucie asked him.

"I don't know any, but I do know a couple of nursery rhymes. Doesn't everybody? Let's try 'Twinkle, Twinkle, Little Star.' But you have to promise not to laugh."

Lucie crossed her heart with her hand. "I promise."

After a shake of his head and a long, blown-out breath, he began the first line.

At first Clementine didn't respond, but then she looked over at him as if somehow recognizing a male voice with a tune in it. Lucie lounged against the pillows too and began rubbing Clementine's back the way her mum often did hers and Amelia's when they were little. It was a soothing motion that had settled tears and fears and bad dreams.

After Chase finished with "Twinkle, Twinkle, Little Star," he began with a Disney tune, "When You Wish Upon A Star." Maybe he thought the heavenly-body theme would put Clementine to sleep.

To Lucie's surprise, it did. Clementine was soon nestled in the crook of Lucie's arm, and her little eyes were closed.

But would she stay asleep?

Chase sang for a little longer, then shrugged. In almost a whisper, he said, "She probably doesn't want to be in that crib all by herself. We should take advantage of her sleeping now in case it doesn't last long."

Chase moved over closer to Lucie, turned on his side and ran his hand through her hair. She could have purred.

Leaning in even closer, he gave her a deep, long, wet kiss that could have led somewhere else if a child hadn't slept between them. When he broke away, he was breathing raggedly, and so was she.

Finally he said, "You're going to make a wonderful mother."

Lucie couldn't help thinking, *And you'll make a wonderful dad.* But she didn't say the words aloud. If she said them out loud, that could be a dream waiting to come true.

Was it a dream she should try to capture? Or should she let their marriage be annulled? Should they go their separate ways?

Maybe in the morning after a few hours' sleep, the answer would become clearer.

Chapter Twelve

When Lucie awakened, Chase was no longer in bed. Had he left?

Clementine was sleeping soundly. Still, Lucie didn't want to leave her on the bed when she went to check in the rest of the apartment for Chase. As gently as she could, she lifted Clementine and laid her in the portable crib. The baby seemed unaware of the move. She stuffed her little fist near her chin and made a sighing sound. Lucie made sure the monitor that Amelia had brought along so she could hear Clementine if she was in the other room was turned on high.

Chase had found the pods to brew coffee and was making himself a mug. He gave her a crooked smile. "Is she still sleeping?"

"She is. I put her in the crib."

She didn't know what to say to him about last night. It had been nice. More than nice, really.

Lucie had brought her cell phone into the kitchen. and now she said, "I wonder if I should text Amelia and tell her everything is okay."

Chase shook his head. "If you don't call her, she knows everything's okay. Let her and Quinn have this time together."

"You're right." Lucie glanced at her phone, where she saw she had a text. She tapped it. It was from Keaton. He wondered if she'd like to have lunch sometime.

"Is that from Amelia?" Chase asked.

"No. I must have missed this last night. It's from Keaton."

Chase frowned. "The guy who took you to that charity event?"

She nodded.

Chase took a few steps closer. "What did he want?"

Her mouth suddenly went dry at the look in Chase's eyes. It was a possessive look.

"He wants to have lunch."

"Are you going to go?"

"Possibly," she answered, not sure at all what she was going to do or even what she should say.

Chase took the phone from her hands and set it on the counter. Then his hands caressed her shoulders and brought her closer. He didn't say he didn't want her to have lunch with Keaton, but that look in Chase's eyes—

"So Clementine is sound asleep?" he asked in a husky murmur.

Lucie nodded to the monitor on the counter. "I'll hear her if she wakes up."

Lucie was already trembling, anticipating his kiss. Last night had been comforting and warm, but this electricity she felt whenever Chase was near her was definitely even better—exciting and extraordinary.

Although he was close enough to kiss her, he didn't. He said, "Lying next to you in that bed last night and not being able to really touch you was torture."

She did know exactly what he meant. Getting close, yet unable to be totally intimate, created an insufferable longing.

"We're close now," she whispered.

"I have to be at a meeting with Jeff and my father in forty-five minutes. All hell could break loose."

"Maybe you need a little bit of heaven first." She couldn't believe she was being this bold. Charles would never believe it of Miss Goody Two-shoes.

Chase, on the other hand, grabbed on to believing it. He slid his hands into her hair, tipped her face up to his and took her lips in a consuming kiss that forced her to think about nothing but him.

She was entranced by his taste—coffee and Chase— by his male scent…but mostly by his passion. Her blouse was fashioned with buttons down the front, and now she wished she'd worn something easier to take off. Chase's fingers fumbled on the cloth buttons as he pushed them through the holes.

They were standing in bright daylight in her kitchen, and she could hardly believe the sensations rippling through her. He was looking at her as he undid the fastenings, at her face, and then down to her breasts, back to her face again. His eyes were hungry, full of smoky desire, and she couldn't wait to fall into it.

This was impulsive, maybe even reckless, but she felt she needed it. She felt she needed *him*. She never knew when might be the last time they could be intimate. He didn't finish the bottom two buttons, simply helped pull her blouse from her shoulders so she could tug out her arms. Somehow she knew he would just rip it open if it got in the way. And even that excited her.

He was staring at her bra, a little champagne number that seemed to go with everything. She liked lace, what could she say? And he seemed to like it, too.

He just stared, ran his finger over the edge and shook his head. "I wanted to go slower this time, but I don't think I can."

"Slow is definitely underrated," she assured him.

When he removed her bra and cupped her breasts in his palms, his gaze was on hers. She knew her eyes grew wider because she couldn't hide what she was feeling. He set the base of his palm on her nipple and rubbed, and she couldn't help moaning. She couldn't let him watch her melt in front of him. She needed the same kind of power. Now she reached for the buttons on his shirt, and much more quickly than he had, she unfastened the placket. When his bare chest was before her, she placed her hands on it and splayed her fingers. His curly chest hair popped up between them, and she slid them up to his shoulders.

"Oh, Lucie, you're driving me crazy," he groaned.

"Isn't that what I'm supposed to do?" she asked innocently.

At that, he scooped her up into his arms and carried her to the sofa. She lay there, staring up at him, as he took a condom from his pocket and laid it on the arm of the couch. Then he unzipped his jeans and let them fall. When he sat down beside her, he pulled off his boots, then the rest of his clothes.

"What about you?" he asked. "Are you just going to watch?"

"I can't just watch," she said. "We only have a limited amount of time. I'm ready to participate."

With a laugh, he helped her rid herself of the rest of her clothes. He stretched out on top of her and kissed the hollow at her neck, the V between her breasts, each of her ribs.

"Chase, we don't have that much time." She was panting, and being so vulnerable, so open with him, scared her. It must have something to do with the daylight. Seeing each other's every expression, hearing each other's every sound.

"Are you embarrassed by me kissing you everywhere, Lucie? Certainly other men have."

"Other men haven't kissed me naked. Only you have, Chase. Only you."

He looked astounded by her words, and then he looked just plain pleased. He kissed lower and lower, until her navel caught his attention. He ran his thumbs along her mound, touched her intimately, and so seductively, she felt like swooning.

Then he asked, "Are you ready for me?"

"Yes, Chase. Yes, I am."

Taking her words to heart, he rolled on the condom, positioned himself and then thrust into her. She wanted to be as close as she possibly could be. She wrapped her legs around him, rocking with him on that sofa. Bringing them both countless seconds of pleasure was all that was on her mind. She wanted to give as well as take. She wanted to take with him, knowing she'd return it all over again. They seemed to want to make up for ten years of being apart. Chase didn't hurry, but pulled in and out to give them both the most ultimate friction and superlative pleasure.

Lucie didn't think she could take any more. Her breaths were coming so fast. Her body was so overheated. Yet still she wanted more. She wanted *him*. She loved *him*.

Chase's thrusts became longer and harder until finally the pleasure overloaded all her senses and she felt as if she came apart in his arms. If he hadn't been holding her, she wasn't sure what would have happened to her. She called his name, and when she did, he found his release, too. They clung to each other breathing raggedly, letting their bodies cool, letting their breaths fall into a more normal rhythm. Somehow he gathered her into his arms and they lay like spoons, tight against each other, holding each other.

"I'd stay here all day with you if I could, but this meeting is important. I'm going to convince my father that Jeff is the man for the job, and it's time for me to go."

"Clementine will probably wake up soon. Amelia and Quinn are going to pick her up after lunch and head back."

Even though she was still in a bit of a daze because of their lovemaking, she realized they weren't talking about what was important—the two of them.

"You want to settle this with your father before you do that interview with the reporter tomorrow, right?"

"Yes. I don't want anything coming out during the interview that would be new information to Dad. I owe him the courtesy of telling him all about my plans first. On the other hand, he has to be willing to listen. That has never been his strong suit."

Lucie suddenly wondered what would happen if she could prolong her stay in Austin, if she could give herself and Chase time to figure out a life…if they could have one together. But her mother was depending on her. The orphanage was depending on her. She had to put her personal life on the back burner, didn't she? She *could* come back to Austin after the orphanage was built.

She had so much to think about.

And when Chase was quiet, she assumed he did, too.

From the monitor on the end stand, she heard little cooing sounds. That turned to babbling, and the babbling turned to a cry.

"She's awake." Which meant there was no time to talk now. No time to talk before his meeting, and no time to talk with a little one needing attention.

"Do you want to shower?" she asked.

"There's a shower at Parker Oil, and I have a change of clothes there. I often have to go from work during the day to an evening meeting."

"I see," she said. Chase's life had been a high-powered one. How easy was it going to be to rev it down to ranch work instead?

They both dressed quickly. Chase made a stop in the bathroom while Lucie picked up Clementine. She was settling the baby in her high chair when Chase came back to the kitchen and said, "I've got to go."

The awkwardness was there again that always came when one of them had to leave. What was it from? Not knowing when they'd see each other again, not knowing what to say, not knowing the feelings would change in the course of an hour or five or a day?

He picked up his cap from the table and plopped it onto his head. "Tell your sister and brother-in-law that their little girl is the cutest in the world."

Lucie smiled.

He kissed her lips slightly, from one corner to the other, and then he pulled back. "I've got a full day today, with the meeting and odds and ends I want to clear up.

Tomorrow's lighter. Why don't I give you a call after my interview? Maybe we can hook up again."

Hook up. Was that what she wanted?

"Chase, what are we doing? Having an affair before our marriage is annulled? It's dangerous and potentially explosive."

"When are you leaving?" he asked, looking as serious as she'd ever seen him.

Her mouth went dry. "Next Monday."

He waited as if he wanted her to say more. But what could she add?

"Are you telling me you'd rather not see me again before you leave?" he asked.

She was so confused about what was propitious, what was best, what was right.

"What do *you* want, Chase?"

After a moment, he responded, "I want to start my new life…one way or another."

With or without her?

Clementine was crying full out now and Lucie had to go to her. Responsibility versus heart's desire. Swallowing hard, she said, "It would probably be best if we end this now."

Chase looked stoically accepting as he nodded. "I'll call you after the annulment goes through."

Then before she could take either a step toward him or Clementine, he was gone.

Out of her life.

Chase couldn't stop thinking about Lucie. That was just the way it was these days. Especially after this morning and the way they'd parted, she was definitely on his mind. At work, he showered and changed, feeling disconcerted about her, but prepared for the meeting with his dad. This wasn't a matter of *ready*. He was simply going to tell his father what he was going to do.

He went to one of the conference rooms to prepare. For the first part of this meeting, Jeff would join them and give the presentation.

A few minutes later, Jeff entered, looking nervous. But he pointed to the interactive whiteboard. "I'm ready for this."

Chase gave him a thumbs-up. "Good. Don't let my father see you sweat. If he sees a weakness, he'll exploit it. Just be honest with him and stick to the facts."

"Will do," Jeff agreed with a nod.

When Warren Parker came in, he looked from Chase to Jeff to the whiteboard to the laptop. "You're not going to give me a chance to convince you not to do what you want to do, are you?"

"No," Chase said with conviction.

"With all due respect, sir," Jeff interjected, "I have a presentation ready that will show you where I intend to take the company. These are ideas I've developed with Chase over the past six months. Of course, you'll have to confirm every venture I want to start."

"What if *I* want to start a venture?" Warren Parker asked with some vehemence. "Don't think you're going to take over. I'm not going to be just some figurehead."

"Of course not, sir," Jeff assured him. "I just want you to know I have ideas to share—about everything, from new projects to overhauling our software system."

Warren rolled his eyes. "So you're leaving me with someone young and eager?" he asked Chase.

"And intelligent and forward-looking."

Warren lowered himself into one of the chairs. "All right, let's get started."

A half hour later, Chase's dad wasn't asleep or barking that he didn't approve of any of it. He was looking pensive.

"All right, Jeff," he said. "You've shown me you have backbone and you're imaginative. Why don't you meet me in my office after lunch around one?"

Jeff knew he was being dismissed. He nodded, closed down his laptop and left the room.

Chase studied his father, unable to read him. "He'll be good for the company, Dad, trust me on that."

Warren eyed Chase and then said, "I'll agree to try Jeff in your shoes for the next three months. If he works out, wonderful. If he doesn't, you're going to have to find me someone else. And the only way I'll agree to this whole thing is if you'll consult with Parker Oil. I'll put you on the books as a consultant, and you can arrange your schedule accordingly."

"Not for the first month," Chase said, negotiating with his dad as he hadn't done before.

He almost thought he saw a twinkle in his father's eye. "Agreed," he said. "One month, and then we'll negotiate what projects I want you to work on."

"Maybe everything will be flowing so smoothly that you won't need me at all," Chase countered.

His father just arched an eyebrow. His face took on a very somber expression. "We have to talk about ten years ago."

Chase thought about what had happened then and what his father had done. He also thought about the fact that his dad wasn't fighting him now about leaving. Maybe because he knew he'd lose him for sure if he did?

"What's done is done," Chase said, ready to forgive because that was right to do. But he wouldn't forget.

"I didn't apologize for it, and that's because I don't know if I did the right thing or the wrong thing. Marrying someone so young wasn't right for you back then."

"Dad—" Chase warned.

Warren raised his hand. "I know. I should keep my mouth shut. Your mother tells me that all the time. But I'm going to say this. Lucie Fortune Chesterfield is a beautiful woman. She was a pretty girl ten years ago and that beauty has just increased. I can see why you fell head over heels then, and why you could now."

Chase didn't protest because he didn't want to lie to his father. Something had happened again now. He just wasn't sure what to do about it or how to handle it. His heart thumped madly whenever he was near her. He was excited whenever he saw her. He wanted to spend as much time with her as he could. Could it really be love?

"Over the years, I have learned a thing or two about women, mostly through your mother. If Florence likes Lucie, then the girl must have a head on her shoulders as well as a pretty smile."

Chase couldn't help being a bit amused by his father's assessment. "She does have a good head on her shoulders."

Warren stuck out his hand. "I know everything can't be forgiven. Nothing's that easy. But maybe we can have a new start. What do you say?"

Chase extended his hand to his father, and as they shook, he felt closer to his dad than he had in years. Would it last? He didn't know, but he hoped it would.

* * *

The following morning, Norton Wilcox introduced himself to Chase in the greenroom about ten minutes before their interview at TXLB began. Chase hadn't given the reporter much consideration because he was still thinking about all the details he had to handle at Parker Oil before he left, as well as his confusion over Lucie leaving. Norton—the man had said to call him by his first name—had been made up with his hair gelled, his navy suit and red-and-blue tie perfect for an interview. Chase had worn black jeans, a white shirt and a bolo tie, knowing he had to look professional as far as the horse rescue ranch went.

Once the lights in the studio were glaring and the interview began, Norton's questions started easy enough. He said, "You're an oil man by experience and family history. Why did you want to get involved in rescuing horses?"

As Chase had explained to his father last evening as they'd talked over dinner—really talked—he related, "When I was a kid, I went to the barn when I didn't get my way or when I had a problem that needed to be solved. I never thought of a horse as just a vehicle for a trail ride. Like any other animal, a horse responds to voice, to touch and to kindness. I learned that early. They are intuitive creatures if you tap into their souls. I like doing that. I felt fulfillment, being able to communicate with them. And when I see one neglected, it makes me angry. That, however, doesn't serve much purpose. My reaction to it does. I rescue the horse and coax it to trust humans again."

Norton looked totally surprised by his answer. "You make the connection sound almost mystical."

Chase shook his head. "Nothing of the sort. Just as people have to learn how to communicate with each other, I had to learn how to communicate with a horse. But once I did, I wanted to use that for good. Gentling horses can benefit us all."

"How so?" Norton seemed to be truly interested.

"I have a friend who's going to be involved with helping troubled youths. When a kid makes a connection, he's helped. Gentling a wild mustang might not solve a teenager's problems. but it can pull him out of himself. It can teach him how to feel productive and worthwhile."

"So you plan to open a nonprofit ranch on the old Schultz homestead?"

"I do. I'm going to refurbish the house and the two barns and soon get started."

"But you can't get started right away, can you?"

A prickling began at the back of Chase's neck and he knew he wasn't going to like what was coming. He kept silent.

Interviewers hated dead air time, and Norton rushed to fill it. "There's a glitch getting a loan for the place, right?"

Chase still remained silent.

Again Norton hurried to fill the air with words. "Apparently you had a secret marriage ten years ago that you thought was dissolved. But it wasn't. You're still married and you need your wife to sign those loan papers. I think our audience would be very surprised to learn who that wife is. They're seeing the photo of you and Lucie Fortune Chesterfield on a split screen now."

Chase glanced toward the monitor. The photo was one of him and Lucie at the South by Southwest Conference.

"Haven't you been dating Lady Fortune Chesterfield again since she's been in Austin?" Norton pressed.

Chase could easily grasp the fact that the photo was a long shot. Lucie was wearing her wig, sunglasses and ball cap. Chase's disguise made him almost indistinguishable. Only one thought occupied his mind. He had to protect Lucie and her family.

He tried to be as nonchalant as he could be. "As your audience can see, Mr. Wilcox, the two people in that photo look nothing like me or Lady Fortune Chesterfield. I don't know where you've gotten your information, but you're mistaken."

Norton studied him with a scowl. "I took that photograph that day myself," the interviewer said in a huff. "And I've been shadowing Lady Fortune Chesterfield. I spoke with someone who saw the two of you at a church function."

This Chase could explain and he could even add some truth to the interview. "If you've done your research, Mr. Wilcox, you know that Lady Fortune Chesterfield is in Austin, setting up a branch of the Fortune Foundation. My mother asked her to evaluate the after-school program at our church to help with the funding. Lady Fortune Chesterfield was at the function and so was I. But we weren't together. Maybe you should have talked to me about this before the interview, so we wouldn't mislead your audience."

"You're the one who's misleading my audience, Mr. Parker."

"I imagine your audience tuned in today to find out about my horse rescue plans. They haven't been misled in the least. I'm sure your station will post the information on your website, but if anyone is interested in the

program or has a horse in need of rescue, just email me."
Chase rattled off his email address.

The tech was giving a signal for Wilcox to wrap up
the interview. Trying to paste on a recovery smile, the
reporter said, "Thank you for coming in today, Chase.
I'm sure our audience appreciates your forthrightness on
everything we discussed."

Chase felt a flush come to his face. He didn't like *not*
being forthright. But for Lucie's sake, what else could
he do?

Chapter Thirteen

After watching Chase's interview, feeling for him as he was ambushed by the reporter, Lucie came to several realizations. She *was* irrevocably in love with Chase. Because she loved him, she couldn't let him put his reputation on the line. He probably didn't realize what was going to happen next. There would be so much fallout that there'd be an absolute media scramble to find out the facts. There would be rumors about their marriage and affairs and engagements, and everything in between. Chase had no idea what was coming.

But she did.

What did Chase feel for her? Did he just want her in his bed? Or did he love her? Did he want their marriage annulled? She didn't, but she wasn't in this alone. If Chase didn't love her, it would hurt and be almost unbearable. But because she loved him, she'd give him the annulment and let him go on with his life.

However, neither of them could continue without the truth. It was about time she followed her mother's advice and let the truth be liberating. She knew the best way to do that was to contact her mother's public relations secretary and let her set up a press conference. But first she'd call her mother and tell her what she was planning.

Chase was pacing his office, realizing that wily reporters, let alone investigative ones, could probably access his phone records to see if he and Lucie had talked. Should he call her and tell her he hadn't known what else to do except fall back on denial?

While he was considering that, his own phone beeped. Taking it from his pocket, he didn't recognize the Texas number. "Chase Parker here."

"Mr. Parker? This is Josephine Fortune Chesterfield. We met briefly last week."

"Yes, we did," he confirmed, wondering why Lucie's mother was calling him. Then a horrible thought hit him. "Has something happened to Lucie?"

"You mean, by way of an accident or that type of thing? No, no, no. I'm sorry if I worried you in that way."

Worried him in the least? If something happened to Lucie, the light would go out of his life. This realization stunned him. Chase's heart had almost stopped when he realized how his world would fall apart if harm came to Lucie…because he loved her. It had taken him too long to realize it. Was he too late? "How can I help you, Lady Fortune Chesterfield?"

"Lucie saw your interview and so did I."

He was silent because he absolutely didn't know what to say.

"Chase?" she asked.

"I was there to talk about the horse rescue. I didn't expect the rest."

"No, of course you wouldn't. You're an honorable man. Mr. Wilcox was out for the ratings. Lucie is terrifically unhappy that you were put in that position."

"That's not her fault."

"I'm so glad you don't blame her. Other men in your position might."

"It is what it is, Lady Fortune Chesterfield. She can't help that the press hounds her and her family. The truth is—I didn't know what to tell him. I'm sure with investigation all of this is going to come out. But at least with notice, you and your family can prepare what you want to say. It gave you a little time if nothing else."

"I see now that that was your plan," Josephine said. "Thank you. Lucie is wasting no time dealing with this and that's why I called. She will be giving a press conference in about an hour at the Crown Hotel's ballroom. I thought you might want to be there."

"Why didn't Lucie call me and tell me?" Was she too upset about what he had or hadn't said?

"My guess is that Lucie doesn't want you to be embarrassed if you don't like what she's going to say. Personally I think you two need to communicate better."

There seemed to be much Lady Fortune Chesterfield wasn't saying, but Chase understood loyalty, and she would be true to her daughter no matter what.

"I don't know whether to be worried or relieved she's giving a press conference," Chase said honestly. "Do you *know* what she's going to say?"

"She hasn't shared everything with me, but she did say she was going to tell the truth. You can infer from that what you may."

"Will you be there, Lady Fortune Chesterfield?"

"No, I'm still in Horseback Hollow. I won't be able to get there in time. But I will be watching."

"Then you'll see me there. I'll be as close to the front as I can get."

"I thought you'd want to be there. Lucie's going to need all the support she can get. After she makes a statement, the press will bombard her with questions."

"I'll protect her. No matter what she says."

"I was counting on that," Josephine said with a smile in her voice. "I've depended on her a bit too much since her father died. I think we're both coming to realize that. She's a woman with her own mind, and I have to stand back a bit now and let her do what she must."

After Chase ended the call, he thought about what Lucie could say, might say, might feel.

Then he headed for the elevator. He had a stop to make before he attended that press conference.

Lucie knew she had to do this. She absolutely had to. If she brought the tabloids down on her family, well, so be it. They'd been through it before. They'd survive. Her mother had accepted her decision and hadn't tried to talk her out of it. Maybe she'd realized she had to pull back a bit. Maybe she'd realized Lucie wanted a different life from the one Josephine envisioned for her. Lucie had realized that she had to find her own life, no matter what happened with Chase. She simply knew she couldn't let him take the fall for their history and what had happened between them the past few weeks. She didn't want him to have to evade or be dishonest. Neither of them had done anything wrong.

To Lucie's dismay, the ballroom of the hotel seemed

to be filled. There were press members with their lanyards and ID badges, cameras and cords, and people everywhere. The cacophony of voices almost made Lucie's head spin. But she emerged from the shadowy corner and walked up to the podium, prepared for whatever happened next.

After she adjusted the microphone, she tapped on it and closed her eyes for a moment against the flashes of light. Taking a bolstering breath, she opened her eyes and put on her best smile.

"Hello, everyone. I'm glad you could join me here today. Ever since Norton Wilcox's airing of *About Austin* yesterday, there have been rumors and gossip about me and Chase Parker. I'd like to settle those rumors and give you the truth."

Any chatter in the room stopped. For so many people gathered, the atmosphere was as silent as that of a church. But Lucie wasn't nervous anymore. She wasn't anxious either. She was doing the right thing.

"I have a tale to tell you and it's not very long."

Reporters held up microphones. She knew some of the people in the folding chairs were recording and photographing with their cell phones. She continued. "It's the true story of a girl who hadn't known much about the world. That girl was me. I'd been fairly sheltered, sent to the best schools, taken care of as if I were royalty. But at seventeen, I felt it was time for me to venture a bit on my own. I signed up for a trip to Scotland. I thought I was ready to be an adult, away from my parents and family. I was enjoying some freedom. My trip leader was Chase Parker. He was twenty-one, and from the first moment we looked at each other, there was attraction there. So much so that we were both a little overwhelmed. So overwhelmed that when Chase asked me to marry him right there in Scotland where I didn't need permission, I said yes."

Many of the reporters in the crowd gave a gasp, and Lucie couldn't help smiling genuinely this time.

"Our marriage was short-lived, however," she went on, "because when Warren Parker, Chase's father, found out, he persuaded us both the best thing to do was to have the marriage annulled. I was sent home from that trip in disgrace because I'd been caught with a boy in a hostel room alone. No one but Mr. Parker, Chase and I knew that boy was my husband."

Again there was a buzz vibrating through the room. But it stopped when she began to speak once more. "Because of circumstances that occurred after that, Chase and I didn't see each other again, not for ten years, not until a few weeks ago, when he visited me and told me he'd just found out that our marriage had never been annulled. He said lawyers were working on putting it right, but he wanted to tell me in person in case the news got out. Chase and I have seeing each other since that day. We've gotten to know each other better than we knew each other ten years ago. And I want to make one fact perfectly clear. When I was seventeen, I fell in love with Chase Parker, and…I'm still in love with him now."

Oohs and aahs went up from the crowd.

"Yes, the annulment is in the works," she went on, "but if it's up to me, we'll stay married forever."

Chase had been sitting about ten rows back. He knew Lucie couldn't see him in the crowd, especially not with the lights and the flashes and everyone wanting her attention. When he heard the words *When I was seven-*

teen, I fell in love with Chase Parker and I'm still in love with him now, it took him a moment to absorb what she was saying.

Reporters began firing questions. "When did you last see Chase Parker?"

"Have you been intimate with him?"

"Did his horse rescue ranch bring all of this to light?"

Chase was not going to let Lucie handle this herself, and he knew what he was going to do. There was no question about it in his mind…or in his heart.

When he stepped out into the side aisle and moved forward, security that had been hired for the occasion stopped him. But Chase took out his wallet and flashed his driver's license.

"I'm Chase Parker, and I have something to say to Lucie."

The burly man's eyes grew wide. He stepped to the side to let Chase pass, and Chase heard the man call, "Good luck."

Yes, he needed luck, but he needed more than that. He needed Lucie to change her life the way he would change his. Would she do it?

Chase pressed his way to the front of the crowd and shouted above all of them, "Lucie. What happens next isn't just up to you. It's up to me, too." Then he ran up the steps to the stage.

She was staring at him as if he were a ghost. "Where did you come from? How did you know?"

"Your mother phoned me," he said with a grin. Then, knowing exactly what he had to do, what he wanted to do more than anything else in the world, he dropped down to one knee.

Immediately the room grew quiet once more.

On his way to the press conference, he'd stopped at the jewelry store. Removing a velvet box from his pocket, he opened it. "From the moment I met you, I was smitten with you. There was something so strong between us that years and distance couldn't erase. When I realized we were still married, one of the things I felt was…hope. I looked forward to seeing you again. Reuniting with you was the most life-altering moment I ever experienced. Because I loved you then…and I still love you now."

Then, his voice ringing out loud and clear, he asked, "Lucie Fortune Chesterfield, will you agree to not unmarry me?"

A genuine smile broke out on Lucie's face, and he could see tears brimming in her eyes.

"Yes, I'll agree to not unmarry you. I'll stay married to you forever."

Rising to his feet, Chase slipped the ring on Lucie's finger, took her into his arms and gave her a resounding kiss. The applause in the background registered only slightly because he had his world in his arms…and that was all he cared about.

Epilogue

One Week Later

Lucie and Chase sat on the fence, watching the horses trot in the larger pasture and in the separate runs from the barn. Chase had settled on the ranch, and his dad had let him borrow hands from the Bar P to quickly make necessary changes for the rescue horses. The sign for the Parker Rescue Ranch had just gone up the day before. Chase wrapped his arm around Lucie's shoulders.

"We're going to take a real honeymoon. I want to take you someplace you've never been." That could be difficult, considering how much Lucie had traveled, but he didn't think she'd ever been to Curaçao or Bali.

"We *are* on our honeymoon," she reminded him.

He laughed. "Sleeping in sleeping bags the first two nights until we had furniture moved into the house wasn't exactly what I had in mind."

"Making love all night, whether on the floor or in a bed, is *my* idea of a honeymoon," she teased.

"Besides trying out the stall in the barn and settee in the sunporch and—"

She jabbed him in the ribs.

He leaned close to her and kissed her temple. "I never thought you'd agree to stay in Austin…to starting a life here with me."

"When you first told me we were still married, I couldn't comprehend giving up the life I was leading. I had so many responsibilities to so many people. I guess I finally realized I don't have to carry the world's concerns on my shoulders. And…Mom and I need a little bit of distance, too. Neither of us really realized what happened after Dad died, the way we held on to and depended on each other, and didn't make a move without the other's approval. It was like we were afraid we'd lose each other, too, so we did everything we could to hold on. But that kind of love soon feels confining. It didn't let either of us stretch our wings. We both realize that now."

"And your mom's not upset you found someone to take your place in Guatemala?"

"No. She knows Jenny Preston. She's worked with us on many projects. She knows as much about the details as I do and about the process. She and Mom will work well together."

Suddenly there was a honking of horns and the sound of cars on the gravel lane.

"Everyone's arriving," Chase said with a broad smile. "This barbecue might not be the best organized in the world, but the important thing is we're sharing our happiness with our family and friends."

"Exactly."

She and Chase hopped off the fence and ran to the front of the house. As they passed the front porch, Chase caught the scent of newly sawed wood. He'd been cutting new baseboards. The inside of the house needed lots of work. He and Lucie had painted some walls and sanded the living room floor. It was work they enjoyed doing together.

As he rounded the lane and peered into the backyard, he grinned. It was ready for company, with picnic tables, benches and canopies. He'd had new appliances delivered to the kitchen two days ago, so that room was ready.

A limo drove up first and he knew his mother-in-law would be ensconced inside. She'd postponed her trip until after the barbecue.

Lucie waved at the couple in the second car and Ella stuck her head out the window. "Are you ready for us?" she asked.

"More than ready," Lucie assured her.

A third SUV parked beside the others. It wasn't long before Amelia, Quinn and Clementine were rushing toward Lucie and Chase.

Chase said, "Come around back, everyone. There's beer, sweet tea and plenty of food."

It wasn't long before Chase's parents arrived, along with Josephine's sister, Jeanne Marie, and her husband, Deke, as well as Josephine and Jeanne Marie's brother, James Marshall. Lucie's brothers and their wives were there, too. All except her bachelor brother Charles, who couldn't get away from London yet.

Quinn said to Chase, "There's a news van parked out at the end of the lane. But I saw you had two burly guys in a truck watching them."

"I hired security for today so we could have privacy. This is the reception Lucie and I never had, never dreamed we'd have. I'm not going to have it ruined by the press."

Lucie and Amelia, Josephine and Jeanne Marie went into the kitchen and soon had the food organized, bringing it all outside to a large buffet table.

Chase heard Jeanne Marie say to Lucie, "I understand you're going to keep working for the Fortune Foundation."

"I am. I'm not giving up my work with children. There are lots of needy kids here in Austin. I'll be helping the Fortune Foundation fund the best ways to aid them."

Chase wrapped his arm around Lucie's waist. "And soon maybe we'll have kids of our own."

They'd talked about that at night as they'd held each other in their arms. They both wanted children, at least three and maybe four.

Lucie's cell phone buzzed and she took it from her pocket. Chase could see her press her video-chatting app. Her brother Charles's face appeared on the screen.

"Hi, Luce. I wish I could be there with you, but I had to congratulate you and tell you I'm happy for you."

"Oh, Charles, I wish you could be here, too."

"I'll visit Texas soon. I just wanted to tell you I was thinking about you. Love you, sis."

"Love you, too, Charles."

After Lucie pocketed the phone, she looked up at Chase and said, "I'm the happiest woman in the world."

He took her hand and pulled her away from the crowd into the kitchen. "What do you think about the Caribbean for a delayed honeymoon, possibly in a month or so?"

She laughed. "I'm thinking anywhere with you would be heavenly."

"After we get the house in order, I'll hire a manager

to live in the apartment above the barn. Then we won't be tied down here twenty-four-seven."

She wrapped her arms around his neck. "I don't mind being tied to you."

He kissed her soundly, certain they were going to have the best happily-ever-after a couple could ever have.

* * * * *

MILLS & BOON®

Desire™

PASSIONATE AND DRAMATIC LOVE STORIES

A sneak peek at next month's titles...

In stores from 10th March 2016:

- **Take Me, Cowboy** – Maisey Yates *and*
  His Baby Agenda – Katherine Garbera

- **A Surprise for the Sheikh** – Sarah M. Anderson *and*
  Reunited with the Rebel Billionaire – Catherine Mann

- **A Bargain with the Boss** – Barbara Dunlop *and*
  Secret Child, Royal Scandal – Cat Schield

Available at WHSmith, Tesco, Asda, Eason, Amazon and Apple

Just can't wait?
Buy our books online a month before they hit the shops!
visit www.millsandboon.co.uk

These books are also available in eBook format!

MILLS & BOON®

Let us take you back in time with our Medieval Brides...

The Novice Bride – Carol Townend

The Dumont Bride – Terri Brisbin

The Lord's Forced Bride – Anne Herries

The Warrior's Princess Bride – Meriel Fuller

The Overlord's Bride – Margaret Moore

Templar Knight, Forbidden Bride – Lynna Banning

Order yours at
www.millsandboon.co.uk/medievalbrides

MILLS & BOON®

Why not subscribe?
Never miss a title and save money too!

Here's what's available to you if you join the exclusive **Mills & Boon® Book Club** today:

✦ *Titles up to a month ahead of the shops*
✦ *Amazing discounts*
✦ *Free P&P*
✦ *Earn Bonus Book points that can be redeemed against other titles and gifts*
✦ *Choose from monthly or pre-paid plans*

Still want more?
Well, if you join today, we'll even give you
50% OFF your first parcel!

So visit **www.millsandboon.co.uk/subs**
to be a part of this exclusive Book Club!

MILLS & BOON®

Why shop at millsandboon.co.uk?

Each year, thousands of romance readers find their perfect read at millsandboon.co.uk. That's because we're passionate about bringing you the very best romantic fiction. Here are some of the advantages of shopping at www.millsandboon.co.uk:

* **Get new books first**—you'll be able to buy your favourite books one month before they hit the shops

* **Get exclusive discounts**—you'll also be able to buy our specially created monthly collections, with up to 50% off the RRP

* **Find your favourite authors**—latest news, interviews and new releases for all your favourite authors and series on our website, plus ideas for what to try next

* **Join in**—once you've bought your favourite books, don't forget to register with us to rate, review and join in the discussions

Visit **www.millsandboon.co.uk**
for all this and more today!